Last Word to
the Wise

Last Word to
the Wise

A Christie Bookshop Mystery

ANN CLAIRE

BANTAM

NEW YORK

A Bantam Trade Paperback Original

Copyright © 2023 by Ann Perramond

Published in the United States by Bantam Books, an imprint of Random House, a division of Penguin Random House LLC, New York.

BANTAM BOOKS is a registered trademark and the B colophon is a trademark of Penguin Random House LLC.

LIBRARY OF CONGRESS CATALOGING-IN-PUBLICATION DATA
Names: Claire, Ann, author.
Title: Last word to the wise / Ann Claire.
Description: New York: Bantam, [2023] | Series: A Christie Bookshop mystery
Identifiers: LCCN 2023006142 (print) | LCCN 2023006143 (ebook) | ISBN 9780593496381 (trade paperback; acid-free paper) | ISBN 9780593496374 (ebook)
Subjects: LCGFT: Cozy mysteries. | Novels.
Classification: LCC PS3603.L344 L37 2023 (print) | LCC PS3603.L344 (ebook) | DDC 813/.6—dc23/eng/20230217
LC record available at https://lccn.loc.gov/2023006142
LC ebook record available at https://lccn.loc.gov/2023006143

Printed in the United States of America on acid-free paper

randomhousebooks.com

2 4 6 8 9 7 5 3 1

Book design by Caroline Cunningham, based on the
original design by Virginia Norey
Frontispiece collage: AdobeStock/redchocolatte

To Eric and our time in the mountains

Last Word to
the Wise

✻

CHAPTER 1

Rather Be Reading

N ever had I so dreaded a trip to the library.

Me, Ellie Christie, devoted reader, bookseller, bibliophile, and library patron since infancy. In fact, had I *ever* approached a library with anything less than delight? I recalled only joy and anticipation.

Now, however . . .

From my frosty nose to my mitten-clad palms, I yearned to turn in my boots and flee. I knew exactly where I'd go. Home to my loft above my family's bookshop, the Book Chalet. Once there, I'd dive into flannel PJs, curl up with Agatha C. (as in Cat) Christie, and read.

It was the perfect evening for a fluffy friend and a good book. Late January snow, fine as icing sugar, pirouetted to my eyelashes. I sighed. Wistful sentiment froze into a mocking cloud.

A night in with a book and your cat? No, no, no . . . Not for you. Not until you've endured this date!

I sighed, launching another taunt.

Hee, hee, ha, ha! Not just a date. A blind double date! In the library!

Every bit of that seemed wrong. Date. Double date. Blind

date. Most of all, the involvement of the library. The library was a readers' sanctuary, like the Book Chalet. It shouldn't be sullied by potentially (no, almost definitely) stressful blind meetups.

I consoled myself. The library had always helped me out. It would tonight too, right? If the date went south, I could . . . what? Excuse myself and hide among the books?

No. I'd be found. The library was open and orderly. At the Book Chalet, I could disappear for days. Shelves reached for the ceiling. Aisles twisted like a maze. Customers could literally find themselves lost among the books.

My imagination turned fanciful, or perhaps just desperate.

A magical library cart, that's what I needed. I pictured a metal cart, rattling to my rescue. I'd jump on. Together, we'd bump down the library steps and clatter through downtown, speeding for the gondola station, where a glass carriage would await to carry me up to the upper hamlet and home. I glanced over my shoulder. Midway up the mountain, lights twinkled through the snow, beckoning like summer fireflies.

I smiled under my scarf. Riding the gondola was always special. *But I had a magic library cart! We'd fly!*

A bookish woman could always dream.

A frigid gust carried away my fantasy. I turned back to reality and my companion in blind double-date dread, striding a few yards ahead.

"We'll be early!" I called to my older sister.

Meg was approaching this evening like an impending root canal or cream pie aimed at her nose: Hurry up and get it over with.

I tried again. "We'll look overeager!"

Meg stopped in the middle of Galena Street, thankfully free of traffic.

"Can I admit something?" Meg asked when I caught up.

"Of course," I said and admired the long views from the middle of the road.

"I'd sooooo rather be home reading."

"You and me both! Let's go hide in the Book Chalet! You can sleep over in the loft and tell me ghost stories like when we were kids."

"Stop," my sister groaned. "Too tempting . . ."

I piled on cozy lures. "Flannel PJs, hot cocoa, a fire in the hearth, Agatha on your lap . . ."

"Now you're just being cruel," Meg said. She countered. "My place is closer. We run there. *You'll* stay overnight. We'll watch a *Masterpiece Mystery* and eat cookies. Gram and Rosie are making a batch right now. Chocolate chip . . ."

It was my turn to groan. Cookies, a mystery, Gram, and my niece . . . that combo sounded divine. Meg and my niece—somehow transformed into a fourteen-year-old—had lived with our grandmother since our beloved Gramps passed away over a decade ago.

The arrangement suited everyone. Gram adored the company and her grandchildren. Meg, a single mom since before Rosie was even born, enjoyed parenting support. Rosie saw Gram as her BFF from another era and was soaking in Gram's secrets to life, bookbinding, and legendary baking.

Since moving back home, I'd benefited too. Delicious dinners. Luxurious leftovers. Movie nights and sleepovers in the coziest guest bedroom in town . . .

"Or, hey, we start on the taxes?" Meg suggested. "That sounds like more fun. Pluck our eyebrows? Except Rosie already tortured my brows *and* convinced me to wear contacts. If my eyeballs freeze, that's it, I'm going home."

I smiled. Misery did adore company. "You'll need your sister to guide you."

"Noble of you. Maybe one of us could slip and sprain an ankle?" Meg slid a boot over snow packed to ice. She looked almost hopeful.

Headlights turned our way a few blocks up. "Get hit in the road?" I suggested.

"Fine by me," my sister muttered.

I slipped my mittened hand through Meg's elbow and tugged her along. As we strolled, I told her about the magic library cart. Her laughter warmed me. The five years that separated us seemed like nothing in our thirties, but a part of me would always be the little sis eager to make her big sister chuckle. I was glad to have her at my side tonight and even happier to be reunited after my years abroad, traveling the world on bookish gigs.

"So," Meg said. "There is *some* hope for this evening?"

"The magic of the library." Carts wouldn't fly, but I believed in the enchanting powers of buildings filled with books.

"Bet I'll still win," Meg grumbled.

When it came to dating, Meg and I lugged around baggage heavier than trunks of books. Since learning of our impending blind dates, we'd been engaged in a bit of dark humor in the form of sisterly competition. Who had the worst dating record?

Meg, hands down, held the lead. Fifteen years ago, she'd been stood up at the altar by Rosie's dad.

Few could compete with that heartbreak and humiliation. However, I'd had a recent surge. First there'd been my long-term boyfriend. I'd *thought* we loved the same things. Bookshops, travel, literary landscapes, each other. I also secretly—foolishly—assumed he'd propose. *Any day now,* I'd think, every few years or so. Only when I stepped up and asked did I learn he wasn't the marrying type. Turned out, he wasn't the one-woman type either.

Our breakup left me adrift, but after some wallowing in tearjerker novels, I moved on. Literally. Last October, I winged back home to little Last Word for my dream job, working with my big sis as fifth-generation caretakers of our family's historic bookshop. I vowed to start a fresh chapter, to seek out new friendships and rekindle old acquaintances. A budding romance even seemed possible.

But then . . . I hadn't even unpacked when murder struck my seemingly idyllic hometown.

My boot slipped. I steadied myself, physically and emotionally.

It was too soon to prod at the scars of last November. *Way too soon to think about dating, too!*

I returned to the fun fantasy. "We need an escape word. If either of us says it, we bolt for the nearest cart."

"Great idea." Meg pondered. "How about 'book'? 'Book it'?"

"Mmm . . . Nice, but we'll be in the library, and supposedly our dates are bookish matches? Presumably, they'll talk books?"

"Dare we hope?" Meg thought some more. "Okay, how about 'ostrich'?"

I laughed. When we were young, our parents swapped out any foul word with "ostrich." Not that our quiet father or love-the-world hippie mother made a habit of cursing, but they got a kick out of "ostrich."

What the ostrich? Oh, ostrich! We're up Ostrich Creek now, girls.

"Perfect," I said, "both in meaning and rarity."

Meg and I stopped in front of a grand-dame Queen Anne with gingerbread trim and fish-scale shingles painted in purples, golds, and leafy green. The Last Word Free Library began its life as a gold-baron's abode. Now, like the Book Chalet, it was a treasure-trove for bibliophiles.

And I wanted to run from it.

"Remind me why we agreed to this?" I asked. Rhetorical question. We "agreed" because we loved our cousin Lorna. Also, because we were too nice and thus susceptible to Lorna's guilt-tripping.

Lorna fell between Meg and me in age, thirty-five to my thirty-three and Meg's thirty-eight. She had a husband, two kids, a nice house, and a Great Dane. What she hadn't found was her *thing*, her life's work. I'd lost count of Lorna's self-started enterprises. Each time, she'd swear she'd found The

One. That is, until problems sprouted and Lorna careened like a moth toward the flames of her next big idea.

Her newest endeavor was Bibliophiles Find Love, matchmaking based on bookish interests. Lorna wanted dating guinea pigs to test her concept before an official Valentine's Day launch. That's where we came in.

Meg quoted Lorna's much-repeated sales pitch in a dire monotone. " 'We'll delight in a full matchmaking package, a private, catered dinner in an exclusive dining space, the public library.' "

"Lucky us," I said, matching her tone.

Although, dinner in the library did sound pretty cool.

"Foolish us," Meg said. "Want to bet we're the only ones to sign up? Well, us and our dates, wherever Lorna found them."

A fresh horror joined my dread. Lorna soft-opened for applications about three weeks ago. What if no one applied? Our cousin had no boundaries. I pictured her plucking random ringless guys from the produce aisle, ski slopes, or street corners.

My boots inched backward. On their own accord—I couldn't be blamed for their actions.

Meg steadied me.

"Maybe," Meg said, "just possibly, Lorna has a winning idea this time. Matchmaking by reading tastes is a great idea. In any case, it can't be worse than our past dating."

Dear Meg was an optimist at heart, which was truly a wonder, and not just because of her dating history. Meg was a reader, a lover of mysteries.

As we climbed the library steps, I held on to my sister's arm. I clung even tighter to my safe and sensible dread.

Can't be any worse? Any mystery reader knows, things can *always* get worse, with a blind double-twist along the way.

✳

CHAPTER 2

Head in the Sand

Meg tugged open the heavy oak door, and we stepped into the vestibule of the Last Word Free Library. The wood-paneled room held back drafts and allowed all-hours book returns in an antique vault. However, the vestibule was more than practical.

It was a portal.

As a kid, the vestibule had been my wardrobe to Narnia, my time-traveling phone box, a wormhole to worlds past, present, and unknown. All the places that books could take me. I might have grown up in a bookshop, but the library was always special.

Meg and I stomped our boots on a rugged runner. To either side, marble tiles gleamed, dark as the deepest waters, spun with silvery threads like celestial rivers.

If we stepped off, we might sink down, down, down . . .

I tore my eyes from their depths. High above, bat wings glowed, the flared globes of an arts-and-crafts chandelier. A sway took hold, though I swore I was standing still.

The portal! I was back inside, but not in a giddy kid *I'm Nancy Drew off to explore a Gothic mansion* kind of way. I had the off-kilter feeling Meg and I were about to step into another world, one without an escape hatch.

"Ready?" Meg drew a breath.

"No." But there was no turning back. We'd promised Lorna.

Our cousin waited on the other side. Lorna tapped a suede boot on floral carpet.

"There you are!" she said. "Finally!"

Finally? Despite our best foot-dragging efforts, Meg and I had arrived right on time, as confirmed by the Westminster Chimes of a grandfather clock.

"Six o'clock on the dot," Meg said.

"Yes," Lorna acknowledged. "But the library closed at *five*. I was here. I *expected* you to be too."

Meg and I exchanged a glance and sisterly telepathy, in which we agreed on two things. One, this was news to us. Two, we wouldn't argue. Lorna would have opening-night jitters too. We smiled and shed our winterwear, which Lorna insisted on taking.

Lorna marched our coats to the circulation desk at the end of the wide entry hall. Rooms spoked to either side—young adult, kids, reference, periodicals, and adult fiction and nonfiction.

I nudged Meg. "Take note: The magic cart will have to detour to circulation or we'll freeze."

Meg grinned. "I'll risk frostbite."

Lorna returned and we composed polite smiles.

"You both look lovely," Lorna said.

We had Rosie to thank. My niece had taken charge of our date looks, deeming us hopeless. *So true!*

Mascara weighted my lashes. Hairspray stiffened my naturally wavy layers. I could still detect a lingering hint of chemical cloud.

Meg smoothed her single-layer auburn locks, which Rosie had allowed to flow loose at Meg's shoulders. "*You* look lovely, Lorna," Meg said.

Lorna did. She also looked dramatically different from her last professional persona, a fiery redhead hawking Lorna's Doom Fire on the Mountain Hot Sauce. Tonight, Lorna could be on her way to a Downton Abbey tea or Harlequin cover shoot. Corn-silk curls cascaded to her boosted bosom. Her dress floated in gauzy layers and romantic florals.

She turned her saleswoman smile on us. Bright, forceful, a touch terrifying. "You girls are in for a treat. Meg, your biblio-match is tall, handsome, and *very* successful! Dashing, like your own Great Gatsby!"

My sister frowned.

Yeah, Jay Gatsby hadn't exactly enjoyed a happy ending.

Lorna bubbled on. "His name is Darcy! Joe Darcy! Get it? Like in that classic by whatshername?"

"Jane Austen," said Meg, looking stunned.

Was *that* how Lorna had found our dates? Scouring the phone book for bookish names? Who would she have for me? A moody Heathcliff? Mr. Rochester? *No way am I playing Jane Eyre!*

Lorna grabbed my elbow. "Ellie, can you guess who I have for you?"

Yes! Who was another leading cad disguised as a romantic? A draft slithered by with an answer. Maxim de Winter! I first read *Rebecca* as a teenager and considered it a romance. Right! I re-read it a few years back and was appalled. Maxim de Winter wasn't just high-maintenance, prudish, and brooding, he was a—

Lorna squeezed my funny bone, hard. "Ellie, I've found you a *doctor*. A doctor of books!"

A book repairer? That sounded promising. I was about to ask for more details when voices sounded in the vestibule.

The portal groaned. Or was that Meg?

Two men stepped inside, joined by wintery scents of frosty air and woodsmoke. One fit conventional definitions of dashing. Tall with a swoop of dark hair, an aristocratic air, and a well-cut wool coat. The other wore tweed from his brimmed cap and scratchy-looking scarf to a jacket with bronzy velvet elbow patches.

From Lorna's descriptions, I could guess who was matched with whom. Meg with dashing guy. Me with tweedy.

Fine by me. I adored elbow patches and bookish looks, and I was definitely off dashing. All good so far, except tweedy's frown was so furrowed it knocked his thick-framed glasses off-kilter.

"I could have run you over," he grumbled, removing the glasses to let fog slip from their lenses. "You should watch where you're going, even in a crosswalk. A night like this . . . The roads are pure ice. My brakes shuddered."

A cautious driver, I told myself, and nodded approvingly.

Tall and dashing waved off the incident. "Thankfully you and your shuddering brakes missed their mark." He turned a beaming smile to we three cousins. "I wouldn't have wanted to miss this date for the world."

Lorna patted her breast, which was appropriately heaving. "Thank goodness you're both here safely and right on time."

On time? Hadn't Lorna just scolded our promptness? I didn't have time to question my cousin.

She tugged us forward for introductions. "Bibliophile and world-traveler Ellie Christie, meet your brainy book doctor, Waldon O'Grady, professor of English literature at Mid-Mountain College. Meg Christie, bookseller extraordinaire, meet your mystery-loving match, entrepreneur and philanthropist Joe Darcy. Joe heads his own wealth-management firm, plus a children's literacy foundation."

Joe thrust a hand toward Meg, an invitation for an old-fashioned shake.

Waldon removed his hat and gripped it in both hands.

"Don't be shy," Lorna declared. "Ellie, get in there! You two are *perfect* for each other."

With that, my cousin shoved me into the greeting I feared most: the air kiss and its oh-so-many ways to mess up. Which cheek? How many kisses? How distant from actual skin? How smoochy?

On the upside, Waldon and I already had something in common. Awkward kissing. Propelled by Lorna, I plunged toward Waldon's left cheek. Caught by surprise, he jerked left too. We swerved—again in the same direction. We wobbled, head-stuttered, ran out of space, and—inevitably—collided.

My too-smoochy kiss landed on his earlobe. Waldon got caught up in my aerosol-stiffened hair. He backed away in wide-eyed horror.

My misery turned to Meg but found no company. Joe Darcy held my sister's hand in both of his. Meg smiled into eyes a romance novelist would describe with a beverage menu: dark espresso. Americano, tall. Those yummy eyes took in Meg the way I'd gaze upon a new book by a favorite author.

With joy that something long-awaited was finally in my grasp.

With heart-fluttering anticipation.

With an I can't wait to gobble you up *hunger?*

I frowned. I was being overly dramatic, I told myself. I was almost convinced when a gong reverberated, loud enough to flutter pages.

Waldon matched my startled jump. Ah, another commonality.

"Bibliophiles," trilled a high-pitched voice. "Appetizers will begin shortly."

Lorna's fellow matchmaker, Marigold Jones, resembled her floral namesake, from her copper hair with its thick fringe of bangs to her leaf-appliquéd cardigan and red ruffled skirt. She was in her forties, I guessed, and a children's librarian by day. The latter comforted me. If she could get kids to sit still for story hour, she could manage four adults on a date.

Marigold led us to the reference room with its dark wood and leatherbound treasures.

I gasped. Candles flickered on shelves, inches from antique pages. Flames blazed and tapers dripped at each end of the mahogany research table.

"Oh," said Meg. "How, ah . . ."

"Romantic!" Lorna supplied.

I supposed "romantic" was a synonym for flammable.

Lorna bubbled on. "Remember when I sold Serenity Flame Candles? Pure soy, high-drama drips. I have a bunch in my garage still. Available for purchase—friends and family discount! Fire sale, ha!"

Lorna was a born salesperson. All she lacked were commitment, a healthy dose of caution, and actual sales.

Marigold directed us to our assigned seats with formal intonations. I was Eleanor J. Christie, Joe was Joseph Harrison Darcy, and my date was Associate Professor Waldon Q. O'Grady, PhD, MFA.

I was across from Waldon, with Joe at my right and Meg diagonally across. Perfect—I could catch Meg's eye and mouth "ostrich."

Except, as the dinner wore on, Meg had eyes only for her date. Meanwhile, Waldon's gaze fixed somewhere between my shoulder and Mr. Darcy's head, as unwavering as his topic of conversation. Waldon spoke only of his literary idol, the great Irish author Samuel Beckett.

Initially, I blamed myself. I should have asked about his middle name.

Instead, after Marigold plunked down Greek salads catered by an Italian restaurant, I asked Waldon (*Dr.* Waldon, he'd corrected) what he liked to read.

Big mistake.

He read Beckett, books about Beckett, and peer-reviewed articles on all things Beckett.

"I'm drawn to the refined absurdity," Dr. Waldon said.

That made one of us. I sipped sensible Syrah and tallied the evening's absurdities.

Candles. Thankfully, their flames were down in number. Marigold extinguished some when she swooped in with plates of pasta.

The meal. The food was delicious, but what sadist chose spaghetti and meatballs for a first date? A date in the library! I twirled a single strand, drenched in red sauce, all too aware of the antique books inches behind me.

My attire. Why hadn't I worn black? Rosie said the sage in my sweater dress set off the hazel in my eyes. More realistically, my eyes were brown and the dress was a one-piece palette for ragu splatters.

Dr. Waldon? Did he make the absurd list? No, I decided, but he was a bore and a reminder that all things have their limits, even talk of books.

I tuned back in and confirmed he was still belaboring Beckett—specifically, his favorite play, *Waiting for Godot*.

Pavlov's yawn rose. I gulped it back. That play! I understood its literary importance, but I'd also fallen asleep in it three times. I'd only been three times, twice with precautionary pre-play naps. I murmured to let Waldon know I was still awake.

Not that he cared.

"Sublime futility," he said, staring toward Mr. Darcy's good hair.

Would he notice if I sank under the table and crawled away? *Doubtful.*

Would Meg? Also unlikely. She and Mr. Darcy locked eyes. Over Waldon's talk of the forever-late Godot, I caught snippets of their conversation.

Meg spoke animatedly of her favorite mysteries. Mr. Darcy listened with apparent rapt enthusiasm. The man was a bookish hero!

And I was an eavesdropper.

I sighed and turned to a favorite distraction, bookish list-making. Topic: favorite Austen novels.

Pride and Prejudice had to be number one. Then? *Persuasion.* Its poor heroine, wracked with romantic regret and already an old maid in her twenties. Meg and I would be beyond ancient by such standards. *What was number three?*

A shift in Dr. Waldon's drone jerked me back. Had his words risen in pitch? A question? I attempted a fast rewind and failed.

"Ah, sorry, what?" Okay, so I was also failing at scintillating conversation.

Dr. Waldon had just stuffed a pasta clump the size of an osprey nest into his mouth. He chewed, thoroughly. He dabbed his napkin, meticulously. Finally, he said, "What are *you* reading?"

My favorite dinner topic! Karma was rewarding me.

"Christie," I said. "Agatha Christie, of course. I've read all her books, but I'm going back to her short stories."

I was about to elaborate when Dr. Waldon made an odd sound. A throat tickle? A bit of Parmesan or pepper gone down the wrong way?

A scoff?

No one would scoff at Agatha Christie. I'd misheard, surely.

"Do you, ah, like Christie?" As soon as the words were out, I regretted them. I'd just broken a key rule of small talk with strangers. Never ask a question that may invite a disagreeable answer.

He shrugged.

Uh-oh . . .

Dr. Waldon laid down his cutlery and tented his fingertips. I braced myself for professing.

"Literarily speaking," he said, and proceeded to lecture. Christie, he contended, was overrated. More of a *popular* author.

Popular was a problem?

"She's the best-selling author of all time," I said. "Over two billion copies sold." The number boggled the mind.

Dr. Waldon raised an eyebrow and a smile. No, correction, a smirk.

I squirmed like a called-out student. "Best-selling after the Bible and Shakespeare," I qualified. "Best-selling *novelist*. She also wrote plays too, as I'm sure you know. *The Mousetrap* still sets the record for longest-running performance." Only the pandemic had temporarily put it on pause.

"Yes," Dr. Waldon said blandly. "I must always remind my students, popularity does not equate to quality."

As he meticulously quartered and chewed meatballs, I rehearsed a retort.

People should read what they like! If you liked a book, then it was quality to you!

I drowned my fuming in a glug of Syrah. I wouldn't convince Dr. Waldon, and arguing certainly wouldn't improve this date.

I did have to ask, though. "Have you read Christie?" What I *really* disliked was people dismissing books they hadn't read.

"Me? I've sampled enough to know. I find her characters and plots . . . silly? Extreme? Jane Marple, for instance. Could an older woman sitting around knitting solve all those crimes from her armchair?"

Yes! And had he just picked on Agatha Christie, to a Christie? We Last Word Christies sadly had no relation to our favorite author, but still—that was personal! In a tiny act of absurd rebellion, I raised my wineglass and whispered, "*Oh, ostrich!*"

"Ostrich? Indeed!" Dr. Waldon suddenly looked interested. "Yes, you're absolutely right, Eleanor. We cannot see what others see, in books or life. To quote the great Beckett, 'Any fool can turn a blind eye but who knows what the ostrich sees in the sand.'"

I telepathed a scream Meg's way: *Ostrich! He said ostrich!*

Meg was too busy glowing.

I aimed my fork at a globby clump of pasta and twirled with

abandon. The candles dripped and flickered. Dr. Waldon resumed talk of Beckett, and I stuck my head in the sand until finally, blessedly, the date was done.

We stepped through the vestibule into frigid air as sweet as a summer's evening. Our matchmakers waved from the library steps. I could have danced, twirled, and skipped.

I politely restrained myself.

Dr. Waldon didn't. He aimed his keychain down the street. A black hatchback issued a cheery *beep-beep*.

Meg and Mr. Darcy lingered, still starry-eyed.

Dr. Waldon frowned their way, then remembered me. "Ah . . . Thank you for the enjoyable evening."

"Thank you!" I said, overcome with smiles. *I was free!*

"Can I give you a ride anywhere?" my date asked. He shot a dubious glance up into the darkness, as if already anticipating shuddering brakes.

My smile could have melted the snowpack. "No, thanks. It'll be good to work off all that pasta."

"All right." Dr. Waldon gave up way too easily. "I'll hope to see you again soon, Eleanor."

With that—and thankfully no more misplaced kisses—he hustled to his car, looking very much unlike someone who hoped we'd meet again. Fine by me.

"Drive safely!" I called out, waving. His car slipped away silently, like it had been designed for escaping dates. I inched into Meg's glow and asked if I should wait for her.

Her cheeks flushed pink from cold, wine, Joe, or all of the above. "Joe and I thought we'd go for a little stroll downtown. We can walk you to the gondola station. Joe? Shall we?"

"We'd be delighted," said Mr. Darcy.

So chivalrous. I'd have none of it. I declined with thanks and enthusiasm. "Have fun strolling. Sounds fabulous!"

It did, but not as wonderful as my impending date with a book, cozy PJs, and Agatha C. The night, I thought with heedless optimism, was looking up.

*

CHAPTER 3

Giving Up on Ghosts

"Your sister is humming," observed Ms. Ridge.

I paused, listened, and grinned. John Denver floated in from somewhere back in the maze of aisles. "Sunshine on My Shoulders," I said.

"Indeed," said Ms. Ridge, raising both eyebrows.

Sunlight bathed my shoulders, lazy Sunday light that promised a relaxing day. The shop would open soon. Agatha and I were arranging display copies in the front window. I set books on pedestals. Agatha judged whether they should remain standing. Her extra-fluffy Siamese cheeks were currently nuzzling a biography of Agatha Christie. The hefty volume toppled. Agatha looked up at me with wide eyes the color of a tropical sea. Innocent eyes, one might think, except for the twinkle of challenge and smug satisfaction.

I righted the biography and admired the subtitle: *An Elusive Woman*. Agatha had good taste.

"Your dates went well," said Ms. Ridge.

To say that Ms. Ridge respected personal privacy was calling ice cold, water wet, or Agatha Cat Christie adorable. All obvious, undeniable facts. In Ms. Ridge terms, these observations neared tabloid-level prying.

Ms. Ridge had come to work for the Book Chalet years ago, drawn by her love of the shop as well as a desire to escape elements of her past. During the unfortunate events of last November, Ms. Ridge's secrets and private life had become painfully public. By tacit agreement, we'd all settled back into her preferred fiction, which was, essentially, fact. Ms. Ridge was a modest and efficient bookshop assistant.

"Meg's date went very well," I said.

"Ah," said Ms. Ridge. Her "ah" implied volumes of understanding about my date. I couldn't let her skip to dire conclusions, which would be logical given her relationship history and mine.

"There was nothing *wrong* with my date," I said. "We didn't click. Not like Meg and Mr. Darcy."

"*Mr. Darcy?*" Ms. Ridge smiled and went off in search of some Austen novels for the Valentine's display. Agatha nuzzled a memoir about trail-running with burros by a local author. I took her recommendation and placed the book front-and-center in the window.

Humming grew closer. Meg strolled in with a book.

"What do you have?" I asked.

"Mmm?" Meg looked up dreamily. "Oh, I found this lovely copy of *The Thirteen Problems*. Joe asked about my favorite Christies. He didn't know this one. Agatha Christie herself put it on her top-ten list. Miss Marple solving crimes from her armchair."

Meg chatted on. Joe was stopping by soon. He wanted to see the shop. Then they'd go to brunch.

"Nice," I said. Like Ms. Ridge's "ah," my "nice" covered territory. Nice that Joe appreciated Meg and Miss Marple. *See, Dr. Waldon!* Nice that Meg was going to brunch, a rare indulgence. Nicest of all: my happy sister.

I turned the door sign to OPEN. Agatha retired to her red velvet pillow in the window, and Meg floated around the shop.

An hour later, however, her humming had stopped.

"Oh dear," Ms. Ridge said, when I told her of Meg's would-be brunch plans. "It's noon."

According to the most accurate among our antique cuckoo clocks, it was three minutes beyond noon.

Faced with evidence of a no-show date, some might have offered bright excuses. Maybe Joe overslept or stopped to help an elderly woman or kittens cross the road.

Not Ms. Ridge. She said nothing. The firm set of her jaw said it all.

That jerk stood Meg up!

Meg had clearly reached the same conclusion. She stomped to the lobby, dressed to leave.

Ms. Ridge tactfully—wisely—slipped away to help customers.

I readied myself to offer sisterly support. If Meg needed outrage, I was there for her! Sympathy, empathy? Absolutely. Cursing? *Joe Darcy was such an ostrich!*

Meg held up her cellphone. "That's it," she said.

"You're calling Joe?"

"What?" Meg's tone implied I'd suggested kitty litter on her cappuccino. "No way, El. I'm a fool. That's the most embarrassing part. I *let* myself get smitten after a single date."

"No! It's him, not you," I said.

Meg jabbed at her phone. When a voice sounded on the other end, she declared, "Lorna, it's Meg."

Uh-oh.

Bubbly sounds from Lorna's end suggested she was praising our dates.

"Lorna!" Meg interjected. "Remove me from your dating list. Please. Thank you."

Lorna's garbles turned to disbelief.

Meg said stiffly, "Yes, I believe you *attempted* to vet him. However, that man stood me up. Remove me from your dating rolls. Immediately."

I totally empathized. Yet . . . Meg seemed pretty upset for a single dinner date in the library. Had something more happened?

Meg's voice rose in volume and pitch. "Oh? You think he has a good excuse?"

I was so caught up gawking, I didn't notice Last Word's preeminent (and only) gossip columnist step up to the counter.

A tsk-tsk alerted me. "That's not good," said Piper Tuttle. Her gleaming birdlike eyes said just the opposite. "Man trouble?"

Yes, but Meg didn't need gossip trouble topping it off. I changed the subject.

"Great book," I said, nodding to a selection from our winter-themed Agatha Christie display. "*Midwinter Murder* is perfect for the season. Or a summer beach read. Any occasion, really."

I might as well have told the cash register. Piper wasn't listening to me. Neither were the other supposed book browsers in the lobby. Sure, some pretended to read back covers, but I knew better. They hung on Meg's next words.

What unfortunate words . . .

"Lorna," my sister said icily. "Unless that man is on his deathbed, I do *not* want to hear his excuses."

Meg stabbed her phone to end the call. Then she looked up, and her cheeks reddened to maraschino cherry.

"Hey, Meg, everything okay?" Piper trilled.

My sister ducked her head and made for the door. "El, I'm going home." The string of cowbells hanging from the handle rattled behind her.

"So, who does our Meg want dead?" Piper asked.

I could have clarified that Meg said "deathbed," not "dead." But that would mean repeating the words. Piper wrote a column for our local weekly newspaper called "Heard about Town." If she heard something twice, she considered it common knowledge and thus fair game for quoting. Or misquoting.

"Nice weather today!" I exclaimed, as if that would distract Piper.

"Unexpectedly *heated* for below freezing," Piper said with a chuckle. "Did I hear that you and your sister are on the marriage market? Arranged meetups in the public library? Do tell!"

I forced a smile. "Our cousin Lorna is starting a new business, Bibliophiles Find Love. Book-based matchmaking. Isn't that a wonderful idea? I'm sure she'd love to tell you about it."

She would. Lorna could spin any situation. Plus, she ascribed to the timeworn falsehood that any publicity was good.

"Book lovers are passionate people," Piper said with wolfish glee. She patted her book. "Let's hope we don't have a midwinter murder of our own."

She left with an unseasonably springy step. I tried to shake off the chill she'd planted in my core. I rang up books, gave reading recommendations, and treated myself to hot chocolate from our Coffee Cantina.

An hour later, the landline rang. I answered. "Hello, you've reached the Book Chalet, where reading is our pleasure—"

"Ellie!" Words tumbled out and a memory swooped in.

The summer before I entered fifth grade, Lorna invited me on a trip to Elitch Gardens, a Denver amusement park. Lorna convinced me to ride the roller coaster even though as a kid (like now) I preferred my thrills from books. For the entire ride, Lorna scream-gabbled. Think *Ellie-we're-going-to-die-open-your-eyes-you-have-to-see-this-I-love-you-we're-going-to-die-auuuughhh!*

That was the voice on the other end.

"Lorna?" I said over the whoosh. "Slow down . . ."

The word coaster rolled on.

"Lorna, please! What's going on?"

"I'm at his house!"

I understood the words, but not their meaning. A pair of customers approached. I smiled at them, raised on my tiptoes, and waved to catch Ms. Ridge's eye. When I did, I mimed a request. *Could she take over the register? Please?*

Ms. Ridge nodded with brisk agreement and a concerned frown.

Mouthing "thank you" all around, I moved to a corner by the door.

"Whose house?" I feared I already knew.

"*His*. Joe Darcy's." She plunged into another free fall. "After Meg called, I raced up here. I told Meg, there must be a misunderstanding. Joe's a catch and my matchmaking system is based on my groundbreaking psychological survey and—"

I tried again. "Lorna, what, *exactly,* is the problem?"

"He's not *here*!"

Every muscle I'd been unconsciously tensing relaxed. My loosened eyes did a 180-degree roll.

"Okay," I said slowly. "That doesn't sound too alarming."

"El, I knocked on the front door and it opened, so I went in. Don't worry, I know the woman who owns this place. I listed it for her when I was a realtor but then she wanted to rent it out instead and . . ."

I waited for Lorna's real-estate thoughts to run their course.

". . . so, the kitchen's a dream but it's *weird,* Ellie."

She paused, my cue to inquire.

I obliged. "Weird how?" If Lorna critiqued a cabinet remodel, I'd fake a bad connection and hang up.

"There's a mess. Not a breakfast mess. Wineglasses and fancy crackers and cheese."

I aimed for reason and calm. "Maybe he went out and didn't tidy up."

"There's wine on a carpet, Ellie. White *sheepskin* in the kitchen! At least, I think it's wine? It's red . . ."

My stomach lurched.

"Ellie, *please,*" Lorna begged. "Come look. I'm outside. I didn't want to be in there with that wine or whatever." She rattled off an address on the other side of the hamlet.

"You should—" *You should call the police,* I would have said. But Lorna had hung up.

I could call the police. But then . . .

Lorna had another trait. She exaggerated. Back on that roller coaster, Lorna had assured me that we were absolutely, definitely, no-doubt-about-it going to perish. When we didn't, she'd sold me on corn dogs—*You'll 110% love them!*—and the Tilt-A-Whirl—*Of course your stomach will be fine!*

Lorna had only gotten more persuasive with age. Why, she'd assured Meg and me that her matchmaking was guaranteed and no-risk. Ha! Still, Lorna was upset and waiting in the cold. I had to go ease her mind.

And mine . . .

* * *

I speed-walked across the hamlet to Moosejaw Lane, which resembled its name. After a short hook, the street followed the edge of Moosejaw Canyon before curving into a dead end. Old-timers had steered clear of building on ledges. Not so the modern crowd. Chalets of glass, metal, and timber clung to the canyon's edge.

Lorna's Kia was parked a few houses up, still sporting its hot-sauce paint job: fiery red decorated in dancing peppers and flames. Lorna jumped out and waved me in like landing a plane.

"I *knew* you wouldn't let me down!" Lorna swung me into an air kiss.

"If something's wrong, we should call the police," I said through minor whiplash.

"It's okay. You're here now." Lorna trotted up the walkway.

"We can't just go in," I protested.

Lorna already was. "I told you, I know the owner, Fiona Giddings. Isn't this a *fabulous* property? Do you think I should have stayed in real estate?"

"I don't know." I didn't. Not about Lorna's career choices or whether we should summon the police, trespass, or deem Joe Darcy a jerk or victim.

"Come on, Ellie," Lorna beckoned.

Lorna was right about one thing. The house was fabulous, if you were into minimalism. White walls, white sofas with thin pillows standing stiffly around a glass coffee table. Glass, everywhere.

"The kitchen's over there." Lorna pointed toward a glossy expanse of snow-white cabinets with nary a knob.

I stalled, scanning the living space. Something was missing. Well, besides Joe Darcy, coziness, and cabinet pulls. "Where are the books?"

Joe Darcy was a book lover. *Allegedly!*

Lorna huffed. "I don't know, El. He *said* he loves books. He signed up for Bibliophiles Find Love. What am I supposed to do, run a background check on his library card?"

Yes?

"He just moved here. He's *renting.*"

I'd hopscotched around the globe for years, renting, housesitting, and bookshop-sitting. I'd carried minimal luggage but I'd always—*always!*—had books, even in the age of electronic texts.

Lorna strode across the bookless space, chunky-heeled boots clonking on pale wood planks.

"Wait, Lorna," I called after her. "What if he's in the shower? Asleep?"

"Win all around! He's hot, plus we'll know where he is. We can apologize."

Apologize? Sure, right after I lectured him about hurting my sister. I caught up with Lorna in a kitchen with high-end appliances and French doors overlooking a deck and the canyon beyond.

Lorna clicked her tongue. "See? Sheepskin. I hope Fiona stain-guarded that. Wine and sheep do not mix."

I shuddered and not just for the unfortunate sheep. A bottle of Pinot stood on the island. Two glasses lay toppled beside it.

The wine spill was a relief, but the glasses weren't the only dis-array. A fireplace set sprawled across the floor, as if kicked.

"It's like he was abducted or something!" Lorna shook her head at the rug.

A shiver gripped me. "It's cold in here."

"That patio door was open a sliver. I shut it."

"The patio? Did you look outside?" The large deck ended in glass panels. The view kept going, like an infinity pool of air.

My cousin sniffed. "El, I think we'd notice a handsome, eli-gible bachelor out there."

"What about beyond the balcony?"

"There's nothing but canyon and . . . Oh!" Lorna paled and reached for my arm. For support, I guessed. I was wrong.

"You go!" Lorna pushed me forward. "You have more experi-ence."

"With balconies?" But I knew what she meant. I had more experience with trouble.

"With bravery!" Lorna released my arm and slid open a door.

Frigid air sliced in. "It was *your* idea to look outside," Lorna said, now shoving.

"It was *your* idea to trespass in his house."

"Yes, exactly. *In* the house. I'll go snoop in the closets if you want. Off you go . . ."

All I had to do was look. When there was nothing to see, I'd return to maligning Joe Darcy. Not abducted or in danger. Just a slobby bachelor who failed to clean up his spills and show up for dates.

I stepped to the door and told myself more stories. A clean-ing lady. That was it. Joe called someone over to clean up his mess. He left the door open for her. I pictured a charwoman straight out of Agatha Christie. Battleship solid. Bearer of a broad Yorkshire accent. Fueled by tea, scones, and hot-burning gossip.

I stepped outside, bolstered with indignation for my ficti-
tious cleaner—with arthritic knuckles and a bad knee, no less!
Wind slapped at my cheeks. Someone had been out before me.
A path dented the snow, smoothed to ghostly by the wind.
When I reached the glass balcony, I clamped on to it like a life
raft.

The earth fell away, a drop of at least two stories. If I had this
deck, I'd sit back by the house and look straight ahead. I'd . . .

I looked down. Color caught my eye. And a lump, softer than
the jagged boulders. I traced a form like a chalk outline. Legs.
Arms outstretched as if soaring.

No! No, no, no!

I staggered backward. One step. Two steps. Three . . . my
foot landed on something round and hard. It rolled and so did
I, flailing first, then going down in a painful thud.

Lorna squealed my name. My bare hands gripped snow so
cold it hurt. One clutched at the treacherous object. A ski pole?
Fishing pole? I pushed it aside, scrambled up, and lurched for
the house.

Lorna caught me in a hug. "Honey, what happened?"

"Someone's down there. Someone fell."

"*Someone?*" Lorna released me. "Oh no! Joe?"

Dark hair. Long limbs. His house. "I think so."

Lorna grabbed her phone.

"Hello?" I heard her say through my head-spinning daze.
"We need an ambulance. A man fell from his balcony. Hurry!"

Lorna gave the address and our names. She paced the kitchen
as she spoke, tidying as she went. She righted wineglasses,
straightened a doormat, and corralled the fallen fireplace tools.

Something wasn't right . . .

Obviously!

I reached out to stop Lorna.

"It's okay, El, I have this." She waved me away and said to the
dispatcher, "Yes, he fell. Hurry!"

Could Joe still be alive? I tallied the elements. The snow, the cold, the angle of his limbs, that drop, the object rolling under my boot. My stomach replayed the moment with a lurch and flip. My fingers mimed a grip. The pole had been heavy. Not a ski pole. Hard, cold metal . . .

Lorna replaced the final fireplace tool with a *clank*.

Or maybe not the last one.

I swayed toward my cousin and blurted into her phone. "The police. Send the police and tell them to hurry!"

CHAPTER 4

✳

Death on the Rocks

I was a bookseller. I faced down scary situations all the time. Payroll, taxes, upkeep of a fifth-generation family shop. I had skills. Lots of them. I was widely read. I was great with reading recommendations and those puzzlers presented by customers. *I'm looking for this book but I don't remember the title. The cover's red? There's a woman in it . . .*

Gravel slid under my boot. The slope pitched. I pinwheeled my arms and resumed my steadying list.

I climbed tall ladders to reach high shelves.

I managed the social-media accounts of a semi-famous bookshop cat!

I looked down again and fought back vertigo. None of these skills prepared me to scramble down a rocky slope in aid of an unmoving man. Well, except for being widely read. That *should* have convinced me not to come down here.

What-ifs had overridden caution and common sense. What if, in the time it took for an ambulance to arrive, Joe took his last breath? What if I could have saved him? Snow was an insulator. I'd read about hypothermia victims who survived in just-alive states under frosty blankets. There was hope. There had to be.

The slope steepened. I lowered to a crouch.

"Be careful!" Lorna yelled from the flat crest of Joe's yard. "You want a hand?"

Yes, but Lorna wasn't about to climb down and offer one. Her boots were suede, she'd informed me earlier. Suede did not expose itself to snowy misadventures. Plus, she didn't do steep. This, from the cousin who'd bullied me onto roller coasters?

"No. Thanks, I'm fine!" I lied. "Watch for the ambulance. Wave them down."

"On it!"

I scootched along, half-sitting. Cold and grit seeped through my jeans and mittens. I stopped on a ledge above where Joe lay. To reach him, I'd have to drop down. I inched to the edge, stretched onto my tiptoes, held my breath, whispered *"Please, please, please,"* and let go.

The few inches felt like miles. I landed in a wobble, braced myself against the wind and dizzying nerves, and removed a mitten. With a trembling hand, I reached for his neck and prayed for a pulse.

My chilled fingers met ice-cold skin. I yanked my hand away as if singed, dropping my mitten. As I reached to retrieve it, my eye caught movement. Paper fluttered on a rock a few feet below Joe. A ripped page? I leaned, squinting at words in large, loopy marker. *I know . . . who . . . I know who?*

Who what? It was probably nothing. Yet what if it wasn't?

Wind waggled the page closer, then back. Carefully, I placed a boot on the next rock down. I was feeling pretty agile until the rock tipped like a seesaw on surf waves. I jumped off and landed on a patch of snow-covered gravel. Good, until the gravel let loose, taking me with it. The rocks and I rolled downhill, sledding toward a drop-off. I dug in heels, palms, fingertips, and elbows until my boots crashed into the sweetest boulder I'd ever met.

"I'm okay! It's okay!" I yelled. Silence responded. Where was

Lorna? Making her way down, heedless of suede? Engrossed in her phone?

I soon got an answer.

"Yoo-hoo!" Lorna trilled. "Officer? Over here! Help! My cousin fell over a dead man!"

* * *

When you're stuck on a slippery slope midway between a corpse and a cliff, time moves slowly. Not a pleasurable slowness either, like a leisurely afternoon curled up with a book.

For something to do, I took stock of my aches. Butt, yep, definitely bruised. Hips? My left hip throbbed. Hands? I held up both. A mitten, knit by Gram in red and green, had protected my right hand. My mitten-less left hand was scuffed and my fingertips were pale, turning icy.

Head? Physically, I was pretty sure I was okay. Mentally, I ached. I couldn't face Joe. Not yet. I felt like I'd failed him.

I leaned back and rested my head on cold granite. A Steller's jay alighted nearby, his blue-black crest tipping inquisitively.

"I can't," I groaned to Steller.

Another fib. I *could.* I could crawl/climb back up that hill. I didn't want to.

Steller cackled in what I interpreted as either a rightful chiding or a birdie pep talk. Either way, easy for him to say. He could fly.

"Not yet." I just needed a minute. Or two. I could close my eyes. Foreboding muttered something about closing one's eyes in the snow . . .

"Hold on!"

My eyelids popped open. I loved fairy tales, but I didn't believe the jay had acquired the ability to speak.

I twisted to look upslope. A man jogged down, hopping from rock to rock, as nimble as a mountain goat. I took in tan combat boots, olive cargo pants, a beige jacket with a logo, dark hair closely cropped, and features as chiseled as the granite. A hero, racing to my rescue, a prince popped from the pages of an outdoorsy catalog.

Steller had been right. I should have gotten up and rescued myself! This man was wasting time on me when he should be attending to Joe.

Except we were all too late to help dashing Joe Darcy.

The boots landed at my side. A waft of fresh soap and piney cologne reached my nose.

"Sam Ibarra. Detective, Last Word PD. Are you hurt?" He crouched and assessed me and our surroundings.

The jay fell silent, perhaps in awe. The detective had gray eyes, the color of granite flecked with gold. It was a good thing I was totally off handsome outdoorsy types. Lorna, on the other hand, was probably up there swooning.

"I'm fine," I said. "I was trying to reach some paper. . . ."

"Paper?" He frowned.

I winced. "I mean, I climbed down here because of that man. He's . . ." Words made it all too real and final.

"Yes, ma'am. I checked him on the way down."

Of course he had. He was a professional, right down to his "ma'am."

"And then I saw some paper by him and I slipped. . . ." I continued.

He reached out a hand.

I hesitated. I didn't *need* rescuing. But I sure wouldn't mind some help. I took his hand and was nearly lifted off my feet.

"What's your name?" His voice was hot-chocolate warm and concerned. I pinched the bridge of my nose. Maybe I had hit my head. What was I doing, comparing his voice to beverages?

"Ellie," I said, dusting grit and prickly grasses from my backside. "Ellie Christie."

He nodded briskly. "Okay, Ellie. Follow my steps. We'll go back up the scree slope. Dig the toes of your boots in the loose rock, okay? Do you climb? Hike? Rappel?"

"I sell books."

He reached back a hand.

Was that a statement on a bookseller's ability to navigate tough paths? "Thanks," I said. "But I'm okay."

To his credit, he didn't question that—no more than he already had. He moved at slow mountain-goat speed. I placed my footsteps in his, repeating a silent mantra. I was a bookseller. Booksellers were tough. I was a Christie. Christies were . . . ? Hardy? Brave? Great with stories!

I told myself a happy mundane fantasy. I was out for a hike, a pleasant walk in the open air with a new friend. I was just fine.

I was, until we reached Joe's ledge. My eyes tugged to his unmoving form. Could he have fallen accidentally? I looked up. Joe was tall. The glass barrier to the balcony wasn't all that high. He could have lost his balance, fallen on that poker.

But why take a poker to the deck?

"Do you know him?" Detective Ibarra asked.

I nodded, biting my lower lip.

"Okay," my rescuer said gently. "You're already a huge help, Ellie. You can tell my boss and me all about him later."

Except I hadn't helped and I barely knew Joe Darcy. I'd smiled hellos. He'd charmed my sister.

I focused on something I could fix. My dropped mitten. I couldn't leave it littering a crime scene. Plus, my hand was cold and Gram had knit that mitten. I wanted it back.

"That's my mitten," I said. "I'll just grab it." Now I hoped for chivalry. Detective Ibarra could offer to retrieve my mitten.

He thrust out an arm to block my reach.

"Leave it." His tone was as firm as the outstretched arm. "We'll return it to you later. Let's get you out of here."

I couldn't argue with leaving. In a few nimble steps, he was up and over the ledge and holding out his hand again.

I took it and held on as we navigated over the boulder field. When we were back to gravel, I reluctantly slipped my hand from his.

I could manage from here. Besides, I didn't want to give Lorna any matchmaking misconceptions.

Detective Ibarra hovered close. "You feel okay? You didn't hit your head? You sure you don't want a hand?"

"My head's *fine*," I assured him, practiced with this go-to fib. "Thank you. You got me over the worst part."

Another lie. My biggest one yet. The worst would be breaking the awful news to my sister.

CHAPTER 5

＊

Death Under the Clouds

I was wrong. There was something worse than breaking the news to Meg.

Not getting to tell her myself.

As Detective Ibarra and I crested the hill, a macabre carnival came into view. Lights flashed from an ambulance and a police SUV. A small crowd gathered on the street. Neighbors, I guessed, and gathering gossipers.

Three figures stood near the house. Cousin Lorna, Police Chief "Sunnie" Sundstrom, and my sister.

Lorna added to my worst-case scenario. Her voice carried in the clear, cold air.

"Being stood up's Meg's trigger," Lorna declared. "Of course she was steaming mad when her date didn't show!"

If I hadn't been huffing and puffing, I might have yelled for Lorna to shush, not that that would have helped.

"A trigger makes us irrational," Lorna was saying. "I have a certificate in wilderness-centered therapy. Meg, if you'd *actually* been stood up, I'd have prescribed forest therapy. Trees soothe anger and anxiety . . ."

My anxiety spiked higher than the pines ringing the canyon.

A man was dead from unknown circumstances, and Lorna was broadcasting Meg's anger to the chief of police?

"Who's the therapist?" Detective Ibarra asked.

"My cousin," I said, trying to breathe while putting on speed. "Meg's my sister."

"Nice to have a therapist in the family." He sounded relaxed, like we could be back at the Chalet with hot tea and cookies.

I surmised two things. One, he was reading too much into Lorna's therapy. Not that I could blame him. Lorna was going on about a "red mist of anger" and the benefits of yelling into waterfalls. *All your negativity flows downstream.* Two? I desperately needed a date with a StairMaster.

I summoned another breath and called out Meg's and Lorna's names.

Lorna raised her arm high and waved back. "Ellie! Thank goodness! You've been rescued. Officer, you're our hero!"

That slowed the intrepid Detective Ibarra. I reached the trio first and wrapped my arms around my sister. Meg squeezed me, hard.

"I'm so sorry about Joe," I said, muffled in her hair. "I should have called you right away, but I wanted to check on him first."

"Oh, El," Meg said. "I feel awful. Poor Joe! There I was, doubting him. Lorna's right. I wasn't myself."

Lorna agreed. "To think, you threatened to quit Bibliophiles Find Love. You're still in, right?"

Meg stiffened.

I broke our hug to shoot Lorna a look of disbelief.

Lorna missed it. She was too busy introducing herself as "Last Word's premier matchmaker" to Detective Ibarra.

If she asked about his relationship status, I'd see red.

Lorna restrained herself. However, she did cast a pointed look at Ibarra's ringless left hand, followed by a raised eyebrow to me.

Chief Sunnie also turned her attention to the detective. She nodded downslope. "Condition?"

He shook his head in an all-too-readable message. "I better suit up and get back down there. Ms. Christie reported potential evidence. Storm's coming in. We don't want it blown away."

He strode to an SUV at the end of the drive.

Lorna watched him go with way too obvious appreciation.

The rest of us inspected a bluebird sky. A storm? What was he talking about? Was he one of those locals who claimed to feel weather shifts in his marrow? I was about to write off his prediction. Then I saw it. A gray tongue poking from behind the highest peak.

The chief spotted the cloud too. She frowned. When that failed to chase it away, she tugged down her signature hat. Sherlock Holmes had his deerstalker, at least in the popular imagination. In his books, not so much. Chief Sunnie had her plaid cap, replete with earflaps and fluffy interior lining.

The chief hailed from sunny California. She'd moved here last year and told the local paper her hopes for her new home. She craved fresh mountain air, small-town charms, wildlife sightings (she especially yearned to see a moose), and a lower incidence of major crime.

Fresh air and small-town charm enveloped us. The chief had achieved those goals. I hoped she'd finally spotted a moose. Even more, I prayed this wasn't a crime.

I registered that she was asking about my evidence.

"There was some torn paper," I said. "It could have been nothing. I only read a few words. *I know who . . .*"

The chief sighed. "I wish this were nothing . . ."

She eyed me, then Meg, with the same look she'd given the cloud, as if our presence boded ill. "I'll get your full statements later, but let me make sure I have the basics. Lorna, you already told me—you set Meg and Ellie up on blind dates last night." The chief shivered under her many layers.

"I did!" Lorna exclaimed. "Matched by my soon-to-be-trademarked Bibliophiles Find Love psychology- and book-based system." She beamed, then remembered the circumstances and swung into a pout.

"Right," the chief said. "And, Meg, you were matched with the deceased?"

Meg sniffled.

"Where'd you go?" the chief asked.

Meg and I let Lorna gush on about our exclusive library dinner.

"Perfect matches, all around," Lorna said sadly. "My system worked. Chief, are you single? Valentine's Day is our official launch. I'm offering exclusive early-bird pricing for new members."

The chief slow-blinked. I recognized this as her gathering-patience move.

I empathized with the chief. With Lorna too. My cousin must be in shock. That would account for her inappropriate fixation on dating. Plus, a dead client couldn't be good for her fledgling business. But mostly, Lorna knew no boundaries.

"Not now, Lorna," Meg said tightly.

Lorna huffed.

Chief Sunnie resumed her questions. "Did anything seem amiss with Mr. Darcy? Did he appear concerned, distracted? Anyone he argued with?"

"No. He was perfectly attentive," Meg said. "Pleasant. Nice . . ."

"And after the library dinner?" Chief Sunnie asked.

Meg scuffed at the snow. She'd worn a patch away, exposing winter-dormant grass. "Neither of us wanted the date to end. We walked around downtown for a bit."

Beeping interrupted her. The ambulance backed into the street. The crowd of watchers inched away, then oozed into its empty spot. Detective Ibarra waved them to a halt. A large duffle bag lay at his feet. He pulled out a Tyvek suit and began tugging it on.

The chief noted his progress. "Ellie, I'll be going inside the house. Your cousin told me things seemed 'off.' She also said that you asked for the police. Why?"

Lorna interrupted. "I've changed my mind on the off-ness. This is surely a tragic accident. Right, Ellie?"

My cousin wanted me to agree. I wanted that too. Death was death, but murder was so much worse.

Still, I avoided Lorna's pointed look and kept to the facts. "Lorna found the front door ajar."

"Loads of innocent explanations for that," Lorna interjected. "Faulty latches. Wind. Absentmindedness . . ."

A bustling British charwoman. All seemed equally imaginary, but I kept going. "The French doors to the deck were also open. There were indentations in the snow, like someone had been out on the deck last night. I went out and looked over the edge and . . ." My stomach dove.

The chief filled in the blank. "You saw him. Okay. Anything else?"

I shrugged. "The kitchen is a mess."

Lorna tutted about the sheepskin.

"Wineglasses were tipped over," I continued. "Plus, I stumbled over something out on the deck. I think it might have been a fireplace poker? There's a set in the kitchen. It was knocked over when Lorna and I arrived."

The chief scowled. "Was?"

Not much got by the chief. I couldn't throw Lorna under the evidence-tidying bus. I was guiltier. I'd touched the poker on the deck, the doors, and the balcony too. I'd walked across the ghostly footprints—twice—and inserted a fallen snow angel.

"We, ah, straightened some things," I admitted.

The chief's slow-blink notched down to glacial.

Meg said, "Wine? The fireplace poker? Nothing was tipped over last night."

My eyebrows rose before I could stop myself.

The chief's disappeared under her cap.

"You were here?" Chief Sunnie asked. "I'm sorry, Meg, we should have finished your account. I thought you walked around down in Lower Last Word."

Meg folded her arms to her chest. She wore her puffer coat, the same as last night. Her hair whipped in the wind.

"We did," Meg said. "We tried the wine bar but it was closed. Joe asked me up for a nightcap. It's lovely to ride the gondola in the dark, so cozy."

Her eyes glazed with tears.

I guessed the chief's brows had rotated to the back of her head.

"And?" the chief prompted.

"That's it," Meg said. "We came here. Talked, had some wine. We made plans to meet at the Book Chalet today and go out to brunch. Then I left. I was going to walk to the gondola station, but Joe insisted it was too cold. He got me a ride-share. There was a driver right up here in the hamlet so the car arrived too soon. We said good night, and the kitchen and fireplace pokers were fine." She sniffled. "So was Joe."

A chill took up residence in my middle.

Meg had been here. If this did turn out to be a crime scene, her fingerprints, DNA, and truth-telling admissions were all over it.

The chief waited for a long minute before asking her next question. "Mr. Darcy was okay with you leaving? He didn't ask you to stay longer? Pressure you, perhaps?"

Meg flushed. "He suggested I *could* stay, but I wanted to get home. He understood. He was a gentleman."

The chief pressed on. "Did he say he was going out afterward? Maybe he met up with someone else? Had them over?"

Meg's reply was firm. "No. I can't imagine that. We talked about how it was late and so cold. He was going to bed."

"So . . . Meg . . . You may have been the last person to see him alive?" the chief said.

"I suppose I may have been," Meg stammered.

Not if Joe Darcy was murdered! I shoved the horrific thought away and clung to Lorna's loads of innocent explanations. *Joe, tipsy, knocking over glasses and fireplace sets, tripping over his own balcony . . . Joe, leaning too far out to admire the stars . . .* Except clouds covered the sky last night and who took a fireplace poker out to admire a frigid view?

I looped my arm through Meg's and tugged her back a step. "We should get out of your way," I said to the chief. *And Meg should get out of her thoughts as the last person to see a dead man.*

Chief Sunnie fixed us with her serious look. "Ellie, Meg, this *could* be an accident. It could be a crime. Whatever it is, *please,* leave the investigation to the professionals. We'll do our job."

"Will do!" chirped Lorna.

Meg and I nodded mutely, but when we were a few steps away, my sister stopped and spoke into my ear, her voice so soft, I might have been reading her mind.

"El, we *have* to help. For Joe's sake."

"We will." If this was murder, we had to help for Meg's sake too.

CHAPTER 6

Elephants Can't Forget

Meg's silver Subaru waited at the end of Joe's driveway.
I jumped in, buckled up, and willed Meg to punch the
gas. My sensible sister pulled into a slow-motion U-turn.

The gossipers turned our way, and I imagined them closing
in like a clutch of friendly zombies. Silently, I urged Meg to *go,
go, go*!

I could have made a faster escape on foot.

Then it struck me. Meg, driving. She rarely drove up to the
hamlet. The mountain road was as twisty as a chain of hairpins.
Like most, Meg preferred the stress-free and cost-free gondola.

"You drove up," I said. Not only that, Meg had been waiting
for me when I crested the slope. "How did you get here so fast?"

Meg snorted. "Is that a critique of my driving?"

I glanced at the speedometer. We rolled downhill at 18 miles
per hour.

"Lorna called me," Meg said. "It was like she was yelling into
a tornado. Words everywhere. Sheepskin and red and then she
said you were down Moosejaw Canyon and Joe was dead."

Meg's knuckles whitened on the wheel. "I jumped in the car
and tailgated the ambulance up the mountain. I've never driven
that road so fast."

"I'm sorry," I said. So much for my heroic move. I'd failed to save Joe and I could have killed my sister.

Meg tapped the brakes, and I saw another hazard, headed straight for us.

A yellow scarf fluttered behind Piper Tuttle like a swarm of canaries. Her spiky platinum hair shone.

I scrunched into my seat. "Hit the gas!"

For a glorious second, the Subaru surged, which only made Meg's brake-tapping more aggressive.

Piper spotted us and waved. Not a nice-to-see-you waggle but a stop-immediately flag down. She stepped into the street for good measure.

I spun fantasies while I still could. Meg could lay on the horn, stomp the accelerator, jump the right-hand curb, and take out that mailbox shaped like a bear.

Of course, my sister would do none of these. The bear mailbox was too cute, and Meg was too much like Mom when it came to stopping for road hazards. Our mother would pull over to mediate a fight—*Let's talk out our differences.* In a move forever in family lore, she once "rescued" a "lost puppy." The pup turned out to be a teenaged hybrid wolf. There are photos of it grinning between Meg and me, strapped into our car seats.

And now Meg was pulling over for a professional gossip, a bloodhound for bad news.

My sister rolled down her window.

Piper patted her feathered scarf and caught her breath. "Altitude," she said.

Piper had a few decades on me, but still her panting and its rationale made me feel better. The hamlet soared some 8,000 feet above sea level. A stroll across town counted as cardio. So did sitting at home, reading a book.

I canceled my mythical date with that StairMaster.

"Is it true?" Piper asked. "Suspicious death?"

"There's been a *tragic* death," Meg said.

I prayed that Piper hadn't learned Joe's identity. I might as well hope for that magical library cart to appear. Piper had to know already. Why else would she be charging up Moosejaw?

Piper did more than confirm my fear. She doubled it.

"That man you went out with?" Piper asked. "The one you were yelling about? Oh my goodness, Meg, look what you've done!"

My sister gaped.

I leaned over to better meet Piper's avid eyes. "A man tragically fell from his deck," I said firmly. "Meg had nothing to do with it. She wasn't there when it happened."

"She didn't need to be," Piper said. "Meg, you *foresaw*. You *knew*! Remember last time? That was murder. Do you think this is too?"

I opened my mouth to issue hopeful denials.

Piper barreled on. "I sensed it this morning too, didn't I, Ellie? And, to think, I picked out the most perfect book: *Midwinter Murder*! You knew too—that book matches all occasions, you said." She tapped her temple.

I wished I could take back all those words, especially Meg's deathbed outburst. But once released, words could never be re-captured. Their molecules were always out there, bumping around, waiting to be remembered or remixed.

There was nothing more to say. We needed to get away. "We shouldn't keep you, Piper," I said, hoping Meg would take the hint. Piper gripped Meg's window with a gloved hand, but she could let go if Meg floored it.

My sister was too busy looking dazed. "I misread everything," she said. "I feel awful."

More words that Piper could gleefully misinterpret. "She's in shock," I said. "Meg, we really have to go. Want me to drive?"

A cheery *beep-beep* sounded. I twisted to look. Lorna's chile-emblazoned Kia bounced toward us at high speed.

"Blocking traffic," I said. "Sorry. Gotta go."

Road rules roused Meg. She apologized to Piper, waved to our beeping cousin, and jolted us down the lane. In my side mirror, I watched Piper disappear into the gossiping fold.

Moosejaw ended in a choice. Turn left and we'd head down the hairpin mountain road to the base village. Turn right and we'd reach the Book Chalet.

The Kia pulled up beside us. The side window rolled down and Lorna leaned over the empty passenger's seat.

"I saved you!" she said.

From Piper? Yes. From trouble . . . not by a longshot.

"Thanks," said my sweet sister.

Lorna exhaled. "This is terrible. Meg, I'm so, so sorry about Joe! Your perfect match! Marigold's a mess. I have to get down there, stop her from abandoning the dating ship. We'll make this up to you, Meg, I promise. We *will* find you your biblio-match."

My sister's mouth fell open like a stunned koi. Before either of us could find words, Lorna's window slid up. The Kia sped off, squealing left and down the hill.

"She's in shock," I said. "She's, ah . . ." I floundered. "Trying to lift your spirits?"

Meg's hands rested at twelve on the wheel. She lowered her forehead to them and groaned.

"She's Lorna," I said. Which explained it all.

My sister sat back. "I know. I know! Lorna's doing her best in an awful situation. That's all any of us can do." She took a deep breath. "Where to?"

My first thought? *Far, far away*. I wanted miles, mountains, oceans between us and any connection to a potential murder.

Paris would do. Meg and I could wander the bookstalls by the Seine. Or the South Pacific resort island where I'd worked in a beachside book shack. Torquay . . . Agatha Christie's home-town. Our parents were there now, on their book-inspired travels and semiretirement. I imagined us all, strolling by the seaside, soaking up Dame Agatha's air.

I stared out the frost-speckled windshield. Toothy peaks glistened in the distance. The hamlet looked as pretty as a postcard. Snow iced the chalets. Gingerbread balconies were trimmed in evergreen swags and holly berries. String lights crisscrossed the little business district, leading to the historic building that had inspired the hamlet's style, the only place in the world I wanted to be.

"Back to the Book Chalet for me," I said. "You should go home, Meg. Gram and Rosie will be worried. I can get out here and walk. I could use the air."

I'd had more than my fill of canyon air this morning. But a stroll through the hamlet would take me by the bakery. I could stop for a brownie or four. I reached for the door handle.

Meg flicked on her signal. "That's where I need to be too. Gram took the bus down to Ridgecrest to visit a friend. Rosie's at Pasha's working on a history project. I don't want to be home alone. I'll . . . dwell . . . I need books and book people."

"To the Book Chalet!" I said, with forced cheer. "There's nowhere better to be."

* * *

Later, I questioned our choice. Yes, the Book Chalet soothed. There were books and bibliophiles, hot drinks, a crackling fire, and our snoozing cat.

There were also gossipers.

Locals arrived with urgent desires for bargain paperbacks, a thin disguise for their real hunger: information. Make that *more* information. They already knew I'd found Joe's body. They wanted details I wasn't willing to dole out. They'd also heard about Meg's outburst, with dubious accuracy. I wouldn't speak of that either.

Faced with my deflections to bookish topics, the gossipers issued news I wished wasn't true. The police were still at Joe's. They'd been joined by a crime-scene tech and were scouring the deck and cliff. From these clues, our story-loving guests constructed wild tales, many involving my sister: Meg, threatening Joe, willing his death, and, worst of all . . .

"It's absurd!" I whisper-huffed to Ms. Ridge. "How can *anyone* imagine Meg as a killer?"

The latest *anyone* had been the mayor's wife, Imogen Royer, who, "off the record," assured me that Meg "had her full support." Everyone, Imogen said, deserved to make one big mistake in life. Like her husband, proposing to install Last Word's first traffic light, Imogen said with a bitter laugh.

Like Meg, letting a lobby full of inquisitive bibliophiles overhear her outburst, I assumed. That is, until Imogen reached across the counter, patted my hand, and said a good lawyer could probably plead Meg down to second-degree murder, maybe even manslaughter.

Ms. Ridge stood on the other side of the counter now. Faced with my unanswerable question, she busied herself tidying an already neat postcard display. Ms. Ridge had firsthand experience with murder accusations—and with sticking her head in the sand to avoid them. If only that strategy would work.

"I know how." Glynis Goodman stepped to the register counter and deposited an armload of books. Tall and upright as a ponderosa, Glynis was Ms. Ridge's neighbor, a devoted reader of thrillers, and a new convert to Agatha Christie.

She tapped the top book of her stack. Two smiling faces filled the cover. A white-snouted donkey and gray-bearded man. One was the author. They were both locals and had remarkably similar goofy grins and big teeth.

Glynis thumped a finger across the title. *Never Make Assumptions: Life Lessons Learned from Trail Racing with My Burro.*

Her finger backed up to underline the third word.

"I get it," I said grudgingly. "People wrongly *assume* all the time. Meg's not a murderer! That's not me assuming. It's a fact."

Glynis gave me a look I read as affectionate pity. "Your sister's a smart, competent woman," Glynis said, swinging her silver braid over her shoulder. Her parka was Barney-the-dinosaur purple and reached to her calves.

"Who says Meg can't murder someone?" Glynis continued.

Me?

Ms. Ridge tsked. "Now, Glynis. Be nice."

"Now, nothing, Katherine," countered Glynis, one of the few to call Ms. Ridge by her first name. "And I *am* being nice. I've given you the benefit of the doubt before too. Ellie, back me up, haven't I said that Katherine Ridge here could be both a killer and the neighbor who shovels my walks?" She gave the last part dire intonation.

Ms. Ridge's smile quirked with a hint of happy wickedness. "I just happened to be out extra early this morning. That wind last night blew up some drifts."

Glynis muttered that she'd set her alarm for the next blizzard.

The two neighbors had a friendly but fierce rivalry: who could clear their block's sidewalks first.

Glynis returned to her main argument. "Agatha Christie would say anyone could kill."

"True." I wouldn't argue with the Queen of Mystery or Glynis Goodman. Even Ms. Ridge nodded.

Glynis pointed to the rest of her bookstack. Four colorful spines of Agatha Christie's. "You have me hooked on her books. That woman was ruthless. I like it."

Across the lobby, a guest strained on tiptoes, trying to reach an upper shelf. Ms. Ridge left to help. Glynis leaned over the counter and whispered conspiratorially. "Good. Ellie, I want to talk to you in private."

Me? She didn't think I could be a killer too, did she?

Glynis drew a book from her stack and again pointed meaningfully to the title. *Elephants Can Remember.* "Says it all," Glynis said. "That Agatha Christie knew her stuff."

I frowned, wondering again if I had hit my head. I wasn't getting it. The story included sisters, but not in a good way. "It's, ah, a great mystery," I said. "Lots of intrigue and secrets."

Glynis nodded. "Yep. I read the back cover and first chapter. Should be more like 'Elephants Can't Forget.' That's exactly what I want to talk to you about. *You* found another body. I understand how you're feeling."

"Oh." My stomach practiced its backflips.

"You get my meaning?" Glynis said.

Glynis was famous—infamous—for her work with our local Search and Rescue. She found the most lost, the folks who might never have been discovered otherwise. The trouble was, by the time she got to them, they were often long gone. As in, dead.

She was saying, "I'm like this elephant here. It's not that you *can* remember. That makes it sound like a choice. You *can't* forget those bodies, I know. You shouldn't either. Finding someone when they're lost for good, that means something. Know that I'm here if you need to talk."

"Thank you," I said, holding on to the counter.

Glynis turned brisk, as if embarrassed by her heartfelt statement. "Okay. That's said. Also, if you want to join Search and Rescue, we always have openings. I've been looking for my protégé. Not that I'd wish my skills on anyone, but, again, these things aren't a choice. They choose you."

"I, ah . . . I need to get in better shape," I said. And I'd already canceled my never-made appointment with that StairMaster. Search and Rescue would be waiting awhile, unless they needed book recommendations.

"Some bodies are close to home," Glynis persisted. "You'd be surprised." She chuckled darkly. "Or not. Finding the close ones, maybe that's your specialty. You don't have to trek far out into the forest."

Silence seemed the best response. I bit my lip to maintain it.

Glynis pushed her books across the counter. I rang them up with wobbly fingers.

Her protégé in body finding? Ridiculous! It's not like I'd gone *searching* for Joe. I went to his house to support Lorna. And the murder last year . . . That hadn't been the same. Meg and I were in the wrong place at the wrong time. Or the right time for our gondola to glide into a murder . . .

I shook off the thought and tucked Glynis's purchases into a Book Chalet tote bag she'd brought along from home. "Thanks, Glynis. I appreciate your offer to talk, I really do. What will help most is figuring out what happened."

"That's for sure," said Glynis. "Resolution. About that . . ."

I braced myself.

"Some folks—not me, of course—might be getting the wrong idea." Glynis hefted the tote to her shoulder. "Have you taken a peek at First Word Last Word this afternoon?"

First Word Last Word was an online community forum for Last Word residents. Think Facebook but hyper-local. There were listings for jobs, services, secondhand items, lost pets, live-stock, grocery sales, sightings of wildlife (and sometimes Big-foot and suspected UFOs), bake sales, and local events. There was also the "neighborhood chatter" page, a nice way of saying gossip spreading like a wildfire through dead pines. Piper Tuttle held court there, fanning the flames, energizing her minions.

I closed my eyes, as if that would chase the monster away. It was as effective as a kid hiding under the covers.

"I take it you haven't seen," Glynis said, interpreting my move. " 'Course, I don't believe word of mouth unless it comes straight from the proverbial horse's mouth."

Meg—the unfortunate horse in this scenario—chose this mo-ment to return to the lobby. She held an armload of padded mailers that reached to her chin. The red in her eyes clashed with her glasses, a mahogany frame called "bookish."

"There she is," Glynis said.

I could have mimed *flee*! But I was lousy at charades and it wouldn't stop whatever was already galloping around First Word Last Word.

"Hi, Glynis," Meg said. "How are you today?"

"I hope you can confirm a rumor for me," Glynis said.

Meg stiffened.

"Did you really cut off a man's buttons?" Glynis smiled. "If you don't want to talk about it, just say 'no comment.' I'll know what you mean."

Meg dropped the mailers on the counter. They slipped like a padded mini-avalanche. My sister hid her eyes behind her hand. "No comment."

*

CHAPTER 7

Love Lies Lost

I waited until after work to ask, and then only when Meg and I were in the most private place around. The gondola. Lights twinkled from the ski slopes and the village down below. One of those lights beamed from Gram's kitchen, where she and Rosie were whipping up comfort food.

They'd found out about Joe's death late in the afternoon. They'd then immediately called, appalled, shocked, and resentful to be "the last to know."

I yearned to race straight to them, to the warm kitchen and comforting hugs. First, however, we had to give statements to the police. I had to ask before we got there.

"So . . ." I said, easing into the question.

Meg had been staring out the window. She sighed, fogging the glass. "Go ahead, ask . . ."

"Buttons?"

Meg rubbed her temples. "This is so very embarrassing."

"It's just us." And all of First Word Last Word, but here in the glass bubble, it was just my sister, me, and the sky. I waited.

Meg squirmed. "Cameron's buttons."

I'd guessed as much. Cameron was Rosie's dad, Meg's ex, the jerk who'd stood her up at their wedding. Button cutting seemed the least Meg could do. I nudged my sister and grinned. "Good for you! How did I not know this?"

"You were back at college. If you'd been here, you might have stopped me."

Meg was to have had an early July wedding, when wildflowers burst across the meadow. I would have returned to college in late August. Meg had waited a while to commit button assault.

"He left everything, including a full closet," Meg said. "Lorna thought it would be therapeutic to cut the buttons off his dress shirts and toss the shirts out the window." Meg gave a wry chuckle. "She'd read it in a book."

Ah, Lorna. Now it made more sense. "Can't argue with books," I said supportively. *Or Lorna.*

"*I* should have," Meg said. "This was before Lorna's wilderness-therapy certification. If she'd had that we could have gone out and yelled into waterfalls. Of course, someone would have seen us doing that too and waited fifteen years to gossip about it. There are no secrets in a village!"

"Miss Marple would agree." I wondered what Jane Marple would think about a digital village like First Word Last Word. Would she find it useful, or were people harder to read online? Some—a lot of—people let loose their inner devils online. Others donned aspirational masks.

I mulled, then the answer came to me, via Miss Marple herself. In *The Mirror Crack'd from Side to Side,* an elderly Miss Marple slips the confines of her caregiver and totters off to explore a new development. The houses and clothes are new and flashy, but people, she observes, are always the same. What had she said? The new world was the same as the old?

Meg wriggled on our wooden bench. "I'll admit, it was momentarily cathartic. But Cameron wasn't around to know! And they were nice shirts that could have been donated. I felt bad about that. Mom, Gram, and I ended up sewing the buttons back on."

I nudged closer to my sister. "And here I thought you had a fun scandal."

"I wish! How come we never get the *fun* scandals?"

Because Meg followed the rules. She was dutiful and cared. Which was why we were on our way to the police station and, I feared, politely inviting in more trouble.

* * *

"Christie sisters." Lottie Nez, receptionist, dispatcher, and one of Gram's favorite sources of information, looked up from her book and announced our arrival to the police station.

The only other person in the lobby was a teenager, slumped to reclining in his molded plastic seat. He kept his eyes on his phone.

"Hi, Lottie," Meg and I said in unison.

Silver strands highlighted Lottie's dark hair. Her earrings danced, fine strands of tiny beadwork. Her mother was a well-known Navajo jeweler.

"How's your mom's new knee?" Meg asked.

Lottie chuckled. "Ma says she's bionic now. I say, if that's so, she should take up flying. Then I wouldn't have to drive her to all those physical therapy appointments down in Ridgecrest."

She and Meg talked knees. Then Lottie asked about our parents. "Enjoying their travels again, are they?"

Mom and Dad had taken early "retirement" to travel the world, following in my path of exploring literary landscapes. Like college kids, they'd saved up and jetted home for Christmas but then set right back out on more adventures.

"They're in Torquay now," I reported. "Agatha Christie's hometown. They're housesitting a thatched cottage with three cats, six alpacas, a bunch of chickens, and garden hedgehogs, and working part-time as tour guides."

Their worldwide bibliophile connections had gotten them the rent-free accommodation. I'd helped with the tour-guide gig, having held that job myself. Typically, it attracted just-out-of-college types, as I'd been. Mom brought the energy and knowledge of a dozen twenty-somethings. Before long, I bet, the tour company would be hiring all retirees.

"Sounds like a lot of work to me," Lottie said. "Thought they were retired."

Meg explained. "It's more like a working retirement so they can travel. Mom needs to stay busy. Of course, Dad would read all day if he could."

"I'm with your father," said Lottie, patting her book. "Days like this, when we're busy, they get me down because I can't keep up with my reading."

Meg and I empathized.

"So," I said, easing into the reason for our visit. "We're here to see the chief. Unless she no longer needs us?"

Maybe it had been a terrible accident. I'd keep dreaming until someone told me otherwise.

"She needs to see you," Lottie said with a certainty that couldn't be good. "She got an unexpected visitor, but they should be out soon. Can you wait a bit?"

Could we? Yes, but I sure wished we could run home to Gram's. My tailbone ached from sledding down a cliff. So did my emotions. Meg's day had been even worse.

"Of course we'll stay," Meg said. "We want to help."

Lottie gestured to a row of molded plastic chairs. My tailbone protested in anticipation. Meg and I sat, and I studied the space. The building dated from the gold-rush days. The floor was milky marble with black veins like rivers. Stamped tin patterned the ceiling. Sounds bounced between metal and stone. The scuff of the teenager's shoes. Meg, rustling in her purse. She took out her Kindle, swiped the screen, and began to read.

My phone held a vast library, yet I knew I couldn't focus on a book. I turned to a side table and well-thumbed magazines. There were two options: *People* and *Police Today*.

People offered "Ten Tips for High-Intensity Workouts, Great Legs, and Intermittent Fasting" as recommended by a country music star.

That wasn't going to happen.

Police Today promised tips for moving up in my law-enforcement career. Nope, I had my dream job. Also: "Top Ten Tipoffs of Deceptive Body Language." That could be useful.

I was up to tip five, "evasive eyes," when the door behind Lottie opened and a woman stepped out. She had red corkscrew curls and a handkerchief pressed to her nose.

The chief stepped out behind her. "Thanks for coming in, Ms. Giddings. I'll call when the medical examiner has finished. I understand how important it is to lay a loved one to rest."

My heart ached for the woman. But why was the medical examiner involved? I hadn't heard of another suspicious death. *I had heard the name Giddings recently . . .* Where? The memory skittered just out of reach.

Ms. Giddings raised a shaky smile that quickly collapsed. "Thank you, Chief. I know you'll do your best for my fiancé."

A fiancé! How awful!

Beside me, Meg put down her Kindle.

Ms. Giddings sniffled. "It's too shocking to believe—for Joseph to die in *my* house!"

Joseph? Joe? Her house . . . Giddings! Lorna had mentioned the name Fiona Giddings.

I gasped. My whisper, aimed at Meg, ricocheted around the lobby. "She owns Joe's house."

Meg stood, her purse and Kindle falling to the plastic seat with a clatter. "Your fiancé? I'm so sorry. What was his name?"

"Joseph Darcy." The words were muffled behind her handkerchief. "Did you know him?"

Meg paled. "I'm so very sorry," she said. Then, softly, "No, I didn't know him at all."

CHAPTER 8

For the Record

The chief invited Meg to her office, a room with soft armchairs and tall windows with a downtown view.

Detective Sam Ibarra led me to a squat, square room with walls the color of dying lavender and a hazy mirror that in TV cop shows would hide a watcher sipping bad coffee.

Or it was just what it looked like—a mirror in need of cleaning.

"Sorry," he said. "My office floors are being redone and they're still sticky."

There weren't any other rooms in a two-story building occupying half a block? I thought longingly of the lobby, with fresh air swooping in from the front door. This room smelled of disinfectant and desperation. A single bulb in a cage flickered from the ceiling.

He noticed my assessment and offered a wry smile. "I know. We could use a decorator."

"You could," I agreed.

We sat across from each other. Gouges and angry ink marks marred the wood table. The detective wasn't as cover-model perfect as I'd thought this morning either. A faint scar etched the stubble on his chin. The flecks in his granite eyes had dimmed to tired. Unfortunately, for me, that made him more human and handsome.

He opened a notebook and asked, "So? You're a local?"

"I am. My family's been here for five generations."

In other circumstances, I might have told him about my gold-miner great-great-grandfather and the single lucky strike he'd turned into a bonanza of books.

"We have something in common," the detective said. "Fourth generation here. My relatives came over from the Basque Country to herd sheep. I still have cousins keeping some flocks going."

He named a ranch and referenced landmarks, and I wished we were in a cozy coffee shop. I'd love to hear about those herding relatives and the Basque lands spreading across the border of France and Spain. I'd visited once when I lived in Paris. The jagged, rocky peaks had made me nostalgic for home.

"So," he said. "Your cousin is starting a dating business. Tell me about your date." He held a pencil to paper, ready to write.

Great. My bad date would have a record.

"I don't think we need to talk about *my* date," I said tightly.

He flashed a smile. "That great, eh? Okay, tell me what went wrong so I can avoid being *that guy*."

"I don't think you could be that guy," I said and immediately wanted to take it back.

Had I sounded flirty? His grin suggested I had.

I'd meant, he wouldn't be a pompous professor who droned on about Samuel Beckett. But that might be wrong too. For all I knew, Sam Ibarra might be named for Samuel Beckett, from a family of Beckett- and absurdity-worshipping sheepherders.

I studied the gashes in the table. When I looked up, he'd sprouted a dimple.

"Oh?" His pencil hovered, as if this were the key moment of the interview. "Please, humor me. I need dating advice."

From me? Ha! A contender for worst dater among Christies? Except now Meg had a murdered date. I had nothing to complain about.

"My date wasn't that bad," I said. "He's an English professor. He talked about his work all night."

Detective Ibarra nodded seriously. "You're right, I'd never do that. My work is confidential."

I raised an eyebrow. "What would you talk about, then, Detective?"

"If we were on a date?" Now he had two dimples and a twinkle.

He leaned back until his chair creaked. "First, I'd insist you call me Sam, which I hope you'll do now too. Then . . . ? I don't know, the family sheep? The weather? My trail-running habit?" His lopsided grin grew rakish. "Nah, I wouldn't bore you. We'd talk about *you*."

My cheeks flared. It was the heat in this room, I assured myself. It was definitely *not* the handsome man dimpling at me.

I said, "Talking about me would backfire. I'd go on about books like my date did last night. I really shouldn't fault him for that."

"What do you fault him for, then?"

The detective was too astute. I *did* fault Dr. Waldon, but I'd take the high road and remain silent. I pressed my lips firm to keep words from blurting out.

Smile lines fanned his eyes. "Aw, come on. I need to know about crimes against dating."

I caved but only because dishing on Dr. Waldon was safer than discussing Meg and her deceased date. "He dissed Christie."

"*Agatha* Christie?" Detective—Sam—Ibarra sounded appropriately appalled. "The chief told me it's a book-based dating service? Bad-mouthing a popular author seems the height of bad form. Especially one with your name."

"Exactly! He also considered 'popular' a problem. Not all

popular books are well written, but if they entertain or bring joy or escape, they're doing what they should."

Sam grinned.

I flushed. "See? I warned you. Get me talking about books and I'll bore you."

He shook his head. "I'm not at all bored. I do, however, have to ask about your sister and her date." He looked almost apologetic.

"What do you want to know?" I asked, resigned.

"Anything that comes to mind." He spread his hands, palms up, as if inviting me to share any and all incriminating clues. "Were there any arguments during the date? Tension?"

I thought of Waldon, fussing that he'd nearly hit Joe on the icy street. That had been a concern for safety. "No," I said, shaking my head.

"And your sister? How did she and her date get on?"

Here was an easy question. "Fabulously."

"How could you tell?"

How could I? I was sure, but it was just an impression, as I told the detective.

He nodded seriously. "Impressions are good. They contain minutiae of truth."

"Poirot said the same thing of intuition," I said, proving my earlier warning that I would always default to book talk. "*A thousand little details . . .* They add up."

"If only I were Poirot," Sam said ruefully. "Help me out. What did your intuition make of Darcy?"

It seemed my intuition had taken the night off. "I thought he was the perfect date. But he wasn't, was he? He had a fiancée."

Sam looked up from his notes. "When did you learn about his engagement?"

"Just now. We met Ms. Giddings in the lobby. Did she know about Joe dating other women?" I felt for her. I truly did. But she had more motive than Meg.

"I can't say," he said.

He couldn't because of the active investigation, or because he didn't know?

I could speculate. "He was living in her house. She'd have a key. If she caught him with another woman, she might have snapped."

"So, you do know her?" Sam said, granite eyes hardening again. "You know she owns the house on Moosejaw Lane?"

Sam was too easy to talk to. I cautioned myself to remember the "Detective" in front of his name. "My cousin Lorna used to be in real estate and knew the owner of the house. Lorna obviously had no idea about the engagement or she wouldn't have matched up Joe and Meg."

He made a noncommittal sound.

I changed the subject. "Did you find that scrap of paper by Joe?"

He had not. "Storm whipped up. My priority was preserving the scene around the deceased. Rest assured, we'll keep searching."

My assurance wouldn't be resting until Meg was in the clear. "You're sure it was murder?"

Sam Ibarra leaned back, chair tipped, fingers steepled. In Dr. Waldon, such a gesture would signal incoming professing. I guessed the detective was debating how much to tell me. Abruptly, he leaned forward. Chair legs thumped. His words struck me.

"It was murder. Mr. Darcy was killed by a blow from a blunt object. Either that or wounded to the point of incapacitation, allowing the perpetrator—or multiple individuals—to maneuver his body over the balcony."

The room was approximately the temperature of Arizona in June, if Arizona had no ventilation. I shivered. *Murder.* The fear that had lurked in dark corners of my mind was out, prowling free.

I closed my eyes and pictured the deck at night. The quiet

snow, the surreal yellow glow, the gaping canyon. A killer, look-ing over the balcony, just like I had?

I pried open my lids and made myself ask. "The blunt object. Was it the fireplace poker out on the deck?"

"Yes."

As blunt as a poker. I'd half hoped he'd refuse to say.

"I fell over it," I said. "I touched it." No wonder my hand had felt singed by the icy metal.

He nodded sympathetically. "So I hear. We'll need your prints. For elimination purposes, you understand."

I understood. Meg, Lorna, and I had left our marks all over a crime scene. Chief Sunnie would be asking Meg for hers too.

Claustrophobia swarmed like hornets. Threatening, buzz-ing. I had to get out of this room. "Okay, but then Meg and I need to go. Our grandmother is expecting us for dinner." I rose, holding my breath, waiting for him to object.

"Dinner at Grandma's. Sounds nice," he said wistfully and got up to hold the door for me.

"Thanks," I murmured, stepping into a hallway decorated in sepia photos, all slightly askew. Unless it was me who was tippy.

"My pleasure," he said and a dimple winked. "Thank you for the dating advice. And for the record? I'd never, ever badmouth Agatha Christie."

✳

CHAPTER 9

Dinner and a Search

D inner at Gram's should have been relaxing. Yellow ging-
ham curtains held back the darkness. The air was warm
and scented with one of the world's finest perfumes: Gram's
famous chicken potpie. I wore fluffy slippers and sat around the
table with three of my favorite people.

Gram pushed a pea around her plate.

Rosie studied her lap, where, I suspected, a forbidden-at-
the-table cellphone lurked.

Meg frowned at the ceiling.

Overhead, soft footsteps sounded as loud as clog dancers
and way more nerve jangling.

Meg sighed. "I shouldn't have invited them. I'm sorry, Gram.
Chief Sunnie convinced me they'd be quick."

The Chief and Sam Ibarra were upstairs searching Meg's
bedroom, with its attached sleeping porch and bathroom. The
footsteps were slow and methodical.

"You have nothing to hide, dear," Gram said. "It was nice of
you to invite them."

Too nice, I worried. After we'd given our statements and
elimination fingerprints at the station, Chief Sunnie had walked

us to the door. We'd almost made it out when the chief asked, ever so casually, if they could come over and take a little look around Meg's rooms.

My too-polite, too-helpful sister said yes.

I reminded myself that Gram was right. Meg had nothing to hide.

Rosie tore her eyes from her lap and picked up a piece of crust, the crowning glory of Gram's potpies. Usually, Meg would say something about manners, forks, and knives. Rosie waggled the crust, so buttery that golden flakes dusted her plate.

"What are they looking for, Mom? I mean, you went out for a date at the *library*. He didn't die there, right? It's not like you're hiding, I don't know, a bloody ax."

Meg winced. We'd told Gram and Rosie that Joe's death wasn't accidental or natural. We had to, given the imminent arrival of two guests not here for the potpie. Meg, however, had refused to discuss any murder-related details with Rosie.

My sister thought she was protecting Rosie, shielding her. I wondered. Rosie was a reader and a Christie. Her imagination could conjure up myriad means of murder.

"No axes were involved," Meg said tightly.

"I *know*, Mom." Rosie heaved with an adults-can-be-clueless sigh. "I heard from Pash, who overheard her mom. *Everyone* knows he was shoved off a deck."

She looked to her mom for confirmation. When Meg gave nothing away, Rosie turned to me. I offered a shrug grimace. *Close enough*. Rosie could hear about the fireplace poker from someone else.

"Harsh!" my niece said. "The police can't think *you* did that, Mom. You're not that strong. You don't go around pushing people."

"No, I don't, honey," Meg said. "But this is how they eliminate innocent people."

"By suspecting them?" Rosie countered. "That's not fair, and anyway, you only went on *one* date." She brightened. "But it went well, right? You should go out more often, Mom."

Meg shuddered.

"No, seriously," Rosie said. "Come on, what do you tell me about horses?"

"Never fall off," Meg said with a thin smile. "Wear a helmet."

Another eye roll, plus a scoff. Rosie said, in a teacherly tone, "If you fall off, get back on. Same goes for you, Mom." She then changed the subject to actual horses and a camp she hoped to attend over the summer. "It's a whole month. You get to camp out with the horses, isn't that great?"

By mentally replacing "horse" with "book" I was able to say that it did sound great. I liked horses. They were beautiful and I liked to pat them and feed them apples. Sitting on them, however, gave me vertigo.

Rosie had no fear. She'd have the time of her life at horse camp. Meg's stumbling block wasn't the horses. It was cost. Camping with horses costs as much as a luxury resort or summer college semester.

Meg had shown us the glossy booklets the other night, when Rosie was out. "Her dad could pay for it," Meg said. "But Cameron would rather take her on their fancy father–daughter vacations, and I don't want Rosie to think she can fall back on his family's money. Look how responsible he turned out."

"You learn wilderness first aid," Rosie was saying now. "Survival skills. Horse care and veterinary stuff and—"

"Sounds great, honey," Meg said, glancing at the ceiling. "We'll get your application in by next week, okay?"

"What?" Rosie looked up from her lap, clearly shocked. "Really? But you said it cost too much."

"Not too much for a priceless experience." Meg smiled at her daughter. To Gram and me, she raised a shrug.

Experiences were priceless. That's how I'd justified flitting around the world on little pay but amazing bookish endeavors. Heck, it's why I reveled in selling books and caring for the family shop.

However, I knew why Meg was caving now. She wanted to wrap Rosie up in the happy anticipation of horses and buffer her daughter from a murder investigation. If only horses could do that for all of us.

Rosie bubbled on about how she'd save up all her pay from teaching bunny-slope ski lessons. "I've been getting some super big tips. Parents want to butter me up so I'll babysit for them. They tip me for that too. I'm in demand."

"Maybe *I* should work for tips," Gram said. "Rosie, I'll donate them all to horse camping."

Rosie laughed. "Thanks, Gram! Tips for napping, that's a great idea! Agatha could earn big bucks."

"Tips for *modeling* cozy reading," Gram corrected, primly patting her fluffy white curls. "I'll knit my own tips hat too. I could sell those."

"Make them extra-big," Rosie suggested.

A scraping sound from upstairs put a stop to our fun. From the sounds of the floorboards, I guessed the police had moved on to the sleeping porch off Meg's bedroom.

Closer at hand, the wicker basket over by the breadbox buzzed for about the hundredth time since we'd sat down to dinner. Gram's phone, on mute but vibrating with incoming texts.

"You should get that, Gram," Meg said.

"I'm ignoring it," Gram declared with a frown that said otherwise. "Rosie tells me that it's legitimate to ignore one's phone. Not like the landline, which I feel compelled to obey."

"You *have* to ignore cell calls," said Rosie, the girl who kept glancing at her lap.

The basket buzzed again. Gram fidgeted like a teenager separated from technology.

"Answer it, Gram, please," Meg urged. "It could be important."

Or, more likely, gossipers.

Gram pushed back her chair. "Maybe I should. I took the landline off the hook before dinner so we wouldn't be bothered." Gram stood and straightened a woolly cardigan in autumnal shades.

She returned, scowling at the small screen. Rosie had helped her magnify the words so each one filled a line.

"Entire books of texts," Gram said, slowly scrolling. "Mostly Suzanne Milford next door, wondering if we're okay. Suzanne informs me that our landline's been busy. She asks if we're being held hostage or under arrest. If I don't answer, she's apt to come over. What should I tell her?"

"That we took the receiver off the hook so people wouldn't bother our dinner?" Meg suggested wearily.

Too late for that. Official feet tromped above us. Gram's phone buzzed again. Rosie's thumbs did a jitterbug inside her hoodie pouch. Blind texting? Teenagers had skills I couldn't dream of.

"A touch too truthful for manners," Gram said. "I'll say we're eating dinner. Maybe she'll get the hint."

Meg looked rightfully unconvinced.

Gram yelled commands to her voice-to-text app as if it were hard of hearing.

"Hello, Suzanne. Nice of you to text. We're enjoying potpie. Talk to you soon!"

Gram held the phone out and said, "Send!"

Then she held it out to Rosie. "Did that send? Did I turn the microphone off, dear?"

Rosie grinned. "Yeah. It's off, but you told Mrs. Milford that we're enjoying Popeyes. Like the chicken restaurant."

"Or the sailor man," I said.

Gram smiled. "Either is fine. Good to keep Suzanne guessing. She's too nosy by half."

Kettle, judging pot. But, then, Gram's nosiness was in the service of good. Suzanne Milford was simply nosy for nosiness's sake. She was probably calling and texting half the block, informing them of Gram's busy signal and Popeye involvement.

Creak, creak, creak . . . The footsteps were moving into the upper hallway.

Meg stabbed a potato.

Rosie peered at her lap.

"Rosie?" Meg said, suddenly cueing back in. "Are you on your phone too?"

My niece was all wide-eyed innocence. "I'm done with dinner, Mom."

"But still at the table," Meg noted.

Rosie flashed a meaningful glance toward Gram.

"This is my *emergency* phone," Gram said. She winked at Rosie, who grinned back.

"I have a history project emergency," Rosie said.

"Is that who's been texting?" Meg asked. "Pasha?"

"Pash and I have been texting tons about history," Rosie said.

Which didn't answer Meg's question. I thought of the article I'd read in *Police Today*, traits of evasion, and Rosie was exhibiting number four. Deflection. Of course, I didn't need *Police Today* to tell me that classic ploy.

Nor did Meg, but she smiled with resignation.

Rosie sighed. "When are they going to be done upstairs?"

Meg rubbed her temples. "You can go up to your room, honey. They won't go in there. Do you want to take a piece of cake with you?"

Rosie blinked at her success. Horse camp plus dessert in her room? "Thanks, Mom!" She jumped up and stuffed her phone into her back pocket. The latter made me feel better. Rosie was hardly a seasoned deceiver.

"Thanks for dinner, Gram," she said, after slicing off a hunk of two-layers of ultimate chocolate comfort. She grinned at me. "Aunt El, see you later? You're staying over, right?"

I hadn't made up my mind yet. I could bundle back up and go out into the cold. Agatha awaited. So did the book I was oh so near to finishing.

"She's definitely staying," Gram said. "It's been an unsettling day. Plus, tomorrow's Monday."

"Yeah, for you guys," Rosie said.

Monday at the Book Chalet meant a day off. I could sleep in late in Gram's cozy bedroom. Agatha would forgive me. She'd guilt me into giving her more treats.

"Cool," Rosie said. "See ya."

Teenage footsteps, as loud as a herd of bison, jogged up the stairs. When Rosie's door shut, Meg leaned over the table and whispered. "I think she's been texting a boy. She's awfully secretive about that phone lately and on it all the time. Gram, has she said anything to you?"

Gram and Rosie were BFFs. They shared everything, including the tricks and ways of their generations. Gram knew all about TikTok and Korean boy bands. Rosie, meanwhile, could pickle anything, bake a cake without a recipe, and reference episodes of *I Love Lucy*.

Gram put down her phone. "No. She hasn't said anything to me. What boy?"

Meg didn't know. "I've tried to ask, but she changes the subject."

Yep, evasive techniques.

Meg said, "I wasn't spying on her, I swear. I just happened to see her phone light up the other day. There was a text with the initial *D* on it. She used to have a friend named Dominica, but she moved away last year and I don't think they keep in touch."

Gram reached across the table and squeezed Meg's hand. "Rosie's a smart, sensible girl. All of these problems will work themselves out. Now, how about cake? I made chocolate with chocolate icing."

Deflection? Absolutely! A good idea? Fabulous!

I cleared dinner plates. Meg put on a pot of decaf—none of us needed more jitters. Gram cut extra-generous slices.

Gram asked, "If Rosie does open up to me, what message do you want me to impart?"

Meg jabbed the coffee maker's button with unnecessary force. "Run from all romance?"

"Now, dear . . ." Gram said soothingly. "There are good partners out there. Look at your Gramps. He may have snored and grumbled, but he was a true gem. And you had a good time with that unfortunate Mr. Darcy, that poor man . . ."

Meg and I exchanged a look. We hadn't had a chance to tell Gram about Joe Darcy's grieving fiancée.

"You eat," I said to Meg. "I'll tell Gram."

Meg answered by digging into her cake.

I told Gram how we'd met Joe Darcy's fiancée.

Gram listened intently with disapproving sounds escalating after each word.

Meg put down her fork. "If Joe hadn't died, when would I have found out? It's mortifying. One date and I was already falling for him like a fool."

"No, no . . ." Gram assured her. "You're honest. You expect the world to be honest."

Footsteps sounded on the stairs. We listened as the steps rounded the foyer and made their way to the kitchen.

"Chief, Detective," Gram said to the two officers who appeared in the doorframe. "We're having cake and coffee—chocolate and decaf. Will you join us?"

Chief Sunnie looked longingly at our plates. Sam Ibarra had on his cleaved granite expression, giving away nothing. He held a plastic zip-top bag.

He caught me looking and raised a smile I read as apologetic.

If that smile was meant to comfort, it had the opposite effect. I tensed. *What did he have?*

"Wish we could join you," the chief said. "But we're on duty still and have evidence to process. Ms. Christie?"

"Yes," said Meg, Gram, and I.

"Meg?" the chief specified. "I'm going to need to take the boots you were wearing the other night and your coat and gloves. I'll give you a receipt for everything."

"What else are you taking?" I asked, frowning at Sam Ibarra.

He held up the bag. I recognized the green sweater Meg had worn last night.

"A sweater for fiber and luminol analysis," he said.

Gram tutted. "That's an alpaca wool sweater. It requires special handling. I hope you'll be careful."

The chief nodded seriously. "We will, Mrs. Christie."

"My sweater?" Meg said. "Why are you taking that?"

Sam answered. "We spritzed this with luminol, which is—"

Gram tsked. "Not a substance natural to the alpaca . . ."

He continued, grim-faced. "Luminol reacts to the iron in blood and will exhibit chemiluminescence if . . ."

Gram, Meg, and I nodded in a get-on-with-it way. We were mystery readers. We knew about luminol. Plus, who hadn't seen *CSI*?

He cut to the ending. "There's blood on this sweater."

I wished we hadn't hurried him. Even more, I wished that Meg hadn't been so nice as to invite a search. Most of all? I dearly wished we'd never agreed to blind bookish dates.

CHAPTER 10

✳

Thorns with Roses

At barely past seven in the morning, Rosie and I stepped out into air so cold, it swiped my breath and froze my nostrils.

My niece yawned. "You don't have to walk with me, Aunt El. It's your day off. You should be sleeping in."

I waved off warm quilts, flannel sheets, and the perfect pillow as if they were nothing. "I have lots to do today, starting with getting Agatha her breakfast. She's going to be grumpy with me."

Rosie's laugh froze between us. Her jacket was open and her bare knees exposed to the chill by designer rips. "Of course she will be. Agatha's a queen!"

"That's for sure." I zipped my jacket as far as it would go and wound my scarf tighter. "And a celebrity. She has more Instagram followers than the Book Chalet does."

"Awesome." Rosie set off at a jaunt, loose limbs showing teenage imperviousness to the cold. "Gram and I could get Agatha on TikTok. We'd go viral. Totally explode!" Rosie mimed a mushroom cloud.

I had to smile at the idea of Gram, Rosie, and Agatha taking over TikTok. "Does it make me sound really old if I admit that 'going viral' and 'exploding' don't sound like things I'd like?"

"Truth? Asking if you sound old? That makes you sound ancient," Rosie teased. "Old Auntie El and her ornery cat, trending!"

As we walked, I admired the frosty sparkle and Rosie's bubbly talk of blowing Gram up on Instagram. "If Mom would just let me join! Pasha showed me these grandparents on Insta. They're in Taiwan, I think. They have a dry cleaner and they dress up in outfits that get left behind. So adorbs!"

"So you'd dress Gram up? In what? We don't get entire wardrobes left behind at the Book Chalet." Our lost and found included a cardigan that could crush any ugly-sweater contest, a collection of baseball hats, lone mittens, and a single wooden clog.

Rosie admitted that they hadn't worked that out yet. "Maybe just Gram, you know, knitting in fun places. Just being Gram. With books, of course."

"Adorbs," I said, testing out my coolness. Apart from freezing my nose off, I had another reason for getting out early with Rosie. I wanted to ask about possible romance. Except I had no idea where or how to start.

When I was your age? No.

Take it from me, kid, relationships are hard. . . . That sounded like a hard-nosed heroine from a noir novel. Plus, who was I to give romantic advice, unless as a cautionary tale.

Rosie checked her phone, typed something fast with two thumbs, and plopped it back in her pocket.

"One of your friends?" I asked. She'd given me the perfect opening.

She shot me a look that said *Yeah, obviously!*

"Your mom thinks you're texting a boy," I said. "Or a girl. Someone new?"

"Why's she think that?" Suspicion etched my niece's brow.

"Has she been snooping? You guys snoop. I know you're looking into Mr. Darcy's death."

And I knew she was changing the subject. I nudged her. "Like
you're not a snooper? You're a Christie too."

"Whatever," she said, essentially agreeing.

We waited at a crosswalk for a car to go by, slow on the ice-
packed roads.

"She's just concerned," I said, as Rosie stepped out like no ice
or treachery or care in the world existed. "Like any mom."

I waited for another "whatever."

Rosie kicked a snowdrift. "Yeah, well, *I'm* worried about her.
You know, I heard everything last night."

An uncool aunt might have feigned ignorance: *Oh, heard
what?* Very uncool aunt could have chastised eavesdropping. As
if a Christie would ever discourage that! Information was always good, even if it was unsettling.

"You heard the police?" I confirmed.

Rosie nodded.

"And your mom's explanation for that bit of blood on the
sweater?"

"Yeah. Mom's such a klutz. Of course she broke a wineglass
on a first date! How embarrassing!"

As Meg had explained, she'd broken a wineglass. The fancy
kind, paper thin and large as a balloon. Joe, picking up the
pieces, had nicked a finger. She'd helped him wrap a bandage
around it.

"A major date disaster," Meg had said to us, blushing. "Or so
I thought at the time."

"I believe her!" Rosie said, defiantly. "Don't you?"

"Yes! It'll be okay." Since I had no evidence to back that up, I
shifted the subject. "Where'd you sit to spy? Third step down?"

This made her smile. "Fourth. The third step has a squeak.
You have to step all the way over it, but then only on the far
outer edge of the next step or it'll groan."

"Ah, good to know," I said.

Rosie flushed. "It was a total kid thing to do, but whatever. I was worried about Mom, and I knew she wouldn't tell me what's going on. She still thinks I'm a little kid."

"Mothers always do," I said and added, "and snooping isn't a kid thing. If the officers had kicked Gram and me out of the kitchen, you can bet we would have been on those stairs listening in too."

Rosie smiled. "Gram is the queen of the snoops." She scuffed her boots and kicked another snowdrift. "You really think Mom's okay?"

"Absolutely," I said. "She had a perfectly reasonable explanation for that blood. The broken glass will be in the trash. The police probably already collected it. That'll totally back up her statement."

"Totally" was an exaggeration. It might prove Meg was klutzy, as Rosie affectionately put it, but Joe hadn't been killed by a fumble with fancy glassware.

"Not that." Rosie stretched her words in exasperation. "I mean, Mom seemed so happy after that date and now she's sad. I want her to be happy. You think she hasn't been?"

Oh. I'd wanted a serious conversation. I sure had one. Rosie wasn't just worried about blood on a cuff. She was concerned with the biggest of intangibles. Love. Happiness. Desire. Dreams . . . My niece was way more mature than I was at her age.

"She was happy about the date," I said carefully. "Even Ms. Ridge noted it."

"Really? Ms. Ridge commented? What was Mom doing, singing? She was singing before she left for the Chalet."

"Humming," I said.

"Oh my gosh!" Rosie said, all teenager, until she reconsidered. "Poor Mom."

I hurried to assure her. "Your mom enjoyed a date, but that

doesn't mean she was *unhappy* before. Of course, she's sad about what happened to Mr. Darcy, but she loves her life. She and I have talked about this. We have our dream job and she's always said she doesn't need a relationship with anyone but you. She means it, Rosie."

"I guess." She sounded unconvinced. "But if she did get in a relationship that made her happy, that would be cool."

We'd reached the cross-street where she'd turn to school. The gondola station was straight ahead, but by chance the conversation had turned in the direction I'd initially hoped.

"It can be hard to express feelings," I said. *Tell me about it!* I'd felt surer-footed falling down a cliff yesterday. "Rosie, you know you can tell me anything, right?" I raised my eyebrows. "Aunt and niece cone of secrecy?"

Rosie's eyes shifted to the left.

Per that helpful article in *Police Today,* leftward glances could suggest a fib and/or evasion. I sensed the latter.

I forged on. "*Is* there anyone you're interested in? Romantically?"

Rosie scowled and kicked another blameless snowdrift.

I plowed on. "You have been texting a lot . . ." If I'd been digging an actual hole, it would have collapsed on me by now.

"Everyone texts," Rosie said. Her tone suggested I'd accused her of life's essentials: consumption of oxygen, water, books . . . "Did you hear Gram's phone last night? She got more messages than me and you're not after her."

I held up my hands. I had a new pair of mittens, in rainbow zigzag stripes. Gram had let me pick from her trunk of knitwear. "I just want you to know, I'm always here for you."

My niece took pity on me. "Yeah, I know that, Aunt El. Thanks, really, but I'm fine."

I wasn't convinced, especially when Rosie continued.

First, she hedged, "It's like, you know, whatever . . ."

Next, she kicked more snow. Then she dropped her bomb.

"Mom's going to hit the roof anyway. If she'd just give it a chance, it could be awesome!"

"Hit the roof?" I asked. But I was too late.

Down the way, two figures waited. They waved, arms high, like they were meeting again after an ocean voyage, not a weekend. And hadn't Rosie just seen Pasha yesterday?

"That's Pash," Rosie said. "And Diego. He's new here, pretty cool. Gotta go. See ya, Aunt El." She held out a fist. I bumped my mitten to hers.

Meg said that Rosie had been covertly texting a contact named "D."

Et voilà! I felt as smug as Poirot. I'd solved the mystery. Diego was tall, lanky, and laughing. But what had Rosie meant about Meg hitting the roof? Had the romance sped ahead? The teenagers jostled and gestured, looking like happy friends.

I'd talk to Rosie again soon. Maybe we could go out for an aunt–niece pizza night. Until then, I had a date with a pampered feline queen.

* * *

Agatha greeted me with an indignant meow that expressed much suffering. She'd been starving, lonely, and deserted.

In the storeroom, her kibble bowls were still mounded with food. Upstairs, three catnip mice lay in the bathtub, and Siamese kitty fluff decorated my pillow.

I called out her fibs. "You had a catnip party, my pillow, and a week of food."

Agatha responded with her wide-eyed desperation look. She won. I opened a packet of kitty pâté in Agatha's favorite flavor, roasted duck.

"Meg needed company," I said as Agatha purred over her gourmet breakfast. "We stayed up late talking."

A yawn overtook me. I'd had coffee at Gram's, but another cup never hurt. I heaped French roast into the coffee basket and told Agatha the day's plans. She was a great listener, and the last time we'd gotten wrapped up in crime, Agatha had pointed out clues.

"Meg's coming up this morning," I said, stifling another yawn. "We need to find out more about Joe Darcy."

Agatha looked up from her bowl and scowled.

I took her look as an indictment of Joe Darcy, not our plan or a desire for more breakfast.

"I know!" I agreed. "Between you and me? He was a cad."

She meowed. I awarded her solidarity with more duck.

"Cheating on his fiancée while living in her house?" I said, pushing the coffeepot's start button. "What a jerk!"

But was that enough to get him killed? Possibly . . . We needed to know more about his fiancée too. Lorna knew Fiona Giddings, but we'd have to wait until later to call Lorna. After her kids got off to school, Lorna returned to bed for what she called her "wakeup nap."

The coffee maker embarked on its leisurely brew. Hiss. Burble. Dribble. I leaned back on the counter and admired the morning light, which almost made the storeroom look like the rustic home-behind-the-shop it used to be. Currently, it serves as a hold-all.

There were staff lockers, painted in primary colors, rescued from a now-demolished elementary school. A long soapstone table that Meg utilized to send out book mail. Gram and Rosie mended spines there too. Their tools, antique hammers, mallets, clamps, and a mishmash of tools from a great-aunt's experiments in blacksmithing hung from pegboard, with painted outlines marking their places.

Then, there was my kitchenette, the perfect "Before" for any Before-and-After home-renovation spread. I preferred to think of it as antique trendy. People paid thousands of dollars for round-cornered avocado fridges. Mismatched tile countertops? Not as desirable. But my oven was 1950s white enamel with a built-in rotary timer.

I cast my eyes up to the beamed rafters and steep staircase

leading into my loft. Where I could retreat for a wakeup nap. A tempting prospect . . .

The coffeepot spluttered. It was right. I had too much to do to go back to bed. While it finished brewing, I got out my phone and did what any twenty-first-century sleuth would do. I googled Joe Darcy.

"There are lots of Joe Darcys," I told Agatha, who'd hopped up to the table to groom her claws. I added "Last Word" to the search. Now nothing matched and LinkedIn was pursuing me.

The coffee maker beeped in triumph. I abandoned my search to fix a mug. Coffee could help anything, even Google.

I was about to savor my first sip when Agatha threw back her ears. Moments later, sharp raps carried through the shop.

I groaned. Had I forgotten to flip our door sign to CLOSED? The knocking persisted, aggressive even for the most book-desperate visitor.

The police? Again? Trepidation skipped at my side as I made my way through the darkened shop. Agatha trotted ahead, her tail puffed to double fluffy.

Rap, rap, rap!

Usually, I would have called out, but Agatha seemed to sense trouble. I kept to the edges of the shop, where the shadows were darkest and someone busy knocking couldn't see me. At the door, I sidled up to a diamond windowpane.

I saw red. So much red, it took me a moment to decipher. Roses. Their petals ruffled. The knocking continued. In between, I heard a muttered "Come on, answer the door."

Agatha was also impatient. She hopped on the bay-window ledge, knocking over a book and mewing.

"Okay," I whispered to Agatha. Louder, I called out, "Just a moment."

I twisted the lock, opened the door, and was knocked back by a nose-full of sweetly perfumed petals.

"Oh!" A woman peered out from behind a bouquet approximately the size of a tea-rose shrub. A scratch reddened her cheek.

"Here!" She thrust the flowers at me as if delivering a court summons.

I took them, feeling like I'd just received a thorny hot potato.

"That's a relief," their deliverer declared. "My boss said, deliver 'em to a *live* person at this bookstore. I about died when I saw that CLOSED sign. What was I supposed to do if you weren't here? They're already a day late, and I'm on a Vespa!"

I peered around the flowers and confirmed her impractical means of winter flower delivery in the mountains.

She kept talking. "I got 'em here as soon as I could. The order came in online after hours on Saturday, but Posey's Mountain Posies wasn't open yesterday. I can't be blamed for that."

"Thanks?" I said uncertainly. Saturday night, late . . . That would have been after our dates.

I peered into the extravagant bunch. Thorns like tiger claws hid among clouds of baby's breath. "Who are they for?"

She frowned like I'd asked a riddle. "Someone who works here?"

My stomach tightened. "You said the order came in late on Saturday? How late?"

The delivery woman raised her palms in apparent frustration. "You ask a lot of questions for someone holding a deluxe arrangement."

"I want to get them to the right person," I said.

She nodded, serious. "You should! People fight over our flowers."

People also killed—and got murdered—over romance and betrayal. I tried a different angle. "Do you know *who* sent them?"

She puffed exasperation. "Look inside. I stuck a card in there, unless it blew off when I was driving up the mountain."

It was a wonder that she and the flowers weren't frozen solid.

"Careful when you go looking," she advised. "Sender requested heirloom stems, *au naturel*. Means we don't clip the thorns. Now, this particular variety, it's our Eternal Remembrance Rose. We took the initial cuttings from Fairmount Cemetery down in Denver. We grow 'em and force blooms all year in our greenhouses. Pretty special, eh?"

"Wow," I mustered. "That is, ah, special. How thoughtful."

How creepy!

She thrust an electronic signature pad toward my unoccupied left hand. "Here. Sign. Prove I found a live body." She chuckled happily.

I scribbled illegible loops with my finger.

"Sure is a big bunch," she said admiringly. "Someone had a *really* good time on Saturday night. Or did something *really* bad . . ."

✳

CHAPTER 11

By Any Other Name

"It's that card that bothers me," said Gram, an hour later. She and Meg had come up on the gondola after I called to tell them about the roses. A dozen thorny stems, frothy baby's breath, and waxy ferns lay before us, sprawled on the workbench. Agatha had a similar pose, but a few inches away. Even she was giving the flowers space.

"The card, Gram?" Meg asked. "Not that they're cemetery clones, like something out of a Stephen King story?"

"No . . ." Gram sounded far away and pensive.

"Or that Joseph Darcy likely sent them, even though he has a fiancée?" Meg scowled at the blooms.

Other, less Stephen King–like petals, might have withered.

"That is more disturbing," Gram allowed. "Ellie, could I see the card again?"

I passed Gram the folded square of paper. Earlier, when fishing it from the thicket of stems, I'd been careful. Even so, a thorn had gotten me.

Meg nodded at my bandaged thumb and grumbled about a gift that drew blood.

My sister—usually sunny—was in a stormy mood. Understandably so.

Gram took the note, adjusted her bifocals, cleared her throat, and read aloud. " 'With appreciation to my favorite Christie.' " Gram paused and frowned. "Not very romantic is it? 'Appreciation'?"

Meg sniffed.

Gram read the rest of the note. " '*Books,* I have often noticed, *are* a great matchmaker.' " She emphasized two words that were written in italic font, different from the rest.

"The sentiment is perfectly logical," Gram said.

Meg and I agreed.

"Why the italics?" Gram mused. "Something doesn't seem right."

That was for sure.

"I hear the words in someone else's voice," Gram said. She cleared her throat once more and read again, this time in an approximation of a fluttery English accent.

"Nice," I said when she was done. "Miss Marple?"

Gram nodded. "Yes, but I don't think it was her. . . ."

Even Meg had to smile at Gram's next reading, done with Belgian-French inflection.

"Poirot?" Meg asked.

"Can one of you look the words up?" Gram asked. "The non-italicized parts?"

I tapped the phrases into my phone in parts, enclosed in quotes: "I have noticed" + "great matchmaker" + "Agatha Christie."

Google popped up results and goosebumps sprouted on my arms.

Meg read over my shoulder and drew a breath.

She read aloud for Gram. "*Murder,* I have often noticed, *is* a great matchmaker. It's Poirot, all right, from *The A.B.C. Murders.*"

"A book about a serial killer? Wonderful. Just when I thought I'd had the worst date ever." Meg removed her glasses and rubbed her eyes.

"Maybe not *serial*," I said. "A multiple killer on a mission." The technicality failed to cheer my sister.

"Right," Meg said, straightening her glasses and her composure. "Into the trash with these." She reached for the plastic wrapping I'd cut open to extract the card.

Agatha perked up. She liked crinkles.

Gram said, "Now, Meg, dear. It's not the roses' fault, and we don't know the full story yet. Besides, there's still a possibility they're from Ellie's date."

I snorted. "Right." When palm trees sprouted on the ski slopes.

Gram bustled over to take the roses from Meg.

Meg looked to me. "Ellie, do *you* want to keep them?"

They weren't mine, of that I was sure. But they were pretty, from a safe distance. Another reason to preserve them struck me as suddenly as the thorn pricking my thumb. "We have to keep them. They add to your alibi. The delivery woman said the order came in late Saturday."

I didn't have to spell it out. Joe couldn't have been dead if he was up in the wee hours ordering flowers.

"Fine," Meg said. Her tone sounded truculent. Her eyes, puddling tears, gave her away. She caught me looking and said, briskly, "We need to know more about Joe. His past too. Lorna should know. She supposedly vetted our dates."

My phone buzzed. I read the text.

"Speak of the matchmaker," I said. "It's Lorna. She says, and I quote: 'Found U perfect biblio-matches! Big news!'"

"What?" Meg mixed incredulity with outrage. "Oh, we definitely need to have a talk with Lorna."

* * *

A few hours later, Meg and I stepped out of the gondola station. Church bells and city hall rang out a duet announcing noon. Up in the hamlet, Gram would be lining up for the buffet and monthly luncheon at the Last Word Historical Society. She planned to learn about mine reclamation, while digging for useful gossip. Meg and I had a date with Lorna and Marigold at the library.

My sister stopped in front of the nearest shop and studied the window display.

I doubted Meg had a sudden interest in fat-tired bicycles made for rolling through snow. More likely, déjà vu taunted her too. I felt it in the form of dread, a return to the library, scene of our dates.

"Let's make a pact," Meg said.

"Sure," I said, admiring a cute but winter-impractical cruising bike with a basket big enough for a picnic, books, and Agatha.

"You don't want to hear what it is first?" Meg asked.

"Nope," I said, grinning at her via our reflections. "I trust you."

"I don't trust myself," she said. "Do *not* let me get bullied into any more dates. Promise?"

I agreed. "But with one condition—"

Our names, trilled at top volume, drowned out my condition that Meg shield me from any more blind dating too.

Venessa Upshaw trotted across the icy street as if her boots bore cleats rather than high heels that made my ankles want to turn just looking at them. She wore a designer ski jacket with a silvery sheen, trimmed in white faux fur. More fake fur rested on her head, curled up like a sleepy snow hare, complete with a bobbing pompom tail.

"Just the sisters I wanted to see!" Ven proclaimed.

I took a step back. Ven was a realtor, under the illusion that she'd sell me on a dream home. Ridiculous for at least two reasons. Last time I glanced at the glossy photos in her window, I couldn't afford an abandoned shack half crushed by a toppled pine. *Make it your own,* the listing headline screamed. Two, I lived above a shop full of books. Location, location, location!

Meg greeted her.

"I can't talk long," Ven said, "I'm on my way to visit a seller—darling place! Ellie, it has your name all over it. Imagine . . . your own private condo on Marshland Court. Mmmm?"

She couldn't help herself, but to my astonishment, I didn't even have time to say no before she let it go.

Ven lowered her voice to a conspiratorial whisper. "I heard what happened."

She and everyone else in town.

"Poor Lorna," Ven continued. "She has the worst luck in business."

Ven was a local. She'd been in Lorna's class in school. I remembered them having a lot in common then: cheerleading, looking good, being popular. They'd been friendly. But actual friends? I wasn't sure, then or now.

"It's awful for everyone involved," Meg said.

"Don't I know!" Ven swiveled, as if checking that we were alone. We were, except for two guys inside the bike shop, seemingly fascinated by gears. Ven leaned closer. "I *knew* him."

I could guess who.

"Joe?" Meg confirmed.

The furry hat bobbled. Ven had met Joe in a trendy new cocktail bar up in the hamlet. "Après," she intoned, of the bar. Regarding whether they were dating, she flicked her hand dismissively. "Nothing formal or matched like you, Meg. We hit it off, you know? We'd text, meet up."

I read between the lines and guessed they hadn't always stayed at Après.

"When did you first meet?" Meg asked.

Ven looked pensive. "Just after the new year? I was celebrating a sale—a ski-in/ski-out property. Quite a commission, but Joe bought *me* drinks." She reached out and touched Meg's arm. "At the time, I thought I was in luck. Now I feel like I dodged a bullet. You too, Meg."

Had word already gotten around about Joe's fiancée? I wouldn't be surprised.

"How so?" I asked, thinking Ven might say more if she thought she was dishing up new information.

Ven's gaze returned to Meg. "You went out with him the night he died. I didn't know he signed up for matchmaking." She shrugged, a *whatever* kind of move that failed to convince me.

"I'm sorry," Meg said. "He didn't mention that he was seeing other people."

Or engaged.

Ven rolled her eyes. "Of course he was. Welcome to the world of handsome single guys, Meg. No, I mean, you and I both dodged a deadly bullet, *the killer*." She looked around again.

A man and a French bulldog, dressed alike in tartan jackets and leather booties, strolled down the walkway. Ven, Meg, and I smiled and cooed at the dog. When they passed, Ven lowered her tone to dire.

"Seems like you got away just in time, Meg," she said.

"And you?" I asked. "Did you see him on Saturday?"

She stroked her hat like it was an emotional support pet. "I texted him Saturday night. I was at Après but the place was dead. I joked he could invite me over. To think . . . The killer could have been there! Or . . ." Ven shuddered.

Joe could have already been dead.

I had so many questions, they logjammed in my throat. *What did he say? Did you go? Did you see anyone? Did you know he was engaged?*

Meg, sensibly, started with a logical and simple question. "When did you text him?"

Ven answered with quick precision. "Eleven forty-eight." She shook her head sadly. "I checked after I heard about his death. And, I know, it was late. I wasn't some *desperate* barfly. Don't get the wrong idea. I knew Joe was a night owl, like me."

A question freed itself from my verbal pileup. "What did he say?"

"He didn't respond." Ven gave an even more unconvincing *whatever* shrug.

Her pocket chirped. Ven drew out a phone in a sparkly case, glanced at the screen, then dropped it back in her pocket. "Buyers," she said with an eye roll worthy of my teenage niece. "Waiting, considering, thinking it through . . . They won't get a house unless they bid high, fast, and often. It's the same with dating. Be bold, ladies, but be careful."

With that she turned to go. She was halfway across the icesheet street when she turned and sang out, "And remember, *if you need a change of abode, I'm the woman to lead you home*."

Meg and I watched as she revved up a Range Rover parked at an angle between a dumpster and a fire hydrant. Like she'd seen us and veered into the nearest approximation of a parking spot. Why? To warn us? To get some kind of guilt off her mind?

"What do you make of that?" I asked Meg.

She frowned. "A night owl? He told me he was early to bed, early to rise. Was everything about him a lie?"

✳

CHAPTER 12

Lunch and a Hunch

At the library, I held my breath and strode through the vestibule without looking up, down, or anywhere around. Totally kid move, my mind chided, the words in Rosie's voice, barbed with teenage scorn. Valid. But why take chances with a portal?

I should have known I couldn't outsmart the library. Déjà vu waited on the other side, tapping a suede boot.

"There you are!" Lorna declared, just as she had on Saturday night.

For a second, I let myself fall into the illusion. We were getting a do-over, a second chance on that fated first date. I wouldn't ask Dr. Waldon what he liked to read, that's for sure. No, scratch that. My date wouldn't be Dr. Waldon, at least not in Beckett-professing form. He'd be the bookbinder I'd imagined, savior of old, neglected tomes.

And Meg's date . . . He'd be a true romantic hero. Single, honest, punctual for brunch dates, and—most importantly—alive.

Lorna yanked me into a hug, and the shiny illusion shattered like an icicle that lost its grip.

"I worried you wouldn't come," Lorna said, releasing me to swoop in on my stiff-backed sister. "You'll be glad you did! I have good news!" She stepped back to assess Meg and deemed her "holding up."

I studied Lorna. Makeup gave her apple-pink cheeks and rosy lips. Her dress was another version of busty Tudor heroine off to a summer garden party. Her tone and smile were as bright as solar flares.

It was her eyes that gave her away. Rather, the tension tightening in the space where a real smile would lift. I wasn't looking forward to breaking our news of no more blind dates, but I was glad we'd come. Lorna needed support too.

"We're just waiting on Marigold," Lorna said. "She's doing something with kids. Puppets, reading . . ." Lorna chattered on, teasing wonderful biblio-date opportunities. On the surface, she was bright and cheery. And loud.

I glanced up the hallway. At the end, a figure sat behind the circulation desk, spine as rigid and straight as a new hardback. An index finger rose toward pursed lips.

Mrs. Harmon!

I fought the childish urge to duck behind my sister. Mrs. Harmon had been anointed head librarian in my elementary-school days. Even then, libraries were moving away from the zone-of-silence model. Now libraries buzzed as community hubs, learning centers, open spaces for all to use and enjoy.

Tell that to Mrs. Harmon. Her shushing finger trembled as if it was taking every ounce of her strength to hold it back.

"You'll absolutely *love* our new dating options!" Lorna boomed.

I tensed, waiting for Mrs. Harmon or Meg or both to snap.

Giggles came to the rescue, tumbling from the kids' room, followed by a half-dozen little library lovers waving paper cut-outs. Dragons, dolls, dogs, cats, and amphibians, dancing on wooden dowels.

Mrs. Harmon lowered her finger and offered a smile that tightened upon reaching the librarian following the kids out.

Marigold carried an armload of stick figures, all slipping and sliding like a writhing bundle of squirmy kittens. She stopped to hear out Mrs. Harmon, whose pointing finger and sharp frown aimed our way.

"That Harmon woman is such a drag," Lorna said, again failing to whisper.

I cringed, thankful that Mrs. Harmon was too busy fussing at Marigold to hear.

When Marigold reached us, she offered a cowed smile and whispered greetings. "Let's go to the staff room. Lorna is treating us all to lunch."

"*We're* treating you," Lorna stressed. "We're a team, Marigold." She regally sailed past circulation, as we turned right and went down a hall to a back room I'd never seen.

The kitchenette inside rivaled mine in terms of eclectic vintage. The appliances weren't the only antiques. Card catalogs lined the walls, like the last of the dinosaurs, huddled together in a cave. Windows overlooked a courtyard tucked behind a tall fence. The library really did have a secret garden!

Marigold laid down her paper figures as tenderly as babies. Then she enveloped my sister in a hug. "I'm so, so sorry about Joe."

Meg squeezed Marigold back. "I am too."

When they released, Meg pressed up a smile. "We hear there's some good news, though. Bibliophiles Find Love is still going? You have new offerings?"

Dear Meg. This was why she couldn't be a killer. She cared too much about others.

Marigold's cheeks flushed. "I hope you don't think we're callous. We debated whether we should shut up shop but—"

"*You* debated," Lorna corrected. "*We* agreed. Joe Darcy's death had nothing to do with Bibliophiles Find Love. We deal in happiness, commitment, love. That's what people need now, more than ever."

Marigold nodded somberly. "It's true. We all know too many people who've been hurt by mismatches, don't we? Like you, Meg, and my dear college roommate, Liv. We used to be such close friends. I truly believe biblio-matching could have helped."

"Exactly!" said Lorna. "Marigold, just remember your favorite authors. They would want us to keep going."

"I think they would." Marigold smiled at Meg and me. "I was telling Lorna. After I heard about Mr. Darcy, I turned to my comfort reads. Books have so much to tell us about love and life." She touched her sternum and inhaled deeply, a move shared by yoga enthusiasts, meditation practitioners, and book worshippers.

On the exhale, Marigold said reverently, "Jane Austen. Oh, and the Brontës! Emily, Anne, Charlotte. So wise . . ."

I thought the Brontës might not be our best role models. Emily and Anne had died young and single. Charlotte's great love had been unreciprocated—and married! She'd sent him love letters. He'd torn them up. His wife, of all people, stitched the correspondence back together. I'd seen them on display at the British Library, safely behind glass. In one, Charlotte had written of her lacerated heart and searing regrets. Yikes!

Lorna cleared her throat.

Marigold snapped out of her literary reverie. "Sorry! I'm going on, aren't I? Our lunch should be warm. I slipped back here and put the takeout boxes in the oven when the kids were practicing with their shadow puppets. They were so creative today. Dominick Watson came up with an entire play involving a singing horse and—"

Lorna interrupted. "What's truly exciting is *lunch*. Marigold, tell Ellie and Meg about your lovely idea."

"Oh, well, it's not much," Marigold said.

"That's what makes it brilliant," Lorna countered, and

spilled the news herself. "Lunch dates. That's our new offering. Casual, fun, light. Plus, it's daylight. No one will have to worry about, well . . ."

Killers on dark balconies.

Marigold busied herself retrieving aluminum trays from the oven and lidded containers from the fridge. "I ordered from the new Palestinian place on Pyrite," Marigold said, plunking down enough dishes for a feast. "We're taste-testing for possible caterers so I got a bit of everything."

Taste-testing was dating support I could happily offer.

Marigold passed dishes.

Lorna remained in sales mode. "Think literary lunch," she said, clasping her hands in lieu of passing along the chicken shawarma. "We'll set the scene. No time wasted worrying about small talk. You'll discuss provided questions. Say, what's your favorite childhood book? Or, if you're not into midday and one-on-one, we're planning some group mixers too. Happy hours with mood lighting and paired cocktails. Hot toddies and Agatha Christie? Lemon drops and Lord Byron?"

Toddies and Christies did sound fun. I worked to keep my face a pleasant neutral. I couldn't let Lorna see any crack in my resolve, especially now. Lorna was in a mode I recognized. Problem solver. Her go-to approach to trouble was to smother it with an avalanche of positives.

"Which would *you girls* be most interested in?" Lorna asked. She held the chicken shawarma close, as if keeping it hostage until Meg or I provided the right answer. "Literary lunch? Bookish brunch?"

Meg looked slightly queasy. Had Lorna forgotten that Meg had waited for a bookish brunch and a date who never showed?

Time for little sister to step up and be bold. First, however, I accepted a tray of tabouli from Marigold. "Lorna," I said, pressing up a smile I hoped would convey warm, loving regret. A version of the classic *it's not you, it's me* breakup. It was us. All of us.

Lorna, pressing us into dates we didn't want. Meg and me, competitors for worst daters. The killer, most of all.

"It's the murder," I said. "Meg and I don't feel right dating under these, ah, circumstances."

Guilt did a jaunt from my head to my heart, sparked by the hurt on Lorna's face. Also, because I'd just used a murder for my personal advantage. Was that wrong? It was surely gauche.

Lorna's expression turned petulant. That actually helped. My resolve stiffened. She would not guilt us back. We—I—had to stay strong.

"We believe in your business," Meg said. "Books are a great connector."

Lorna pouted. She still held the shawarma hostage. "Yet you're dropping out? Deserting us?"

"Until Joe's murder is solved, yes," Meg said.

There went Meg, being too nice again. She'd left an opening for future blind-date disasters.

Lorna made a skeptical *hmmm* sound.

Meg reached over and snagged the chicken. "You can help us look into the crime," Meg said. "Both of you."

"How?" This was Marigold.

Lorna was aggressively mixing the cucumber salad, and I was thinking that dating and murder did have something in common. Even on the sidelines, innocent friends, bystanders, cousins, and salads could be wounded by the fallout.

Meg explained that we needed information on Joe. "We have a lot of questions only you can answer. Why did Joe sign up for matchmaking? How did you match him to me?"

Lorna dropped a single cucumber slice on her plate and passed the dish to Marigold. "No mystery there. He signed up and you matched. Simple. What are you thinking? I picked him up hitchhiking and invited him to dinner with you?"

Maybe? I kept my eyes on my plate. I couldn't let Lorna read my thoughts. Also, the food was divine.

"We did quite a bit of advertising," Marigold said. "Online.

We put up flyers around town. In Ridgecrest and Lone Creek too. We've been getting a lot of interest, even now."

"That's right," Lorna said. "Joe thought our one-of-a-kind service sounded like a marvelous way to meet intelligent, interesting women. And he did. I'm so sorry for what happened to him, but it was nothing to do with our matchmaking."

"But he lied," Meg said quietly.

Marigold looked up from drizzling vibrant green sauce over her meal. "What?"

"He was engaged," I said. "Lorna hasn't told you?"

Sauce dripped over the side of Marigold's plate, fragrant with mint, garlic, and parsley. Marigold didn't notice, which was answer enough.

So was Lorna's sour-pickle expression. "I was about to tell you, Marigold," Lorna said. "Then I got delayed at the police station and when I finally got here, you were busy with children and doll day."

"Shadow puppet hour," Marigold corrected automatically. She noticed the spill and jumped up to tear paper towels from a dispenser.

Lorna waggled a chastising finger that would have made Mrs. Harmon proud. She aimed it at Meg and me. "You two should have told *me* about Joe's supposed engagement! We're family! Those police officers surprised me when I went in to give my statement this morning. I bet they were laughing at me after I left. The forgotten cousin no one thought to tell."

Lorna was right. We should have called her.

"It was late last night," Meg said weakly. "When you texted this morning . . . It seemed better to say in person."

"I was embarrassed, professionally and personally," Lorna said.

Marigold looked up from her scrubbing. "A fiancée? But . . . how? Why? Are we sure?"

Because he was a common cheater! I answered Marigold's

other question. "We're sure. We met his fiancée last night at the police station. She looked devastated."

Marigold dabbed at the table, though it now looked spotless. "That poor woman . . ."

"Oh, please!" Lorna said, surprising us all.

"Don't look so shocked," Lorna went on. "People cheat every day. But how about this? I don't think Joe was a cheater."

"But the fiancée—" Marigold stammered.

"Was she a fiancée?" Lorna interjected. Her smile reminded me of Agatha's right after she stole my pillow. Smug, sly, triumphant.

Lorna basked, then said, "The police told me this supposed fiancée's name. I *know* her. Marigold, I bet you do too."

Marigold's eyes widened. "I couldn't! That means I would have known about her fiancé, about Joe."

Lorna sat back, like a queen bestowing information. "Fiona Giddings. The theater director down in Ridgecrest? Don't you do puppet stuff down there?"

"Yes?" Marigold said shakily. "The kids put on an Easter shadow puppets performance, and I heard Fiona was engaged. I don't think I ever met the gentleman."

"Maybe there's a reason for that," Lorna said. She paused to treat us to a meaningful look.

When she didn't explain, Meg asked, "What reason?"

Lorna dabbed her lips before responding. An air-dab, I thought. Her lipstick remained intact. "Fiona's an *actor*. She tells stories for a living."

"Okay . . ." Meg said.

"Well? What if she made him up?" Lorna said.

Meg and I sold stories as our business. We didn't create fictional fiancés.

Meg and Marigold mirrored my skepticism.

Lorna rolled her eyes, as if we were the outlandish ones. "Did any of you see an engagement announcement? I didn't. Plus, and I'll say this only to you ladies, Fiona Giddings is unreliable. You can't trust her word. Back when I was doing real estate, she listed the Moosejaw house with me. I put in a lot of time and effort and then one day I took a buyer over and what did I see? A new lockbox and a short-term renter. Fiona got testy and said I must have misinterpreted our agreement. I didn't. She wanted what she wanted. She didn't care what was real."

"She wanted a fiancé so she made one up?" Meg said, shaking her head.

Marigold looked appalled. "That's awfully suspicious of you, Lorna. Fiona's a nice woman. She's generous with lending the theater to community groups. Besides, people change their minds on big decisions like real estate."

Lorna snorted. "Ellie, Meg? Is there such a thing as being *too* suspicious, even of *nice* women?"

Meg answered. "No. Miss Marple would agree."

"Exactly," said Lorna in a case-closed tone. She waved a carrot stick at us. "You can't trust a soul. Except for you ladies. Meg, I'll have you know, I stuck up for you and told the police all my theories."

I wasn't sure that helped Meg. As a real fiancée, Fiona made a fine prime suspect. However, by the time we reached the baklava course, I'd consoled myself. If chills creeping up my spine counted as soothing. A delusional faux fiancée would be an even better suspect.

The chills circled my neck. A delusional killer might also lash out at her fake-fiancé's final date.

✳

CHAPTER 13

Persuasions

"This seems too easy," I whispered to Meg.

She looped the plastic ribbons of a trash bag into a tidy bow. I boxed up leftovers that Marigold and Lorna insisted we take home to share with Gram and Rosie.

I tallied our wins and revelations. Free lunch. Delicious leftovers, including a carton of baklava that weighed as much as Agatha C. Christie. A spine-tingling suspect. All that, and Lorna was letting us leave without weighty dating guilt?

The last wasn't just too easy. It was too good to be true.

Something was up.

"Before you go . . ." Lorna positioned herself in the doorframe, blocking our exit like a cat elegantly stretching in front of a mouse.

Marigold joined Lorna, her hands twisting anxiously. "Lorna and I have a little problem. . . ."

I looked around for that magical library cart.

"It's Marigold's boss." Lorna tipped her head back in the direction of the circulation desk.

Marigold flushed. "Mrs. Harmon is just thinking of the library." She turned entreating eyes to us. "It's the dating, you see, and serving food and, well, the murder. Mrs. Harmon says those don't align with our library mission, and we can't host our dates here anymore. So . . . we were thinking . . ."

Oh no! No, no, no!

I backed up. A card catalog blocked me. Dozens of little knobs poked at my back like nubby teeth.

"We need somewhere bookish," Lorna said. She tented fingers like a cartoon villain—one plotting the destruction of my serene world. "Romantic. Atmospheric. Lots of books . . ."

Meg attempted to hold back the inevitable. "I'm afraid the Book Chalet wouldn't be convenient. We're too busy during work hours, and Ellie lives above the shop now and. . . ."

And there was no way I could sleep knowing Lorna was downstairs lighting up the lounge with candles and questionable dates.

"I *know* where Ellie lives," Lorna said. "It's so sweet she can live there. Such a perk."

Yes, I enjoyed a perk. A privilege. I had the best apartment in town, rent free.

Lorna patted her curls. "So nice for you, Ellie, to be able to fall back on the family business. That bookshop, it's all about *love* and *family*."

Her message was as gentle as a slap. Lorna was family. We loved her.

"And you found your thing, Ellie," Lorna said with a frown. "I've always been so envious of that."

True too. I'd always known my love for books and bookshops.

Lorna sniffled dramatically. "Do I have to *beg*? Can we *please* use the Book Chalet?"

"No!" The word burst from my lips. Everyone gasped, even me, right before I leaped to overcorrect. "I mean, no, you don't have to beg, Lorna. Of course, you can use the Chalet."

What had I said? Where was that do-over?

Lorna preened.

I attempted damage control akin to sticking my finger in an exploded levee. "It'll be after hours, right?"

"Yes, yes, you won't even notice us," Marigold said. "We'll bring our own dining tables and food. We'll clean up and leave everything spotless, I promise."

I had no doubt that Marigold would be conscientious and careful. But since she'd brought it up . . .

"There are some, ah, Book Chalet policies," I said, making them up on the fly. "We don't allow candles. House rules."

If Lorna required written proof, I'd race home and type up a policy manual. Agatha could second the motion with her pawprint. Although I'd have to bribe her. Agatha was drawn to candles. All the more reason to ban them.

Lorna muttered about the lack of support for her prior candle enterprise. Had she not seen our family's vast candle hoards? The electric could go out in dozens of blizzards and we could read by candlelight for weeks.

Marigold nodded seriously. "I completely agree. Lorna, it's a good policy. No open flames or wax around precious books. A love of books is our entire business model. I promise you, Ellie, we won't be any trouble."

My lips raised in an automatic smile. My head bobbed in affirmation. My mind screamed warnings.

No trouble with matchmaking and blind dating? I'd believe that when books flew, which I dearly hoped they wouldn't.

* * *

Meg and I fled the library so fast, I didn't have a chance to peruse the new books shelf.

"I had to offer," I said, when we were safely away and weaving back to Gram's via residential streets.

"You did," Meg agreed. "*We* did. I'll come chaperone if you want."

I wanted that, desperately, but I couldn't be such a wimp. "I'll be fine," I said with false bravado. Anyway, we had bigger problems. "What's your take on Lorna's theory? I thought Fiona Giddings was truly upset."

"We read a lot of mysteries," Meg said.

Yes, we did, and my reader's imagination had been spinning terrifying tales. Fiona, the deluded killer, sobbing for her victim. Fiona, under the cast of an amnesiac fugue, forgetting she'd slain the man she loved.

"Mystery writers count on readers deceiving themselves," Meg said. "Maybe we saw what Fiona wanted us to see, what we expected."

Fiona, the cunning killer, toying with us. I knew it!

"Or . . ." Meg paused at a curb. "It's like Poirot said."

"Murder brings people together?" I asked grimly.

A truck revved past, kicking up salty grit that sprayed my boots, but it was a shocking thought that made me step back. *Poirot had been wrong!*

"Not that quote," Meg said. "Didn't he say that the most obvious explanation is usually right? What did we think we saw in Fiona? A grieving fiancée? That's likely the truth."

Sympathy splashed over me, followed by devil's advocate resistance.

"But why live apart?" I asked as we slipped across the street. "It's only thirty minutes to Ridgecrest, but a lot closer to live together."

Meg gave a disdainful sniff. "So he could hang out at after-ski cocktail bars and sign up for matchmaking without Fiona knowing?"

Yeah, that sounded like the obvious explanation.

Meg and I turned into a residential block. The cottages here dated from the gold-rush days and were painted in candy-shop colors. Yellow and pink. Red and white with a marshmallow trim of snow on top. Birds sang. The canyon sparkled around us.

"Or he loved Last Word," I said, waving a hand and the bag of baklava at the scenic street. Even knowing what we did, part of me wanted to find the good in Joe. For his sake, but also for Meg's. She'd been whistling John Denver after that date. It couldn't all have been a lie.

Meg kicked at a snowdrift, reminiscent of Rosie. "He did compliment the town. He said it was quiet for his work." Meg took aim at another clump of snow and muttered, "More lies."

Likely so. Before coming down to meet Lorna, we'd googled Joe Darcy. A lot of Joe Darcys. We'd eliminated a racecar driver, a music executive, a ninety-year-old with a TikTok presence Gram admired, several long-deceased Joes, and one in jail for train robbery in Scotland.

Only two websites seemed to match "our" Joe Darcy, supposed investment manager and founder of a literacy-for-kids nonprofit. Both websites had the vibe of those stock pictures that come with photo frames. Glossy, perfect, and false.

On the financial site, a trio of good-looking business execs squinched seriously over a graph. A placeless corner window looked out at blank blue sky. The other—Let Kids Read—featured young children sitting cross-legged, engrossed in books.

"Did he say *anything* specific?" I persisted. "Anything about Ridgecrest? The house?"

"Like if his fiancée had given him season tickets to her theater?" Meg picked up speed. I hustled to keep up.

I caught up just as Meg's boot slipped on invisible ice. I reached for her arm to steady her.

She held on longer than it took to traverse an icy patch of sidewalk. "He said he liked his house. It had a great view. A great deck."

My shudder rippled into my sister's.

"We went out there," Meg said. "Onto the deck. I told the police they might find my footprints in the snow."

"Only I trampled over them," I said. Always the helpful little sister, that was me.

We were nearing Gram's. Beyond a neighbor's blue spruce, I spotted a white picket fence still decked out in pine swags. Gram, Meg, and Rosie lived in a turn-of-the-last-century Victorian. The home was two stories, with clapboard the color of August goldenrod and scrollwork trim like new-fallen snow.

Meg slowed. "We stood at the balcony. It was freezing, but there was that magical light. You know, when the clouds are so low they trap in the glow of town?"

I knew. I'd walked home in that light. Correction, I'd skipped home, giddy to return to Agatha and my date with a book.

I added balcony-fingerprints to the list of evidence accumulating against Meg. The broken glass. The drop of blood. Meg's footprints on the deck and in his kitchen. Her unfortunate words, blurted to gossipers. *He better be on his deathbed!*

I had to know. "Did you make a fire in the fireplace?"

Meg groaned. "Yes. And before you ask, I used the fireplace tools. I told the chief everything."

I tried snow-kicking therapy but picked the wrong snow to mess with. A pillowy exterior hid an icy core that sent pain through my toe. I bit back a yelp.

Meg sighed. "After we put away the leftovers, we have to go see her, Ellie. We need to persuade her to tell us about Joe. The *real* Joe, or whoever she knew."

I didn't have to ask who. Fiona Giddings. Foreboding didn't just tap on my shoulder. It yelled in my face.

There were all sorts of reasons we shouldn't visit Fiona. If she really was Joe's grieving fiancée, she'd hardly welcome a visit from Joe's last date. And if she was faking or delusional? I shivered to think how she might react.

Either way, Fiona could be a killer.

"We can take her some flowers," I suggested. "Isn't Posey's Posies on the way out of town?"

My sister smiled. "Good thinking. We can ask about those roses too. Two birds, one flower stop."

I was pleased by Meg's praise, but had she forgotten the original idiom?

One stone, two dead birds.

✳

CHAPTER 14

A Lucky Strike

Meg drove out of town at twenty-five miles per hour. She fully braked at each stop sign and looked all ways. Last Word's lack of traffic lights was a point of pride for locals. So was civility. One could spend longer than any red light at four-way stops, stalled by drivers all politely gesturing for the others to go.

No, please, you. No, no, you go! Please, go! You were here first. You were here ten minutes ago!

We navigated two such politeness blockades before passing out of town. A vintage sign marked the exit. On it, a friendly marmot waved against a backdrop of chalets and peaks. The landscape also changed. The canyon narrowed and twisted, hemmed in on one side by a rocky cliff and the other by Camp Creek. Today, the creek's rounded boulders glistened like orbs under icy shells.

We passed a campground, some stables, and then Meg flicked on her lefthand turn signal, way ahead of time.

"Such a cool old building," I said as we waited for a truck to pass.

The shop was like a fading flower, drooping toward its last days but still pretty. Pink paint peeled from aged clapboard.

The entire structure leaned. Depending on one's perspective, the building might be standing up to gales or sinking into a well-deserved nap.

"It has a story," Meg said.

"Oh?" All houses did. I liked to think they absorbed the daily tales that went on within their walls.

"Back in the gold rush days, a woman by the name of Goldy Strike lived here," Meg said, turning into a gravel lot. "She got a mining claim—hard to do for a woman back then. It was near Crowley Gulch. You know, down around that road that leads out of the hamlet? Great-great-gramps knew her. I saw her name in his Chalet guest book. She liked travelogues."

So had Great-great-gramps, who'd fashioned his chalet after etchings he'd admired in books. So did I . . . I thought I already liked Goldy Strike.

"Did she hit it rich?" I asked.

Meg turned off the car. I remained belted in my seat, watching a neon rose flash in the shop's window. I wanted to hear the end of Goldy's story.

Meg's "mmmm" sounded ominous. "Goldy Strike got married. Right after that, she struck one of the biggest seams found in these parts, but legally it all belonged to her husband. He ran off with the money and a cabaret singer. It's said Goldy went mad. I don't know if that's so, but she moved up into the mountains to stake another claim. She was still panning the same creek bed until the day she died."

I pictured Goldy, fingers blue with biting cold, sifting gravel. Desperate. Or mad with determination to show that cad up. Either way, it was sad.

Meg was saying, "The remains of her cabin are still up there, just off the Gone Lonesome Trail. It's rumored to be haunted."

Ghostly shivers still gripped me as we approached Posey's Posies. When the door swung open with no one in sight, I bit back a yelp.

A moment later, the delivery woman from this morning appeared. "Darned door doesn't latch," she announced. Then she spotted me. "Hey, it's you! Ever figure out who sent you that big bunch of Eternal Remembrance?"

"That's why we're here," I said. That and to establish Meg's alibi, but I figured we shouldn't lead with murder.

"You want a thank-you bouquet, am I right? I have just the thing." She disappeared into the shop before we could correct her.

Glass cases lined a spacious front room, blinking with high-tech monitors, filled with floral arrangements fit for a royal wedding. There were tropical beauties, lilies in unreal colors, and starburst chrysanthemums as big as I'd seen at flower shows in Japan when I'd taught English and literature there.

"Amazing," I breathed.

The woman smiled. Her hair gleamed bluish black under fluorescent lights. She wore a sweatshirt with the image of a skull sprouting daisies and an embroidered name, SHELLY. "Bet you were judging us by our exterior, weren't you?"

"No," I fibbed. Lesson learned. *Again.* Never judge books, people, or flower shops by their covers.

"We're outta dahlias," Shelly (I assumed) informed us. "You want tulips, you're gonna have to wait till next week or until they're bloomin' in Holland." She cackled.

I continued to marvel. The place was unreal, like we'd fallen through a portal to a floral wonderland. "Where do you sell all these? Who buys them?"

When the words were out, I worried they might sound rude.

Shelly tugged an apron on over her skull. "We sell 'em to whoever can afford 'em. The pricier they are, the better they sell. The mansion set likes to one up each other."

That, I could picture.

Shelly added, "We sell regular posies too. Like your roses, only usually not so many in a bunch."

"About those roses," Meg said, turning her attention from a

case filled with birds of paradise. "We *think* we know who sent them, but there was no name on the card. We don't want to thank the wrong person and cause . . ."

"A fight? Jealousy and rage? Gotcha. Let me see what I can do." Shelly rounded a counter that had probably been there since Goldy Strike's days.

A desktop hulked like a brontosaurus. She pushed a button and it wheezed.

"She takes her time warming up," Shelly said, patting the machine. "While we wait, you wanted a bouquet? Something to say thank you?"

"Actually, we need condolence flowers," Meg said.

"Something small," I added, cautioned by Shelly's talk of millionaire pricing.

Shelly nodded as if she'd judged us as soon as we pulled up in Meg's old Subaru. "Chrysanthemums or lilies. They're the go-to for condolence, but lilies'll drop pollen and they're toxic to cats."

"Mums," Meg said firmly. "Colorful, I think. Purple? Pink? Something a little uplifting?"

The desktop gave a death groan. Shelly took this as its summons and typed in enough to fill a page. "Okay. Book Chalet. Upper hamlet. That's you?"

That was us.

"Order came in online on Sunday, 12:03 A.M." Shelly squinted at the gasping desktop. "We're high-tech now. Can take spontaneous off-hours orders anytime. 'Course, we're not open all the time. That's why your order arrived when it did."

"Anything else?" I asked, wishing I could see the screen. "A name? Credit card?" An alibi was only as good as it was verifiable.

Shelly squinted closer. "Nope. Paid for with a gift card. We don't track those. Other people's romance, that's not our business. We stick to flowers. What you do with 'em is up to you."

I sagged.

Meg nudged me. "This is good. It narrows down the time of, ah . . . living." She raised a weak smile at Shelly, who eyed us suspiciously.

"You said condolence," the florist said. "What kind exactly?"

"A death," Meg said.

"A death?" Shelly rapped stubby fingers on the counter. "And you're from that bookshop. Are you those bookshop gals who found the murdered man last year?"

Oh dear. We nodded.

"Wait . . ." Shelly drummed harder, a hollow *thump, thump, thump* that made me think of bones. "Didn't I hear there's been another murder? Some woman snooping around found his body. That was you two? *Again?*"

"Not entirely," Meg said. "But, yes, we knew the victim. He had a fiancée. She lives in Ridgecrest. We're on our way to see her."

Shelly kept one eye on us as she pulled out pink and purple mums, spikey fern fronds, and puffs of baby's breath. When she was done, she held up a blank white card. "Guessing you'll want to spell out who you are?"

What could we say? When Meg and I hesitated, Shelly prompted: "Dear so-and-so? What's the name of the fiancée?"

"Fiona," Meg said. "Our deepest condolences for your—"

"Fiona!" Shelly bellowed. "Aw, no!" She slapped the counter. The mums shuddered in their plastic. "Her honey is *dead*? He's the murdered guy?"

"I'm sorry. You knew him?" I asked. Clearly Shelly did.

Shelly returned to her flower cabinet and took out more mums, fancier, frilly versions. "This's sad. Real sad. That man came in every Thursday and had flowers delivered to 'my beloved Fiona.'"

A draft skittered around. I reminded myself that I didn't believe in ghosts. Certainly not the ghost of Goldy Strike, a woman betrayed.

"Thursdays?" Meg asked.

"Yeah, odd day, right?" Shelly said. "Either it was because he'd see her soon or she was working on the weekend. She's some theater sort. If she had a play, he'd have me write *Break a leg*. Sweet. So sweet!"

She rang up the mums.

Meg paid.

I asked, "What kind of flowers did he send?"

"Two *au naturel* stems of Eternal Remembrance, our reddest of roses." Shelly held a receipt out to Meg, but her eyes bore into me. "Just like those roses you got."

✳

CHAPTER 15

Two Blind Mice

Lorna had given us Fiona Giddings's address. "An apartment above the Ridgecrest Theater." Lorna had sniffed dismissively. "She could have sold her house in Last Word for a fortune and gotten herself a nicer place. It's not like her Last Word place is sentimental. It was her great-aunt's vacation home."

Meg and I had been happy to hear of Fiona's living arrangement. Work and home in the same place gave us a better chance at finding her.

Meg's bossy navigation app took us on a route through Mid-Mountain College. We passed by stone buildings with gothic aspirations and a quad with crisscrossing pathways. A session must have just let out. Students and faculty streamed across the quad, making for the cafeteria on the other side of the road. Meg stopped at a crosswalk with a veritable disco of flashing warning lights.

I sank low in my seat.

"What are you doing?" Meg looked over to find me reclined to window level.

"Nothing." As if the mother of a teenager would buy that.

"Ah . . ." Meg said. "You still haven't heard from Waldon? It's early days, El. I wouldn't give up on him yet."

I'd given up but not in the way Meg thought.

She saw a break in the academic procession and sped on at twenty miles per hour.

"He was a bore." I raised my seat a few inches so I could see more than winter-bare treetops. "He talked only about Beckett."

Meg's voice held a smile. "We'd never, ever bore anyone with talk of Agatha Christie."

"Never, not us." I grinned. "But here's what he thought of Agatha Christie."

I gave her a blow-by-blow of Dr. Waldon's dismissals.

"No!" Meg punched the gas. The navigator ordered a lane change, followed by a rapid turn. Meg obeyed, then said, "How rude. I hope you enjoyed *something* about the evening."

"There was a moment of fun." In retrospect, at least. I told her about "ostrich" and delighted in her laughter.

"Oh my gosh, he said 'ostrich,' and I missed it!?"

The bossy navigator lady ruined our fun. *You have reached your destination.*

Meg's smile dropped. My stomach flipped. A perfect parking spot waved us in. We couldn't even circle the block and delay.

On the drive down the valley to Ridgecrest, Meg and I had been buoyed by the alibi Joe's roses provided. What we couldn't figure out was his relationship with Fiona.

A man who sent weekly flowers seemed pretty serious. Either that or he was serious about deceiving Fiona. Either way, we were about to deliver unwelcome news.

We stepped out to a stiff breeze gusting down from the mountains. Ridgecrest, despite its name, sat in a broad valley. I gripped our chrysanthemums, which suddenly seemed too small, for condolence and for fending off a killer.

"She wouldn't attack us," I said as we approached the theater. "She'd give herself away."

"That's the Christie spirit," said my sister.

We climbed marble steps worn smooth and swayed in the middle. The theater was red brick and a former opera house, as announced by a marble frieze three stories up: Calder Opera House, 1898. Double doors gave nothing away. No sign saying OPEN or CLOSED or the hours. No bell to ring or knocker to thump. Windows on each side displayed a dark lobby.

The wimp in me thought, *Great, time to leave!*

Meg tried a bronze knob, and its door swung open. "Guess we're invited in," she said.

The last time I'd fallen for *The door was open, let's go in*, Lorna and I had discovered a corpse.

"What are the odds," I mumbled.

Meg didn't hear. She was already inside.

With a sigh and a shove from déjà vu, I followed. Old-timey music, tinny and faint, quavered in from somewhere deep in the building. Scrolled plaster ceilings rose high above. Posters of long-ago operas and plays graced the walls. A gift shop selling playbills, T-shirts, and books occupied one corner. Mannequins in nineteenth-century dress gathered in a back corner. Other than the mannequins, no one was near.

"Hello?" Meg called.

I looked around, half expecting a mannequin to reply.

Meg started toward a door beyond the gift shop. "Stairs to the upper level are through here. Lorna and I had season tickets a few years back. Remember when she dabbled in ghost tours?"

I didn't remember, but I could add up that information. My summation? We were in a haunted opera house.

We entered a small lobby dominated by stairs as wide as the room, leading upward. Portraits and more mannequins stared from all around.

Meg whispered, "Lorna felt the cold breath of a spirit here. . . ." My sister's eye roll suggested her skepticism.

Frankly, I was with Lorna on this one.

"Hello? Fiona?" Meg called again. She sighed. "This was a bad idea. We should have called. It's rude to show up unannounced."

"We're not on a social call," I said, peering into a phone-booth-sized gilt nook that I guessed was the original ticket office.

Meg started to say something. A scream cut her off.

We froze. My feet, heart, and head argued. Feet and head lobbied for dashing to Meg's car. My heart had me again following Meg, sprinting up the steps.

The steps ended on a landing. To either side more steps rose. Scary fun-house steps, steep and narrow, enclosed by walls a sickly mauve etched with cracked plaster. My heart—previously on board with a heroic rescue—had second thoughts.

"Which way did that scream come from?" Meg asked, head spinning between the stairs. "Either way leads up to the balcony seats, but there are separate offices on each side."

I had no idea. If pressed, I'd say the direction was up.

Suddenly, a cacophony of sound proved me wrong. Not up. All around. A scream warbled, like a *Phantom of the Opera* moan. Feet ran, or maybe hooves. A herd of horses?

"Soundtrack?" I bellowed as organ music joined the din.

"*Someone* turned it on," Meg yelled back. "That first scream sounded real."

All the more reason to run back to Meg's car or summon the police. "Which way?"

Meg chose the stairs to our left, two at a time. I dropped the flowers and ran after her.

More mannequins greeted us, as well as doors. One opened to inky darkness, the other to an office filled with light and modern office equipment mingling with vintage furnishings. I heard footsteps on hollow boards, which made me realize the noises had quieted. The clomping horses and feet were gone. Only the organ played on.

"Hello?" Meg called again. "Anyone here?"

I sure hoped someone was real.

A woman's voice cut across the music. "Give that back! Stop!"

That didn't sound like a soundtrack.

"The other side," Meg said. "Quickest way is to cut across the balcony."

Which, as I'd guessed, was the door opening into darkness. Once inside, my eyes adjusted and dim light filtered up from a stage below. We were in the nosebleed seats. Rows of antique seating fanned out in tight, curved rows.

"Watch your step," Meg said. "Don't get near the balcony. It wasn't safe when Lorna and I were here."

I doubted it was safe now, and not just because of the balcony. The organ music abruptly stopped. Tinny music played on from somewhere below. Closer by came sounds of a scuffle. I fumbled for my cellphone, aiming to turn on the flashlight.

I never could find that icon . . .

Meanwhile, my sister hurried toward danger. I could just make out her shadow.

"Wait," I called as Meg disappeared into the dark.

A scream that froze my blood echoed through the cavernous building. It was followed by worse. Sickening thumps and thuds.

"Meg!" I squeezed past seats and twice tripped on electrical cords snaking across uneven floorboards. I tried not to think about the soggy boards. If I moved fast, would it be like running over thin ice or hot coals? Having done neither—and never wanting to—I could only hope.

Hope fizzled when I reached the other side. The stairs plunged downward. So did Meg, running toward a woman lying on the landing.

Red hair splayed like a halo. *Fiona.*

"Is she okay?" I yelled down. She obviously wasn't, and my

phone finally found its flashlight. Now I struggled to turn it off with shaking fingers. Calling 911 was easy. There the three numbers sat on my recent calls list.

Meg knelt at Fiona's side. "She's breathing."

Breathing was good. Wonderful!

Meg looked up and her face was pale. "Someone shoved her, El. I saw someone push by her and run!"

Not good. On the other end of the phone, a calm female voice inquired as to my emergency. Déjà vu threatened to push me down the stairs too.

"We need an ambulance," I told her. "And the police. Please, hurry!"

✳

CHAPTER 16

Long Gone

I needed to do something. Hovering over Meg on the cramped landing wasn't helping anyone's mood. Fiona was still unconscious. Meg sat beside her, stroking her hand. The mock-candle sconces flickered as if someone—something—were trying to blow them out. Silence pressed in, proving more unsettling than the previous racket.

"I'll wait outside," I announced. So that didn't sound entirely cowardly, I gave myself a purpose. "I'll flag down the EMTs and give them directions."

"Great idea," said Meg, her worried gaze fixed on Fiona.

"Yell if anything happens."

"I will." Meg looked up at the duo horror-house stairways. "You too, but I'm sure whoever was here is long gone."

Long gone . . .

I repeated the words as I made my way down the main steps, head swiveling like a nervous owl. Meg was right, surely, yet I imagined I felt a presence.

Only a mystery-reader's imagination, I assured myself. In a book, the culprit would stick around, watching. Where? Behind those mannequins? In the old box office? A secret door behind a portrait, their eyes staring out from dusty oil paints? A read-er's imagination was a treasure, except at the scene of a crime in a haunted theater.

I was so focused on a lurking menace I almost did the un-thinkable and stepped on a book. I yelped, pulling my foot back just in time. The book lay facedown, its spine straining. Instinc-tively, I reached to help it, then again drew back.

A book. How had we missed it before? We'd heard a scream, but even under stress we would have noticed a fallen book. Which meant someone had recently dropped it. The shover, fleeing? The book could be evidence.

I squatted and tilted my head to read the upside-down cover. *The Mousetrap, Stage Play with Annotations.*

Not a novel, a script. Agatha Christie's famously long-running play, the one Dr. Waldon had dismissed as unliterary entertainment. Who would take it, only to then toss it on the steps? I yearned to turn it upright and close its straining cover.

I talked myself back. I would not tamper with another scene. I edged far around it, then jogged until I was out the door.

A mountain breeze nibbled at my ears.

I replayed *The Mousetrap* as I paced up and down a few squares of sidewalk. The characters had secrets. Of course! Ev-eryone had secrets in an Agatha Christie. In real life too.

Joe Darcy sure did. He'd presumably kept secrets from Fiona. He'd only known Meg for an evening, but he sure kept a whop-per from her.

What was Fiona's secret? Something that got her attacked? Something to do with Joe's death?

Tires squealed. I spun, expecting the ambulance. An older model pickup rounded the corner and skidded to a stop behind Meg's car. Before I could wave off the double-parker, sirens filled the air.

I trotted down the walkway, raising my hand high to flag down the ambulance. Three EMTs exited. They opened all the doors, adjusted jackets, hauled out bags, and—to my eyes—took way too long in their preparations.

When one, a slender woman with a stern expression, headed my way, I pointed. "A woman was shoved down the stairs. My sister's with her." I gave directions to the landing.

The woman nodded and aimed a finger-pointing wave to the men, who lumbered up laden with bags. I relaxed. Help was here. Fiona would wake up. She'd tell the police what was going on. Meg would be cleared of all suspicion. Case closed.

I smiled to myself, happy with this story, until I felt a presence behind my shoulder. I spun.

"What are *you* doing here?" Not my nicest greeting.

Detective Sam Ibarra's lip quirked all the same. "I could ask you that." He wore jeans and the boots that had bounded down a canyon to rescue me. Red flannel plaid poked from a buckskin-tan uniform jacket.

My question stood. What *was* he doing here? Ridgecrest had its own police force. Had he come to see Fiona too?

He raised an eyebrow.

I'd asked him first, but I answered anyway. "Meg and I came to express our sympathies to Fiona Giddings. Are you here to see her? She was shoved down the stairs. She's injured."

"I am aware," he said grimly. "I heard the radio call. I didn't think you and your sister knew Fiona Giddings."

"We don't," I admitted. "But after we met her at your station last night, we thought we should, ah, visit her."

We *should* have come up with a convincing reason for visiting a stranger if questioned.

"I see," Sam said, his lip twitching to another smile.

"We brought flowers," I said, too defensively. Then I remembered. *The flowers.* I'd littered another crime scene.

"You want to tell me something?" he asked with mild amusement.

My cheeks warmed. "I dropped flowers on your crime scene. But you'll see—they're mums, condolence flowers!"

"This is getting to be a habit." His smile sprouted a dimple. "You, me, you dropping stuff at crime scenes. We could do better."

I caught myself smiling back. No! I would not be taken in by a cute smile or that dimple. We were meeting at crime scenes, and Sam Ibarra probably still suspected my sister of murder. Well, I could disabuse him of that.

"On the way here, we established an alibi for Meg," I said.

"Oh? Care to share?"

I did. I met those twinkling granite eyes and told him about the roses. "The florist has a record. They were ordered after Meg was safely home, by a man who was obviously still alive." I waited. A beat passed, during which the detective failed to jump up and down with alibi glee.

"You just have to find the ride-share driver who took Meg home," I said. "He'll have a record and—"

"We have." He remained serious.

"Great!" I waited. Now would be the time for him to say something. I didn't expect an apology, but a simple thanks-for-doing-my-job would be nice.

He shoved his hands in his jeans pockets and rocked in his boots. "You said the sender paid with a gift card, but the card didn't have a name or credit card attached to it?"

"They're the same kind of roses Joe Darcy sent to Fiona." I added, paraphrasing Miss Marple, "Any coincidence is worth noting."

"How many kinds of long-stem roses do they sell there?" Sam asked.

Meg and I hadn't asked that. I heard Shelly's voice, now in teasing tones in my head. *Our reddest of long-stem roses.* Maybe they were the most popular.

"I'm sure you can figure it out," I said. "You're the professional."

"Yeah . . ." he said, dragging out the word. "About that. Didn't my boss tell you and your sister to stay clear of this?"

I remained silent.

"Right. Okay, how about this? I'll look into the roses. That way, you and Meg can return to bookselling. Investigating murders isn't safe. *You two* could have been hurt in there." He softened the chastisement with a smile. "That and, by your own admission, you keep dropping incriminating evidence at crime scenes. *Some* might think you're involved."

I inwardly cringed. Flowers, mittens, prints . . . We'd left them all.

But there was something neither of us had touched or dropped. "There's a book on the stairs. It wasn't there when Meg and I first went in. The shover must have dropped it."

Now he looked interested. "Did you touch this book?"

"I did not," I said, feeling unreasonably smug in this achievement. I bobbed my chin toward the crime scene. Hint, hint . . . He should get in there and investigate.

He gazed that way, looking almost wistful.

"Wish I could. I used to work down here. Switched to Last Word PD in December. The Ridgecrest chief and I, well . . ." He shrugged, letting me read into that. "I'd catch a mountain of trouble if I went in before Chief Abernathy trampled all over that scene. You could tell me what happened, though. Like we're two friends meeting on the street."

He smiled like he meant it. "Please, Ellie? It could help with the murder investigation."

How could I say no to a please, those dimples, my name said with such hope, and the chance to help?

I told him about the noises. "Maybe background sounds for a play? It was unnerving. Screams, horses, an organ. But there were real sounds too." I described the yelling, footsteps running away, and Fiona tumbling down the stairs.

"You saw this alleged perpetrator and the fall?" he asked.

"*I* didn't see anything," I admitted, ignoring the "alleged." "I was trying to turn on the flashlight on my phone. Meg ran ahead of me."

He scowled. "So, your sister was alone with the victim?" The chilly wind frolicked around his words.

Before I could note that the shover was there too, sirens screamed around the corner. A police car parked behind Sam's truck. Two men got out. One, looking approximately the age of my niece, jogged by us. The other, a top-heavy man in a Stetson, sauntered up.

He tipped his hat to me and blatantly ignored Sam.

"Ma'am, you called this in?" A navy uniform strained against his ample top and sagged over skinny legs. He hiked up a utility belt that would have been safer on suspenders. He introduced himself as Chief Abernathy, Ridgecrest PD.

"I did. My sister and the emergency personnel are inside with the victim." Movement caught my eye. The front door opened and Meg stepped out, looking dazed.

"Meg!" I rushed to her and met her at the steps. She clung to the railing.

Sam and Chief Abernathy walked our way, as if competing to see who had the most swaggering saunter. Men! This was not the time for petty turf skirmishes.

"How's Fiona?" I asked.

Chief Abernathy spoke over my words. "Did you see who did this, ma'am?"

Meg's head bobbed in the negative. I caught my breath.

"Fiona regained consciousness," Meg said.

"Thank goodness." I thumped a hand to my heart.

Meg's head kept shaking. "She's confused. The medics say she has a concussion. She kept saying that someone broke in. She tried to stop them."

Chief Abernathy beat me to my next question. "Any description of the perp?"

Meg shook her head. "I saw a shadow, maybe a dark jacket? Fiona said something similar. Someone in a dark coat, hood up."

I glanced at Sam Ibarra. He frowned at my sister in her dark hooded coat. He raised a pointed eyebrow to me.

Oh, come on! So what if Meg had a black jacket? He couldn't possibly think . . .

He caught my eye and offered a hint of a shrug. Not an apology. An admission. He'd thought it!

"I better get in there," Chief Abernathy said, puffing his chest. "You ladies, stay here."

"Look for a book," I said. "On the stairs. It's evidence."

"A book?" Chief Abernathy and Meg asked as one.

"Technically, it's a script," I said. "*The Mousetrap* by Agatha Christie. You can't miss it."

Abernathy swaggered forth.

Meg touched my elbow. "Ellie, I didn't see a book."

What? She clearly wasn't thinking straight. I tried to picture Meg, staggering down the steps, dazed, relieved. . . . But oblivious even to a book? I urged her to sit down.

Meg sank to the cold steps. I sat beside her. Sam remained standing, scanning the street as if it might tell us what happened.

Three college kids walked by, oblivious to the disturbance. A hatchback rounded the corner, whisper quiet with tinted windows and dust-speckled black paint. It inched by Sam's truck, paused, then peeled out like a windup bug.

"What kind of car was that?" I asked to make conversation.

"A rubbernecker's," Sam grumbled.

Next came a minivan that honked at the emergency vehicles blocking its lane and a dog-walker who acknowledged us with a grunt as his poodle sniffed our step. I nudged closer to Meg.

A few minutes later, Chief Abernathy stomped back out and pointed at me. "Miss. Yes, you, miss. Where's this so-called book?" The finger turned to Sam. "You. You can leave my crime scene."

Sam Ibarra smiled so pleasantly he might have been watching Agatha Cat Christie romp in a flower-filled meadow. "I'm fine here."

He upped his look of serenity. A peaceful smile. An almost beatific gaze. Except . . . his right nostril flared. If we were friends, I'd let him know he had a tell.

Chief Abernathy turned and stomped back inside.

Sam touched my arm. "Be careful around him. Abernathy goes after the first suspect he finds. Full blinders to anyone else."

And *he* didn't? The man who'd just considered the possibility that Meg shoved a woman when I wasn't looking? Or did he think we'd both done it?

My mental retorts fizzled in the face of his concerned gaze.

I would be careful. Of Chief Abernathy and stealthy shovers and a hidden killer. I'd take care around cops with dimples too.

Inside, Meg and I nearly ran into Chief Abernathy, who blocked the entry to the stairwell foyer.

He stepped aside, waving a hand like a snarky gameshow assistant. *You've won a fabulous crime scene!*

A stretcher blocked my view of the landing. Voices floated down, including a quavering voice I recognized as Fiona Giddings's. Thank goodness! Even if she couldn't remember details, surely she'd say that Meg and I hadn't shoved her.

"Well?" the chief demanded. "Where's this *book*?"

My finger pointed before my eyes registered. Everything was the same. The staring portraits. The unsettling mannequins. The stairs, just like when Meg and I first saw them, empty of a book.

"It was right there," I said, making a move toward the stairs.

The chief's arm flew out, blocking me.

"Up there," I said. "On about the twelfth step. I left it because it could be evidence."

"Okay," Chief Abernathy drawled. "Where's it now? Walk off on its own, did it?"

It made no sense. Could the EMTs have grabbed it? But they wouldn't stop for a book in an emergency.

"You saw it when you left the first time, El?" Meg said, touching my elbow supportively. "What about when you came back in?"

I froze. "I didn't come back inside. Not until just now."

"But I called down to you," Meg insisted. "Fiona was regaining consciousness. When you didn't answer, I figured you'd run out to meet the ambulance."

I steadied myself on Meg and turned to take in the room. The mannequins stared back in mocking expressions. The portraits taunted, and darkness seemed to giggle from the ticket booth.

Chills tickled up, down, and around my neck like little mouse feet.

"Meg," I said, gripping her arm harder. "That wasn't me."

✳

CHAPTER 17

Making Assumptions

The next day, I vowed to start afresh. Tuesday was our Monday, the beginning of a new week. By most accounts, it began like a good day at the Book Chalet should.

Agatha snoozed on her red velvet pillow in the window, luring in customers. Readers relaxed with their books. Bibliophiles browsed, coffee percolated, pine logs crackled, and I set myself two goals.

One, to hand-sell *Never Make Assumptions* and turn the burro-racing memoir into a local bestseller.

By mid-morning, goal one was going great. Five happy readers had gone home with signed copies. Pretty good for a seemingly niche hobby, but the life lessons and love between a man and his four-legged best friend were universals.

The trouble was goal two: turning my mind from all thoughts of crime.

Some goals are setups for failure. Even when talking up *Never Make Assumptions,* crime slipped in.

Words would come from my mouth: *You'll adore these heartwarming life-lessons from a man and his burro.*

Meanwhile, questions swarmed my head: *Who killed Joe? Fiona? But then who shoved Fiona? An accomplice? Why?*

More words: *Zeke and Bartholamule live right here in Last Word.*

Treacherous mind: *Who stole the script? Were Meg and I literally steps from a killer?*

For once, working in the Book Chalet was no help. *Not* thinking about crime in a shop that specialized in mysteries was like trying to ignore an elephant when one stomped on your foot. That and locals wouldn't let me forget. Word had spread that Meg and I had tangled with another crime. Details had gotten around too, including the peripheral involvement of Agatha Christie. Already, members of the Mountains of Mystery book club had come around, looking for the novella version of *The Mousetrap* contained in the collection *Three Blind Mice and Other Stories.* They'd just had their monthly meeting and needed to pick a new read.

I knew from our last murder that the club members wouldn't stay home, curled up with their books. They'd be out to crack the case. I told myself that this was a plus. More suspicious minds looking for clues was always good. So was selling more Christies.

I was putting in an order for a dozen copies of *Three Blind Mice and Other Stories* when the cowbells clanked. I looked up, registered our newest guests, and ditched goal two for good.

Chief Sunnie removed her ear-flapped cap, and her curls haloed her head, floating from static. Detective Sam Ibarra's dark hair was so cropped, it couldn't go anywhere. He ran a hand through it anyway and scanned the lobby. When his eyes landed on me, a dimple flashed.

For a moment, I let myself imagine they were here for books. *Relax, get lost in a book,* that was our motto at the Chalet. We were a readers' refuge, a retreat from the troubles of the world. Work, strife, inclement weather, murder investigations.

Sam's expression froze back to granite. My fantasy retreated. This was an official visit.

I rounded the register counter and met them at the new releases display.

"Is your sister here?" Chief Sunnie said.

Meg? Why ask for Meg? Released from any hope of goal two, my brain listed all the wrong reasons. *Last known person to see Joe Darcy. Fingerprints on a murder weapon. Blood on her sweater. Present at the scene of a shoving.*

But Meg had alibis. The roses and me. Well, partially me. I'd admitted that I lost sight of my sister in the darkened theater. Because she was running ahead heroically! Honesty had its drawbacks.

I rested a steadying hand on a display table. "Why do you want Meg?"

"We just need to chat with you both," Chief Sunnie said. "We have some updates. Some additional questions."

She sounded casual. With the chief, casual could mean serious as a bloodhound catching a scent. But chatting and updates didn't sound like *We're here to arrest Meg Christie.*

"She's reshelving, I think," I said. "I'll text her."

I tapped out: *Police here. Want to chat . . .* Then I erased the three dots, lest they look too ominous.

The chief picked up *Never Make Assumptions.* She grinned and held the front cover up to Sam. "Ibarra, this what you do? It's something people actually write books about?"

My phone buzzed with a thumbs-up emoji from Meg. I looked up in time to see pink rise to Sam's chiseled cheekbones.

"Yeah," he admitted. "But I'm nothing like Zeke Vaca there. He and Bartholamule are legends. They've crushed every trail race from here to Saskatchewan."

For the first time this morning, I forgot entirely about crime. A smile overtook me. Detective Sam Ibarra trail-raced with a burro? I pictured them cresting peaks, weaving through aspen groves, fording icy streams. How intrepid. How adorable!

I couldn't help myself. "How far do you run? Who's the lucky burro?"

"Ha!" the chief said. "Lucky burro. Good one!"

Sam's blush raced to the tips of his ears. "I team up with a donkey from my sister's ranch. Her name's Jessie-Belle. The donkey. Not my sister. We run the marathon distance and above. We're not a team for speed. We're plodders. We just keep going."

"Like any good detective," Chief Sunnie said, placing the book back on the stack. "Slow and steady wins the race. Ah, there she is. Meg, we have some questions."

Meg had one first. "How's Fiona?"

Now my cheeks warmed, but with shame. I should have asked about Fiona instead of quizzing Sam about his running companion.

The chief scowled. "Best if we talk somewhere private."

That didn't sound good. My stomach tightened, but when I followed her gaze out the window, I understood. Down the street, past a toddler wobbling in his snowsuit, canary yellow fluttered our way. Piper Tuttle, on the gossip path!

Meg spotted her too. "Storeroom," she said.

On the way, we passed Ms. Ridge. "Can you handle the register and Piper Tuttle?" I asked.

"One of them." Ms. Ridge smoothed her immaculate apron as if checking her armor.

Usually, we left the storeroom door ajar for Agatha. I shut it, and we took seats around the worktable. Sunlight streamed in the tall windows, turning dust motes to glitter. Curly plastic ribbons decorated the table, peeled from the sticky strips of mailing envelopes. Meg had been preparing mail orders. These days, we got a lot.

Some of our distant customers had visited Last Word or used to live here. Others were bibliophiles who had us on their bookshop bucket list. Still more probably couldn't find us on a map but appreciated our selection and online shelves.

I wrapped a mailer ribbon around my ring finger and wondered what book-mail gift was winging its way to a reader.

Chief Sunnie got right to the point. "Fiona Giddings will be okay."

Meg and I exclaimed our relief. I released my makeshift ring and rose. Good news called for a celebration. A fresh pot of coffee would do. Plus, Meg and I needed to keep alert.

"She'll be breaking out of the hospital right about now," the chief continued. "A friend is to watch over her. Head injuries, you know. They can hide their seriousness. One moment, you're walking around fine, then wham, you're down again."

Sam nodded. "Also like murder investigations."

"Yep." Chief Sunnie drew out her notebook. "I'd like to hear about your theater visit. In case it touches on our investigation."

"In case?" Meg said. "Fiona was attacked. That *must* relate to Joe's death."

The chief made a noncommittal noise. "Never make assumptions?"

Meg sighed and started with the theater's unlocked doors.

I interjected. "First we stopped at the flower shop. Meg has another alibi, Chief. Did Detective Ibarra tell you?"

The roses stood by the sink. I hefted the vase and carried it at arm's length to the table. Even so, a thorn snagged my sleeve.

The chief took a sniff. "Pretty. Ibarra, we confirmed their sender yet?"

"We have not." He shot me an apologetic smile. "I'm looking into it, I promise."

I'd hold him to that. I started the coffee maker and willed it to hurry. It gurgled and hissed, signaling it would take its sweet time.

"So," the chief said, "possible alibi. Then you went inside the theater. You heard something. . . ."

Meg described the scream and ensuing sounds. "They stopped one by one."

"Timers," Chief Sunnie said. "There's some test system for sound effects. Ms. Giddings said she punched them all when she spotted an intruder, trying to scare them off. Now, were you upstairs in the north side of the theater before the sounds started?"

I took a moment to work out cardinal directions. Then I realized what she was asking. Upstairs before the sounds? Were *we* the intruders?

"No!" Meg said. "We didn't go upstairs until we heard the scream."

Chief Sunnie smiled. "But you had a bigger purpose than simply delivering posies to Ms. Giddings."

Not a question. She knew us too well.

"You were snooping around about Joe Darcy's death," Chief Sunnie said.

"We just want to understand him," I said.

"Don't we all?" said the chief. "But now I have a new difficulty. You two at the scenes of *two* crimes."

That was a problem. But Joe was still the bigger mystery. "Have you learned anything more about him?" I asked. "His work? Personal life? *Anything?*"

The chief's frown suggested she didn't appreciate playing interviewee. "I have my best tech guy on his trail."

So she didn't know either.

"We don't have a good grip on him *yet,*" the chief stressed, "but I can tell you what he wasn't—not the head of a kids' literacy foundation like he told you, Meg. At least not a registered foundation."

"Too good to be true," Meg said through a sigh.

The coffee maker drowned her out with its grand finale. Spits, burbles, wheezes, and a triumphant beep.

The chief cocked her head and frowned at another sound. "What's that? You have mice?"

An insistent scratching came from the door, like claws on a treadmill.

"Big mouse," Sam observed.

Not a mouse, but their sworn enemy. "Agatha." I rose to get the door. "She doesn't like to be shut out."

She wasn't. The door had a kitty flap, but Agatha refused to muss her queenly whiskers.

Another sound filtered through the door. *Shhhhhh!*

The chief raised her finger to her lips. On surprisingly brisk and silent feet, Chief Sunnie stepped to the door and swung it open.

Piper Tuttle held Agatha in her arms. Agatha pinwheeled her paws to get down. After a tangle in Piper's feather scarf, she galloped to her treat bowl and yelled her demands.

Piper smoothed her feathers. She had demands too. "Chief, give me exclusive first-reporting rights and I'll tell you everything I know about Joseph Darcy. I guarantee, I have juicier info than your tech guy."

* * *

"*Another* fiancée, in Durango?" Meg's voice was muffled. Her elbows and glasses were on the table, her head in her hands. Hair curtained her face.

"I'm just getting started," Piper said. "With a man like that, there *will* be more. I already have a whiff of a girlfriend in Reno."

Meg groaned. "I was smitten with a man with two fiancées, and a girlfriend in Reno?"

The chief looked equally pained. "How did we miss this?"

Sam grimaced.

Piper preened. "Likely not on record. There's no crime in loving love."

Sam said, "You say this other fiancée is in Durango? That's over two and a half hours away, almost three. How'd he manage it?"

Meg looked up. "He traveled a lot, he said. For his work and the philanthropy."

Agatha hopped to the table and rolled onto her back between us, playing a favorite game. Kitty roulette. Few human hands could resist her creamy belly fluff. Nine times out of ten, hapless hands ended up in the grip of kitty claws and kicking back feet.

Her blue eyes flashed. I waggled my finger at her. Fool me once . . . Or twice or umpteen hundreds of times.

Sam reached out.

"Be careful. It's a trap," I said.

His lip quirked. "Oh yeah? I'll risk it."

His fingers' funeral.

He reached. I held my breath. Agatha C. Christie purred and allowed him to give her arm massages.

I glanced at Meg. *Was she seeing this?* Sam Ibarra was a burro runner and Siamese whisperer.

Meg was pinching the ridge of her nose. "I wonder if Fiona knew?"

If she did, she had a whopper of a murder motive. But then someone had pushed her down the stairs. One of Joe's other girlfriends? I said as much.

"Something to look into," Sam said.

He'd momentarily taken his attention from Agatha, displeasing the queen. She wrapped all four paws around his forearm. I imagined her kitty fantasies: lioness taking down a wildebeest. We occasionally watched nature documentaries together.

"Agatha," I warned. "Be nice." I got up to rattle her canister of treats.

The lioness released her prey in favor of shrimp-flavored kibbles.

"Thanks for the rescue," Sam said.

"Far more dangerous than when you climbed down that canyon to rescue me," I said.

Piper twinkled at us. "Aw . . ."

Chief Sunnie tapped her notebook. "Ms. Tuttle. How did *you* find this out?"

Piper drew out her moment of glory. She patted her scarf. She examined her manicured nails and sparkling rings.

"I am a professional," she said. "A journalist."

I grinned. "A professional, top-league gossip."

Piper raised her coffee mug. "Thank you, Ellie. Darling of you. Gossip is an art and a science, so often underestimated."

We clinked mugs.

Piper launched into a list of informants that would have made Gram and Miss Marple proud.

"Basically," Piper said, "I started from what I knew. A name and *supposed* occupation. But my main clue? He signed up for a dating service and had questionable dating ethics. That meant he likely joined other services."

Piper reached over to pat Meg's hand. "No fault of yours, Meg, or your cousin's. Nice folks are easier to trick. So . . . I put out the word on First Word Last Word. I asked if anyone recognized him. From there, I let the trail find itself." She smiled around the table. "Easy."

"Easy," the chief repeated grimly. "I'll need the fiancée's name and contact information, plus whatever you have on the Reno woman."

"You might have a hard time speaking to the fiancée," Piper said.

"Oh, she'll talk to me," the chief said. "This is a murder investigation."

"Why, Piper?" Meg asked quietly.

Piper leaned in. "Because, my sources say, she sold her house and abruptly left town last month. No one knows where she went. Another mystery . . ."

"Great," the chief said. "Just what we need."

Piper smiled. "I'll let you know when I find her."

✳

CHAPTER 18

A Date with Trouble

Piper left with the police, off to show the chief's best tech guy the ways of gossip networks. Her parting words remained, curling and heavy like a Sherlockian fog.

You're lucky, Meg. Lucky he died after one date or he might have reeled you in too.

"I don't feel lucky." Meg cradled her mug. The coffee would be tepid now, if not cold. She'd barely taken a sip.

I attempted to lighten the mood.

"There are more murder suspects," I said, peppy as a cheerleader, amping up the crowd when her team was down. *Yay, more potential killers!* "Once Detective Ibarra confirms those roses, you'll be off the hook for good." I beamed and clasped my hands.

Meg said, "He's not having much luck with the roses, is he? And everything we learn about Joe makes him murkier. Engagements, girlfriends, Reno . . ."

Rah, rah, rah yelled my inner pep squad. Volume and baseless enthusiasm wouldn't convince Meg or the police.

I looked to my mug. Miss Marple smiled knowingly from its side. Would Jane Marple care that she couldn't prove a clue? No. She wasn't beholden to legalities and forensics. She knit up the pieces, the clues and incongruities, odd coincidences and intuitions.

"Joe juggled multiple relationships," I said. "Multiple types of relationships too. Meeting up with Ven. Joining Bibliophiles Find Love. Juggling a long-distance girlfriend and two possible fiancées . . . That tells us something about him."

Meg snorted. "He's a multitasker? Not a commitment-phobe?" She rolled her eyes. "What a catch."

He was committed to something. Love? An addiction to playing Prince Charming? Those real-life stories of secret double lives always fascinated me. Two families. Two mortgages and holiday schedules. Multiple birthday parties and anniversaries. I'd take the click-bait every time. I wanted to know the *how* but most of all the *why*. In some cases, it seemed like the double-lifers got caught up, unable to extract themselves. They *had* to keep going until a slipup pulled them under.

I didn't know Joe Darcy, but he hadn't struck me as a pulled-out-by-the-tide kind of guy.

My eyes wandered to the roses. Shelly said Joe sent Fiona a few stems each week. He'd ordered Meg an extravagant dozen. Classic wooing behavior, if one overlooked the creepy cemetery-clone part and modified Poirot quote. He'd also either missed or ignored Ven's text, teasingly inviting herself over.

Had he been instantly smitten with Meg? I recalled that flash impression from our first date. Joe Darcy, eyeing my sister with wolfish intensity.

Meg was special. A gem inside and out.

What had Joe seen in her? Kind, smart, well-read, funny . . . A single mom, a business owner, a very rusty dater. A target? Piper's words swirled up again. *Lucky* . . .

Meg reached out and tickled Agatha's belly fluff.

"You must be feeling somewhat lucky," I said.

"Or fatalistic," Meg said, but she grinned. "Aggie, you have a new boyfriend, don't you?"

Agatha aimed a back-paw bunny kick at Meg's hand. Her attacks were all play, an act.

Meg scooped Agatha up for a cuddle. "Mmmm? Is the handsome detective a good guy? Should Ellie flirt with him?"

I snorted but let that pass because it was nice to see Meg smile. Also, because Agatha was wise and discerning. I hoped she was right and that Sam Ibarra was as honest and dedicated as he appeared.

A *tap-tap-tap* startled us all. A patchwork quilt of color appeared in the squares of the door's paned window. Copper hair, leaf-green coat, fingers waggling in dandelion-yellow gloves.

I waved to Marigold Jones and rose to let her in.

"I hope it's okay," Marigold said, slightly breathless. "I parked out back. I have some date-night supplies to unload. Chairs, tables, linens, candles—" She held up her hand before I could protest. "Faux-flame battery candles. We'll be all set for Friday!"

"Friday?" I repeated with a dread rarely attached to everyone's favorite weekday.

Marigold's brow creased. "Didn't Lorna call you? We have dates. Is it okay? Do you have other plans?"

Yes! A quiet night in with Agatha and a book.

I pressed up a smile. "I haven't heard from Lorna, but it's okay." It had to be. I'd offered up the Book Chalet and my peaceful evenings.

"You're the sweetest!" Marigold declared.

Not if a devious part of me wished Lorna would have a change of heart about the dating business. As penance, I offered to help Marigold unload.

She waved off my offer. "I'm dressed for the cold." She balled her fist and raised her bicep like a weightlifter. "Plus, I'm a puppeteer. A few folding tables are nothing compared to a fifty-pound puppet."

I held the door, the least I could do. Meg washed up from our impromptu coffee gathering. Agatha groomed her ruffled belly fluff.

"I need to get to work," Meg said, drying her hands. "I have to get my mind off all this."

Good luck with that. "Don't try to *not* think about the thing you don't want to think about."

Meg took a second to work out my convoluted advice. "Okay, then. I'm off to wallow in self-pity. I'll let distraction drag me to shore."

"Is everything okay?" Marigold asked after Meg left, Agatha trotting at her side, ready to provide distractions.

Marigold answered her question before I could. "Of course it's not! Lorna told me about Fiona and the trouble at the theater. How frightening! Is she okay? Are you?"

I reported that Fiona was getting out of the hospital soon. "Physically, she'll be okay."

Marigold tutted. "Emotionally, though? That poor woman! Betrayed. Attacked in her own theater! I feel awful for her and for the involvement of BFL."

I translated BFL to Bibliophiles Find Love. "You and Lorna didn't turn Joe Darcy into a rampant seducer," I assured Marigold.

"Rampant?" Marigold looked up from a box that appeared to hold table linens.

Time to break more unpleasant news. "Piper Tuttle was just here." I paused so Marigold could ready herself for incoming gossip.

She looked even more confused. "Who?"

I could have hugged her. How refreshing to find someone untouched by the gossip blaze of First Word Last Word. "Piper is our local gossip columnist?" I prompted. "She writes for the newspaper and on First Word Last Word, the online community forum."

"Oh!" Marigold said. "The 'Heard About Town' column? I've seen that. She does get around."

She did. So did Joe Darcy. I said, "Piper learned that Joe had another fiancée, over near Durango."

"*Another? A former* fiancée?"

"That's still unclear. Piper's working on the details. The police will be too." I wasn't a gambler, but if I were, I'd put my money on Piper finding out first. "There might also be a girlfriend in Reno."

Marigold pulled out a stool and sat unsteadily. "He *said* he was single and looking for a bookish match. Lorna's going to have to adjust her survey."

"I don't know how any survey can catch a liar," I said.

Marigold shook her head sadly. "A shared love of books should do that."

People would always hide secrets or tell stories, to themselves and others. My inner pessimist, in league with bad-date experience, told me that. However, my inner cheerleader still wanted to rally. "Biblio-matching is a great idea!" I proclaimed. "And your questions are spot on, Marigold. We don't know yet—those relationships might have ended before Joe joined Bibliophiles. Everyone has a past."

We needed to figure out Joe Darcy's.

Marigold brightened. "Thank you, Ellie. Lorna and I appreciate your support." Her pocket chirped. She drew out a phone with a marigold-printed case. "Lorna's out front." She grabbed her tote bag.

My phone buzzed a second later. I read the text: *SOS*. The sender: Ms. Ridge.

* * *

The register counter, Agatha, and a feather duster separated Ms. Ridge and Lorna.

"You'll have a great time!" Lorna was saying. "We'll match you to your true bookish love."

Agatha's tail swished. So did the feather duster, which Ms. Ridge gripped like a broadsword. She'd go down fighting.

"Lorna," Marigold said. "We agreed. No pressuring folks to date."

If Cupid had recruiters, they'd resemble Lorna. Angelic edged with frightening fervor, armored in bouncy blond curls and a flowing wool coat of fiery red. All she needed was Cupid's arrow or a net.

Lorna turned to Marigold and me. "Ms. Ridge loves books," she informed us with crisp enunciation. "She's single."

Ms. Ridge raised the feather duster higher.

I suspected Ms. Ridge had recently rekindled a certain reading friendship, but it wasn't my place to say.

Instead, I said, "Ms. Ridge, could you check on the Reading Lounge? I think there are books to reshelve."

There were always books to reshelve. Upstairs in my loft at night, I imagined the books moving around on their own. Hopping to nearby shelves, visiting friends in other genres, gathering in stacks for spontaneous meetings. Whatever the books got up to was preferable to customers "helpfully" reshelving, stuffing books onto any shelf they considered close enough.

Ms. Ridge mouthed "Thank you." Still clutching the duster, she edged around Lorna with all the wariness of dodging a rattlesnake.

Marigold said, "Lorna, I've just learned something shocking. Joe Darcy had another fiancée."

Lorna frowned, but quickly recovered. "Sounds like he was a man eager to commit."

"Or just the opposite," I muttered.

Lorna ignored me. "Marigold, we've discussed this. Our business needs positive energy. We're love brokers!" She waggled her fingers at Marigold as if hypnotizing her into compliance.

"Of course," Marigold murmured, clutching her tote bag tighter.

"Good!" Lorna said. "That's the spirit. Ellie, did you hear our *wonderful* news? We have fresh biblio-matches. The Book Chalet will be the hottest place to be this Friday."

"I heard," I said.

"You'll be here," Lorna said.

Rebellion took up a stand. I didn't *have* to be here. I could hide out upstairs. Except my loft lacked a door . . . I could flee down to Gram's!

My cousin looped an arm around my shoulder and squeezed hard. "Ellie . . ." Lorna crooned. "We need one more lady to fill out a six-person evening Friday."

Years ago, I took a self-defense course. In theory, I could escape. Jerk my elbows down, collapse my shoulders, swivel, and either run or thrust a knee or raven-claw fingers at my attacker. Of course, I'd never do any of those to my cousin, least of all the kneeing and jabbing. I loved Lorna. Plus, we had a lifetime of family events to attend together.

I scoured the lobby. There had to be someone willing to fall for a free meal with the possibility of lifelong commitment and/ or dating disaster.

Two men browsed the Valentine's display. Their shoulders brushed, and they smiled over the back-cover blurb of the same book. A happy couple. I scanned on. A woman wrangled two giggly toddlers. She didn't have time . . .

Lorna tightened her grip.

"If I hear of anyone, I'll let you know." I attempted a shrinking move.

"*You're* free." Lorna released me, but only so she could step back and stare me down, daring me to lie.

"Lorna," Marigold warned again.

Lorna huffed. "Fine. But we need one more lady. We need to look desirable, exclusive. Like *everyone* wants to be here but only a few lucky couples can get in."

She left to check on the table linens. I exhaled in relief. Marigold browsed a rack of postcards with images of Agatha Christie book covers.

Evil Under the Sun. Murder on the Orient Express. The A.B.C. Murders. They twirled by in art-deco imagery and primary colors and so many crimes in between pretty covers.

"These give me an idea," Marigold said. "We could host an Agatha Christie date night. We could provide some fun facts. Conversation starters for biblio-daters to discuss."

I loved Christie trivia. I could already imagine fun multiple choice quiz questions. Name Agatha Christie's first dog. (A) Prince Albert, (B) Fido, (C) George Washington, (D) a cat named Marple. "I could help," I said before thinking.

Marigold smiled. Unlike Lorna, she didn't pounce on my moment of weakness and sign me up for dates.

Although it did seem fun . . . Like naming a terrier George Washington!

Maybe I'd found my dating criterion, my line in the romantic sand: Must Love Christie. At the very least, it would weed out Dr. Waldon.

Out of the corner of my eye, I saw a customer approach. "Ven," I said, surprised to see her. Ven wasn't a frequent book buyer, and she'd already unloaded her I-dated-Joe confession on us.

Ven set her stack on the counter.

"I heard what happened at the theater," she said, shaking her head and dipping her voice to a whisper. "And right after I warned you and Meg to be careful!"

I shrugged helplessly. What could I say?

"Is it true?" Ven continued. "Was Fiona Giddings engaged to Joe?"

That was an even trickier question. "She said she was."

Ven made a disgusted sound and pushed her books toward me.

Two paperback romances and three nonfiction titles from our Valentine's display. The latter fell into the category that used to be dubbed "self-help." Under our mother's classification, they were "self-discovery, metamorphosis, and personal blossoming."

"Fiona Giddings doesn't seem Joe's type," Ven huffed.

When I asked why, Ven had the grace to blush.

"She's so . . . artsy and academic. He was so . . ." A sad, dreamy sigh escaped her perfectly made-up lips.

"Dashing? Dapper?" I supplied.

Ven was pretty, polished, and popular, a former prom queen. By looks alone, she and Joe Darcy would have made a stunning couple. Yet apparently he hadn't gone out of his way to woo her. I felt for her. And for me! If Venessa Upshaw couldn't find her match, what chance did I have?

The cash register was curling out a receipt when an idea struck me like a smack to the forehead.

Ven. Single. Purchasing romances and a book titled *Date Like a Girl Boss*. She wasn't swearing off dating. Time for me to play matchmaker.

I caught Marigold's eye and gestured for her to join us.

"Ven," I said. "This is Marigold Jones. She's Lorna's partner in Bibliophiles Find Love. She was just telling me about an exclusive date night."

I turned to Marigold. "Ven's the hottest realtor in Last Word. She's also fabulously single and a book lover." I glanced pointedly at Ven's bookstack.

"Oh, I am too," Marigold said, fluttery. "Not a realtor, I mean, or hot, but I'm a book lover. That's why I believe in Bibliophiles Find Love. Readers will always have something to talk about, and bibliophiles are emotionally intelligent, empathetic, passionate, and imaginative. Oh, but you know that."

Ven frowned. "I can find my own dates."

"Of course you can," Marigold said. "You don't *need* a matchmaker. But if you're looking for true connection, books require commitment and engagement. So does love."

Ven nodded. "I'm done with the liars and noncommitters, let me tell you. Is it too much to ask for simple honesty?"

"Absolutely not," Marigold said. She drew a three-ring binder from her tote. "A gentleman just signed up. He's looking for long-term love. He favors biographies in his reading, which I think shows a firm interest in truth."

Marigold flipped through dozens of pages.

Did they have that many applicants? My fantasies of Friday nights committed to my to-be-read stack fizzled.

"He bought a house here recently," Marigold was saying. "He's a successful hotel developer. Handsome too, not that we emphasize or judge income or looks."

Ven's face morphed from polite smile to complete disinterest. Which I read as just the opposite.

"You could fill out our biblio-match survey," Marigold said. "We'll give you the first date for free. I know we've just met but I *feel* you'll connect with this gentleman."

I crossed all my fingers.

Ven played disinterested. Marigold threw in a second date.

"Sold!" Ven declared, just as Lorna reappeared.

Ven and Lorna swooped in for air kisses and thrilled hand-clapping about Ven's date.

"Lorna, I heard you called in Joe's murder," Ven said. "How shocking for you, and at the Moosejaw house . . ."

Simultaneously, she and Lorna uttered variations on "such a gorgeous property!"

"Maybe Fiona Giddings will finally sell now," Lorna said. "She wasn't ready when I listed it for her."

"She won't be now either," Ven said, red lips pursed. "She's moving in tomorrow. I just drove by. The cleaning crew told me."

"What?" I blurted. "She's moving into a murder house?"

✳

CHAPTER 19

Glass Houses

"Don't say 'murder house' around realtors," I informed Meg the following afternoon.

New snow sparkled as we stepped out of the chocolatier's with a basket of goodies for Fiona Giddings. The sweet offerings would hopefully convey all we needed to say: Welcome to your new home. Get well soon. So sorry for your loss. Apologies for going out with your fiancé. *Good luck living in your murder house!*

Yesterday, Ven and Lorna had leaped on my poorly considered wording like mothers chastising a foul-talking five-year-old at the holiday table. Houses were not to be stigmatized by deaths of any kind, natural or unnatural. Not even supernatural. According to Ven, hauntings required no disclosure under Colorado real estate law.

"I can see that," Meg said. "The house didn't kill anyone."

"That deck didn't step in to help," I said, moving behind Meg to allow a group of skiers to pass. They thronged by, bright and chatty as parrots, gear clacking, jackets rustling.

"I still can't believe she's moved into that house," I said.

Meg said, "At least it shows she's okay. Moving takes effort."

"Or she's not thinking straight," I countered. "She had a head injury."

"We'll soon find out. *If* she'll see us. I can't believe Piper told her my name. Now I have to confess and apologize. Okay, I totally believe Piper told her. I just hope Fiona will see us. See *me* . . ."

Piper had stopped by the Book Chalet earlier, along with three other members of the Mountains of Mystery book club. They'd just dropped by Fiona's.

"To welcome her to town," Piper claimed, with her posse backing her up. "And to invite her to join the book club."

Uh-huh. Just four friendly bibliophiles stopping by a murder house to invite a shoving victim to a mystery book club. No ulterior motives there, like squeezing Fiona for clues.

Fiona, it seemed, also hadn't been fooled. She'd blocked them at the threshold, saying she needed to unpack. A good strategy in the moment, but resistance only made Piper more determined.

"Fiona will let us in," I said, bold despite Piper's temporary defeat. "You were both wronged by Joe. You already have something in common. Plus, she probably wants information from us."

"All we don't know about Joe and the attack at the theater?" Meg said.

I raised the basket. "We have a secret weapon. Chocolate."

The basket contained a box of mixed truffles, hot cocoa mixes, and homemade marshmallows dipped in milk chocolate and toffee crumbles. Who could resist?

Meg and I had indulged in samples at the shop, and I felt emboldened by a rush of sugar, caffeine, and optimism.

Fiona would let us in. She'd reveal something she might not realize was important, the key to all the crimes . . .

This happy fairy tale carried me along until we reached Moosejaw Lane. Then I remembered Little Red Riding Hood, skipping off with her basket, oblivious to the waiting wolf. Early versions of the tale had Little Red offering up info that spelled her and her granny's gory doom. In all renditions, the message was timeless: beware of smooth-talking wolves.

Fiona had been injured. She was a victim. She could still be a murderer with an agenda.

When we reached her house, Meg rang the doorbell and waited, long enough for me to formulate a better plan. I was about to suggest we take our chocolates and run, when the door opened a crack.

Fiona Giddings peeked out with narrowed eyes. Her gray sweatsuit coordinated with the pallor of her skin. Her red curls sagged from a messy bun. A ragged strip of neon-pink tape covered her left temple.

"I'm not joining a club or giving interviews or selling the house," she declared and moved to slam the door in our faces.

A club and interviews. Those pointed to Piper and her posse. Selling the house? Had Ven been by too?

Meg said quickly, "I'm here to apologize. We're from the Book Chalet and—"

Fiona interrupted. "You're here to apologize for that book club? They said they predicted my fiancé's death! Crass! Then they wanted to come in and 'sense' more crimes and discuss Agatha Christie!" She touched her bandage and winced.

"They're enthusiastic mystery readers," I said. I wouldn't apologize for that.

"We were at the theater the other day," Meg said. "We heard you scream and tried to help, but we took the wrong set of stairs."

Fiona stepped back. "Why were you there?"

Now Meg looked pained. "I'm Meg Christie. That's why I'm apologizing. I, ah, met your fiancé the night he died."

I thrust out the basket. "We brought chocolates."

Fiona stepped aside with a heavy sigh. "You better come in. We can talk in the kitchen."

The kitchen was just about the last place I wanted to revisit, after the deck and the drop-off. I imagined the room frozen as it had been when Lorna and I arrived. Red stains on sheepskin. Murder weapons sprawled in front of the hearth. Perhaps some new ghastly flourishes. Ribbons of crime-scene tape or a connect-the-dots game of evidence markers.

When we stepped in, I saw that Joe's minimalism had been replaced by a mess. Fiona led us around a stack of luggage. A suitcase gaped open to a mound of clothes, like Fiona had tipped up a drawer and tossed in its contents. An open box revealed edges of paper and books. At least *she'd* brought books.

The kitchen had also been cleaned, then re-cluttered. Grocery bags and boxes crowded the counters.

"Tea? Coffee? Something stronger?" Fiona asked. Before we could answer, she said, "I'm having sherry. I'm not supposed to with my head, but I think I deserve something sweet."

"I'll join you," said Meg, to my surprise.

Meg wasn't a mid-afternoon drinker, but this was sherry. Miss Marple would prescribe a glass or two for shock and distress, which we were surely about to inflict.

A half hour later, we sat around the island on high chairs that could double as torture devices. Fiona steadily turned a bottle of sherry to half-empty. Meg did the talking. The chairs reminded me I'd recently sledded on rocks.

Meg was describing Bibliophiles Find Love. "Of course, our cousin and her partner didn't know that you and Joe were . . ."

"Engaged?" Fiona topped off her glass. I wondered if we should intervene. She had a head injury.

She pushed the box of chocolates toward us. Meg and I took truffles.

"I am *so* sorry," Meg said.

"Not your fault." Fiona gulped sherry like a tequila shot.

Except for the sherry and resisting the truffles, she seemed to be taking this surprisingly well. No tears. No wailing or recriminations. Maybe she was on something to dull her nerves. Then she really shouldn't be downing sugary booze. Under the ruse of pouring myself more, I moved the bottle farther from her reach.

"How long were you engaged?" I asked.

Fiona shrugged like she might not recall. Then she said, "Five months and two days. Joseph Harrison Darcy asked me to be his wife on my birthday, after one of my plays. That's how we met. He came to a performance and sweet-talked his way backstage to meet me. I guess it was all an act. Or he got cold feet." She stared out to the frozen deck.

I followed her gaze and squelched a shiver. Meg and Joe had stood out there, admiring the snowy night and its magical light. Then he'd gone out again and someone had struck him with the poker. A visitor he invited in? A burglar? *Someone who already had a key because she owned the house . . .*

I turned back to find Fiona eyeing me. It was a good thing her chairs required abs-of-steel to scoot them back. Otherwise, my flinch might have sent me careening.

She raised a half smile.

I fumbled for small talk, anything other than *Did you kill Joe?* "Lovely house!" I exclaimed, channeling Lorna and Ven. "Great kitchen. Nice and open." *To falling down a ravine!*

Meg saved me from myself and asked, "Do you plan to stay in Last Word?"

Fiona made a disgruntled sound. "For a while. I'm on leave from work. Forced exile, more like. And I don't feel safe in my theater apartment. That breaks my heart. I love that place." She swiped at a tear, the first I'd seen.

Here, I could empathize. "I live above the Book Chalet," I said. "We had a break-in last year. It was awful, violating. Do the police in Ridgeway have any answers?"

Fiona frowned. "The chief says it was probably teenagers. There've been break-ins around campus. I did leave the door open. You two walked right in, apparently."

That created an awkward silence.

Fiona twirled her glass. Rings in colorful gems and hammered metal graced all fingers except her bare left ring finger. Which meant nothing, as Lorna would say. Not everyone wore an engagement ring.

Or she tossed it into the canyon with Joe's body!

I wriggled in my seat.

Meg said gently, "Do you know who might have hurt Joe? Someone from his past? A past relationship?"

Fiona's face hardened. "Have you been talking to that gossipy book-club woman? She claimed Joe had another fiancée. Ridiculous! He told me when we first met, he had an ex who wouldn't let go. That was one of the reasons he didn't want to broadcast our relationship."

She stood abruptly. Metal chair legs grated against tile. "People can make up stories. You, my colleagues, the police—none of you knew Joseph like I did. He probably thought he was going to the library for a book discussion that night you met. Bibliophiles Love Books, is that what your cousin's business is called? Joseph was widely versed in literature and the arts, theater . . ."

She sounded dreamy, angry, and in total denial.

I touched Meg's arm. She took the hint.

"We should go," Meg said. "We're so sorry to have bothered you and brought up all . . . this."

I slid gratefully from my seat.

Fiona escorted us to the door. "Thank you for coming," she said in a slightly slurred monotone.

We zipped jackets and wound scarfs, and my eye caught on a business card and a familiar face.

"Venessa Upshaw came to visit?" I asked.

"Who?" Fiona frowned and looked around, as if another guest might linger behind the stacks of boxes.

I pointed to the card. "She's a realtor?" *And another woman who dated your fiancé.*

"Oh, her." Fiona shook her head. "What is it with people in this town wanting to barge in? Are you all aggressively friendly?"

Or aggressively nosy. My cheeks warmed. Meg and I would fall in that category, except we'd brought chocolates and had a noble purpose. Justice!

I tuned back in to Fiona, who was saying she'd practically had to throw Ven out.

"She insisted on seeing the kitchens and bedrooms. Said she'd write me up a free home valuation. Why would I sell?"

My mind chimed *murder house, murder house*.

Meg's phone buzzed. She fished in her pocket, looked at the screen, and stepped off to one side.

Fiona gave a look of bleary exasperation. Now we were uninvited guests overstaying our welcome too. I decided to add pushy questioner to the list. Fiona might never let us in again.

"Do you know why someone would take your copy of *The Mousetrap*?" I asked.

Fiona's eyes cleared to hardened. "You know about that? Did *you* take it?" She took a step toward me. I backed into the sideboard.

"No, no," I said, raising a palm. "The police must have told you. Someone took it. I reported it missing."

"Is that why you're here?" Fiona stepped closer.

"Ellie." Meg tugged at my sleeve. "We need to go."

I was all for that. I burst out the door as Meg issued hurried thanks and best wishes.

Outside, it was Meg who surged ahead.

"What's wrong?" I said, jogging to keep up. "Did you hear Fiona accuse me of taking her script? What's so important about it?" I valued Agatha Christie, but that script hadn't looked like a precious vintage edition.

Meg stopped at the end of Fiona's walkway. "That was Luna Perez, the secretary at Rosie's school."

I froze from my limbs to my lungs.

"Rosie left early," Meg said.

I melted a little and exhaled. That didn't sound like my world's best niece, but it wasn't the horror I'd been imagining.

"With a man," Meg said. "She sneaked out and drove off with a strange man."

*

CHAPTER 20

Looking for Trouble

Meg took off down Moosejaw. I jogged after her, but didn't get far. A pickup truck with two-toned panels rumbled up the lane. It slowed, did a rattly U-turn, and pulled up beside me. A window rolled down. Sam Ibarra dimpled. Then he read the room—rather, the icy sidewalk—and turned serious.

"What's going on?" he asked.

I raised a hold-on finger. "Meg!" I called. "Where are you going? I'll catch up."

Meg stopped and frowned. "Home?" She retraced a few steps back toward me. "I'll run to the gondola, then get my car, and—"

"Hold up there." Sam was out of his truck. He eyed Fiona's house. "What are you doing here? Is everything okay?"

Easy answer: no. But then my mind skittered, wondering what he meant. Who was he worried about? Fiona, bothered by nosy booksellers? Or the other way around? Innocent booksellers visiting a murder suspect?

"We're fine," Meg said. "We're in a hurry."

Fine? Hardly. Rosie ran off with a stranger, and my sister was lying to the police. "Meg . . ." I pitched her name as a plea.

"El, I'm sure she's okay," Meg said, puffing a frosty, frantic breath.

I turned to Sam. "It's Meg's daughter, Rosie. She's only fourteen. She skipped out of school with a man. We don't know who."

The detective stiffened. "Did she go willingly, or do you have reason to think this was an abduction?"

My stomach mimed Olympic springboard diving. Leap, lurch, and drop. In the background, Rosie's words. *Mom's going to hit the roof.*

I should have told Meg. No, first, I should have run after Rosie and pressed her for more. What if she'd dropped me a hint—hoping I'd stop her—and I'd let her down?

"We have no reason to assume she's in trouble," I said, trying and failing to convince myself.

Meg's "Ha!" fell between a sob and a threat. "She's in trouble. She'll be grounded until she's forty."

A beep. Meg leaped on her phone. She read the screen and sagged. "Rosie's not at the ski center. That was her boss. I need to go get my car. I'll check her friends' houses."

"I'm coming too." No way was I letting Meg go out stress driving on her own.

"I'll take you down," Sam said. "You'll get there faster, and we can decide if this warrants an Amber Alert."

Meg shook her head in *no, no, no* resistance to it all.

I took her arm and tugged her toward the truck. "Thank you," I said to the detective.

He held the door. I got in first and realized I'd committed myself to the middle place on a bench seat.

"Sorry about the ride," Sam said, as I buckled a lap belt. "My work vehicle's in the shop."

Meg slid in beside me, staring at her phone, willing it to send news. If she'd been paying attention, she would have stomped air brakes all the way down.

Sam Ibarra drove fast but confidently. I trusted him, or at least his driving. The old truck? Not so much. The vehicle swayed like a canoe on a choppy sea. It also lacked suspension or shocks or whatever gave modern vehicles a smooth ride. Every pebble felt like rolling over a boulder.

To take my mind off the jolts, hairpins, drop-offs, and my wayward niece, I questioned the detective. "What were you doing at Fiona's house?"

"I asked you first, remember?" He swung the truck around a hairpin that hooked downward like a carnival flume. I slid into Meg, then Sam. In both cases, I didn't mind. Meg was soft in her puffy coat, Sam as solid as a guardrail.

At least, I hoped the guardrails were solid. I kept my eyes straight ahead, focusing on trees.

When the truck and I regained equilibrium, I said, "We took Fiona some condolence chocolates. Do you think she and Joe were really engaged?"

He smiled. "Good switch of subjects there. You could be an interrogator."

I took that as a compliment. Then I realized he hadn't answered the question. "Well? What do you think?"

The truck rattled over a patch of icy gravel. He removed a hand from the wheel to rub his jaw. "Your cousin proposed that theory. I must admit, we hadn't considered it. Not often that someone makes up a fiancé. Especially since she'd have to know it would make her a stronger suspect in our eyes."

"She could have done that to throw you off," I said. "By making herself a suspect, she then looks more innocent."

He took his eyes off a curve to grin at me. "Now, that's a devious theory. I like it."

We swayed down a hairpin. I attempted to sound nonchalant as I gripped my seatbelt. "I can't take full credit."

"Oh? Your cousin again?"

"Agatha Christie." I was about to provide examples from her

stories, but then realized. "You *still* haven't answered my question. Were they engaged?"

We surged down a relatively straight stretch. Pines leaned in from both sides as if straining to overhear.

"Okay," he said. "I'll admit to you, I might not have questioned it. Especially now since we have that other fiancée in the picture. If we could locate her."

"She's missing? Hiding? What if she's here? She's a great suspect." My hopes surged, even as Sam tapped the brakes to allow a wide-hipped van to pass. Our truck edged within inches of a precipice. I forced my eyes and hopes to look straight ahead.

"Did Fiona tell you anything you think I should know?" he asked.

Fiona had guzzled sherry and remained dry-eyed except about her theater apartment. But I wouldn't judge anyone for failing to stick to a grieving script.

I said, "She was really upset about the missing screenplay. She wants it back." I left out the part about her accusing me of theft. The detective had enough suspicions.

"Did she say why? She told us it was 'just a script.'" His fingers mimed quotes. "If it was just that, why'd someone steal it?"

"I wish I knew." More than that, I wished I'd picked it up. My initial book-rescuing instincts had been right.

We'd reached the base village. I relaxed my full-body clench. Meg looked up in surprise.

"Oh," she said, "that was fast."

When we pulled up to the goldenrod house, Meg jumped out. Gram flung open the doors, arms waiting for a hug. My heart sank. Rosie wasn't here. I slid across the seat.

"Ellie, wait." Sam held out a business card. Gold flecks and concern warmed his granite eyes. "My personal cell number is on the back. Call me, anytime, for anything, and, please, let me know if you find her—and especially if you can't."

CHAPTER 21

✳

Premeditation

Gram wore her frilly turquoise apron and a tight smile that failed to mask her concern. Still in our coats, Meg and I followed her to the kitchen.

Gram put on the teakettle. "It's not time for Rosie to be home from school yet."

"Gram," Meg said with strained patience. "Rosie left school early. That's why we're worried."

"Yes, I know, dear," Gram said, setting out the cookie jar. "But, as far as we know, Rosie doesn't know that we know she's not where we expect her to be."

I sorted out when, where, and who knew what about whom. Was Gram suggesting that sweet, smart Rosie—world's best niece—might stroll in at her usual hour, acting like nothing had happened?

That would take cunning, nerves of steel, and darned good fibbing skills. My niece was wise, but was she conniving?

Meg paled. "You think she's done this before? Has she said anything, Gram?"

"No, no," Gram said. "She hasn't done or said anything that I've noticed. But I know Rosie—we all do. She'd never intentionally hurt you or make you worry, Meg."

Guilt had been lounging on my shoulder, heavy as lead. Now it jumped up to kick at my conscience. I had to tell Meg. I cleared my throat. "I talked to Rosie on her way to school the other day."

Meg looked up. An impatient *And!?* flashed on her face. Meg was too polite to let it out.

My cheeks could spark a wildfire. I'd royally messed up. "I was hoping to get her to open up about whomever she's been texting."

Meg's *AND?* flared in silent all-caps and bold.

"She didn't tell me," I said. "But she said something that worried me. I planned to talk to her more later. Over pizza or . . ." I had to just say it. "She said, '*Mom's going to hit the roof.*'"

Meg caught her breath.

Gram pursed her lips.

The teapot whined.

Meg had draped her puffer coat over a chair. She grabbed it. "Rosie was right. Roof. Hit. Let's go, El."

I'd just sunk into my seat, preparing to indulge in some nerve-soothing gingersnaps and selfish relief. Meg hadn't blamed the messenger, even if I did.

I jumped up. "Where are we going?"

"Her friends' houses, favorite places. Friends first. I'll try to reach their parents if you'll drive?"

Gram hugged us both. "I'll call around too. Ms. Ridge should know so she can keep an eye out. I'll tell my birdwatcher friends as well. I have a feeling that Rosie's simply going the wrong way on what she thinks is the right road."

The wrong way. I prayed Rosie wasn't about to crash.

In the car, Meg checked the time.

"Almost four o'clock. Rosie and her friends usually hang out after school. I wouldn't have expected her home for another hour or two. Gram's right, if Luna hadn't called, I wouldn't have known to be worried."

Meg gave directions to the house of Rosie's BFF, Pasha Witten.

"Why *did* Luna call?" I asked, aiming Meg's old Subaru toward a familiar neighborhood. The Wittens lived near the house where Meg and I grew up. Mom and Dad still owned our family home. As part of their globe-trotting early retirement, they had been renting it out to fund their travels.

As we passed their street, I forced myself not to turn the wheel automatically.

"*Why* did Luna call?" Meg repeated my question with incredulity.

I rephrased. "I know, because of the man. But what made her worry rather than assume he was a, say, cousin picking up Rosie for a family event or dentist appointment?"

Impressions were important. Intuitions mattered. Fear was like that too, sometimes subconscious, an animal sense of danger.

Meg looked up from her phone. "Good question. Luna didn't call immediately. She thought maybe Rosie went out for the late lunch period. But then, it kept bothering her. She checked for approved absences and didn't see any. She worried because Rosie looked . . ."

I glanced at Meg. "What?"

Meg repeated Luna's description like she was tiptoeing over a thin frozen lake. "Excited but furtive? Like Rosie was 'ducking from a lightning storm' was how Luna put it."

Ducking wouldn't stop a strike. I sped up, only to slam on the brakes when Meg pointed to a log house tucked amid pines. A deck curved around the front and sides. Lights glowed inside, including in an upstairs room with lace curtains. I willed it to be a loft retreat filled with giggling, gossipy friends, including Rosie.

Meg rapped a bronze knocker shaped like an acorn.

"No one answered when I called," Meg said. "Maybe they're not home from work—"

The door opened. Rhea Witten wore scrubs and a hassled

expression. I recalled that Rhea was a surgeon at the Ridgecrest hospital and that she originally hailed from Greece.

"Meg!" she said, dark eyebrows unfurrowing from their frown. She turned to me with a smile I recognized: too big, bright, and tight. She'd forgotten my name. As someone who regularly blanked on names and faces, I empathized.

"Ellie," I said, pointing to myself. "I'm—"

"Rosie's favorite aunt! Of course! She raves about you and your world travels."

I blushed at the highest of compliments. *Favorite aunt.* "Now the homebody aunt," I said.

"With a knack for finding bodies, I hear." A shiver rippled under Rhea's scrubs. "That poor man, shoved from his deck. Was it a robbery? I have a friend who lives up that way. She doesn't feel safe. She says it's those vacation rentals. You never know who's around."

Meg interrupted. "Rhea, we're looking for Rosie."

Rhea's eyes widened. "Rosie? What's happened?"

For a doctor, Rhea Witten wasn't exactly soothing.

Meg rushed through an explanation about Rosie and the unknown man.

Rhea turned and bellowed upward. "Pasha? Come here, please."

"Hey, Ms. Christie, Auntie Christie." Pasha jogged downstairs. Her dark hair was tied back in a knot. She wore pink sweats and oversized slippers.

Meg repeated our problem, adding a forced smile. "Rosie didn't tell me she was leaving school. I'm worried. You understand."

Unsettlingly, Pasha did understand. Her frown mirrored her mom's. "A *man?*"

"Is she dating anyone?" I asked. "Someone with a 'D' initial?"

Pasha's frown deepened to *What are you talking about?*

"Diego?" I suggested. My *et voilà* Poirot moment fled under Pasha's single snort.

"Diego?" Pasha said. "He's crushing on lame football players. I told him, soccer and skateboard boys, they're the coolest."

Pasha was a skateboarder. Her mother smiled at her, the unworried adoration of a parent whose daughter liked sporty kids her age.

"And Rosie?" Meg asked. "She's been texting a lot. She always says it's with you, Pasha, but is there someone else too?"

Another shrug but accompanied by a cloud across Pasha's young face.

"Pasha Fatima Anja Witten, if you know something . . ." Rhea folded her arms across her chest.

Four names? Rhea meant business, in naming and in warnings.

"No, I don't! Sorry, Ms. Christie!" Pasha bit her bottom lip. "I thought maybe . . . You know, maybe Rosie had another best friend? Other than me?"

She remembered her teenage toughness and said, "Whatever. That's cool."

"No," Meg said soothingly. "You're her best friend. I'm sure of that."

"I really wish I could help." Pasha shuffled to her mother, who put her arm around her. I couldn't bear their matching earnest looks. I gazed over their shoulders, into their home. Unlike Joe Darcy's sparse place, the Wittens' house was comfortably cluttered. Throw blankets and pillows. An open newspaper, piles of magazines, and stacks and stacks of books.

In fiction, sleuths from CIA operatives to snoopy neighbors were aways feigning restroom emergencies to access medicine cabinets. There, they discovered prescriptions and poisons, from which they deduced both personalities and crimes.

If you asked me, bookshelves provided the best insights. Books pointed to who people were, who they wanted to be, and whether they read up on poisons.

"What about books?" I asked Pasha. "Has Rosie changed up her reading?"

Last I'd known, Rosie was into manga and graphic novel renditions of the classics.

Pasha launched an eye roll that took her head and upper half with it.

Was she suggesting I'd asked the most absurd question ever? Her mother seemed to think so.

Pasha's eyes returned to level, and she said, "Oh! My!—"

"Pasha . . ." Rhea cautioned.

Pasha sighed. "Rosie and me? We used to read the same books, like our own club. Last month, I found the most awesome series! It's incredible. I can't even!"

"What's the series?" I asked, unable to stop my book curiosity.

"The Tales of Two Monsters," Pasha reported, thrilled to be asked. "It's, like, Frankenstein's monster, but in Paris. He thinks he's the only one to survive this plague, but then he goes to London in a hot-air balloon and he finds another monster and . . ."

Pasha bubbled on about what sounded like a fabulous mashup of Charles Dickens, Mary Shelley, and wild imagination. In other circumstances, I'd have asked for details. I might even have risked boring a teenager with literary trivia.

Mary Shelley had written fantasy beyond Frankenstein. She'd set a book in our time. In her imagined twenty-first century, people still traveled by carriage but also in hot air balloons with feathered wings. That is, until a plague hit and one man was left alone.

Just as well I didn't bring that up. Rhea already looked appalled.

"Should you be reading that?" Rhea asked.

The combined "Yes!" from myself, Pasha, and Meg made Rhea blink.

I softened our response. "*Read what interests you,*" I said.

"That's our motto at the Book Chalet. Read what makes you happy."

"Or unhappy enough to change the world!" Pasha thrust fists to her hips. "Plus, Mom, there's survival stuff too." She mimed eye jabs and well-placed knee kicks. Her mother brightened.

"So . . ." I said, bringing Pasha back to the question. "I'm guessing Rosie didn't want to read the series?"

Pasha lowered her voice to scandalized. "Rosie's reading romance. The kind where high-school sweethearts break up and meet the wrong people and then find each other again and get married!" In case we hadn't clued in to her feelings, she added "Cringe!" and a gagging sound.

Meg issued a wry smile. "Anything can happen in fiction, Pasha." She nudged me, a cue to go. So much for my bibliodetecting.

Before we left, Meg asked Pasha about Rosie's favorite hangouts.

Pasha shrugged. "Here. Your house. Lookout Point? That new ice-cream shop up in the hamlet too. Winter Freeze. Everyone cool hangs out there." She laughed at the ice-cream cool joke and looked like a little kid again.

"Ice cream in winter," Meg said, when we were back in the car. "If that's the extent of Rosie's teenage rebellion, I'll be the luckiest mother around."

"You already are."

"Romances." Meg groaned, sounding like Pasha. "I like a good romance, but I know fiction when I read it. What if Rosie thinks she's in love with that man?"

I had no answer. I concentrated on getting us safely up the mountain. Unlike Sam Ibarra, I inched around the hairpins and edged away from drop-offs.

That's why I take the gondola. I exhaled with relief when we reached the top and a welcoming scene. Pretty chalets. Happy window-shoppers and skiers. A sled dog, pulling a young man on a snowboard, both of them grinning wildly. The hamlet looked like a place where nothing bad could ever happen. Of course, I knew better.

Meg's phone rang. She pounced on it.

"Ms. Ridge? Yes?" Meg's next words weakened my limbs. "Thank goodness!"

"She's there?" I asked.

Meg nodded. I braked at a crosswalk, glad to let my arms firm up from rubbery relief. Pedestrians ambled past. One group stopped midway and took photos down the street, toward the Book Chalet.

Since no one was behind us, I waited for another group to pass and listened in on Meg's side of the phone call.

"But she's safe?" Meg was saying. "All right. Yes, thank you, Ms. Ridge."

"She's at the Book Chalet?" I confirmed.

"Yes, and she's fine, safe, never in danger. Ms. Ridge is calling Gram, but she won't say what's going on. She claims I need to see for myself."

More pedestrians approached the crosswalk. I *should* have done the polite thing and waited. I stomped the gas and surged on until the Book Chalet came into full view. When it did, I braked, hard.

A cluster of people stood outside.

"Is that a carriage?" Meg asked. My braking had jerked us both forward. She leaned farther, straining to see.

Beyond the crowd stood a high-wheeled carriage that might have rolled in through a portal from Jane Austen's time. The hamlet business owners' association had hired a similar carriage around the holidays. Santa and two horses with fake antlers and red noses had delivered holiday gifts to kids and meals to seniors.

The only holiday on the horizon was Valentine's Day. I frowned. "Do you think it's Lorna? Something for her dates?"

Meg jumped out as I pulled into our loading zone. I parked and joined the crowd angling for photos. The carriage sported twinkling strings of lights and was drawn by two mules the size of Clydesdales. The mules were magnificent, but there was something even better now: Meg, hugging Rosie.

My heart swelled. Tears of happiness prickled. I could have watched them forever, but then I noticed a thorn in the scene. Specifically, the man in the driver's seat.

It couldn't be!

I was seeing things. A winter mirage. A stress-induced illusion.

He wore a black wool jacket and matching beret. His hair, sandy-blond, was Ivy-League clipped with a rakish side part. His lips pursed in a smile wrinkled with haughty petulance. I rubbed my eyes, hard, and willed them to open to a different scene. They did, but the difference was Piper Tuttle at my side.

"Will you look at that?" the gossip columnist breathed. "Now, there's a man our Meg could happily throttle, don't you think?" She raised her cellphone and snapped photos.

I still couldn't process what I was seeing. *Maybe if I blinked some more . . .*

Piper broke my stunned spell. "Cameron Winfield," she marveled. "When it rains it pours."

Cameron. Rosie's father. The man who'd abandoned Meg at the altar.

*

CHAPTER 22

Poor Timing

"Mighty big team of jackasses there." Glynis Goodman took Piper's place at my side. The gossip had moved in for close-up shots and overheard quotes.

"Do you know who that is?" I asked.

"*Uh-huh.*" Glynis stuffed her hands deep into her parka pockets and rocked in her boots. "I know the long-eared pair really well. They're good guys. Reliable. Trustworthy. Katherine Ridge filled me in about the other one. For Katherine, she was steaming mad. So mad she didn't care if Tuttle overheard."

Cameron stepped down from the carriage, smiling at Piper's camera. Meg stood with her arms folded. In a cartoon, a dark cloud would billow over her head, shooting lightning, hail, or daggers. Rosie made gestures of pleading and placating.

"Ms. Ridge was right to be mad," I said. "Meg got a call saying Rosie left school with a strange man. Meg was frantic. We had no idea Cameron was in town."

"So I heard," Glynis confirmed. "I stopped by the shop before this crew arrived and was about to join the hunt for Rosie. Not in my usual search-and-find way, mind you. I knew Rosie would be okay, smart girl like her. Nope, I was about to unleash my inner Miss Marple. Human nature . . ." She tapped her temple. "What does Rosie Christie care about, I asked myself. Books. Her family . . ."

That tugged at my heart. Whether the rest of us liked him or not, Cameron was Rosie's family.

The onlookers shifted and drifted, moving on to other scenes. I continued to stare. Cameron looked pretty much the same. Tanned from ample time relaxing on beaches or ski slopes or both. Smile, bright white, defaulting to assured and flirtatious. He looked good, I hated to admit.

"What's he doing here?" Glynis asked.

"No idea. He shows up to take Rosie on splurgy vacations every year, but those are scheduled."

And much built up. Cam counted anticipation as a big part of his dad time. He'd take Rosie to places Meg couldn't afford and frankly had little interest in. Theme parks. Fancy cruises with Grandmother and Grandfather Winfield footing the bill. Spring breaks in Palm Beach, where his parents had a seaside mansion.

"Ms. Ridge said he lives in Florida now?" Glynis shook her head as if that was a strike against him. She was a local—mountains, snow, and golden aspens ran through her blood.

"That's his landing pad," I said. "He's more like a wealthy couch surfer, except it's yachts and penthouses instead of sofa beds. He travels a lot, presumably for the family business. He attends parties, makes connections."

"What funds all that? What's the family business?"

"Old money," I said with a shrug. I wasn't actually sure, but I knew the family fortune dated back to the days of mining and railroad barons. Now, I assumed, they invested, moved money around, tucked it away in businesses, banks, and tax-free vaults.

"Ah," Glynis said. "I'm forming a picture. A rogue, like from the old novels."

New novels and real life too.

Glynis tapped her temple. "He wants something. He strikes me as a man out for himself."

"He is," I said.

Over by the carriage, Meg looped a protective arm around Rosie. Her other hand gestured. I deduced she was telling Cameron to take his mules and go.

"I better go offer my support," I said. "Make sure Rosie and Meg are okay."

"I'll do the same for Morse and Endeavour," Glynis said.

Morse and Endeavour? I made a note to meet their mystery-lover human. As I neared the unhappy family, Rosie slipped from her mother's hold.

"Hey, Aunt El," Rosie said. She grimaced. "I'm really, really, really sorry I worried you guys. I didn't think you'd notice."

Gram had been right. Rosie thought she could ditch school without anyone knowing. I drew my niece into a full squeeze and breathed in the scent of her hair. Peach and honey shampoo with traces of hay. "We're just glad you're okay."

Meg's voice cut through our hug. "El? Can you and Rosie stay here and watch the mules? Cameron and I need to speak in private."

"Mom . . ." Rosie's voice was pleading. "Just come to our dinner, please! There's candles and appetizers and Dad and I worked really hard."

Meg glared at Cameron. He raised his shield of white-toothed charm. "Megs . . . We can talk at my place. All night if you want. It's right up the street and much more private."

"Just over on Moosejaw," Rosie chirped. "Endeavour and Morse will take us. It'll be romantic. Remember? You and Dad went on that Christmas carriage ride as your first date? There was a guy in a beret singing 'Jingle Bells' in French?"

Cameron touched his beret.

Morse and Endeavour issued snorts, repeated by Glynis.

"We'll talk in the Book Chalet," Meg said, as icy as the mountain wind.

Rosie wisely bit back more pleas.

Cameron smiled like he'd gotten his way. "I'd love to. Thank you for the invitation."

Meg stomped to the door. Cowbells clattered. Cameron languidly strolled in behind her. Beside me, Rosie hid behind her hands.

"Hey," I said, nudging her. "Which one of these guys is Morse?"

She removed her hands and offered a smile that expressed both gratitude and oh-my-gosh-you're-so-obvious. I appreciated both.

"This guy." She patted the nearest mule. His haunches reached my chin. Lips—whiskered and velvet—fluttered. "He likes apples but I already fed him all we had." She kept a hand on his neck and said, "Honest, truly, Aunt El, I thought Mom would be here at work. All you guys do is work! Where were you?"

Taking chocolates to a grieving widow and/or murder suspect.

Glynis had a better answer. "I'm guessing, young Christie, they were out looking for you."

Rosie's cheeks blazed. She murmured something.

"What, honey?" I asked.

My niece slumped. "Dad *said* it would work. He's been planning this, like, *forever*. He said we needed something big and grand. Like in the books!"

"Not the books I read," muttered Glynis. Morse and Endeavour waggled their heads. "There's not always a happy ending, in books or in life."

Rosie already knew that. She'd correctly predicted her mom wouldn't be happy. I wanted to bombard her with questions. There was only one I could ask.

"So that's who you've been texting? Initial D? Dad? *Et voilà!* I solved the mystery."

Rosie smiled at my lameness, teenage bravado returning.

A familiar two-toned truck eased down the street. Sam Ibarra parked by Meg's Subaru and made his way toward us.

I tried not to beam at him. He noted Rosie, smiled back, and joked to Glynis. "Got a permit for these mules, Goodman?"

"Not my mules." She chuckled. "If they were, I'd say these boys can do what they like."

Sam turned his smile on Rosie. "Miss Christie. You're okay?"

She flushed red. "Yeah." Then the implication clicked. "Oh my gosh, did Mom call the police?"

"We ran into Detective Ibarra after your school called," I said to Rosie. Guilt prickled. He'd been worried for Rosie too. "I was going to call you." Then something else occurred to me. "Wait . . . you two know each other?"

Rosie straightened. "Yeah. We met when Detective Ibarra and Chief Sunnie were searching Mom's rooms. I told them exactly when Mom got in after her date. I'm her alibi. I woke up because she was whistling." Rosie rolled her eyes. "Mom's a romantic. She just won't admit it."

"Whistling," I said, heaping on meaning. "Evidence of an enjoyable date." I turned to my niece. "She has another alibi too, Rosie. Detective Ibarra is working to confirm it."

Sam rubbed the insides of Endeavour's ears. The mule's eyelids drooped and he practically purred. "Still no way to connect that gift card to our victim," he said. "No record he bought it himself. He could've paid cash, of course, or received it as a gift. Either way, no record unless we find a witness."

Minor details. "Your mother was home when her date was ordering her roses online," I told Rosie.

"Cool," said Rosie.

"So, what's going on here?" Sam asked. "I saw the crowd. Thought I should check in case anything was wrong."

Something was very wrong.

Rosie flushed and studied her boots.

I said, "Meg's, um . . ." What to call Cameron? Meg's cheating, lying, deserting ex? Not in front of Rosie. "Rosie's *father* turned up unexpectedly. This is . . ." I gestured at the carriage and again debated. A romantic disaster? A mule-drawn wreck?

"Bad timing," Rosie said sullenly. "If the school hadn't called Mom and she'd been at work like usual, it could have been okay. I mean, look!"

She gestured toward the carriage and mules.

Sam nodded sympathetically. "Bad timing? I hear you. It happens to the best of us." He winked at me.

What did that mean? My cheeks took it as a sign to flush.

Cowbells came to my rescue. Meg stomped from the Book Chalet.

"Uh-oh," Rosie said.

"Rosie," Meg called from ten paces away. "We're going home."

I dug out the car keys and handed them to Rosie.

"You want to press charges?" Sam asked Meg. "Sounds like noncustodial interference."

My sister looked startled. Surprise turned to narrowed-eyed interest.

"Mom! No!" Rosie turned to me. "Bye, Aunt El. Come visit when I'm grounded forever?"

I gave her a quick hug. "Good news for your favorite aunt. I'm guaranteed to see you every day until you're fifty."

Rosie groaned and trudged after her mom. Cameron stepped out of the Book Chalet as they drove away. He stood in the doorway, waving, playing the part of a forlorn, deserted dad.

"Guess you have things covered here," Sam said. "Unless you need any assistance with him?" He nodded toward Cameron, now engrossed in his phone. I hoped he was contacting Morse and Endeavour's owner and booking a plane ticket out of here.

"I've got Ellie's back in case any jackass problems arise," said Glynis. "Unless you two kids want to take a carriage ride. I'm a qualified mule handler. I could steer."

Was that a blush on Sam's granite cheeks? I knew it was on mine.

"Ellie? Eleanor? Yoo-hoo . . ." My name floated in from up the street.

For a moment, I considered hiding behind the mules. It was too late. Instead, I issued a too-bright anxious smile.

"Your biblio-match," Sam observed.

Dr. Waldon was tweedier than before. Corduroy pants, impractical-in-snow loafers, a tweed jacket open to a tweed coat over a tan sweater, topped with a nubby beanie. He could blend into tumbleweed. He greeted Sam Ibarra with a hand-shake (all of two shakes) and me with a stiff wave.

Glynis avoided an awkward greeting by moving behind Endeavour's broad neck. I envied her.

Dr. Waldon surveyed the scene. Bookshop. Carriage. Me and a police detective. Two massive mules and a purple-clad woman actively ignoring him. "What's all this? An event for your book-shop? How delightfully absurd! I see no books."

"Hi, Waldon," I said, dragging out my mulish manners. "How nice of you to stop by. You know Detective Ibarra?"

Waldon did. "He grilled me about our date. I told him I didn't see you kill anyone." He laughed.

If I had, he wouldn't have noticed. I could have committed the perfect crime! I smiled. "Have you come for a book?"

"I was in the neighborhood." He studied a spot beyond my shoulder. I fought the urge to turn around and look.

Instead, I examined his claim. *In the neighborhood?* We were halfway up a mountain. No one happened by on their way to the grocery store. "Oh?"

"I came to see my colleague," he said archly. "She was injured in a fall."

I chided myself for another assumption. He hadn't been lying.

"Fiona?" I asked.

"Yes," he said with an air of bored irritation. "Since I had to come all the way over here, I thought I'd drop by and see this *famous* bookshop. See if you have anything *I* might be interested in perusing."

Glynis poked around the side of Endeavour. "All books are worth a peruse."

Endeavour bobbed his head. Sam appeared to stifle a smile.

Dr. Waldon issued Glynis the smile equivalent of a pat on the head. The man was either braver or less wise than I thought. Glynis towered over him in height and force. She also had two massive mules at her side and wouldn't take kindly to an overt insult of books.

Dr. Waldon adjusted his beanie. "I, ah, also wondered, Eleanor, if you received my flowers?"

"Flowers?" My heartbeat sped to a trot. *No! He couldn't possibly mean . . .*

A delivery must have come in today, while we were out. Orchids requiring some absurd care regime of ice cubes and spritzing. A carnivorous flytrap we'd have to feed. "*Meg* received roses." I emphasized Meg's name, daring him to contradict me.

"I sent roses too. A dozen, bloodred, with thorns. Cemetery roses! Such a ridiculous option, I couldn't resist." The professor took my gape-mouthed shock as an affirmative. "Good. I see you got them."

"*You* sent them?"

He brushed invisible dust from his tweed. "Your reaction tells me that my little mystery worked. I do believe I've just proven a point about Agatha Christie as well. She doesn't supply enough clues. Not even the most brilliant reader could unravel those mysteries."

"You didn't sign your name," Sam said icily. "It wasn't any Christie's fault that no one knew who sent them. I wasted several hours of a murder investigation trying to track down the sender."

Dr. Waldon clasped his hands. "So you *did* figure out my little linguistic ruse, Ellie? Clever. Although, I provided blatant clues with the differential font. Detective, why were you so concerned? Was it because the quote was about murder?"

"Murder?" Sam frowned.

Waldon shook his head as if impressed by his own brilliance. "That was happenstance, I assure you. Such odd coincidence. I'd say *delightful* if it wasn't so aptly morbid."

Sam, correctly detecting that he wouldn't get a straightforward answer from Waldon, turned to me.

I sighed. "Waldon altered a quote from a Poirot novel. *The A.B.C. Murders*. In it, a killer taunts Poirot. There's a series of seemingly random killings in towns chosen alphabetically from the train schedule." I could easily summon the sentence. I'd played it in my head so often. "At one point, Poirot says, *Murder, I have often noticed, is a great matchmaker.*"

"I substituted 'books' for 'murder,'" Waldon said. "And corrected the grammar accordingly. *Books, I have often noticed, are a great matchmaker.* A better sentiment than the original, no?"

"I'm not so sure," said Sam.

Cameron had wandered over to listen in. He offered a scornful sneer. For once, I agreed with him.

Waldon frowned. "What's wrong? Eleanor, we met on a *book matchup*. You do like books?"

I didn't "like" books. I *loved* them, and I agreed entirely with the sentiment. There was one big problem, though.

Sam Ibarra rocked on his boots. "Guess I can cross that alibi verification off my list."

✳

CHAPTER 23

Talk of Murder

The next morning, Meg, Agatha, and I sat in the Reading Lounge before opening. A fire danced in the hearth. Agatha snoozed in the nearest fireside seat. Meg and I held steaming mugs of Earl Grey with lots of milk.

Tea, my sister, Agatha, and a wintery wonderland viewed from a cozy armchair. It should have been relaxing.

"He's been here a week. An entire week!" Meg exclaimed.

Agatha's ears flew back.

Meg put her mug down with such force, I worried. For Meg, of course, but also for my favorite mug. It had a rosy background, two crossed knitting needles, an image of Miss Marple, and an appropriate quote.

I think, my dear, we won't talk any more about murder during tea. Such an unpleasant subject.

Miss Marple was wise, as always. However, this morning, I respectfully disagreed with her. Talk of murder might be more pleasant and fruitful than discussing Cameron Winfield. It was also a more urgent topic. Last night, I'd told Meg about Dr. Waldon destroying her rosy alibi. She was too distracted by Cameron to care.

"So, Rosie knew that Cameron was in town?" I asked.

This time, Meg picked up the mug and cradled it. Citrusy bergamot scents floated my way, launched by Meg's sigh.

"Rosie's known for over a month. A month! All this time, they've been plotting. He convinced her they had to keep it secret. He manipulated our daughter into secrets and lies. You get why I'm so upset?"

I got it. But there was something I didn't understand. "He's been here a week. How come no one saw him and told you or Gram?"

Sure, Cameron rarely graced Last Word, but he grew up here. People would recognize him. He also wasn't the kind of guy to stay in with a good book.

"Remember his friend Sanjay Reed?" Meg asked.

I did. When I was around Rosie's age, Meg had been newly dating Cameron and hanging out with his friends, including the dashing Sanjay. I'd had a huge crush on Sanjay, right up until he sided with his pal in wedding desertion.

Meg was saying that Sanjay's family had a cabin out in the backcountry. "Except it's not exactly backcountry anymore with all the new homes out that way. The cabin's done up with electric and plumbing now too, I guess. Rosie said her dad and Sanjay went ice fishing. Have you ever known Cameron Winfield to fish, let alone sit out on a frozen lake? More likely, they hauled in a bunch of booze and snacks and pretended they were teenagers again." Meg sighed almost wistfully.

Cozied up in a cabin by a lake sounded nice. I'd pack books and hot cocoa mix. However, I thought I'd pass on being a teenager again.

Outside, a peachy sunrise morphed to clear icy blues. Meg stared into it.

"Rosie said that Cameron is staying on Moosejaw?" I asked. "Do you know which house?"

I didn't like the coincidence of Joe and Cameron staying on the same street, but it had to be just that. Coincidence.

"A place at the end?" Meg said. "I don't think Moosejaw's very long. I'll have to go see him sometime. Rosie's upset that I rebuffed their dinner. But good grief, how could he ever think that was okay? I was so stunned at the time. I had no words."

I had all sorts of words, none appropriate for a quiet morning in the Reading Lounge. Besides, we had a guest.

Marigold buzzed in and out, happily decorating for tomorrow night's three-couples date. It wouldn't be fair to ruin her buzz with gripes about romantic failure.

The ruffle of paper alerted us to Marigold's return.

Meg took a deep, calming breath and sipped her tea.

"You're sure you're okay with me hanging the decorations early?" Marigold asked. Book pages trailed behind her, threaded on long lengths of red string. They were clipped on the ends like regatta flags and stamped with red hearts. "You don't think anyone will object?"

"Object to books?" Meg asked.

Marigold eyed her craft project with unease. "Chopped-up books. Some people might find it sacrilegious in a bookshop, but I only used pages from books that the library was going to toss out otherwise. Deaccessioning always makes me so sad."

"This way the books live on," I said encouragingly. "You've found them a new purpose."

Marigold glowed, cheeks as peachy as her cardigan. I got up to help her. Agatha decided she should offer her services too. Batting at string and messing with ladders were her specialties.

Meg took charge of cat herding. I held Marigold's ladder as she used a long pole to loop her paper strings up and over high crossbeams.

"It's like rigging for puppets," Marigold said. "And here people mock puppetry as a frivolous, silly art."

"No art is frivolous," Meg said.

Agatha agreed, especially art involving string, her great but forbidden love. Our aunt's kitty had nearly perished after swallowing some Christmas ribbon. We were saving Agatha from herself, not that anyone in love ever thanked messengers of sense and safety.

Marigold climbed down from the ladder and looked up. "What do you think?"

"Lovely," Meg said.

I agreed. "Magical. Our customers will love it."

Marigold bustled off to make more.

Meg stretched, fingers clasped high over her head. "I guess I can't stay here *all* day complaining about Cameron."

I grinned. "You could . . . I could bring you cocoa and scones and you could borrow some of Gram's work slippers."

Meg smiled back. "Tempting, but I'd rather work and figure out what he wants. He always wants something."

"No one can hide a secret from Christies," I said. I hoped that was true, both of Cameron and a killer.

* * *

Meg headed for the lobby. Agatha resumed her important morning work (napping on a high shelf), and I returned our mugs to the kitchen, with an ulterior motive of snagging an extra cup of coffee. I'd stayed in last night, pleading off dinner at Gram's. I had a date with leftovers, Agatha, and a book, I told Gram.

True. I'd also wanted to give Rosie and Meg time alone and myself some time to think. *Oh, I'd thought . . .*

Problems stampeded around my head all night, so many I'd taken to counting them like sheep.

Murder, assault, suspicion on my sister. A missing script. Joe and Fiona. Cameron! The only solved mystery—the sender of the roses—had only brought more trouble.

Voices reached me as I pushed through the storeroom door.

Marigold sat at the worktable, stamping hearts onto bunting. Ms. Ridge stood by the lockers, tying on her crisp work apron.

I greeted Ms. Ridge.

"Is Rosie okay?" Ms. Ridge asked. "I was so delighted to see her, I didn't ask what she was doing with those mules."

I noted that Ms. Ridge tactfully avoided mention of Cameron.

I briefly explained what I knew. The secret texting. The surprise dinner date that Meg, of course, had refused.

"Aw . . ." Marigold was threading paper flags onto thin red string. "That sounds rather sweet. Like something from a book."

"Indeed," said Ms. Ridge. Her tone suggested that she and Marigold were thinking of different genres.

Marigold rolled a rubber stamp over a red ink pad, then thumped it onto some flags. Hearts all around. "Meg did seem stressed this morning. What did this Cameron gentleman do? Is there a chance Meg could forgive him?"

In romance novels, that's how it would happen. A couple met, preferably in cute circumstances. Sparks flew, followed by betrayal or misgivings or a stadium-cam proposal gone horribly wrong. The relationship was doomed. Then, happenstance, Cupid, or—best of all—truth and true love brought them back together.

That wouldn't be happening for Meg and Cameron.

"Cameron Winfield deserted Meg at the altar," I said. "He flew off to Cabo San Lucas and lounged on a beach for months, even after Meg told him they were having a child together. He sees Rosie about once a year to take her on vacations. He convinced Rosie to sneak out of school yesterday and terrified us all, thinking she'd been abducted."

By the end of my abbreviated list of Cameron highlights (lowlights), Marigold gripped her cardigan in a clenched fist. "He is *not* a candidate for Bibliophiles Find Love."

"No," I agreed, pouring myself more coffee. Then something occurred to me. "Marigold," I said, "yesterday you showed Ven a dating application. Do you have Joe Darcy's?"

"Yes . . ." Marigold said cautiously. She rose and went to the sink to scrub a red-stained thumb.

"Could I *see* his application?" I asked.

Marigold fluttered like her pages. "I suppose there's no harm now. He won't be dating with us again. If you think it could help . . ."

I didn't know what to think, but I thanked Marigold.

She dried her hands, then rummaged in her bag. The three-ring binder seemed even more stuffed. *I'd be hosting blind book dates forever!*

Marigold drew out a page but seemed reluctant to hand it over.

Ms. Ridge reached for it. "I'll make a copy."

Marigold held it to her chest. "I'm afraid it's incomplete. You'll think we cut corners. The rest of our applicants filled out Lorna's about-to-be-trademarked book-focused psychological survey, just like we advertise. Her survey truly provides insight and invaluable matching."

I had little hope in finding truth from a dating profile, especially Joe Darcy's. I still wanted to see it. Lies were revealing too.

"I'll take it," Ms. Ridge said firmly.

With a sigh, Marigold handed it over. Ms. Ridge carried it to the copy/fax/printer over in the corner. According to my fanciful mother, the machine had multiple personalities along with its multiple functions. Mom contended it needed a soft touch, kind words, and time to itself.

Ms. Ridge pressed its buttons with force. The machine bleeped, flashed, and did her bidding. Ms. Ridge in efficiency mode was not to be questioned.

What the copier couldn't do, however, was spit out what I

wanted. Information. Revelation. Ms. Ridge handed me a page that was disappointingly sparse.

Joe's name was given: Joe H. Darcy. His company, JHD Financial, would lead to the stock-image website we'd already found. Ditto his supposed literacy nonprofit.

He hadn't listed a fiancée. No line for that, though.

I stared at the page. Under favorite reading genre, he'd written *Mystery*. Favorite author, Agatha Christie. Like running a kids' literacy foundation, those answers seemed so promising. Or too good to be true.

"Why didn't he fill in the full survey?" I asked.

Marigold aimed her stamp at pages and thumped with extra force. "Lorna wouldn't want me to tell you . . ."

All the more reason to say. I took a cue from Chief Sunnie and waited Marigold out.

Ms. Ridge finished her coffee, washed her mug, and issued a silent goodbye.

Marigold stamped until she ran out of both ink and resistance. "Okay, but can this stay between us?"

I remained silent.

My approach worked. "You're her cousin so I guess it's okay," Marigold said. "Anyway, it's nothing bad. It's romantic! But, you see, it wasn't exactly Lorna's algorithm or survey that did the matchmaking. Joe *asked* to meet Meg. Lorna advertised that she was related to the famous Book Chalet Christies. When he came in for his interview, he talked about the Book Chalet. How beautiful it was. How he'd seen Meg and she was so beautiful too. He really wanted to meet her, but said he was too shy to do it on his own. He wanted to get it right. Through books. See? Sweet?"

Famous Book Chalet Christies. That was nice. And my sister was undeniably gorgeous inside and out. But something was wrong.

"He'd already seen the shop?" Had he been here? Watching?

I thought about last year and another man who'd skulked in our shop. That hadn't ended well.

"Yes," Marigold said uneasily. "But everyone knows and loves the Book Chalet! He said it was the loveliest bookshop he'd ever visited. I agree! Books and love . . ." She touched her heart.

"He told Meg he hadn't seen the shop," I said. "She was going to show it to him on Sunday morning."

"Maybe he wanted a private tour?" Marigold suggested. "He was a romantic?"

He was a liar, but I hadn't discovered anything new in that.

Unless I had. It seemed unlikely, but maybe he had been telling the truth.

Could he have honestly fallen for Meg and his only lie was fibbing about seeing a bookshop? What if he wasn't engaged? Maybe Fiona was telling stories. Her colleagues had insisted she take a break. Perhaps they thought she was unstable.

I knew someone who'd have an opinion. "Marigold, do you have a contact number for Waldon O'Grady?"

She looked up from glumly clipping pages. "I do! Ellie, I'm so glad! Dr. Waldon reached out last night and asked if he could have a date do-over. He's so scholarly and important too. He's taking over the theater, I've heard. I know you said you were refraining from dates, but now that you ask. . . ."

"No, no," I insisted. "I don't want a date. I just need to talk to him. A friendly chat."

Marigold raised her heart stamp. "That's exactly what Professor Waldon wants too."

He did? I kind of doubted that.

"Just a conversation," Marigold continued. "He's afraid he was overbearing about Samuel Beckett on your last date." Marigold looked perplexed.

"Maybe a smidge," I said.

Marigold smiled. "He's a professor. That's his job. Here's the sweetest thing—he said that nerves make him over-profess. Isn't that cute? That's why he sent you the flowers. They are lovely, look at them!"

I saw thorns and thought about cemeteries and Stephen King. Then I calculated my options. I could say no. I already had. But then Waldon might very reasonably refuse to speak with me, and I needed to know more about Fiona Giddings.

Marigold was saying, "We have an open table tomorrow night. One of our couples canceled. They were from out of town and signed up for our new book-romance package to re-ignite the bibliophile spark but then found out, well . . ."

That one-quarter of the previous dating party was murdered, another quarter was a prime suspect, and a third quarter droned on about Beckett? I supposed I should include myself in that dating disaster—the fourth quarter had skipped gleefully home, more thrilled with a date with her cat and a book.

"Of course, we could simply remove the table," Marigold said, "but we're hoping to look popular. Lorna says we need buzz. Better positive buzz."

Marigold twined her fingers anxiously. She looked so darned hopeful.

I *knew* I'd regret this. "Okay. I'll have dinner with Waldon. But just as friends, talking about books." And Fiona Giddings and hopefully a murder, a shoving, and a missing script too.

✳

CHAPTER 24

Déjà Date

Friday evening, velvet night draped the wall of windows. Marigold's paper bunting wafted overhead like constellations of hearts and words. Lanterns with faux flames flickered on three round tables and pine logs crackled. I sat across from a man in tweed.

Dr. Waldon reached for a toast square topped with goat cheese and a drizzle of honey. I raised my wine and realized I'd downed half the glass.

I lowered the Pinot and grasped for something to say. I knew the problem. Well, other than us failing to click. Waldon had promised Marigold he wouldn't speak of Beckett. I'd promised myself that I wouldn't interrogate him until at least the main course.

We'd already exhausted the most basic small talk. Weather: *sure is cold*. How our days went: *fine*. Road conditions: *icy patches*. Appetizers: *tasty*.

Waldon had eaten most of the appetizers, and we needed a more substantial topic. I reached for the booklet at the center of our table. Inside, our matchmakers had included the menu and bookish conversation starters.

"Shall we try one of the prompts?" I asked.

Waldon continued to chew, more extensively than a bite of toast and cheese required. He swallowed, reluctantly. He dabbed his lips, refolded his napkin, and sighed. "We *should*," he said.

I scanned the list.

What's your current read? Him? Beckett, for sure. Off-limits.

What's at the top of your to-be-read list? More Beckett, I assumed. I couldn't remember mine. My to-be-read stack was so tall, I used it as my nightstand.

Who is your favorite fictional character? Miss Marple. I already knew the professor's thoughts on her.

Waldon helped himself to the last breadstick.

Why was I waiting? I knew what I wanted to talk about. I replaced the booklet and asked, "How well do you know Fiona Giddings?"

He frowned. "Fiona? We work in the same department."

I tried again. "You went to see her. That was nice. It must have been out of the way for you."

"It was."

Nice of him to visit or out of his way?

Marigold floated by and refilled my wine. "Are you enjoying the ambience?" she asked, smiling up at her décor.

"It looks magical," I said.

"Hacked up books?" Waldon said with a smirk. "I appreciate the absurdity."

Marigold's smile faltered, then she waved a finger at Waldon. "Now, now, Professor, remember what you vowed . . ."

Way to call him out, Marigold! I hid a smile behind my wine.

Waldon's face pinched in petulance.

When Marigold moved on to another table, I returned to my interrogation. "Meg and I visited Fiona. We heard she's taking a leave from work?" I expected the shortest answer possible. A "yes" or apathetic shrug.

Dr. Waldon brightened. "She is. She resisted, but we all agreed it's for the best. She's not fit to manage students and the theater. I'll be taking over for the rest of the semester."

"So I heard. You'll be putting on the plays Fiona scheduled? *The Mousetrap*? It's one of my favorites."

Waldon snorted. "I wouldn't put my name to such . . ."

Fun? Entertainment? A cracking good mystery?

"Trifle. My students demand a play of more intellectual rigor."

"What's your play? A Beckett?" I watched him. For a second, he looked like a little boy asked about his favorite comic. Pure delight.

Then his face pinched up again. "I shouldn't say. But you must come see it. I *insist!*"

Marigold saved me from committing. She delivered salads and an encouraging smile.

When she'd moved on to Ven's table, I said conspiratorially, "You can tell me. Is it *Waiting for Godot*?"

Waldon was taking aim at a cherry tomato. He put down his cutlery. His eyes twinkled. "No, not *Godot*."

"Really?" Maybe I would go see it.

Dr. Waldon searched the room, spotted Marigold leaving, and said, "Since you ask, we'll be performing Beckett's *Endgame*. When it came out, critics praised it as the play *Godot* fans had been waiting for."

Godot fans, waiting for something other than Godot? Had Waldon just made a joke? A giggle escaped my lips.

Waldon looked like he'd found a lemon in his salad. Nope. Not a joke.

"Sounds delightful," I amended. "Why don't you tell me about it?"

He sighed. "Eleanor, I'm afraid I talked too enthusiastically about Samuel Beckett last time we met. I will not bore you with him tonight."

I raised my assessment of Waldon for his honesty and self-awareness. Except he just *had* to keep talking.

"Not *everyone* can appreciate Beckett. We should talk about something else. Something less challenging. Those questions in our date guide, perhaps?" Waldon eyed our centerpiece grimly.

I turned the booklet to him.

He read and smiled. "Ah."

Yep. I returned to a safer topic. Murder.

"You must have been surprised to see Fiona's fiancé Saturday night. When you encountered him outside the library?"

"I was not surprised at all. I didn't know he was Fiona's fiancé. Later, of course, I was shocked. To think, he was actually real. . . ."

"Real? You mean you doubted whether they were engaged?"

Waldon waved a hand. "I doubted whether he corporeally existed. I wasn't the only one. Some in our department postulated that he was a fiction, a figment of Fiona's, how should I put it? Eccentric imagination?"

A forkful of salad froze midway to my mouth. "What do you mean?"

He shrugged. "One of our colleagues got engaged a few years back. She went over the top, if you ask me. It was gauche. Parties. Showers. Such build-up and drama for what's essentially a legal agreement. Fiona was enthralled. We postulated she invented an engagement of her own. It was a logical assumption."

"Logical?" None of that seemed logical to me.

"Yes. Entirely logical. Fiona refused to bring her betrothed to departmental events. She made excuses. He was too busy, too important, too devoted only to her. . . ." Waldon pointed his knife at me. "In all the time we'd known her, Fiona hadn't had a serious relationship. Suddenly she was 'engaged' to an entrepreneur and philanthropist?"

Such collegial support. I felt indignant for Fiona's sake. The problem was, my moral high ground was underwater. I'd thought pretty much the same thing. So had Lorna.

Waldon meticulously dissected his salad. I mulled and found a flaw in *his* story. "But surely you heard her talk about him. You knew his name? Why didn't you recognize that?"

"Joseph is a common name."

"Darcy?" Waldon was an English professor. Surely the name Darcy would draw his attention.

The professor shrugged. "I have little interest in such things. Our administrative assistant, Delphine, may know. She's wildly fascinated by mundane personal matters. You might say she's nosy. You'd get along."

Laughter rose from Ven's table. I heard Meg's and my names amid the giggles.

I turned. Ven's date wore a flashy suit and equally high-end smile, which he raised in my direction, along with a wink.

"Oops!" Ven swung around. "Were your ears ringing, Ellie? This is Amir. He's a hotel developer. London, Dubai, Tahoe, Last Word . . ." There was the slightest slur to her words, wine on her breath, and likely wild dreams in her realtor's heart.

I prayed for Amir to be a sentimental, looking-for-love romantic in the cutthroat world of hotel development.

Amusement flickered across his handsome face. "Venessa was telling me, you and your sister are super-sleuths. Here in this little village?"

"They are. They're probably investigating right now," Ven said. "Is that why you're here, Ellie? Scoping out suspects?" She raised her wineglass in salute.

"What's this?" Lorna appeared, presumably to refill water glasses but I knew better. She'd been keeping an eye on me. "What's Ellie doing?"

"Enjoying a delicious meal," I said firmly.

"I should hope so," said my cousin. "Bookish connection! That's why you're here, right, Ellie?"

"Absolutely," I vowed. *And to talk about murder.*

Lorna beamed at Ven and Amir, then swooped over to the young couple on our other side.

"Oops," Ven whispered. "Sorry for blowing your cover." She giggled, not at all sorry.

"No cover to blow," I fibbed. "I'll let you enjoy your meal." I nodded to Amir, who was already doing so.

When I turned back to Waldon, I found him eyeing me with smug satisfaction. "So that's why you're interested in our Fiona? You think you can solve a murder?" He leaned over the table. "I can help you with that. I've been reading Agatha Christie."

* * *

Marigold interrupted to deliver our main courses and their lengthy backstories. Chicken from a ranch over the mountain, cooked in local cream and white wine. Haricot verts with Colorado garlic. Potatoes grown in the high-altitude valley to the south.

During her recitation, I imagined what Waldon might have read. Had he come around to the ways of Miss Marple? Been impressed by Poirot?

"Enjoy!" Marigold said.

If talk turned to Christie, I thought I just might.

Waldon arranged his linen napkin. He leveled knife and fork above the chicken.

"Agatha Christie had it all wrong." He took a bite and let me chew on that.

I bit back a sigh. A free meal was never free. "Oh?" I said mildly. "How do you know?"

"As I said, I read Christie. After the police visited, I decided to see if their plodding approaches to crime intersected."

Plodding? Chief Sunnie with that ear-flapped cap covering the best little gray cells around? Sam Ibarra, bounding like a mountain goat to my unnecessary rescue? Most absurd of all, Agatha Christie, plodding? Never! Her books frolicked in mayhem, death, and misdirection.

"Which books did you read?" I asked, a much more polite question than "Are you kidding me?"

He dabbed a napkin to his lips. I guessed Poirot. He had a Poirot-like fastidiousness.

"Miss Marple," he said, again proving that I shouldn't make assumptions. "Short stories. Basically, an elderly woman sits around. Her friends tell her stories they think might perplex her. Predictably, she solves them. Just like that." He snapped his fingers.

"*The Thirteen Problems*," I said. The book Meg had wanted to share with Joe. He *said* he'd been interested. Now I doubted everything about him. I wished Miss Marple were here to help.

"Not that." Waldon shook his head.

"It has another title too," I said. "*The Tuesday Club Murders*. That's Miss Marple's group of friends. They get together on Tuesdays for dinner and to discuss perplexing crimes or puzzles. There's a wonderful new series that pays homage to it. A group of retirees examine cold cases. *The Thursday Murder—*"

Waldon interrupted. "The title's not important. Agatha Christie was wrong, and thus so were the approaches of her detectives. It's to be expected."

I gazed up at the flickering faux flames. Pages softly wavered, like butterfly wings. Why had I let myself be tricked into thinking Dr. Waldon O'Grady would change?

"Agatha Christie had no formal education," Waldon was saying. "Certainly she had no training in literary critique and analysis. She was basically homeschooled, by herself." He tutted disapprovingly.

"All the more remarkable," I countered. "Her mother didn't want to teach her to read until she was eight. Agatha learned by herself at five. She loved a challenge. You know how she came to write mysteries? Her sister, Madge, told her she couldn't do it. Agatha proved her wrong."

"Mmm . . ."

"She had an innate understanding of human nature," I continued. "As did her sleuths."

Dr. Waldon laid down his cutlery. "But no firsthand experience in law enforcement. She was a woman, fantasizing at home, indulging in a hobby."

I gritted my teeth. "She based a number of stories on real-world crimes. She worked as a chemist in World War I. She knew a lot about poisons."

Why was I bothering to argue? Why did I even have to? No one ever critiqued Stephen King for lack of firsthand experience with possessed pet cemeteries and killer clowns.

"So, what's *your* approach?" I asked. We did, after all, have the rest of this dinner to get through.

Waldon sat back. "I could offer instructive concepts from Beckett."

I gestured for him to proceed. We'd both ditched our dinner vows. Murder and Beckett were back on the table.

Waldon steepled his fingers. "As you *might* know, Beckett examined the tropes of the detective story and turned them on their head. For instance, was the victim even dead? Magnificent! I propose to do the same."

I could say with stomach-turning certainty that our victim was dead.

"Murder is not logical," Waldon continued. "Therefore, it cannot be deduced by such, no matter what your Poirots or Marples say. Thus, *obviously,* the killer is the most illogical person possible, the most comedically absurd."

I stopped my eyes from rolling. Oh, please! That was his great revelation? "The least likely suspect? Every mystery reader looks for them. Or the most likely, who then seems the least likely." Personally, I liked to sit back and float along as a reader, letting the fictional sleuth do the heavy detecting work.

"Ah," Waldon said. "But I said most *illogical,* not most *unlikely.*"

That seemed to be splitting hairs.

He sipped more wine. "Your sister is too obvious."

Good. We agreed on that.

"You're a possibility," he said.

"Me? Why on earth would *I* hurt a stranger?"

"To get away with it?" His smile said he was only humoring me. "For the twist ending? But no. There's only one least-likely person of importance."

Person. That let Agatha off the hook. I waited.

"Me," he said smugly.

I nearly choked on a sip of water.

Waldon's lips quirked. An unlikely, unexpected sound came from his lips. A laugh. "You're asking yourself, did I do it? I have no motive and I will issue firm denials, but now you consider it a possibility. That's good. I *could* have. I'm smart enough to know I could get away with it."

But he did have a motive, an absurd, convoluted one. He'd taken over Fiona's theater. Would he kill Fiona's fiancé—basically a stranger—to get her to step down?

I recalled our first date. Waldon and Joe, entering the library. Waldon, grumbling that he could have hit Joe, unable to brake quickly on an ice-slippery street. Unless he hadn't wanted to brake . . .

Waldon patted his lips. "Yes . . . Fresh thinking, that's what you need."

I was thinking I liked boring, Beckett-professing Waldon a whole lot better.

He waved his knife toward me. I forced myself not to lean back.

"I also have a clue. The trite, common kind, like your Miss Marple would enjoy."

I narrowed my eyes, suspecting a trick.

Waldon smiled. A true, delighted grin that wiped years and arrogance from his face. "I visited the theater a few weeks ago.

I was inspecting the stage, and I overheard Fiona yelling in the back."

He was right. Miss Marple feasted on eavesdropping delights. "What was she yelling?"

Waldon kept his tone level. *"Where's my ring? I know you took it."*

I sat back, shaken.

Waldon said, "Like I said, she's dramatic. I might have thought she was practicing for one of her plays, but when she met me out front, I could see she'd been weeping." He smiled. "Real tears. Our Fiona isn't that good an actor."

✳

CHAPTER 25

Deep Reading

The next morning, silence thrummed from the Reading Lounge. The Saturday Slow-Depth Readers were midway through their hour-long read. Every other Saturday, a group of three to twenty members met to read together.

Each member chose their own book. They never discussed their reads. In fact, no talking was allowed, or distractions of any kind. No phones. No checking of email. Even gazing out the wall of windows was discouraged—a true test of will.

Their mission was meditative. Each word was to be savored as slowly as possible, sometimes several times repeated. Their organizer touted the many benefits to mental and physical health and, most of all, to reading enjoyment.

Someday, I'd join them—preferably during a week when real-life murder and mysteries wouldn't derail my reading concentration.

I strolled slowly along the center aisle, gazing down each row, meditating on all the stories and worlds their books contained. At mystery, I stopped to greet a shop landmark, a marble bust of Poirot. Mom had found him at an antiques store years ago. She'd gotten him for a good price because one side of his immaculate mustaches was chipped.

I stood by Poirot and we listened to the silence, which was really quite loud when you paid attention. Cuckoo clocks ticked. The cash register dinged, the sound of a book going to a new home. And . . . the softest of sounds coming from the lounge: delicate snoring.

I knew that snorer. Gram was a Slow-Depth Reader.

Her snores were soon overtaken by footsteps as subtle as a moose tromping through autumn leaves.

An arched bookshelf filled with tomes the color of a rainbow trimmed the entry to the Reading Lounge. Glynis Goodman marched through it. She clutched a book and her rustling purple parka.

She stopped beside me and Poirot and raised a shushing finger. "I'm breaking the rules." She eyed Poirot like he might judge her and nodded farther down the aisle. Two rows down, she ducked into Fantasy and Flights of Fiction.

"What's going on?" I whispered. Around us, shelves rose to the ceiling, crowded with books of all sizes. Sagas the size of cement blocks. Wispy chapbooks of celestial poetry.

Glynis glanced over my shoulder. The row hooked to a dead end and a secret reading nook with the comfiest armchair in the shop, cleverly disguised in faded floral upholstery, a sagging seat, and scuffed clawed feet. A floor lamp with an amber shade tilted beside it. A curtain in gold velvet could be drawn partially across.

Earlier, I'd been back here to reshelve a space comic.

"The nook is empty," I said.

Glynis grinned. "Not for long. I *need* to finish my book. I had to leave. Deandra was about to call me out."

"She'd speak?" Deandra was serious about the hour-long code of silence among her readers.

"She'd give me the silent eye," Glynis said. "That woman can stare you down like a mountain lion. No blinking. All the while, you get the idea she's not really there—she's still in her book."

Glynis—who'd faced down the wild and death—shuddered.

"But I'm almost at the end. I have to flip pages. I *need* to know what happens."

I understood. I ushered Glynis to her nook and returned to the lobby. In the window, Agatha meowed. Agatha has many meows. *Feed me. Admire me. Let me ignore you in your selfie. Wake up!* This, I interpreted, was her incoming-friend-who'll-feed-me-treats meow.

"Who is it?" I asked. A half block down, I spotted Meg.

I checked the nearest cuckoo clock. My punctual sister was over half an hour late.

"Sorry!" Meg said, when she bundled breathlessly in.

"No problem," I said, but I feared Meg had one. I bet I knew the problem's name too. "Cameron?"

Meg stuffed her coat into the lost and found shelf under the register. "Yes! He was waiting outside the house this morning in his car. He wanted to take Rosie skiing."

"Did you let him?"

"No!" Meg sounded appalled. "She's grounded! Not just by me. The school gave her detention for skipping out."

"They should give Cameron detention too," I said.

"I agree." She rubbed her temples. "I talked to her principal yesterday. He said I need a court order if I want to restrict Cameron from picking Rosie up. I don't want to go that far. What would my complaint be, anyway? That he's being nice?"

"Suspiciously nice," I murmured.

The cowbells clonked and chilly air swept in, along with a sunny couple. I recognized them as the young daters from last night.

"Did you enjoy your evening?" I asked, after exchanging greetings.

The woman took a moment, but then clued in. "You were there too. You and your date were so connected!" She patted her partner's arm. "We're already engaged but we went for the 'book ambience' dinner."

Her companion spoke up. "The lady who sold us the dinner package said it was the most exclusive dinner in town. She was right."

They'd returned to explore the shop in daylight. I warned them about readers, silent and hidden in nooks. They started their adventure by taking selfies with Agatha. Agatha obliged, treating them to her orneriest frown. No one dared tell Agatha that her frowny face was adorable.

Meg smiled. "Maybe Lorna really is on to something. And you? You and Waldon connected, eh?"

"We found a common topic of interest."

"What would that be?"

I may have mumbled.

"Murder?" Meg said. "I should have known."

"And sleuthing," I said. "Get this: Waldon, for all his highbrow protests, is a classic eavesdropper." I told her about the overheard argument about a ring.

"Interesting," Meg said. "Did you notice Fiona's ringless ring finger?"

I had. "Maybe it was petty theft? Like the chief down in Ridgeway suggested? But Fiona didn't seem convinced of that." I wasn't either.

Meg said, "So, did your Dr. Waldon, illogical detective, have any other clues?"

I told her about the invisible fiancé theory. It was a good lead-up to Waldon's most absurd proposal. "He says that Agatha Christie was all wrong," I said. "It's not the most unlikely suspect, it's the most *illogical*, which, by the way, is him."

Said in the daylight, the words no longer sparked goosebumps.

Meg frowned at me. "He was just being pompous, right?"

That question had spun through my fitful sleep last night. "Yeah, I think he wanted to seem clever. He's wrong, though. About Agatha Christie, of course, but also himself. He has a logical motive—far-fetched, but still a motive. He wanted Fiona's theater. Now that she's on leave, he has it." I told Meg that we were also invited to *Endgame*.

"An absurdist, one-act tragi-comedy," I said, paraphrasing Waldon. "The play *Godot* fans were long waiting for."

Meg laughed. "Waiting for—that's great! I'm also glad you're probably not dating a killer."

"We're *not* dating," I said. That, I knew for sure.

Customers arrived, looking for recommendations, my favorite part of bookselling. Meg held down the register and selected inventory. Every week, new books arrived in the world. So many reading temptations.

When I joined her behind the counter, I glanced at her laptop. I expected to see her browsing *Booklist, Kirkus,* or our favorite book clubbers and influencers.

Her screen showed a dome-shaped tent amid red-rock mesas and saguaro cacti.

"You're running off to the desert?" I asked.

"I wish," Meg muttered. "Actually, no, I prefer mountains and snow. I'm looking for Cameron's parents."

In the desert? Elaina and Holden Winfield lived in Palm Beach, where their gated community had the Florida equivalent of a moat. The Intracoastal Waterway on one side, ocean on the other.

"I know . . ." Meg said, reading my skeptical thoughts. "I called their housekeeper this morning. It took a lot of pleading and cajoling but she finally told me that they're *glamping* in Arizona. She claimed not to have the name of the resort." Meg clicked to another screen. "If you were Holden and Elaina, would you go for a Desert Star Glamping Dome with a king-sized feather bed or a luxury cave with *two* king-sized beds and an anti-gravity float tank?"

"If I were Holden and Elaina . . ." I shivered at the thought. The Winfields had that effect. They were chilly. If they didn't already live in Florida, I'd say they went to Arizona to warm up.

"Why do you want to talk to them?" I asked.

Meg sighed. "I need to know *why* Cameron's here. Cam's parents might know. He supposedly works for them and lives in their guesthouse when he's not globetrotting. I need to track them down."

"Someone ask for tracking?" Glynis trooped in, coat on, book clasped in her hand, glum look on her face.

"Did you finish?" I asked her. "How was the ending?"

She hung her head.

I'd read her book, one of the fun *Thursday Murder Club* series inspired by Miss Marple's Tuesday Club, the series I'd attempted to tell Dr. Waldon about. There were murders, obviously, but in the end, friendships and justice prevailed. Mysteries were uplifting that way.

"It's over," Glynis said. "No telling when the next one'll come out."

I understood that sorrow.

Glynis said, "Deandra was right. I should've read slower."

A murmur of soft voices filtered in. The Slow-Depth Readers filed past. Glynis moved behind the card rack, which failed to hide her six-foot purple-clad frame.

Conversations passed by. I caught some words. A man bragged of only reading two chapters. A fan of women's fiction one-upped him. "I read a single paragraph of only two lines."

"I read a single word," said a familiar voice. Gram patted her curls. She looked well rested, as well she should from a full-snoring nap.

Deandra brought up the tail end. "See you next time, Glynis?" she asked the card rack.

"I'll do better," Glynis mumbled.

"There are proven health benefits to meditative reading," Deandra said. "Lower blood pressure, enhanced calm and concentration."

They were probably still in hearing reach when Gram said, "Long naps have the same effect. You could try my approach, Glynis. I feel like I slept for days. I hope I wasn't snoring. . . ."

Glynis, Meg, and I assured her she never snored. Why ruin Gram's great naps with the truth?

Glynis turned back to us. "What's this about tracking? I need cheering up, something to do. You need someone found?"

I looked to Meg. She eyed Gram. "If I tell you, this has to be a secret—especially from Rosie."

"I'm fabulous with secrets," said Gram.

Right, like she was a silent sleeper. But this was a secret for Rosie's sake, as Meg was explaining.

Meg laid out her limited facts. "Here's all I know: They're 'glamping,' somewhere in Arizona. It'll be exclusive, and they have no cell reception."

"*Very* exclusive," I said. Some people paid big money to be cut off from the world.

"I'm on it," Gram declared.

Glynis considered. "I could try to help out. You say they're alive and well?"

"Alive," Meg said. "Not lost to themselves, only to me."

"Finding folks alive would be a treat," Glynis said. She told Gram how she might be handing off her body finding to a pro-tégé. Me.

"Ellie has many skills," Gram said kindly.

"But not body finding," I said.

Gram and Glynis smiled—whatever-you-say-dear sorts of smiles. They left together, chatting about their respective methods of tracking.

"Folks follow rivers," Glynis said. "They go downhill, thinking it'll get 'em someplace. I often look there first."

"I find that people are unfailingly predictable yet surprising," Gram said.

"Truth!" Glynis held the door for Gram, and they stepped out.

Meg chuckled. "What have I unleashed?"

"Research and information gathering," I said. And hopefully a few minds closer to finding out the truth.

✳

CHAPTER 26

Lies and Consequences

The Slow-Depth Readers set the tone for our Saturday. Hours passed by quietly, as midwinter days should. Readers dozed in the lounge and drifted through aisles, discovering, lingering, savoring their pages. Ms. Ridge wiped down shelves with a lemony dust rag. Agatha napped and snacked and napped some more. Meg and I worked mostly in silence, mulling real-life mysteries.

At half-past two, the door opened with a clang of cowbells. Gram, Glynis, and Marigold Jones burst in.

"We got 'em!" Gram proclaimed, raising a mitten-clad fist.

Marigold giggled. "No one can hide from Search and Rescue, a bookseller, and a librarian!"

"Dynamic trio," said Glynis.

Grinning, I greeted them. Meg, who'd been back in the shelves, heard the little celebration and joined us.

"Go ahead, Marigold. You tell the story," Gram said generously. "You found the phone number."

"No, no, please, Mrs. Christie, you tell them. You got the tip about the resort," Marigold urged. "And Glynis, you knew that K-9 trainer."

I blinked. What had they found? Why was a search dog in-volved?

"But Marigold, you used the *database*," Gram said with a touch of awe. "I could never have done that."

"Glynis could have," Marigold said. "Her girlfriend is a coder."

We had a politeness impasse on our hands, the big-reveal version of the four-way stop sign.

Meg had the solution. "How about we get some hot drinks and take them out on the porch? Then you can tell us sequen-tially?"

"Fine idea," Gram said. "Gals, I think we deserve whipped cream on our cocoa and chocolate sprinkles too."

"You two certainly do!" Marigold said.

"No, you, dear," said Gram.

Still in their coats, they bundled off toward the Coffee Can-tina.

Ms. Ridge drifted over. "I'll watch the register."

I felt bad leaving her out. "Would you like to join us? We can put out the bell for customers to ring." As a mystery-reader, I might suspect the worst in people, but I couldn't help believing the best in bibliophiles. Our inventory was unlikely to walk out the door during a short debriefing on the porch.

"I'm fine staying out of murder investigations," Ms. Ridge said, smoothing her immaculate work apron.

"This involves my ex," Meg said.

"I'm even happier to avoid that," declared Ms. Ridge.

We didn't argue.

When we'd settled on the porch at a table for four, Meg said, "So tell us in order of discovery."

No one else was on the all-season patio, where the current seasons were arctic drafts under a tropical sun. I'd turned on two heat lamps over Marigold and Gram. Burning heat and blasting chills made for almost temperate. Gram had kept her coat and hat on. Glynis was down to her shirtsleeves and basking.

"Glynis and I called Lottie Nez over at the police station first," Gram said. "She has family in Arizona. She called them and inquired about outrageously priced glamping resorts. Turns out they have one right next door."

"A home run on your first try?" Meg said.

"Nope, we struck out." Gram had called three more resorts. Glynis contacted a friend in the park service. From there, Gram moved on to members of her knitting club and Glynis drilled down to a K-9 dog trainer.

"Eventually," Gram said, "we arrived at the place we should have started."

"That's how it always is," Glynis said. "Once you find out where you need to be, you know where you should have been."

"Where's that?" I asked.

"The library," said Gram, nodding to Marigold.

Marigold practically glowed. "Glynis and Mrs. Christie had already done most of the legwork. We knew who *not* to call. I just had to look up resorts with glamping that allowed small dogs—your not-in-laws have a Pomeranian—"

Gram interjected. "One of the knitting club members knew that. The Winfields never travel without that little dog. Once they did and it bit its sitter and the pool cleaner."

Marigold chimed in. "Our clues. Glamping. No phone reception. Pomeranian accessible."

They clinked their mugs.

Gram lowered her voice, although we were alone except for sparrows flitting on a pine outside. "After each lead, I got on the phone and *lied.*"

Meg apologized for involving Gram in lies.

"Don't be silly, dear. Miss Marple had no qualms about fibbing for the greater good, nor do I."

Meg and I shared a smile. We had a term for Gram's sleuthing: Marpling. Like her fictional idol, Gram could find out a lot from behind a cover of knitting needles, gardening shears, or books. And, it seemed, through cunning deception too.

"Outstanding," said Glynis.

"Thrilling to observe," agreed Marigold.

Gram had a dollop of cream on her nose and resembled a devious, delighted elf. "I pretended to be the Winfields' house-keeper. I said I simply *had* to speak with them."

"She was wonderfully starchy," said Marigold.

"Right out of Agatha Christie," agreed Glynis.

Gram thanked them again. "I debated between fluttery and starchy. I decided exclusive resorts would respond better to a firm hand."

"My motto for most things," said Glynis.

"So?" I asked. The suspense was making me fluttery. "Did you talk to the Winfields? Do you know what Cameron's up to?"

Gram patted a napkin to her nose and smiled serenely. "No, dear. That's up to Meg. The Winfields have a spa appointment at three, at which time the nice young woman I spoke with will take a camp phone to them. It's a phone with better reception. I didn't need to know the details. I only wanted the number."

Marigold drew a long necklace from her coat and opened a pocket watch. "It's almost time! We wrote down the number, Meg." She pushed a ripped half of lined yellow paper across the table.

Outside, the wind kicked up. The sparrows flew off with a gust. A draft squeezed in and toured the room, fluttering the paper and reminding me of the page I'd tried to grab near Joe's body.

"What do I say to them?" Meg asked. My sister eyed the tele-phone number as she might a rattlesnake.

Gram reached across our table and patted Meg's hand. "I'm afraid that you, my dear, should stick to the truth. That's not always well received."

✳

CHAPTER 27

Camping Out

Gram, Marigold, and Glynis decamped to the Reading Lounge to warm up by the fire. Gram had an audiobook to "catch up on." Translation: She'd bookmark her spot and nap to soothing narration. Glynis wanted to get hooked on a new read. Marigold had more dating to plot.

Before Marigold left, she hugged me. "Thank you for participating last night! It went *so well,* don't you think? We're on a good path now."

I hoped so.

"I'll get out of your way too," I told Meg. She'd want privacy.

"Don't go, please," Meg said. "I need backup support. Holden is usually jovial enough, but Elaina's terrified me since high school. She'll answer, I'm sure. She's the enforcer of the family." She pushed back her glasses and checked her watch. "Five more minutes."

She turned to the windows and the wintery scene.

I lowered my eyelids and let the heat lamp carry me back to a summer's day that started off warm and sunny. Meg's would-be wedding day.

We'd decorated an arch and placed it in the meadow outside

the Reading Lounge. The air smelled of wildflowers, grass, and sun-warmed pines. Birds sang, and a hundred folding chairs stood on a patch of mostly level lawn, Dad's obsession for months before.

Holden and Elaina—always Mr. and Mrs. Winfield to me—sat front and center, stiff as marble statues propped in the tippy seats. With every minute their son failed to show, my limbs had turned closer to Jell-O. The Winfields stiffened until rigor-mortis-like rigidity had them standing, then leaving without a word.

"Will they even know what he's up to?" I mused. They surely hadn't clued in to Cam's plan to flee his own wedding. If they had, they would have saved themselves the front-row embarrassment. They could have saved Meg even more mortification and hurt.

Back then, when it became painfully clear that Cameron wasn't injured, lost, stranded with a flat tire, wounded by a wildlife attack, or ill—unless you counted frozen feet in July—Elaina and Holden Winfield wrote Meg a check and jetted out of Last Word. Their money more than covered the wedding but didn't come close to picking up the pieces.

"Probably not." Meg rapped her fingernails on the table. "They're not a share-y kind of family, but I don't know who else to call. I tried Sanjay earlier. He insists Cam's here to be an 'awesome dad.' If that was true . . ."

I checked outside for pigs with wings. Only the sparrows and an anxious squirrel who looked like he wanted to tell me something.

Was I making assumptions again? I'd jumped to the conclusion that Cameron was up to no good. What if he was telling the truth?

"Is Cameron having any health problems?" I asked.

Meg frowned but filled in the leaps of logic I'd left out. Okay, maybe not the flying pigs and messenger squirrel, but she reached the same point.

"What are you thinking?" Meg asked, a furrow etching her brow. "Cameron had a brush with death and it made him a better person? He is turning forty soon. . . ."

"Isn't forty the new twenty?" I'd been picturing more of a mind-altering tumor.

"Something to ask." Meg picked up her phone, drew a breath, and entered the number. Beeps filled the space, then silence, as if the phone also feared contact with Elaina Winfield. After a few seconds, scratchy rings blared.

"Hello." *Elaina.*

I sat up straighter. The squirrel did too.

"Elaina," Meg said. "This is Meg. Meg Christie, calling from Last Word. I—"

"Yes," said Elaina. "I was informed you would call. Is there a problem? My son and granddaughter are well?"

Meg rushed to apologize. "Yes, I should have said right away. They're fine. Everyone's okay, it's just . . ."

"Holden and I are at a *health* spa," Elaina said. "We went out of our way to be distraction-free."

Translation, Meg was a distraction. Well, so was their son! I mouthed "school" to Meg.

Meg nodded. "Cameron is here in Last Word. Did you know? He didn't tell me beforehand. I found out when he took Rosie out of school. I thought she'd run off with a stranger. The police were nearly involved."

The line crackled. I imagined sparks sent off by Elaina's bristling.

"The police? That sounds rash," Elaina said with stiff disapproval. "Rosie is happy to see her father?"

Meg shot me a frustrated look. "Yes, but . . ."

"Then why are you calling, Meg?"

Meg pinched the bridge of her nose. "Why is he here, Elaina? Why did he show up now? Your granddaughter and I deserve to know."

I issued a supportive two thumbs-up. Yes! Meg could stand up to starchy Elaina Winfield.

Silence stretched, as if Arizona had frozen over.

Finally, Elaina cleared her throat. "Now is not a good time for us."

"It's not a good time for us either," Meg said. "It's a very bad time, and I don't need more problems. Why is he here?"

In the ensuing silence, I communed with the squirrel. He twitched his tail and looked nervous. I agreed.

When Elaina spoke again, it was through a burdened sigh. "Holden and I are encouraging Cameron to take more responsibility in his daughter's life and his own. There are certain financial decisions and encouragements involved."

Meg and I raised eyebrows. The squirrel clasped its paws.

"Financial encouragement?" Meg asked. "You're bribing him to be a better father?"

A haughty huff blew through the line.

Elaina launched into talk of trusts. Revocable. Irrevocable. Their management and distributions. She could have been speaking Greek. No, scratch that. I spoke a few words of Greek. I could say hello, thank you, inquire about bookshops, boats, taxies, and directions, and order a delicious meal.

A murmur broke in. I pictured an anxious spa attendant with a tight schedule and the task of ensuring forced relaxation.

"Yes, yes," Elaina snapped. To us, she said, "Holden and I have stressed to Cameron that our family business requires a *responsible* and *worthy* heir."

Meg winced. I almost—*almost*—felt sorry for Cameron. He was the only child, the irresponsible heir. With frosty parents like the Winfields, no wonder he acted out.

"He hasn't been acting responsible since he got here," Meg said crisply. "He encouraged Rosie to lie to me and skip school."

The squirrel and I could have cheered.

Elaina huffed. The background murmurer made concerned sounds.

"I must go," Elaina declared. "We'll talk at a more appropriate time. Later, when Holden and I have returned home and Cameron and our lawyer can participate in the call."

The phone rattled and fizzed, as if Elaina had tossed it into hot spa rocks. Static followed, frizzling into silence.

"Them, their lawyer, and Cameron?" I repeated. "That'll be a fun talk."

Meg rubbed her temples. Then she straightened. "I'm going to speak with Cameron. I should have done this before. I had my head in the sand."

I gulped down the last of my drink and switched off the lamps. Giddy cold whooshed in.

"Then I'm coming too," I declared. "I'm your backup."

* * *

"Stomping off in a huff is great until you get there," Meg said.

Especially when you didn't know where you were going. Meg and I stood at the end of Moosejaw Lane, just a few houses up from Fiona's. The lane ended in a large roundabout and four chalets.

Meg frowned. "Rosie said he was renting a place at the end of the road."

"Eeny meeny miny moe?" I suggested.

My sister groaned. "Ring doorbells and ask if there's a man named Cameron around I can chew out?" said Meg. "Sorry, El. I rushed off without thinking."

"Happens to the best of us," I said. "Do you have his number?"

"I did . . ." Meg admitted. "He gave it to me and I tossed it in a recycling bin."

"Recycling's good," I said, ever supportive. "Okay, we can figure this out. Look for clues." What those would be, I wasn't sure. Sand from his latest beach retreat? A carriage drawn by massive mules? I was considering the time-honored snoop method of peeping in windows, when a clue trilled our names.

"Meg! Ellie!" Ven Upshaw waved from a canyon-side chalet to our right. "You're here to see Cameron?"

She trotted down the walkway, high-heeled boots clacking and oblivious to ice. She grabbed Meg first and swung her into enthusiastic air kisses. "Ellie!" she grabbed on to me. "You and your date were so *cute* together. What a teddy bear he is!"

A teddy bear who suggested he might be an illogical killer.

Ven said, "I'm here on business. Don't get the wrong idea."

"Wrong idea?" I asked. Admittedly, I wasn't at my sharpest today.

Ven patted her hat, an elaborate faux fur circle that looked like a koala napping on her head. "I was just showing Cam some listings. We're just old *friends,* reconnecting."

Duh! Of course. Ven and Cam were more than friends, or Ven hoped to be. Her lipstick looked freshly applied, except for a smudge on her lower right lip.

My sister smiled tightly. "So Cam's buying a house here?"

"He's interested," Ven said brightly. "I have some lovely properties, including an absolutely adorable cottage in your price range, Ellie."

Sure she did. And Agatha C. Christie could fly.

"I'm not looking," I said firmly.

"Meg?" Ven asked. "Are *you* interested? Now that Cameron's back, your living situation may change. . . ."

"No!" my sister said, also leaving no question.

Ven patted her koala hat and looked way more pleased than a realtor without a sales prospect should.

"You warned me to be careful," Meg said. "You should be too, of your heart. Cameron isn't the most reliable of men."

That was putting it politely.

Ven waved a dismissive hand. "People change, Meg. I'm not going to let past disappointments drag me down."

"What about Amir?" I asked. "He seemed nice." And handsome and wealthy.

Ven's face clouded. "He got called out of town. I also refuse to wait around. None of us are getting any younger." Her pocket buzzed. "Sorry, client calling! Live in the now, ladies!" With that, she trotted toward a Range Rover parked down the lane.

Meg sighed. "I hope she knows what she's doing. She always liked Cam. Remember how she'd flirt with him when we were in school?" She started toward the door. "Well, I tried to warn her."

"When do any of us heed warnings?" I said. Like us, visiting Cameron and expecting him to tell us the truth.

Meg knocked with extra force. I firmed my resolve. Last year, we'd untangled the motives of a killer. We could stand up to a man still trying to grow up.

✳

CHAPTER 28

Glass Houses

The front door was frosted glass. A ghostly blur appeared behind it, and Sherlock Holmes strolled into my thoughts. *The world is big enough for us,* he'd said. *No ghosts need apply.*

Yet here a ghost was, forever haunting Meg's life and relationships.

The door swung open.

"Hey, babe, want to show me another—" Cameron wore sage-green canvas pants and a navy mock-neck sweater. His hair was damp and it took him a moment to register that we weren't Ven. When he did, he switched on the high-voltage charm.

"Meg, Ellie, what a pleasure!"

"Cameron, we need to talk." My sister stepped inside without an invitation.

"Come in, come in," Cameron said, playing the gracious host. "I knew you'd come around and visit, Meg. And Ellie too. Double the delight."

I doubted that. As a kid, I'd sometimes tagged along on Meg and Cam's dates. Mom encouraged Meg to take me. Now I got why. I'd been the perfect age to act as chaperone spy, and Meg had been so young, or so it seemed now—ninth grade! Cameron would shoot me petulant glares when Meg wasn't looking. I figured one simmered now, hidden under his smiling, handsome mask.

He led us to a kitchen that resembled Fiona's, with different clutter. Pizza boxes formed an architectural structure by the trash can. Piles of protein bars, veritable troughs of electrolyte drinks, and apples escaping their bag cluttered the countertops. I recognized it as the mess of a temporary house-camp. Easy meals that didn't require loads of ingredients or cooking.

Cameron's stay in this rental might be temporary, but what about Last Word? On his island lay glossy real estate flyers, along with two mugs. Maybe Ven had been here solely for real estate. I glanced at the top pages and prices that used to make my eyes bulge. Now they seemed all too common.

Cameron caught me looking. "If only we'd bought here sooner, right, El? Could have made a fortune selling. I guess we left too soon."

Cameron sure had.

Maybe I had too. When I'd left town after high school, Last Word was just being "discovered" by the wealthy vacation-mansion set.

"Coffee?" Cameron held up a carafe.

"No coffee," Meg said. Fog clouded her glasses, reflecting her steamed-up mood. "This isn't a social call, Cameron. What are you doing here?"

He turned on his beaming smile. "What am I doing? Thought I'd do a little skiing this afternoon. Why don't you and Rosie join me? Rosie said she's shredding the slopes. Ven wanted to show me some properties, but I can put her off for *you.*"

My sister stiffened. "Rosie is grounded for skipping school. And properties *here?* Do you have that kind of money, Cameron? Will your trust pay for a million-dollar chalet? Will your parents?"

Cameron flashed a bright-white smile, ignored Meg's question, and poured himself a mug of coffee. "Ellie? Coffee?"

I accepted. I never turned down coffee.

"Milk's in the fridge," Cam said, his hosting apparently done. "Feel free to look around the house."

Translation: Feel free to leave us alone.

"I talked to your mother," Meg said. "She said something about trusts and a financial incentive for seeing our daughter?"

For the briefest of moments, an emotion flickered under Cameron's suave smile. Something dark. Irritation? Anger? Worry?

He recovered to smooth and changed the subject. "You talked to my parents, eh? How's the glamping? Can you picture it? I heard they have a temperature-controlled yurt with a private attendant." He said the last with a touch of scorn, as if he'd turn away such luxury.

"I'm not here to talk about your parents," Meg said tightly.

I backed away. Cameron had offered me free exploration of the house in exchange for getting lost. I might find something informative, and I could always hear if Meg needed me.

Mug in hand, I drifted through a living room furnished in vacation-rental lux. Leather sofas. A big-screen TV suspended on one wall, a life-sized photo of a longhorn on another. Light drew me onward and into a surprise, a step-down sunroom overlooking a grove of aspens. Sliding doors led to a deck, delightfully on flat ground.

Unlike our all-season porch, this room was posh, warm, and cozy, with designer leather chairs and a fireplace with a flickering blue flame. I was drawn to the other prominent feature: a telescope capable of spying on the moon, although it was aimed toward the woods.

I strolled over, closed one eye, and peeked through with the other.

The scene that popped up was so unexpected, I jumped back as if electrically shocked.

A nearby stand held binoculars and a guidebook to western birds. I set my mug there, gripped the telescope, and focused in again, careful not to move the lens. The scene was the same as before. Not a hollowed-out tree with a sleepy owl. Not a mule deer, elk, or squirrel. The telescope bored through trunks and branches to a kitchen three addresses down, but practically a neighbor thanks to a bend in the canyon.

A house I recognized.

Lorna and I had first stood there, looking for a tardy brunch date. Now Fiona was there. What was she doing? I watched with a sticky feeling of voyeurism as she yanked items from her freezer.

An ice tray, which she glared at, then emptied into the sink. Next, a bag of cherries, dumped one by one into the sink.

What did she have against ice and cherries?

Fiona dismembered two more innocent bags—organic vegetables?—and what appeared to be a box of Girl Scout cookies. If she tossed Thin Mints down the disposal, I'd race down there and intervene!

Maybe I should anyway. Fiona looked frantic, wild, desperate. She faced the freezer, one hand rubbing at her forehead as if in pain.

She had suffered a concussion.

I debated. I could run down there and check on her. Yeah, and then I'd be that character in horror films who trots out alone to check on thumps in the woodshed. Nope, I'd wait for Meg to finish her talk/argument. Speaking of which . . .

Silence filled the house. A sudden panic struck me, like I was a kid, discovering she'd been left behind.

"Ellie?"

I whirled. "Meg? I'm down here. The sunroom."

The spying-on-the-neighbors room.

Meg entered with a sigh as gusty as a mountain gale. "Let's go. Cameron's mother just called. There's no way he'll tell me now. I'll just have to keep Rosie safe on my own. Like always."

She turned to leave.

"Wait. You have to see this."

My big sister humored me. "What is it? A bird? Deer?" She smiled. "If it's a moose, we should call Chief Sunnie."

"We might have to call her anyway. Look."

I stepped back while Meg focused.

She drew a breath. "Fiona . . . ? Why's she pouring granola on the counter?"

So, Fiona had moved on to pantry items? I took up the binoculars and stepped to the window. "I didn't aim the telescope there," I said. "It was like that when I looked."

Meg made a disgusted sound and stepped back from the scope.

I'd just focused in on Joe Darcy's granola: organic coconut with flax. Meg was right. We shouldn't rubberneck at a personal breakdown. I moved the lens through the landscape seeking to redeem my conscience with a real wildlife sighting.

Here, there were loads of clues. Scars—dark and oval—ringed aspen trunks, evidence of winter-hungry deer and elk. Pinecone parts mounded under a squirrel's dining tree. Footprints big and small wove across the snow like embroidery. I followed one path so tromped it qualified as a wildlife interstate. It and smaller trails spoked to a common point. The backyard of the next house down.

Aha! I focused in on a wildlife smorgasbord. Seed feeders dangled from the deck, suet balls from limbs, and what looked like a corn crib, nestled under an oak. Birds flitted around their buffet. Chickadees and sparrows. A towhee, kicking a snow-free patch under a pine. I was about to show Meg—look, innocent bird peeping!—when a dot of red flashed.

I focused on the source, a camouflage-patterned rectangle the size of a box of matches. The red flashed again. A game camera, I guessed, activated by the towhee, who was kicking like a river dancer.

I was so engrossed in watching the bird, I didn't hear Cameron enter the room.

"Nice views, eh?" Cameron had a mug of coffee and a smile that didn't reach his eyes.

"Nice view of your neighbors," Meg said.

"Yeah, it's a wildlife party out there." Cameron stepped to the window. "Saw a fox just this morning. The neighbor puts out food. It's illegal but none of my business."

"And your other human neighbors?" Meg asked. "Do you watch them too? Like the person three houses down?"

"Never met the guy." Cam gave a nonchalant shrug.

His words zinged through me. *A guy.* "So, you saw *him*? The former resident is no longer living there."

"No longer alive from what I hear." Cameron gazed out at the forest. "Nice view up here. Ven says she has a house coming up for sale on Moosejaw."

"Cameron!" Meg thrust her fists to her hips. "A man was murdered. If you know *anything,* you have to say. Did you see him there with anyone?"

Cameron smirked. "Other women? Worried who your date was dating, Meg? I hear he got around with fiancées."

Meg huffed and turned to go.

"Hey," Cameron said soothingly. "Don't stomp off. You want to know what I saw? Let's have dinner. Just you and me, Meg."

He stepped to the telescope and put his eye to the lens.

"Funny what you see when you look into other people's lives, isn't it? You'll see, Meg. I'm on your side. I'll protect you."

* * *

Outside, the world seemed normal enough. A woodpecker knocked at a dying pine. The air smelled of woodsmoke, and the peaks sparkled.

I felt tippy, like my feet might start off in opposite directions. "What did he mean?" I asked Meg.

Meg stopped at the end of the sidewalk and wound her scarf tightly around her chin. "Who knows. Maybe he saw me the other night with Joe. That's not secret information. I told the police, and I certainly wasn't around for the murder."

"Of course not!"

But a worry nibbled. Cam wanted something. Money was on the line. His easy lifestyle too? "What if he threatens to say he saw more? You and Joe on the balcony?"

"The police know that too, El." Meg stomped down Moose-jaw. "He can't tell them anything new without lying. Unless he saw someone else, but why hold that back?"

The logic—or illogic—of Cameron Winfield wasn't for me to understand.

Meg said, "You know Cam. He always wants to *seem* like the good guy. Here's what I predict: he'll say he's doing me a huge favor by not telling the police I went out with Joe Darcy. Then he'll be miffed that I ruined his big heroic gesture by already telling the police."

Meg nodded toward the neighbor's house. "Like these folks feeding wildlife. He'll hold on to that bit of info in case it's ever useful. Say he throws a party and the neighbors complain about noise. He'll point out what a nice guy he's been for not tattling to Parks and Wildlife."

I slowed to study the house. It looked lived in rather than a temporary roost. A wire snowman waved from the front stoop. A sign reading WELCOME TO OUR NEST hung by the doorbell. The mailbox gave the name as "Redwings."

The name sparked recognition. Not of faces—I had a *terrible* memory when it came to people—but of book lovers and their genres. A jovial man who liked Cold War–era spy thrillers and photographic collections. A woman who special-ordered books written by her niece—until Meg and I started stocking the niece's backlist of culinary cozy mysteries.

Meg was grumbling about Cameron. "Does he think I'll tell his parents how great he's being so he can take his money and run off again? Although . . . if it stops him from messing with us, maybe I'd take that bargain." She huffed. "I'll have to have that dinner with him. Give a little so I can figure out what's going on."

"Did he explain anything before his mother called?" I asked.

"He said that *he* decided to come here. That it was 'time,' and his parents 'supported' him." Meg added skeptical quotes.

As we approached Fiona's, I said, "Do you think we should—?"

At the same time, Meg said, "We should stop and see—"

Sister syncopation. I finished our thoughts. "Fiona."

A woman in a glass house, currently tearing up her kitchen. She could be a killer, but she also might need help.

※

CHAPTER 29

Lost Sentiments

Fiona answered her door with a vacant look, a neon-orange bandage on her temple, and scissors gripped in a fist.

"You two," she said dully. "The book women."

The theater woman had aged a decade. Dark half-moons dipped under red-tinged eyes. Her corkscrew curls sagged.

"We were in the neighborhood," Meg said with assertive cheeriness. "May we come in?"

Did Meg not see the scissors?

"The house is a mess." Fiona reached her scissor hand to her hair, realized she was about to stab herself, and frowned. "Sorry. I was . . ."

She laid the scissors on the entry table. Mess sprawled across it. Ven's business card, slightly crumpled. Coins, keys, and the contents of a handbag. Lipstick, comb, compact, and wadded bunches of receipts.

"I'm a mess." Fiona assessed herself as if just now noticing. Leggings frayed at her knees. Her shirt in oversized denim had too many wrinkles and misaligned buttons.

"Maybe we can help," Meg said gently. "Have you lost something?"

Fiona shot a frown at me. "You said you didn't have my script . . ."

"We don't," I said. "But you're looking for something else, right?" *The Mousetrap* couldn't be hidden in a bag of frozen cherries. A ring, on the other hand . . .

"How did you know?" Fiona's voice dripped suspicion.

Meg smiled. "It just seems like you are."

Fiona led us through the living room, where sofa cushions lay scattered. The kitchen looked worse in wide perspective, like a twister had spun through. Or a madwoman . . .

Fiona gestured vaguely toward the tall chairs around the islands. We sat. I ignored protests from my still-sore backside.

"Do you want something?" she asked. "Water? I have sparkling water. Somewhere . . ."

"How about you sit?" I said. "I see some seltzers over there. I'll get them."

Cans of lemon soda lay among strewn slices of bread. I plucked them out and set them on the island.

"They should be still cold," Fiona said. "I just took them out." She threw up her palms. "You're right. I'm looking for something. It's driving me crazy! I'm sure it must be here. You know that feeling?"

Meg and I nodded.

"I once lost my keys holding them in my hand," Meg said.

"Remember when I lost Gram's clip-on pearl earring in the garden?" I asked Meg.

"Ellie was seven," Meg told Fiona. "We had a tea party in the garden, then noticed the missing earring. We trampled every flower looking for it. The pair was our grandmother's favorite."

"Did you find it?" Fiona looked interested, like us finding a long-ago pearl among peonies would give her hope.

"We did." Meg grinned at me.

Even all these years on, I still blushed. "Under a sofa cushion," I admitted. "We found it a few weeks later." After digging up part of Gram's garden and bringing in an uncle with a metal detector.

"We didn't trace my steps back far enough," I said. "I'd been on the sofa reading while Gram made our tea."

"*Before* . . ." Fiona looked thoughtful.

Thanks to Waldon, I could guess Fiona's lost object. I caught Meg's eyes and touched my ring finger.

Meg nodded. "Little things disappear so easily," she said. "Flash drives, necklaces . . ."

"Rings," I said, cutting to the chase.

Fiona blinked at us. "Rings? That's what I'm looking for. My grandmother's engagement ring."

"Not your own engagement ring?" Meg asked, voicing my surprise.

Fiona studied her sole ringless finger. "Both? Joseph designed a custom ring for me. He was going to use the diamond from my grandmother's ring. I rarely wore her ring. The stone was too big. Who complains about that, right? But the setting jutted up and I worried I'd snag it or lose the stone."

She swallowed, hard. "Joe's design was white gold with little diamonds surrounding my grandmother's, like a flower. He was so proud of it."

I thought she didn't seem exactly keen about dismembering her family heirloom.

"Then it went missing?" Meg prompted. "From your apartment at the theater?"

Fiona twisted her other rings. "I kept it in a box in my nightstand. I *know*, I know. Not a good place, but I liked having it nearby."

Her gaze turned to my fingers and their solitary ring, a twined silver band I bought in Ireland. I wore it on days that could benefit from good luck. I touched the ring and willed it to work.

Fiona's gaze moved to Meg's hand. "That's pretty too."

Meg's silver band featured a small inset stone that sparkled in tones of clear lavender to midnight purple.

"My daughter's birthstone," Meg said. "I got it when she was born. It's amethyst, just a clear quartz until iron is added. That's what I want for my girl. Strength. Inner beauty."

Fiona rubbed her eyes. "You understand, then. It's the *sentiment*. Not the stone or its worth, although my diamond could have paid my rent before I got the college job. I never would have sold it. It's all I have from my family. It *has* to be here."

Here. Where Joe had been living.

"You think Joe took it," I said gently.

Her lip trembled.

"I'm sorry," I said.

She swiped at a tear. "No, you're right. At first, I thought he'd taken it to get reset—as a surprise. He said he hadn't. He claimed I'd lost it and ruined his design."

Claimed. She hadn't believed him. "You argued," I said. And Waldon had overheard. But had he done more than listen? Waldon might dismiss Miss Marple, but he was a snoop, and any good snoop would have tried for a peek at Fiona's elusive fiancé.

Fiona confirmed the argument. "I feel awful about that now."

But she still thought he'd taken the ring. She was tearing up bags of frozen fruit looking for it.

My sister said gently, "Was there something else? Another reason you suspected Joe might be responsible?"

Fiona sniffled loudly. I scanned the mess for tissues. Finding none, I spotted a roll of paper towels behind a hill of loose granola. I rescued the roll and handed it to our hostess.

Fiona ripped off a clump and held it to her nose. "Money went missing from the theater account. I blamed my box office manager. She had access to the account. We had quite the blowout. She quit in a huff. Now I wonder . . ." She snorted into the towels.

Those little mouse feet pitter-pattered up my back. A box office manager would know her way around the theater, especially the antique ticket stall at the bottom of the stairs. She could have hidden there, waiting for her chance to retrieve the dropped script.

But why? Petty payback? Burglary and assault were far from petty. And murder? Could all the crimes lead back to the theater?

"What do you wonder?" Meg asked. I opened my mouth to repeat my speculations, then realized that Meg was addressing Fiona.

Fiona twisted the wad of paper towels. "I wonder if I was wrong. Joseph said it *had* to be her."

Ah, Joseph said, did he?

Fiona was saying that Joe also advised against going to the police.

Meg and I shared a glance. We wouldn't make Fiona say it, but she thought Joe took her theater money too.

Fiona sniffled louder. "Then I discovered a problem with my savings account. Someone stole my debit number apparently. I'm still fighting with my bank to make it right. Aren't they supposed to cover theft?"

Meg and I could only shrug.

Fiona rubbed her eyes. "I want my ring back most of all. That can't be replaced. Joe said I must have put it down somewhere and forgotten. I didn't. I *am* unorganized, but I didn't move my ring."

She stared out the doors to the deck.

I conjured a cold image. Fiona, fuming late on Saturday night, coming to town to resume the ring argument, finding Joe with Meg.

Were we sitting with a killer? I almost hoped that Cameron was up the street spying on us.

Fiona slapped her palms on the island.

Meg and I jumped.

"It was that note!" Fiona said testily. "If it hadn't put awful ideas in my head, Joe and I wouldn't have argued. None of this might have happened."

"What note?" Meg asked. "What did it say?"

Fiona shook her head. "I can't even be sure what it said. That's why I need my script back. What if the note was simply about the play, and I argued with Joseph over nothing?"

"Tell us," Meg urged. My sister's smile was warm, caring, encouraging.

I attempted a similar contortion. Like we were three friends, chatting in a torn-up kitchen. Meanwhile, my nerves danced around Fiona's words. *None of this might have happened? Like her, murdering Joe?*

"Ellie and I deal in books," my sister was saying. "We can assure you, people have wildly different interpretations of the same words."

I returned to known territory. "You never read the same book twice," I said. "The words are fixed, but you're a different reader every time you see them."

Fiona nodded. "Someone classical said that about rivers. You never step in the same river twice. Who was that?"

I resisted the urge to google a literary question and willed Fiona to return to the note.

She shrugged. "Why not? I'll tell you. What more can go wrong?"

Oh, so much.

"I held the annual open house at the theater about two or three weeks ago," Fiona said. "I found it after that. A note, handwritten in all caps stuck in my director's copy of *The Mousetrap.*"

Fiona was saying that the whole theater had been open to the public. She added, defensively. "It wasn't a free-for-all. My theater students were there to chaperone. That balcony can be dangerous. The railing's not secure. It's such a long fall . . ." She glanced at her balcony—solid yet still deadly—and shuddered.

Meg drew her back. "Fiona? What did the note say?"

She blinked at us. "The note? It said, 'He's not who he says he is.'" She held up her palms. "You *are* the right people to tell. You've seen *The Mousetrap*?"

"Seen and read," I assured her.

"You'll get why I thought it was about the play at first. We won't talk about it, of course."

Meg made a lip-zipping gesture. There was a tradition as long-standing as *The Mousetrap*. Audience and cast members— and especially reviewers—were asked to keep the plot twists and ending a secret.

Fiona said, "I was busy with the open house. I put the note back where I'd found it. The next day, I opened the script and saw someone had highlighted the page too. Pink highlighter, not a color I use. It was the scene where the character Paravicini tells the innkeepers—*you should know who sleeps under your roof.* In the margin, someone had written, *Who sleeps under your roof?* That's when I thought . . ."

"Joe," Meg said.

Fiona said, "I let him stay here for free. He paid at first, but later, after we were engaged . . . How could I charge him?"

"Of course," Meg said soothingly. "What did you know about him? His past?"

Fiona flushed. "I thought he was a busy businessman and philanthropist. But now I hear all these awful things. There's *you*," she said, pointing to Meg. "And those other women claiming to be his girlfriends."

She shook her head. "Joe told me he had some exes who wouldn't give up. I understood. I have an ex like that."

I raised my eyebrows. A jealous ex could be a great suspect. Meg inquired.

"You know him," Fiona said. "The police told me *you* went

out with him." She pointed to me now. "Waldon O'Grady? Watch out. You go on a few dates, and he'll assume you're a couple forever."

I decided I liked Fiona's chairs after all. They were so heavy there was no way I could topple over. I gripped the armrest and attempted to sound calm. "Waldon? You went out?"

She flicked her hand, as if ridding herself of a fly. "We had dinner a few times. And he'd sit with me at the cafeteria and invite himself to my office. He likes to talk about his own importance. When I met Joseph, I told Waldon we could be friends and colleagues only."

"How'd he take that?" Meg asked. I was glad she had. I was too scared to ask.

"Waldon wouldn't listen. He kept showing up and assuming I'd have dinner with him or see some play *he* liked so he could prove how great it was. Finally, I had to get rude. We haven't been friends since."

"Did you see each other at the theater?" Meg asked. "Work together?"

Fiona sniffed. "He'd show up to critique what I was doing. He never liked my selection of plays or my community outreach. I let other groups use the space. Choirs. Kids' productions." She frowned. "Well, I did. Waldon got his way, didn't he? He convinced the chair I'm unfit in my grief."

"Did he really never meet Joe?" I asked.

Fiona cracked a wry smile. "Complained about that, did he? No, I didn't introduce them. Why would I want to after Waldon started that awful rumor."

"What rumor?" I feared I knew.

"That Joseph was my fictional fiancé." Fiona shook her head. "Waldon had the whole department laughing at me."

"But why not show off Joe?" I asked. "Wouldn't that have shut Waldon up?"

Fiona scoffed. "Shut up Waldon? Is that possible? Joseph

said it would be more fun to make Waldon squirm, keep him wondering and envious. Anyway, Waldon would have come up with some ridiculous story, like I hired an actor, that Joe was too good for me. Too wealthy, too handsome, too perfect."

Her expression hardened. "You know what makes me so mad?"

I could think of a lot of things. She could too, apparently. Her hands fisted and I was glad she no longer had those scissors.

"Waldon O'Grady was right," Fiona said. "And now he has my theater."

✳

CHAPTER 30

A Heavy Knowledge

Fiona gazed at her fists like a baby discovering fingers. With marvel and delight. "You know what? I *am* mad. Thank you!"

She stood abruptly. Her chair tipped. I held my breath, waiting for the crash. Fiona caught the top rung. "I'm glad we talked this out. I feel so much better, but don't tell anyone. You won't."

An order, one I planned to disobey.

"That you feel better?" Meg asked.

"No! That I was tricked. I'm a professor. I can't be seen as a fool." She frowned at her trashed kitchen, then at us. "Okay. Thank you for coming."

Meg and I took that blatant hint and got up.

"But you'll call the police and tell them about the ring and the box-office manager and especially Waldon?" Meg asked. "It's important they know everything."

"Yes, yes, of course," Fiona said. "Bye-bye now." She herded us from the kitchen, arms held wide.

"Chief Sunnie will understand," I said, slipping into my coat. "She's kind and savvy and—"

"Uh-huh. Thanks again." Fiona stepped too close, forcing us back and over the threshold. She pushed the door closed.

"Take care and please call the pol—" The door cut Meg off. On the other side, locks turned.

Meg and I left in stunned silence. At the turn onto Upper Main, I felt we were far enough away to safely debrief.

"Joe took her ring?" I asked, dosing the words with disgust and incredulity. "Why? And her savings too? How did he think he'd get away with that? She was on to him."

Meg skated over an icy patch. "What could she do?"

"File charges, kick him out!" I bristled on Fiona's behalf. Okay, she could be a killer, but she'd been treated awfully.

"She'd have to tell someone first," Meg said. "You heard her. She's embarrassed to be a PhD taken for a fool. Doesn't she know her Shakespeare? 'A fool thinks himself to be wise, but a wise man knows himself to be a fool.'"

Meg paused at the ski center and we gazed out at the view. Skiers zipped down the slopes. Dusk settled in the valley. Soon, the peaks would glow in my favorite optical trick, the alpenglow, the special light that lingered after the sun dipped under the horizon.

"If Joe were still alive, he'd have sweet-talked her," Meg said. "Convinced her that she lost that ring, that he was Prince Charming. She's questioning him now because he can't talk her down. She won't call the police, I can pretty much guarantee that. She'd be happier if no one knew."

"We know." Chills brushed my neck.

How far would Fiona go to keep her embarrassment a secret? I checked over my shoulder, suddenly sure she'd be there, scissors in hand. The sidewalk was clear except for a giggling group of teenagers in ski gear.

"Then there's Waldon," Meg said. "Where's the line between persistent and stalker?"

That didn't help my chills. "I think he's bad with social cues." I reconsidered. "Or he doesn't care about cues and does what he wants."

"I agree with Fiona," Meg said. "Be careful around him." She took my arm and we started walking again. "I'd never tell you who to date, but maybe you shouldn't see him again until we're sure he's not a killer?"

"We don't have any plans," I said.

Except, at the end of our last date, Waldon had said he'd see me soon.

By the time we reached the Book Chalet, I'd made a decision. "I have Detective Ibarra's private number. I could call him, tell him what we just learned."

"Wonderful idea." Meg smiled at me. "I'd offer to be your backup, but I think you'll both be happier on your own."

"Oh, please!" I said, using Rosie's teenager tone. "I plan to talk about murder."

"Your go-to date conversation," Meg teased.

I rolled my eyes. This was definitely *not* a date. Still, I was relieved that Meg hadn't asked to come along. As a suspect, she shouldn't spend time chatting with a lead detective. But there was another reason too. Yes, I planned to talk about murder and Joe and Fiona, the box-office manager, and Dr. Waldon too. However, I'd also let the detective know about a potential witness with a magnified view. Cameron.

Meg couldn't do that. She'd look like a finger-pointing ex. Worse, if Rosie found out, she'd be livid. I sighed. I was putting one of my most treasured titles on the line. World's favorite aunt.

*　*　*

I retreated to my loft to call Sam Ibarra.

Book browsers and readers filled the shop. Ms. Ridge was taking a much-deserved tea break on the gusty porch, Meg held down the register, and Marigold and Lorna had commandeered the storeroom, plotting a happy hour like generals strategizing an attack.

Lorna's voice filtered up to my loft. "Stealth matchmaking,

Marigold. That's our tactic. Our clients think they're mingling, but really we're moving them into place. Like chess pieces."

Romantic pawns? I definitely needed firm plans to be else-where during that mixer. I kicked off my shoes and stretched out on my newest old acquisition, a pine-green velvet fainting couch salvaged from a friend's attic clear-out. The couch was a glorious Victorian mashup—part plush lounger, part scrolled wood throne. It fit perfectly under the dormer window looking out over the hamlet.

I ignored the view and stared at Sam Ibarra's card with his personal number on the back. He did say to call, for anything.

Down below, Lorna's voice rose in volume and excitement. "I have a surprise, too! You'll love it! Our new secret weapon. Love potions! I whipped some up this morning with essential oils and put them in the cutest little spritz bottles."

She chattered on about diversifying their profits.

Uh-oh . . . Was Lorna already shifting her business model? I wondered if Marigold knew to be worried. More worrisome was Lorna armed with oily potions in spritzing form.

A new sound pattered up the steps. Little cat feet. Agatha stopped on the top, spotted me, and bounded over to leap onto my lap.

"Are you my support crew?" I said to her. "We're calling your boyfriend."

Agatha purred and stomped out biscuits. I dialed and counted rings. One, two, seven . . . I was about to hang up.

"Ibarra speaking."

My index finger had been touching the end-call button. I yanked it away. "Detective. Ah, Sam. This is Ellie. Ellie Christie. From the Book Chalet and . . ."

And trouble on the cliff and the body and the failed flower alibi and the missing-now-found niece . . . That Ellie. Now with new clues!

He sounded amused. "I haven't forgotten. What can I do for you, Ellie?"

I had a shorter list for that: *Clear my sister. Catch a killer!*

"Meg and I learned some information," I said. "Could I meet with you? I could come to the station."

Why had I said that? No way did I want to return to the dying-lavender interview room. Before he could take me up on that convenient offer, I blurted, "Or we can meet somewhere nicer?"

A chuckle. "Nicer than the station? I suppose there are such places. You're at the bookshop?"

I was.

"Do you have dinner plans?"

I did not, other than mooching off my grandmother. One of these days—when the killer was caught and Rosie wasn't grounded—I'd get my act together and host my family for dinner.

I admitted to no plans.

"Perfect," he said. "How about I buy you dinner? You name the place."

That sounded an awful lot like a date. "Wouldn't that be against regulations?"

"I'll be off duty."

I countered. "What if I bought *you* dinner?"

A chuckle. "That sounds like bribing an officer of the law."

An off-duty officer, I might have argued, but my stomach rumbled. I wanted dinner. Even more, I needed to unburden myself of heavy information. Agatha looked back, her cinnamon face in full frown. *Yes,* I silently admitted. *It would be nice to see Sam Ibarra again too. Somewhere other than a crime scene or interrogation.*

He was asking about my favorite place.

I thought fast. Somewhere casual, cozy, and private. "Do you know Cliff's?"

His words carried a smile. "My favorite. When do you get off work? I'll pick you up."

✳

CHAPTER 31

Just the Facts

Back at the mule-drawn carriage disaster, Sam Ibarra had empathized with Rosie about bad timing. He sure knew what he was talking about. The man had perfectly awful timing.

No, scratch that—I did.

I was outside, locking up the Book Chalet, when a rattling two-toned pickup pulled up. That would have been perfect timing, except I had company.

"Look, it's that handsome detective," Marigold said, as Sam got out.

"Ooohh . . ." Lorna crooned. "Ellie! Perfect timing! I have a new love potion you can test out. Here, let me get it . . ." She rummaged in her purse.

The truck wheezed and clicked. The wind kicked up a howl, and a dog barked down the way. None of these noises would have stopped Lorna's words from slicing through Sam's burgundy knit cap and on to his eardrums.

At least I could stop her search for the potion. "No," I said through clenched lips. "No potions. We're meeting about the murder."

"Well, get that solved so you can talk about something nicer." Lorna waved. "Detective! How sweet of you to take our Ellie out to dinner tonight. I was just telling Ellie how lovely she looks."

Not exactly. Lorna had been interrogating me about *why* I was "dressed up" and looking nice.

What did that say about my usual attire? I was dressed for Cliff's, a log cabin that masqueraded as a locals' dive bar and served up the finest comfort cuisine around. I wore jeans, woolly-lined boots, and a sweater, pretty much my standard uniform. But, also, fresh mascara and hoop earrings, which had likely tipped off Lorna's matchmaking senses.

"Lovely," agreed Sam Ibarra and dimpled at me. "Shall we, Ellie?" Wisely, he hovered near his truck, well beyond Lorna's air-kissing and love-potion reach.

If we acted fast, we might escape Lorna's matchmaking clutches. I started for the truck.

Lorna blocked me. "Detective, Marigold and I are planning some *fun* matchmaking events right here at the Book Chalet. Happy-hour mixers! We'll let you know the time and date."

"Lorna," I said. "Detective Ibarra is investigating a murder. He doesn't have time."

"Then you better get moving," Lorna said, stepping aside.

That was too easy flashed through my head moments before a cool mist hit the back of my neck.

Lorna waved a spray bottle. "Have a magical night!" she trilled.

Sam rounded the truck and held the door for me. He sniffed as I got in.

"What did she spray on you?"

I inhaled and my nose wrinkled. Rose petals, hot pepper, and something metallic.

"Nothing to worry about," I said and hoped that was true. If I found love, I wanted it to be real, not provoked by a potion.

* * *

Cliff's Log Cabin was a family affair, like the Book Chalet. Gram referred to the current owner as "that nice young man." Wayne Cliff was in his early seventies, by my estimation. A waitress named Honey on the late side of sixty showed us to a booth.

"Nicest table in the house," I said, when we'd slid in on opposite sides.

"Reserved just for you, hon," said Honey, and handed us plastic menus I could recite by heart.

Sam looked slightly bashful, like he'd been caught out. "I called ahead."

I was glad he did. Our corner nook looked out over the valley. The base village twinkled below. A moon just shy of full cast the pines in silhouettes.

Sam ordered lemonade.

I told Honey I'd take a moment.

"Don't let me stop you from something stronger," Sam said. "I'm driving you home and then myself down the mountain. Have a beer, wine, one of those famous cocktails."

Cliff's made "old-fashioned" cocktails, but not the trendy type found in urban bars. Their concoctions included ingredients like evaporated milk, pickle juice, and splashes of beer. I might smell like a potion, but I wasn't going to drink one.

When Honey returned, I ordered a glass of white wine. We both got Cliff's specialty, green chile cheeseburgers and onion rings.

If this were a date, I might have forgone a stack of fried onions and a burger dripping with hot chiles and molten American cheese. Or maybe not. If I'd learned anything from my bad dating record, it was that people should be true to themselves and truthful about their motives.

With that in mind, I said, "Meg and I visited Fiona Giddings again today."

Sam raised an eyebrow and an onion ring. "Visited or went looking for clues?" His granite eyes glittered, even under Cliff's dust-dulled lanterns.

"Both," I admitted. I waited for him to repeat Chief Sunnie's admonishments about staying away from crime.

He didn't. Instead, he gave me the perfect opening. "Why? What made you go back to see her?"

Cameron's peeping-Tom scope! But suddenly I felt reluctant. What if I did get Cameron in trouble? How big a crime was withholding evidence or obstructing a murder investigation? Trouble for Cameron would mean pain for Rosie. On the other hand, I wasn't about to obstruct a murder investigation for the sake of Meg's flighty ex.

Sam sat back in a padded bench, watching as if my internal debate was playing out on a reel.

"How about this?" he said. "You tell me about your day, a simple chronology, step by step. Where you went. Who you saw. What you learned. No interpretation." He smiled. "Just the facts, ma'am."

I laughed. "What show was that from?" I could remember books, but I was lacking in classic TV trivia.

"It's associated with *Dragnet*," he said. "People think it's Joe Friday's most famous line, except he actually never said it." He grinned sheepishly. "My granddad loved that show, and it's still a good line."

It was. I could get behind just the facts. I fortified myself with onion rings and did what I'd hopefully never do on a real date. I droned on, through every step of my day.

Sam took down Cameron's address. He listened patiently while I told him how I'd seen a towhee and sparrows, paths through the snow, and the red wink of a camera's eye in the neighbor's backyard. I recited each detail in a neutral monotone.

He was clearly interested in some facts more than others.

Sam narrowed his eyes as I described Fiona tearing up her house, her missing ring, and her dealings with Waldon.

He outright frowned when I told him about my second date with the Beckett professor.

By the time I got to the part he knew—me, calling him—our dinners were long gone.

"Dessert, hons?" Honey swooped in with a smile crinkling her wrinkles.

The man across the booth raised an eyebrow to me. "Will you help me with a skillet apple pie?"

After unloading all that information, I deserved a treat. "Yes! With ice cream?"

He dimpled. "Good plan."

"Two spoons and a skillet, coming up, hons." Honey tottered off.

My dining companion studied the night outside the window. After a long while, he turned back to me. "Sorry, I'm being a bad dining companion, aren't I?" He shot me a dimple. "I did say, though, if we ever went out, I'd ask all about you."

I grinned. "You sure heard about me. What about you? What did you do today?"

He considered. I guessed he was tallying up what to keep confidential, professionally as well as personally.

Honey arrived with a tray. Two bowls and three spoons, one the size of a shovel. "Ice cream on the side," she said, plunking down the bowls. I'd expected that. Nothing was allowed to mar Cliff's crackling crust.

Honey deposited a sizzling skillet between us and ordered us to enjoy. Spiced apples bubbled under a golden topping that was a closely guarded family secret.

Gram had sweet-talked the recipe from Cliff. The secret: pour caramel over the pastry before baking.

"What?" Sam asked, lip quirking up. "You look like you're holding back."

"A pie secret," I said. "I'll never tell."

"Maybe someday you'll reconsider." He graciously gestured for me to serve myself first.

The sugary pastry crackled. I scooped out perfectly baked apples, spiced with cinnamon, cloves, allspice, and a dash of cardamom (Gram also snagged that secret).

"My day . . ." Sam Ibarra sat back in his booth seat. "Well, I can tell you it started with my cat, waking me up at five-thirty-five."

I grinned and handed him the spoon. "Tell me all about your cat."

Saturday night in the best booth at Cliff's. Ice cream, pie, and a man who listened to my concerns and liked cats. This was still definitely *not* a date. But if it were, it had the right ingredients.

✳

CHAPTER 32

Sunday Hunch

Sunday mornings, the Book Chalet opened an hour later. This Sunday, I slept like someone who'd unburdened herself of just-the-facts to a handsome detective. Sam Ibarra would be on the job. I could linger in bed. Just a little. A half hour, after which I could read under the covers.

Tell that to Agatha C. Christie, early riser.

Four paws, impossibly heavy, pressed into my chest. Whiskers tickled my nose. A furry forehead met mine.

"It's Sunday," I groaned. Watery gray light filled the loft. Snow blanketed the skylight. My quilts were perfectly warm. I twisted to check the digital clock sitting atop my to-be-read nightstand. "It's only seven. Please? Half an hour?"

Agatha had a buffet of kibble downstairs. She wasn't starving, no matter what she said. I squeezed my eyes shut and pretended not to feel her stare.

A minute—maybe an hour—passed. Paws pressed. How did she make twelve pounds feel like fifty? A purr rumbled. I knew better than to peek. I was almost drifting off when Agatha sprang from my chest like an Olympic springboard diver.

Oof!

But the quilt cushioned most of the blow and was oh so warm and cozy. I could almost believe the lie I told myself. *Ha! I'd won! Sleep was mine!*

Right.

Agatha meowed from the fainting couch. No, not a meow. A bellow to which she added paws and claws scraping on window glass, a sound just shy of nails on chalkboard.

I groaned. "What is it? A bird?"

Agatha meowed again. Her attention-someone-is-here meow. That someone could be a sparrow. However, when Agatha paused to rest her paws, noises a sparrow couldn't make filtered in. A faint creak. A rattle and clonk. Cowbells? The front door?

Agatha meowed again. Translation: *Finally! A hero has arrived to save me from starvation!* Cat feet pounded down the stairs.

Meg had the day off. Ms. Ridge wouldn't be in until nearer to eleven. Who was here?

I threw on a robe and slippers and raced after Agatha. Only when I was halfway across the storeroom did it occur to me that maybe I should be worried and/or armed.

I scanned the room. Books, books, and more books. I wouldn't put them in danger. A broom might do. A tool from Gram's pegboard of book repair? A mallet or hook-headed hammer? That would require crossing the room and getting within swinging distance of an intruder. My eye fell on red. Waldon's cemetery roses. I pictured myself tossing them at an intruder's face like thorny mace.

"Shhhh . . . Aggie, shhhhh . . ."

I recognized that shushing. Thank goodness I hadn't tossed roses.

"Rosie?" I called. "Is that you?"

My niece stepped in with a look of chagrin. Agatha bounded before her, meowing her feed-me-now meow.

"Hey, Aunt El. Sorry! I tried to be quiet."

"No one gets by the guard cat," I said and rewarded my feline alarm with a packet of her favorite roasted duck.

My niece slipped from her parka. Her hair was mussed and she wore a hoodie multiple sizes too large.

"Have you broken out of house arrest?" I asked. "Do I have to call the authorities? You know this puts me in a loyalty co-nundrum. Favorite niece or favorite sister?"

Rosie pulled out a stool and sat in a slump. "Noooo . . . No conundrum. Mom's letting me out for jobs. It's not fair, you know."

"The world of work?" I teased. "Yep, totally unfair unless you do what you love." I was lucky. I adored my job. I dearly hoped Rosie would have that. Lorna too, although I was beginning to think that searching was Lorna's passion, like Glynis and the thrill of the hunt.

I held up a container of baked goods. "Muffin? They're homemade."

Rosie laughed. "Gram's homemade."

"Best kind."

Rosie chose chocolate with caramel chips—cake disguised as breakfast. I picked blueberry crumble—breakfast cake with healthy blueberries and streusel. I zapped them in the micro-wave, put out butter, and got the coffee going.

"It's not fair that Mom won't give Dad a chance," Rosie said. "He's really trying hard."

Oh dear. I hadn't had coffee yet. I'd *never* have enough coffee for this conversation. "Relationships are complicated," I said. So trite, so eternally true.

"Whatever," Rosie mumbled through a mouthful of muffin. She twisted to check a cuckoo clock. A teenager, checking old-fashioned ticking technology. I deduced that Meg had confis-cated Rosie's phone.

"So where are you working?" I asked. "The Ski Center?"

Rosie covered a yawn. "Yeah. Brutal! The bunny-slope kids get lessons before opening. But I came up even earlier to see you." She paused to allow me to appreciate that.

"I'm honored." I was. Rosie was a teenager, able to sleep past noon. Even without Agatha's four-paw alarm, I would have been awake sooner than I wanted.

Rosie frowned at my attire. "I didn't wake you up, did I? Gram and Mom are up, like, before the sun. I tried to keep those cowbells quiet!"

"You didn't wake me." I nodded to the furry culprit, polishing off her gourmet breakfast. Then my pre-caffeinated brain clicked on an incongruity. "You came in the front?"

"Ah, yeah . . ." Polite teenager-speak for *duh*.

I knew she'd come in that way. What perplexed me was the *why*. The front locks required two keys and were persnickety— "high-spirited," my mother called them. We usually came in through the back if the shop was closed. Did Rosie even have front-door keys? Teenagers considered keys ancient relics. I couldn't see her willingly carrying around a bundle like an apartment manager.

She wriggled on her seat. "Can you keep a secret?"

I *could*. The question was, *should* I? I waited her out.

After barely five beats, Rosie groaned. "I lost my keys. I borrowed Gram's extra set. I don't want Mom to know. Anyway, they're not *lost* lost. They're probably at Dad's or maybe here or I don't know." She shrugged. "They're somewhere. Someone'll find them."

Lost keys, with a murderer on the loose. My stomach tightened. Rosie apparently hadn't made that connection. Just as well.

"Do they have your name on them?" I asked.

"Nah, just my library card. Oh, and an old ski pass. I think they're at Dad's. Mom says I can't go there until they 'work things out.'" Rosie's massive sigh predicted when that might happen.

I added lost keys and *someone* finding them to my list of problems. Were we up to thirteen yet? Would Miss Marple please stop by to sit by the fire and solve them?

I turned to a mystery I hoped Rosie would clear up immediately. Why was she here, visiting me, before her already too-early work hour?

"Is there something you want to talk about?" I asked.

Rosie broke her muffin into acorn-sized chunks. "I only have two hours of bunny-slope classes. Then I have to go back to house arrest. Unless I have another job. Can I come here and work after? Mom said it was up to you. I'd do anything!"

A happy reason! Plus, the coffeepot was beeping its success. I heated milk in a mug.

"Anything?" I asked. "You'd clean the top shelves?"

She wrinkled her nose. "Yes."

"You'd remove dead moths and dust motes? Scrub bathrooms?"

Full-face wrinkle but a nod. Rosie was desperate to get out of the house.

I grinned. "Take glamor shots of the shop and Agatha and help me with social media posts?"

"Awesome!" My niece beamed. "That'll take all afternoon. We need the right light."

"Absolutely." And I needed some happy niece time.

*　*　*

I'd invited a niece. I got a photographer more exacting than a prima donna director of a couture fashion shoot.

"More light on Poirot's mustaches," Rosie ordered. "No, the other mustache. Up a little . . ."

We stood by the mystery aisles. I held a whiteboard, onto which I beamed a flashlight that then cast diffuse light on our bust of Poirot. The great Belgian detective sat on his pedestal, which put him approximately at my chin height. Rosie had found another stand with a broad top. It stood beside Poirot and would soon hold one Agatha C. Christie.

I moved my board and light until Rosie said, "Okay, hold that. Right there. Don't move! I'll go get Agatha."

My right arm held the flashlight over my head. My left arm extended the whiteboard just right so light reflected on Poirot. Both arms ached. Doubts bloomed.

Agatha had a cat's sixth sense for humans wanting her to do things. She responded with doing what *she* wanted, usually just the opposite.

"This is absurd," I told Poirot.

"The very definition. How fabulous!" A tweed cap appeared over the top of my whiteboard.

Of all the times for Dr. Waldon to visit. Not that anytime would be ideal. I thought of Fiona's warning. *Be careful around him.*

"Hi, Waldon," I said. I lowered the board slightly. "Have you come for a book?"

He held up a satchel of scuffed tan leather. "I have come prepared with my own."

At the Book Chalet, we celebrated reading. We championed a motto of read-what-you-like, discover, explore, relax, get lost in a book. We never pressured our visitors to buy. We hoped that perusing first chapters—and second and third—would do the selling for us.

But to bring his own books to a bookshop?

I noted a thermos poking from the bag and guessed he was also forgoing our Coffee Cantina. So much for supporting his local bookshop.

"Ah," I said, unable to muster much enthusiasm.

"We should have—" he started to say.

Rosie, thank goodness, cut off whatever Waldon was about to propose.

"Cat influencer, coming through! Lighting assistant?"

That was me. I raised the board.

Waldon covered his nose, grumbled about dander, and scuttled toward the lounge.

Agatha perched regally on Rosie's shoulder. I had a disloyal—but totally reasonable—thought: *This is never going to work!*

Once again, I was proven wrong. Rosie, smart girl, sprinkled cat treats on the pedestal. Then she plunked down Agatha.

"Action!" Rosie raised my cellphone.

Agatha nibbled kibble. When she was done, she sat up, bestowed a smug frown upon us and Poirot. She then raised a back paw, flashed Poirot, and proceeded to groom her undercarriage.

"Brilliant!" I exclaimed. This was going great! At that moment, Agatha flexed her toes, wobbled, overcorrected, and leaped to Poirot's shoulders.

Agatha and Poirot teetered. I dropped my lighting gear and grabbed Agatha. Rosie saved Poirot, and in the end, we were all safe and laughing. Except for Agatha, who wriggled to be let down, then jumped back to her original pedestal.

Rosie snapped photos of Agatha pretending like she'd intended every move.

"Best shots ever!" Rosie crowed. Then her face creased in a frown.

I turned. We had an audience. Chief Sunnie and Sam Ibarra looked on with amusement.

"Miss Christies," the chief said, nodding to us all. Rosie, me, and the feline queen. "We're hoping to ask you a question or two. Ellie, is your sister here?"

I looked to Sam. His face had hardened to all-business granite. I mentally revised. This wasn't a visit from Sam who ran with donkeys and woke to a twenty-pound tabby, but Detective Ibarra, investigating serious crimes.

"It's Mom's day off," Rosie answered defensively. "She needs a day off!"

"It's okay, Rosie," I said. "How about you get some photos ready? Instagram won't know what hit it later."

My niece folded her arms across her chest, a picture of stubborn. She wasn't going to be brushed off that easily.

"Maybe you can both help us, then," the chief said. "Rosie, we're looking for your dad. Any idea where he might be?"

"Dad? Why?"

I bet I knew why. Because *someone* had tipped them off about his telescope. My cheeks warmed. My heart sped to trotting. I didn't want Rosie to know that someone was me.

"Rosie," I said. "Could you go watch the register?"

"Why?" my niece repeated, aiming the question at the detectives.

"We're just talking to folks," said the chief with an easiness that set me on edge. "Folks who may have seen something important but don't realize it."

Or they did know and were holding back for some selfish reason. Would Cameron really hinder a murder investigation just to force Meg to have dinner with him? A murder investigation in which she was a suspect? I knew what the answer should be. Of course not!

Of course he would!

"What would Dad see?" Rosie demanded. "He didn't know the dead guy."

But he'd seen him. I edged close to my niece. I would have put an arm around her, but she looked as prickly as Dr. Waldon's cemetery roses.

The chief smiled. "That's what we want to know, Miss Christie. I've found that people mix up what they see. Takes us asking them to repeat themselves. Then we can decide what's important."

"Just the facts," Sam murmured.

I shot him a smile. "Cameron is renting a place on Moosejaw," I said. "Or maybe he's skiing?"

"We went to the Moosejaw house," Sam said. "No one answered the door. Neighbors reported that he threw a duffle in his trunk and drove off this morning, early. No mention of skis. Any idea where he'd go?"

I looked to Rosie. Her stony expression rivaled the detective's. They'd get nothing out of her.

I had an idea where Cameron might be, but I wouldn't say it in front of Rosie.

"Officers," I said, "why don't you come to the storeroom with me? We have customers." *And gossipers and a bristly niece.* I turned to Rosie. "Would you do me a huge favor and help Ms. Ridge out front?"

She scowled. She and I both knew that Ms. Ridge was just fine.

"More work hours . . ." I said in a too-obvious attempt at a bribe. "We'll need help all afternoon."

"Fine," Rosie muttered. She plucked up Agatha and trudged toward the front.

I led the officers to the storeroom and closed the door. They took seats on the same side of the table, declining my offer of coffee. I leaned against the counter by the sink.

Chief Sunnie said, "I spoke to Cameron Winfield a few days ago. He neglected to mention he'd seen the murdered man."

For something to do, I grabbed a dishcloth and swiped at an already clean countertop.

"Mr. Winfield was aware that Meg went on a date with Joe Darcy," Chief Sunnie continued.

Also not a question, but I affirmed that Cameron had known, both about Meg and Joe Darcy's other relationships. That reminded me. "Have you found Joe's other fiancée?"

A smile flickered on Sam's face. He'd caught me changing the subject again.

"We found her," he said.

His pause gave me time to fantasize that they'd found her here in town, ready and able to murder her triple-timing ex.

"Found her in Costa Rica," Chief Sunnie said. "She's at some kind of nature resort."

I sagged with disappointment.

The chief read my reaction. "Yeah, lucky for her, as she's not exactly broken up about his death. In fact, she was going to go raise a mai tai to it."

"Why?" I asked. "Did he steal from her too?"

"Active investigation," the chief said curtly. "We can't divulge that."

I bet he had.

The chief smiled, a sign she was getting serious. "Right now, we're interested in *clarifying* Cameron Winfield's earlier statement. I need to ask again. Did you or your sister know Mr. Winfield was in town before the mule-and-carriage show?"

"No," I said. "We had no idea."

"So," the chief said. "Neither of you could have told Mr. Winfield about that double blind date in the library?"

"No, how could we? None of us knew he was here except—" I caught myself and spun to the sink, under a poor ruse of washing out the dishcloth.

Except for Rosie, co-plotter in the world's worst wooing plan.

"Mr. Winfield's rental vehicle got a ticket that evening," Chief Sunnie said conversationally. "It was parked a block from the library."

My heart leaped. "It's a small town."

The chief nodded. "Sure is. Nothing remains a secret for long." She leveled her gaze at me. "If we can't find Mr. Winfield, we'll need to talk to your niece. Do *you* know where he is?"

"No, but I have a place you could try." I described how Cameron had hidden out at Sanjay's cabin when he first got to town. "It's by Cresson Lake. I don't know the exact address but I'm sure you can find it."

The chief turned to Sam. "You know this lake?"

He nodded, "Jessie-Belle and I run hill-training over that way."

The chief smiled. "If we need an undercover operation, we'll send you and a mule."

"Donkey," Sam corrected rather archly. "Jessie-Belle is a standard donkey."

The chief dipped her chin in apology but didn't bother to hide her grin.

I smiled too. Last night, I'd learned more about the famous Jessie-Belle. She was gray with white spots. Her favorite treat was peanut butter pretzels. The best she and Sam ever finished in a race was fourth place.

Always the bridesmaid, Sam had said. *Never a podium spot.*

He met my eye and a dimple appeared. Was he thinking fondly of his running pal or of our dinner? When he'd dropped me off at the Book Chalet, he'd thanked me for the investigation tips and an enjoyable evening. I'd had a nice time too. So much so I'd let myself fantasize about the possibility of getting together again without me as informant. I warned myself to be careful. Sam seemed nice, but then, so had Joe. The detective could just be after my clues or sticking close to the sister of a suspect.

Chief Sunnie made motions to go. She adjusted her jacket, firmly secured her flap-eared hat, and nodded to her partner.

"Yeah," Sam said, as if she'd spoken. "Just one more thing. We talked to Mr. Winfield's neighbors, the couple with the camera. It has a data card, rarely swapped out. I downloaded it. We'd like you to take a look. See what you think."

He retrieved his phone from an inner jacket pocket, tapped the screen as if this moment had been planned all along, and held the phone out to me.

If I hadn't been leaning against the counter, I would have backed away.

"Go ahead," Sam said gently, practically putting the phone in my hand. "Scroll past the fox."

"Lovely creature," the chief said. "And that moose, my goodness. Now, there's a handsome guy. I have *yet* to see one myself."

"We could do a moose stakeout, boss," Sam said. "The homeowners say that young bull visits a lot."

They bantered about moose and snacks for stakeouts and wildlife.

I held the phone like it might reach out and bite. Heart thudding, I scrolled past wildlife—indeed, a lovely fox and handsome moose—and there he was.

"Cameron Winfield," Chief Sunnie said, unnecessarily. She couldn't see the screen, but she could interpret my horrified stare.

During the awful events of last November, she'd shown me another nighttime image. That had been so pixelated and dark I could tell myself the person in question was unrecognizable.

Not so with these photos. Cameron, bright and clear, hands in the pockets of a ski jacket, hiked down the well-tromped wildlife trail.

"Motion-sensing camera with high-quality night vision," Sam said, as if camera specs would make it better.

Chief Sunnie rose and joined me. With a stout finger she pointed out the day and time.

Earliest morning on Sunday. The day Lorna and I found Joe Darcy dead.

"Then he returns, you'll see, exactly thirty-four minutes later." The chief smiled at me. "I get it. I was told enough last year. Folks around here feel inspired by the great outdoors and go tromping around at all times of day and night. Still . . . Do you run with that donkey at night, Ibarra?"

Sam did not. "Jessie-Belle wouldn't want to risk her ankles, tripping on roots."

"Smart lady." The chief left my side to pace slowly around the table. "You ask me, it's dangerous for anyone in the woods at night. Can you think what Mr. Winfield was doing, Ellie?"

Oh, I could. I was a mystery reader. I could imagine just about anything. I pictured Cameron, stomping off to confront Joe, warning him away from Meg. Striking him? Shoving him? That dark path plunged on, all the way to Rosie. My niece could never outrun the label of Daughter of a Killer.

In real life, Cameron was a cad, but he wasn't violent. If anything, he was a coward. He ran from his wedding. He enlisted Rosie as backup for his surprise appearance.

I said, "He might have seen something at Joe's house and gone to check. He hinted as much to Meg. He likely didn't realize the seriousness and then didn't tell you because he was embarrassed."

Or he'd held back information in case he could use it for his own benefit later. That fit Cameron too. I trusted the detectives to get the truth out of him.

"He had no reason to hurt Joe Darcy," I said, as much to myself as the officers.

"Jealousy?" Chief Sunnie suggested. Her pacing had taken her to the ends of the storeroom. She paused to inspect Gram's pegboard of tools.

I addressed Sam. "He left Meg on their wedding day. Why would he care if she went out with another man years later?"

The chief answered. "Why would he rent an expensive house, take his daughter out of school, and hire a Christmas carriage? I'm no romantic expert, to be sure, but I'd call that making an effort, wouldn't you, Ibarra?"

"A big effort," Sam said. "Misguided, but huge. I might even say desperate."

They were quite a team. In sync with their timing. I handed Sam's phone back. The chief checked hers and cursed under her breath.

"What?" Sam asked.

"The moose," she said, head shaking with regret. "He's there right now with a girlfriend, the Redwings say."

Sam did a lousy job of hiding his smile. "Choices, choices . . ."

"No choice," the chief said with a sigh. "We need to talk to Cameron Winfield, ASAP."

She stepped to the door. "Thank you, Ellie. I'll admit, at first I thought you were steering us anywhere other than your sister." She chuckled. "Or trying to rid your sis of a pesky ex."

"No!" I protested. To the chief's raised eyebrows, I amended, "Okay, a little, but only because I know Meg didn't kill anyone." I opened the door, more than happy to usher them out.

Rosie stood at the threshold, Agatha frowning in her arms. "Neither did Dad! Dad wouldn't hurt anyone!"

My niece pushed past us, pausing only to let Agatha hop onto the worktable. She grabbed her coat from the rack and stomped to the back door. "I'm going home!"

I gripped the doorknob to stop myself from running after her. I couldn't lie to Rosie. She'd see right through me. I did suspect her father of lying, conniving, and holding back key information.

I turned to the officers. "The killer has to be someone else." Then I added words I never imagined I'd say. "Prove Cameron's innocence. Please!"

✳

CHAPTER 33

On the Hook

M s. Ridge and I closed up shop in the usual way. We
dimmed the lights and announced last call for book purchases at fifteen minutes before six. Customers stepped out
into the night, most with tote bags filled with books. A reader
raced to the mystery aisle. She'd started reading "just a page or
two" around mid-afternoon. Now she was hooked on her book
and wanted the other installments in its series. I rang up her
purchases while Ms. Ridge got ready to head home.

I was bidding our customer good night when I saw Meg
coming down the street.

I always loved seeing my sister, but worry panged. *What was
wrong now?*

"I spent all day at the house," Meg said, cheeks flushed with
the cold. "I needed some air so I rode the gondola up."

That should have soothed me. I sometimes took the gondola
just for fun, down the mountain and up again, watching the
sunset or the moon dance on snow.

Meg said, "I shared the ride with tourists. We talked about
snow and palm trees. Imagine, no murder! Maybe we should
hide out in the gondola until all these mysteries are settled. We
could give out book recommendations and trivia."

"Public service while hiding in plain sight," I said. It sounded lovely. A magical glass bubble where trouble couldn't find us. For an absurd moment, I imagined that's where Cameron was. Except he wasn't the sort to sit still and appreciate. He'd likely also forget to pack snacks and a book.

Ms. Ridge returned, dressed for a snowy winter's night. She stopped to greet Meg. "Is there anything I can do to help, Meg? Anything at all?"

"Want to take in a cranky teenager as a houseguest?" Meg asked. "Just for a little while? Say, until she gets a full scholarship to college?"

Ms. Ridge smiled serenely. Easy for her. She wasn't facing teenage wrath and college tuition.

"Rosie's a Christie," Ms. Ridge said. "She merely wants the truth to come out." She frowned out the window. "Snow's getting heavier. I better get home and beat Glynis to those sidewalks."

Meg, Agatha, and I gathered at the window and watched her stride off under streetlamps and dancing snowflakes.

"You know," I said, "I used to think that her beating Glynis to the shoveling was oblivious kindness, like Ms. Ridge was simply up early and wanted exercise and thought she was doing Glynis a favor."

"Oh no," Meg said darkly. "She's up early, all right, but there's premeditated competition going on there."

I had to smile. "At least they both know where they stand." I wished I did. I told Meg about the police coming by. "It's my fault they're looking for Cameron. I—"

Meg interrupted. "It's Cameron's own fault, El."

True. "But I told the police where he might be, and Rosie overheard. Does she hate me?"

"Oh my goodness, of course not!" Meg said. "You're her favorite aunt."

"I'm her only aunt."

"Beloved aunt, then. You did the right thing. I told Rosie about the telescope at her dad's house. I said he could be a key witness. A hero."

A hero. I wished I'd thought of that. "This is why you're the wise big sister and world's best mother," I said. "I did beg the police to arrest someone else."

Meg sighed. "That's more likely than hoping for a hero in Cameron Winfield."

I dimmed lights and went to sort out the register. I liked this time of the day, when the shop settled into quiet.

"You had a good Sunday," Meg said, watching me count bills.

"Snow in the forecast and gossip in the air will do that."

I recorded the day's take and moved the money to the antique safe that loomed behind the counter. As our New Year's gift to the shop, Meg and I had sprung for a full replacement of the locking mechanism. We no longer had to hold our breath, cross all fingers, and hope the safe felt like opening.

Still, habits die hard. I patted the safe and silently thanked it. According to our mother, the safe was "sensitive" and required praise and affirmations.

"Want something to drink?" I asked Meg. "Decaf? Tea? Warm apple cider with a cinnamon stick? We could sit in the lounge."

Meg smiled. "Hot apple cider sounds divine, but I'm due back for dinner. Come with me? Rosie isn't mad at you, El. She's grumpy at the universe, that's all."

Only the universe and a too-helpful aunt.

Still, I loved dinner with my family. I wanted to make it up to Rosie. How? By telling lame aunt jokes? Letting her beat me at chess or dominoes after dinner? Ha—as if I *let* her. She crushed me.

"Gram's making Swedish meatballs," Meg said.

How could I resist?

"I'd love to," I said. "But is it okay if I eat and run? Eat and

gondola? I want a quiet night in with Agatha. All this dating . . ." I'd had one blind date, a let's-be-friends meetup (with a
guy who might be a stalker and suggested he was a killer), and
a dinner that might have overlapped into police-informant territory. Hardly a dating whirlwind.

"Let me give Agatha some treats and grab my coat," I said.

A knock interrupted my plans. Make that, the sound of a
giant woodpecker attacking the front door. *Rap, rap. Rap, rap,
rap.*

I looked to Meg and mouthed "Hide?"

Too late. Figures appeared at the front window, cupping
their hands to the glass.

Meg unlocked the door to Lorna and Marigold. Lorna
swooped us into kisses. Marigold waved. A pom-pom the size
and color of a cantaloupe bobbled on her hat.

"I'm so glad we caught you! We drove up. I told Marigold, if
I floor it, we'll make it before closing."

"She did," Marigold said with tight laughter. "We made it."

Riding with Lorna at the wheel—even under non-flooring-it
circumstances—was scarier than any roller coaster. Roller coasters, at least, stayed on tracks. Lorna drove like she approached
her businesses. All out, veering and careening.

"We have exciting news," Lorna said. "Go ahead, guess what
it is."

I indulged in a moment of wishful thinking. *Lorna was going
to hold the dates at her place? They could return to the library? Lorna
had resumed her throw pillow business, this time with bookish images?
I'd buy armloads!*

But I knew the answer. "More dates?" Floundering hope
grasped for a life raft. "Next weekend?"

Next weekend would give me time. I could make firm plans
to be elsewhere. Gram's. Another town. A cabin in the woods.
The best booth at Cliff's with Sam Ibarra? Would he have any
interest if I wasn't doling out clues?

"Close," Marigold said, "but it's even better!"

Two weeks from now? Never again?

"Mixer Monday!" Lorna crowed.

"Monday?" I repeated. Today was Sunday. Monday was mere hours from now. "Next Monday?"

"Tomorrow!" Lorna patted my shoulder. "Cocktails. Mingling. Loads of fun conversation starters. We need to capitalize on our success. Leap on it! Look how great our last matchmaking session went. Perfect!"

Meg and I were supportively nodding like synchronized bobbleheads.

Lorna said, "We have great momentum going. No murders. No troubles."

I gulped back an anxious giggle and thought of those signs in danger-filled workplaces like mines or explosives factories: no accidents in X days.

Lorna was saying, "That awful incident with Joe had nothing to do with any of us. Fiona's fall proves that. All we have to do is keep up the positive image. Positive press!"

"We invited Piper Tuttle," Marigold said, clasping hands tucked in yellow and gold mittens. "She says she's very much looking forward to it and won't mention murder. She's signed up some friends too. From her book club?"

Meg rubbed her forehead.

"Mysteries," Marigold said. "That's our theme for the evening."

"But no talk of murder?" I asked. Impossible, not with their theme and especially not with Piper and her book-club friends from Mountains of Mystery.

Marigold frowned. "Well, we can speak of fictional mysteries. Those are the best."

Meg and I resumed our enthusiastic head-bobbing. Fictional murder was definitely better.

"We considered a treasure hunt," Marigold said. "What do

you think? Players would have clues to a mystery book. Then they'd hunt it down in the shop. I promise, we'd put everything back. Unless, of course, you want to make some sales."

"Win-win!" declared Lorna. "Always be selling!"

A shudder rippled up my middle. Cocktail-tipsy guests, racing around the shop pulling out books. Plus, sales implied that someone who worked at the Chalet would be around to ring them up. Like me. *I had plans.* I just didn't know them yet.

"Or bookish bingo?" Marigold said with a worried frown. "Would that be better? Or a more casual quiz. Folks can mingle in the lounge and move around to quiz questions as they like."

"That sounds great," I said. "Less competitive, lots of chances for interaction." So much better than running around pulling out books. Now that I'd complimented the idea, how would I get out of it?

"Oh, Ellie," Meg said, nudging me. "Too bad you have that *thing* tomorrow night."

My sister delivered this line in a stiff monotone. She'd never be an actor, but I could have hugged her.

"Yeah," I said, doing little better with the spontaneous fib. "Really too bad about that."

"What *thing*?" Lorna demanded. "Ellie, you *have* to be here! It's bad enough that Meg's dropped out." She held up a palm. "Totally understandable, Meg. But Ellie, I need you all in. Remember? Positive image?"

I murmured more regrets.

Lorna's boot tapped. Her eyebrow raised. She wanted details about my *thing.* So did I!

"Ellie's going out with that nice detective again," Meg said. "Right, El?"

Marigold beamed. "That's wonderful! Then we know where he's taking you!" She giggled.

A sinking feeling dropped all the way to my ankles.

Lorna patted her bouncy curls. "I spoke with Detective

Ibarra this afternoon," she said, ignoring Marigold's giggling shushing. "The detective is single, he reads, and he agreed right away to attend our mixer. Well, after consulting with his boss. That's either a red flag for mother issues or he's a good guy who follows the rules."

Meg cringed and mouthed "Sorry" to me.

Lorna was saying, "*He* thought our mixer was a splendid idea. You know, Detective Ibarra gave me his personal number after he took my statement about Joe. He said to call anytime, so I did." She fixed me with a your-move stare.

Remorse wriggled. I'd been caught out fibbing. I'd also been silly. I'd let myself think that Sam Ibarra made an exception in giving me his personal number. Because he was interested in my insights . . . or, to be honest, in me.

I studied my feet and mumbled.

"What's that, Ellie?" Lorna said, cocking her head.

She'd heard, but I owed her.

"How fun!" I said, forcing a bright smile. "I'll be here, then. Looking forward to it!"

Lorna looked as smug as Agatha after securing a third breakfast. "With a police officer in attendance, nothing can go wrong. Plus, Detective Ibarra is awfully nice to look at. Rugged! Look how he rescued you from that crime scene, Ellie. Good press all around!"

Ahem.

At the sound of a throat clearing, we all looked to one another. One by one, our heads shook. *Not me,* repeated four times.

The sound came again, this time with approaching footsteps.

"I shall be attending too."

Waldon?

The Beckett professor strolled in from the dark central aisle. "What . . . ?" I managed. What was he still doing here? I summoned Mom's good manners and said, "I'm sorry, I didn't know you were still here. We closed at six. I dimmed the lights . . ."

"I assumed you had electrical problems," he said. "I was engrossed in my reading."

"That's what we like around here," Meg said, covering for my clear unease. "What did you find to read?"

He'd *found* the book he'd brought from home.

He held up a biography of Beckett entitled *Damned to Fame*. "My personal copy. I was rereading the footnotes. Most delightful. One hundred and twenty-five pages of them."

Lorna beamed. "You and Ellie have so much in common!"

No! No, we did not.

Waldon tucked Beckett into his satchel, wrapped his tweedy scarf twice around his neck, and capped off his rumpled head with the brimmed hat. He looked ready to step out onto a wind-swept moor.

Or emerge from hiding in a darkened bookshop.

"Where were you?" I asked. "I checked the aisles."

"A most unlikely nook with a curtain and floor lamp at the end of . . . what is the aisle called? Flights of Fantasy?"

Meg smiled at him. "Fantasy and Flights of Fiction, but I like your version."

He gave a pleased nod, then touched the brim of his hat. "Eleanor, I look forward to seeing you tomorrow. We'll interrogate the detective. He won't see it coming." He gave a small bow. "Ladies."

As soon as the door shut behind him, I hurried to turn both locks.

When I returned, Marigold said, "He's sweet on you, Ellie, and such a serious scholar. Oh, but Lorna, maybe we shouldn't have invited the policeman."

Lorna flicked her hand. "Competition is good. This is what we want as matchmakers and daters. Ellie's playing one off the other, selecting her perfect match. Ellie, just remember, when it comes time to pick, give credit where it's due: Bibliophiles Find Love."

Meg's phone beeped. "Gram," she said. "We should probably get going to dinner, El." She frowned and scrolled. And scrolled some more.

Thanks to Rosie, Gram used an app that transcribed speech to texts. Which meant texts of epic length and sometimes scandalous mis-transcriptions.

"What is it?" I asked.

Meg read aloud. "Swedish meat baldies in oven."

Swedish meatballs. My stomach rumbled, and I grinned, enjoying the fun while I could. I feared bad news was coming.

Meg summed up. "The police found Cameron. He was at Sanjay's cabin."

Right where I'd sent them.

Meg sighed. "They took him to the station for questioning."

I braced myself. "Does Rosie know?"

Meg turned the phone screen to me. I stepped closer to read. "Lottie Nez says holding him for buttered noodles?" I frowned. "What? Noodles?"

"Keep scrolling," Meg said.

I frowned at the next lines: Gram what? The police took Dad? Send. Send!

"Ah," I said. "Rosie came into the kitchen and Gram tried to cover with talk of dinner?" Followed by urgent message sending. I could picture the scene, including my niece's stormy young face.

Meg shook her head. "Phones are always listening in now."

People too, including Dr. Waldon. How long had he been eavesdropping?

"On second thought," I said, "I think I'll stay in tonight. I need Agatha time." I didn't want to aggravate Rosie's bad mood.

"Chicken," Meg said, interpreting my cowardly-aunt move. "Can I hide out with you?"

If only. "Popcorn and denial party in the loft?" I offered.

Lorna had been following our exchange with a scowl. Her hand flew to her mouth. "Wait! Is Cameron under arrest? Meg, did *he* murder Joe?"

"Of course not," Meg said. "Cam's a potential witness. His rental house has a telescope. He may have seen something and didn't realize. You know how he is." She said the last part breezily, as if discussing Cam's absentmindedness, a man who misplaces sunglasses, car keys, wedding engagements, key clues to a murder. . . .

"Phew!" Lorna thumped her chest.

Marigold continued to clutch her lapels.

Lorna gripped Meg's arm. "You can tell us all about Cameron's witnessing on the ride down. Come along, Meg. I'm driving."

Meg shot back a look of trepidation as Lorna maneuvered her to the door. Marigold followed them out, with a parting wave to me. "See you tomorrow, Ellie! It'll be great! You have two dates!"

✳

CHAPTER 34

Mixing It Up

Once, Agatha Christie nearly missed a banquet in her honor. The event was held at the Savoy Hotel in London. Very posh. Exclusive too. A door guard failed to recognize Agatha Christie. Denied entry, the Queen of Mystery wandered the halls, anxiously wondering if she should just go home.

I *so* empathized.

Not that the party downstairs was in my honor. Nor could I rush home. I was home, pacing my loft. Oh, but I understood balking nerves chanting, *Wouldn't it be so much nicer to stay in?*

If I didn't get to the mixer soon, Lorna would come up and haul me down.

"We really need a door," I informed Agatha.

Agatha lay on my bed, smug with the knowledge that she'd soon occupy my pillow.

"A trapdoor," I said, glancing toward the spot where the stairs opened directly into my loft's plank floor. "We'll add a kitty opening."

Agatha scowled.

"Ellie?" My name trilled up.

Lorna! "Coming!" I rechecked myself in the mirrored doors

of my wardrobe. Should I change again? Was my sweater-dress and tights combo too formal? Too informal? Too warm? Too—

"Do you need help with makeup?"

Lorna would decorate me like a flocked Christmas tree. I had to get down there.

"Wish me luck," I said to Agatha.

She yawned and stretched, rubbing it in.

"You look lovely," Lorna said as I descended the stairs. "Here, you're only missing this." She raised her right hand. Her thumb depressed on a spray bottle before I could duck. Mist hit my neck.

"Musk," Lorna intoned. "With undernotes of vanilla, cedar, and old books. I'm calling it Paperback Passion. What do you think?"

"I think you shouldn't spray people without asking."

"*Pish.*" My cousin closed her eyes, touched her sternum, and inhaled deeply. On the exhale, she said, "Breathe, Ellie. Smell the paperbacks . . ."

I could smell paperbacks in any aisle in the shop. What I smelled now was musk, which Lorna had added with a leaden hand.

"Please," I said, "I'm serious, Lorna. No spraying around our inventory. Customers don't like their books to smell like anything except paper and ink."

"Oh! I have a scent for that too: vintage pages. There's patchouli and—"

I thrust up a hand, stop-sign style. "No patchouli. It's polarizing." Mom had gone through a patchouli phase when I was a teenager. I'd never seen my parents so divided.

Lorna chose not to hear. She grabbed my arm and led me to the lounge. At the archway, we paused to admire.

"Look at the crowd!" Lorna said with satisfaction. "I sold tickets at cost. I want to get folks hooked on subscription plans. True love doesn't happen overnight."

I murmured my agreement and took in the room. Nearly

two dozen people filled the lounge. Armchairs clustered in groups of two and four, interspersed with bar-height tables. Piper Tuttle and Mountains of Mystery members formed a half circle by the windows. They faced inward, eyes scanning the room. Waldon stood alone by the fireplace. No sign of Sam Ibarra. Maybe something had come up. Or he'd decided that the Book Chalet and Bibliophiles Find Love held no leads and thus no interest.

That would be for the best, I told myself. I had no business even thinking about relationships until I'd firmly relegated my past disasters to the history shelf.

Lorna squeezed my funny bone. "Ellie, remember, there's one key to success tonight."

Just one? I tried to guess. Smiling? Flirting? Refraining from destroying egos with my knowledge of literary trivia?

"Remember: You are *not* Glynis's protégé." Lorna looked me in the eye. "I've heard the talk going around town. No finding bodies, Ellie! Not tonight. We are rolling with our positive no-crime vibe."

"No crime, no bodies," I repeated, wriggling from her grasp. "I'll do my best."

* * *

"Agatha Christie poisoned pink gin," I said a half hour later. I raised my cocktail glass to Waldon.

He sniffed his with a look of disgust. "I can see why the victim didn't notice."

"Yep," I agreed too cheerily. "It's pure gin with a dash of angostura bitters for color. Sailors used to drink it."

Waldon curled his lip.

I issued myself a mental caution. Pink gin was dangerous. Not that I expected a poisoning. At least, I hoped not. But it was potent, and I'd been sipping too fast to fill awkward silences.

Waldon straightened his sports coat (tweed) over a woolly

sweater (heather brown) and said, "A pity that police detective isn't here."

I tempered my agreement. "Why?" Waldon surely wasn't attracted to Sam Ibarra's dimples.

"He could tell us about the case." Waldon swirled his drink and added, "But then, I doubt he knows anything enlightening. They're plods, the police. Unimaginative. A smart criminal could get away with so much."

"Oh?" Detective Sam Ibarra stepped up, looking anything but plodding in dark-wash jeans, leather shoes the color of port, a sweater in midnight blue trimmed with a band of abstract snowflakes in red and white. Steam rose from his mug, scented with cinnamon and lemon. A hot toddy, I guessed, probably the non-alcoholic version if he was driving and/or investigating.

"Dr. O'Grady," he said, turning to Waldon. "Take care when spreading unsubstantiated gossip. Innocent people can be harmed."

Waldon huffed. "Is that a word to the wise, Detective? I am a professor. I am not a *gossip*. Ellie and I were merely saying that the police have failed to produce results."

I hadn't said any such thing.

The detective winked at me. "We're moving along nicely, I'd say."

My cheeks warmed. Just when I'd convinced myself that Sam Ibarra was only after my clues, he brought out a wink and words I couldn't interpret. I turned to a safe subject. "Have you tried any of the quizzes, Detective?"

"Please, just Sam," he said. "I'm off duty."

Waldon sniffed. "You won't know the answers. They're all obscure trifles only a pulp-fiction reader would guess."

Only fans of mysteries and Agatha Christie.

"I'll try my luck." Sam reached for a booklet decorated in a collage of Agatha Christie covers.

"What was the occupation of Agatha Christie's second husband?" he read aloud. He smiled. "Police detective?"

Waldon scoffed. *Yet, he hadn't known earlier.*

I dropped a hint. "He did dig up dirt. . . ."

"Gravedigger?" Sam grinned.

"Close enough!" I exclaimed, ignoring Waldon's huff. "He encountered some tombs. He was an archaeologist, Max Mallowan. Agatha Christie met him through friends and a journey on the Orient Express. He was about thirteen years younger than her, but devoted and true."

"Nice," said Ibarra.

"After her money," muttered Waldon.

Waldon was wrong. It had been true love. To Sam, I said, "Agatha assisted with his archaeological digs. She wrote several books based on their travels, mysteries and nonfiction too."

"I'd like to read those," Ibarra said. "I enjoy travelogues."

Was that the heart of the Book Chalet, thumping along with mine?

Marigold fluttered up to us, looking quirkily cute in a mustard skirt and sweater set with leaf-green tights. "Is everyone having fun with the quizzes?"

Sam and I said we were.

Waldon muttered about inconsequential trivia.

"Oh, well . . ." Marigold said. "I'm sorry, Dr. O'Grady. You're a serious scholar. These questions are just for fun. Speaking of which . . . did you happen to receive my email about the annual children's shadow-puppet performance? For Easter? Fiona Giddings let us use the theater last year. Can we schedule with you?"

"No," Waldon said curtly. "Puppet plays are not appropriate. The theater is for scholarly endeavors only now."

Marigold went pinker than the gin. "Of course, of course . . . We'll ask the elementary school or a church or . . . Well! I should check on other couples."

I frowned at Waldon. Couldn't he let some kids have an hour at the theater?

He raised a haughty chin. "Eleanor, shall I get you another drink?"

"A hot toddy?" I asked. I glanced at my nearly empty gin glass and added, "Non-alcoholic, please?"

Waldon departed.

"Is he always that good-natured?" Sam asked.

I checked that Waldon was out of earshot. "I think the trivia game set him off. He didn't get any right. He likes to have all the answers."

"That would be nice," said the detective.

I was about to read another trivia question, when his attention shifted.

"There's a surprise," Sam said, nodding toward the archway. "Your cousin invited Cameron Winfield?"

I gaped. My mind did the talking, with appropriate indignation.

Cameron. Here? At a private event in our bookshop?

I registered the woman possessively gripping his arm. *With a date?*

But that date might explain his presence. "Ven Upshaw probably invited him. I doubt Lorna would." Lorna had urged Meg to cut off Cameron's buttons all those years ago. My cousin might be flighty with her business endeavors, but she was steadfastly loyal to family.

I looked around the room, wondering if anyone else had noticed this shift in the mixer. A silly thought. The Mountains of Mystery members stared at Ven and Cameron like a school of ogling fish.

Ven steered Cam toward the drinks table. He wore a smarmy smile and a mock turtleneck in a pale oatmeal color that highlighted his tan. Ven was adorned in hoop earrings the size of bracelets and a silky top made for literal navel gazing.

During our just-the-facts dinner, I'd told Sam about Ven visiting Cameron's rental house. A "work" visit, or so she'd said. Now I elaborated. "Ven's liked Cameron since high school. She joined a biblio-match date here the other night, but that man's out of town, so . . ." I let the detective fill in the rest.

"Ah." His tone was mild, but he watched the couple with interest.

If Sam Ibarra were Miss Marple, what links would he be knitting? I asked, "Did Ven tell you she texted Joe Darcy the night of his death?"

If only Joe had responded . . . Meg would be off the hook. Joe might be alive. Except Ven had flirtatiously invited herself to his place. If she'd gone over, would that have stopped the crime or would we have two murders?

I wondered if Ven had allowed herself to think of either possibility. Maybe that explained her bold determination to get out, live life, and date.

"She told us," Sam said and stopped at that.

I took the hint. He might be off duty, but he was on the case.

So were the Mountains of Mystery book-clubbers.

"Incoming," I murmured to Sam as four women and three men swept across the room like an inquisitive tide.

The detective at my side took a step backward.

Piper reached us first. "Do you see those two? In an Agatha Christie mystery, one of their cocktails would be poisoned."

My stomach tightened. "Don't even think that, Piper," I chastised.

Piper harrumphed. "As if you haven't, Ellie Christie?"

The book-clubbers backed her up, murmuring like a Greek chorus. I decided I shouldn't try to lie in front of seven savvy mystery lovers and a police detective.

We all watched as Ven and Cameron squished themselves into a wingback made for one, hands on knees, ankles intertwining.

"Such a display," said Piper with a glee I'd reserve for stacks of newly released books. She patted her heart and a pin all the book-clubbers were wearing. At first glance, the pin looked like mountains with a moon in between. Trace the outline, though, and two *M*'s dotted with an *o* appeared, the logo for Mountains of Mystery.

"You don't have on your pin," Piper observed. She lowered her voice a half decibel. "You're undercover?"

Why did everyone think I was investigating? Probably because I was.

Sam stifled a grin. To Piper and the mystery readers, he said, "You are too, I assume? As a group, you might be a bit obvious."

Piper beamed. "Good. That killer should know we're on the lookout. Nothing's going to happen in our favorite bookshop."

The chorus concurred.

I appreciated that. Lorna would too, although I wouldn't tell her that half her guests were here to look for a killer instead of book-matched love.

Piper lowered her voice to a true whisper. "This truly is *the place* to be tonight. If I were the killer, I'd be here. I'd stick close to the investigation." She nodded at me, then Sam. To the group, she said, "Mystery readers, let's fan out."

They scattered, with Piper homing in on Ven and Cameron like a gossip-seeking missile. He issued a bright-white smile as fake as a three-dollar bill. Cameron was putting on a show. To Piper, at the moment, but also to everyone here, including Sam Ibarra and me.

But what was he trying to say? That he was innocent and had nothing to hide? That he was a romantic catch and Meg should take notice? That he no longer wanted to woo my sister? He'd rented a house, giant mules, and a carriage. Giving up so quickly seemed unlikely, even for Cameron.

I sighed and turned to Sam. "Would you back me up if I booted him out?"

His lip quirked. "Sorry, I'm an officer of the law. I cannot condone or be a party to booting."

I was the keeper of a reading refuge where all were welcome. I couldn't boot him either. Plus, I wanted to keep an eye on Cameron.

"Did he tell you anything useful?" I asked.

"Ongoing investigation," Sam said, but his headshake suggested no.

"Is Cameron under suspicion?" I willed Sam's head to keep on shaking. I focused on that chiseled chin and an appealing shadow of beyond five o'clock stubble.

His smile dipped to tight-lipped and apologetic and said way more than I wanted to know. Cameron was a suspect, as was Meg. I scanned the room, thinking of Piper's words. *So was everyone here.*

CHAPTER 35

Games Afoot

S am was attempting to guess Agatha Christie's favorite drink (straight cream) when Waldon returned. He balanced a dinner plate loaded with canapés atop two steaming mugs.

"I was delayed," he announced. "So many people wanted to discuss the new theater schedule and my unique interpretation of *Endgame*. Let me tell you about the first act. . . ."

The play only had one act. Waldon droned on about the opening image. Long minutes in, Sam touched my arm and murmured something about mingling. I reconsidered his "hero" status. A true hero would have swept me into his arms and taken me with him. Or tipped a drink on my sleeve, necessitating my escape to the restroom.

I could be my own hero. I was considering a toddy sacrifice when Waldon said, "Good."

"What?"

"That tedious detective is gone."

I blinked. Waldon had purposefully bored away the competition? The professor was more self-aware—and conniving—than I'd realized.

"We have a lot to talk about," he said.

I raised an eyebrow.

"Murder," intoned Waldon.

Where would Waldon and I be without murder? "Do you have a new theory?"

"I have a firm suspect, thanks to this mixer." Waldon nodded toward Ven and Cam's armchair display of affection. "Isn't that your sister's former paramour? I heard that the police questioned him. His *performance* tonight convinces me."

I waited.

As expected, Waldon served up his theory. "Obviously, what we're witnessing is a variant on the criminal returning to the scene of the crime. Except no one's at the actual scene except Fiona and her breakdown." He leaned close. "Do you know? When I arrived, she was peering in your front window?"

"Fiona? Here?" I looked around with unease. "Did you talk to her?"

Waldon had not. "I approached. She scurried away, acting like she didn't see me." He shook his head. "Dismally poor actor. Now, him . . ." He quirked his chin toward Cameron. "He's here to taunt us."

Or the professional detective in the room. Sam's mingling had kept him within listening-in distance of Ven and Cameron.

"We should try to eavesdrop," I said, expecting Waldon to scoff.

"Champion idea." He raised both hands and wiggled air quotes. "I will be doing so ironically, of course."

Lorna intercepted our path to sleuthing, ironic and otherwise. She beamed at Waldon and made a disgusted sound to me. "Can you believe *he's* here? Cameron!"

"Yes," said Waldon.

I had to agree.

Lorna tapped her boot. "I could have found Ven a much more suitable date! I would have kicked Cam out too, but Marigold said Ven looks so happy. Marigold's too much of a romantic for the matchmaking business. Of course, Meg is appalled."

"Wait, what?" I stammered. "You told Meg?"

"More than told her. I texted a photo of their shenanigans. She said she'll handle it."

"She's not—" *She's not coming up here,* I was about to say, when Ven trilled the answer, slightly slurred at the edges.

"Meg! Hey, there!" Ven waggled her arm high, causing Cameron to put down his drink.

Meg stood at the arched entryway, fists balled at her hips.

I deserted Waldon and hurried to her. "Don't bother with Cam. He's not worth the fuss."

My sister straightened her posture. "I do not intend to *fuss.*"

All eyes watched as she strode to Cameron. "Cam, you wanted to talk. Okay, let's talk. Now."

Cameron issued his best flirty look. Lids lowered. Smile at toothpaste-commercial bright. "Megs," he said. "I knew you'd come around." He slid from the seat and Ven's grasp and stood to drape an arm around Meg's rigid shoulders.

She shrugged him off.

"Megs . . ." he repeated. "You need what I have to offer. . . ."

Meg took Cameron by the elbow and marched him away. Out of sight, the storeroom door slammed. The lounge was silent except for the low chatter of the huddling Mountains of Mystery and Ven's vexed huff.

Ven struggled up from her now solo seat. I offered a hand.

"Explain that to me," she said, smoothing her silky top. "Haven't Cam and your sister been over since their wedding disaster?"

"More than over," I said.

"Well! So am I!" Ven straightened her shoulders. "I am so done with people who take me for granted and show no respect!" She spun and stalked out of the lounge. Lorna trotted after her.

"Mmmm . . ." Waldon and his snack plate appeared at my side. "What does he want from your sister?"

Now, there was a non-absurd question. "I wish we knew," I said.

Marigold fluttered in and thrust a tray of canapés at us. "Have some," she insisted nervously. "*Please,* enjoy. You're still having a good time?"

"We are," I said, a slight fib. "Everything's beautiful. These look delicious." I took a cheese shortbread. Waldon took three to add to his mound of snacks.

"Thank you, Ellie." Marigold shot me a grateful smile and avoided Waldon's smirk. After she moved on, Waldon leaned close.

"If I'm murdered, remember this moment," he said.

"What?" I eyed the canapés. If he crocked off from overindulging in buttery, cheesy cookies, he couldn't blame anyone but himself.

"That woman with the ridiculous name," Waldon said. "Did you see? She couldn't look me in the eye."

"Marigold?" I felt better. Waldon really was absurd. There was no way he was a calculating killer. "Why on earth would Marigold murder you?"

"I denied her use of the theater for her so-called performance. I saw what happened last year. The children brought real rabbits and glitter."

I was with him in an aversion to glitter. It had no place around books. "I think you're safe," I said.

"You're probably right," he said, rather regretfully. "But Cameron Winfield should watch his back. His date didn't look happy, not like those women falling all over our detective friend."

Three women gathered around Sam Ibarra. He appeared to be reading quiz questions. They giggled.

I bit back a sigh. I had no right to be disappointed. Lorna, not Sam, had invited me. We just happened to be at the same mixer.

"Let's go sit by the fire," I said to Waldon. "You can tell me more about *Endgame.*" I needed time to think, and Waldon could profess with or without my complete attention.

He chatted happily about post-apocalyptic set design. I mulled loose threads and open questions. Once, when I slipped away to the restroom, I listened at the storeroom door. Meg's voice filtered through, tight, tense, frustrated. Back in the lounge, Sam's circle of women had decreased to one, a blonde in a little black dress. Waldon interrupted his own act and went on a lengthy hunt for desserts.

Finally, Marigold rang her gong and announced the end of "our delightful time together."

Guests departed, a few arm-in-arm. The Mountains of Mystery left as a clump, off to "debrief" at Piper's house. Waldon announced a need for the restroom. The blonde went to fetch her coat, and Sam and I found ourselves alone in the lounge.

"Interesting evening," he said.

"Piper and the mystery readers had quite a time," I agreed.

"Your sister's okay?"

Worry twisted in my middle. But Meg was surely fine. She could handle Cameron. Hopefully, she'd gotten information out of him.

"I listened at the door a while back," I reported. "She seemed okay. As okay as anyone arguing with an ex."

The blonde poked her head in. "Taxi's already here, Sam."

"Be right there, Nina."

Sharing a taxi . . . I pressed back more unjustified disappointment.

Sam turned to me. "I want to check on Meg before I go."

I wanted that too. I hurried ahead, knocking on the storeroom door as I pushed through. I needn't have bothered. The room was empty except for a mess of food containers.

"Would they leave together?" Sam asked.

"Noooo . . ." The word bumped down the stairs from my loft.

"Meg?" I called out. "You're up there? Alone?"

"No." A beat passed, then a smile in Meg's voice. "I'm with Agatha. We have your pillow, El."

Agatha meowed confirmation.

"Ms. Christie?" Sam said. "This is Detective Ibarra. Where's Mr. Winfield?"

Shuffling ensued. Meg's feet and a fluffy Siamese appeared at the top step. Agatha blinked slowly at Sam, a kitty version of *I love you* kisses.

"Gone," Meg said, clomping down the stairs. "And good riddance! I'm going home, El. Thanks for Agatha time and your pillow."

"You want a ride down?" Sam asked. "I'm sharing a taxi. There's room for another."

Meg politely declined.

"I can drive you." Waldon stood at the door in his tweedy outdoor layers.

"Thanks, Waldon," Meg said. "But I want to take the gondola. Time alone to clear my head."

"Very well." Waldon turned to me. "Eleanor, it has been a fruitful evening. We shall do this again."

Back at the front door, I stood with Marigold and Lorna and waved. Sam and Nina climbed into a Jeep taxi. Meg trudged off into the night. Waldon unlocked a black hatchback, illegally parked in our loading zone.

With a cop in attendance! Waldon had nerve.

The car started up with the hushed whirl of an electric engine.

Where had I seen that car? Our first date at the library but where—
Lorna nudged me. "Wave to your date, Ellie."

I dutifully raised my arm. Waldon pulled out under a streetlamp and realization sparked. The Ridgecrest Theater, waiting outside while EMTs treated a stricken Fiona. A car had crept by. A rubbernecker, Sam called the driver.

Had that been Waldon?

I watched until his taillights disappeared. "Come on now," Lorna said, nudging me. "Don't look so sad. You'll see him again."

Sad wasn't my emotion. Shock grappled with denial.

On autopilot, I helped Lorna and Marigold clean up. My cousin grumbled about comping Ven for more dates. "She was stomping mad, but honestly, it's her fault for bringing an unmatched date! Thank goodness, Meg took care of Cameron. . . ."

We stashed tables, tidied, rinsed, and washed. Meanwhile, my thoughts dwelled on the theater, the shover, the script thief lurking in a hidden corner. I attempted to talk myself back. We'd seen a car driving slowly. Even if it had been Waldon, he worked at the college and the theater. He was an eavesdropper. It made sense that he'd rubberneck too. And the timing . . . That could have been mere coincidence. Chance . . .

I told myself all that but Miss Marple's words kept floating in my head. *Take note of coincidence.*

✳

CHAPTER 36

Done and Dusted

"Alone at last," I said to Agatha C. Christie.

I'd changed into flannel PJs, my bathrobe, and slippers and was down in the kitchen making peppermint tea. Agatha wanted a snack after her long evening's nap.

The teapot whistled. Agatha meowed. I turned off the stove, doled out shrimp-flavored treats, debated between popcorn and yogurt, and decided on the latter. I'd nibbled on canapés all night.

Agatha had already inhaled her treats. She trotted to the back door and settled into a loaf position.

When you get a new roommate, it can take a while to notice their quirks. In Agatha, I'd initially seen the obvious: cute, fluffy, long-haired Siamese with a great resting frowny face and puttering purr. Later, she'd revealed her hobbies. Stealing my pillow. Photobombing selfies. And staring at doors and floor grates with a look suggesting ghosts or rodents.

Agatha stared at the door with wide-eyed horror. Like a Stephen King clown grinned on the other side.

"I'm not falling for it," I told her. "You don't want to go out. It's cold."

Agatha rarely ventured outside. In the summer, she might sun her whiskers on the stoop. Last year, however, she'd run off to chase a clue.

The hairs on the back of my neck prickled. Agatha upped her game and pawed at the threshold.

"Nope," I said firmly. "Nothing's out there. You're messing with me." I could prove that to Agatha and myself and take out the trash. On the other hand, maybe Agatha sensed wildlife. A fox or racoon or . . .

I stepped to the door, cupped my hands to the window, and squinted into the dark. The porchlight had burned out last week. Getting a replacement bulb was on my list of things I'd been too busy to do.

"What is it?" I asked.

Agatha jumped to the counter and puffed her tail to double fluffy.

Not helping, I thought.

But maybe Agatha was warning me. I unlocked the door and inched it open. "Hello?"

The silence of a winter night spoke back. Darkness devoured all light. A flashlight hung by the switch. I swung its beam around, illuminating what should be there. The chubby blue spruce. A path tromped by boots. Icicles like swords, trimming the eaves. Our bear-proof trash containers about ten strides out. A dark lump . . .

A lump with feet!

My heart took up bass drumming and residence in my throat. Shoving aside concerns regarding monsters, murderers, and the snow-worthiness of my slippers, I raced outside.

The lump was a man. I recognized his hair, chin, and a nose shockingly similar to Rosie's. Red speckled the snow. Sparkles danced across my vision.

I remembered Lorna's advice. Breathe. I could not—*would not!*—faint on a crime scene. I dropped to my knees beside Cameron, felt for a pulse, then called 911.

The voice on the other end was familiar. Anxiety almost made me blurt, *Hey, remember me?*

"A man's hurt," I said. "At the Book Chalet. I need an ambulance, please hurry!"

"Stay on the line, ma'am," the dispatcher said. I struggled out of my robe, draped it over Cameron, and apologized to my friend on dispatch. I had to make another call.

Sam Ibarra answered on the second ring. "Ellie. Hey, everything okay?"

My first thought: He had my number in his contacts. That brought a puff of delight. Second thought: Of course he had my number. I was Last Word's new finder of bodies!

"Not okay," I stammered. "Can you come back? Cameron's been attacked."

* * *

Midnight should have passed with me under my quilts and Agatha snoring in my ear. Instead, I was in a private waiting room at Ridgecrest Memorial Hospital.

Gram sat beside me, steadily knitting.

Rosie slouched in a seat across the room. Arms folded, ears muffled under headphones, eyes glued to an endless scroll on her phone. Meg paced a hall with walls a sickly chartreuse and floor tiles in a splatter of beiges. So many colors and patterns in the world and someone had chosen those, under flickering fluorescent lights, no less, in a place where people already felt unwell.

For the briefest of microseconds, I wished Waldon were here. We could discuss absurd design choices.

Meg looped back and squeezed Rosie's shoulder. "He'll be okay, honey."

"You don't know that, Mom," Rosie said, scrolling onward.

Footsteps made us all turn. Not a doctor, but Sam Ibarra. His stony face sent my stomach into a roller coaster plummet.

Meg sank to a seat beside Rosie. "How is he?"

"He'll recover," Sam said.

"Can I see him?" Rosie asked.

"I'm sorry." Sam looked like he truly meant it. "That's up to the doctor. She's still in there with him." He jutted his chin toward the door to the lobby. "Ellie, Meg, I need to speak with you."

Gram's knitting needles clicked at higher speed. "Rosie and I will come get you if the doctor comes out."

We pushed through swinging doors into a large but awkward lobby between hallways and elevators. The walls were stark white, the floor tiled black. Floor-to-ceiling windows probably offered stunning mountain views in daylight. Now they reflected wavery images of us.

Meg and I perched on a stiff sofa.

Sam took a chair facing us, his face unreadable. "Mr. Winfield sustained contusions to the back of the head."

Meg said, "Contusions? Could he have slipped? It's icy back there. I should have sprinkled more rock salt or kitty litter or . . ."

"He didn't slip," Sam said. "The chief texted this." He produced a phone from his inner pocket. "The woman I left the mixer with, Nina Harten, she's a crime tech with the sheriff's office. Chief asked her to sign up for your cousin's matchmaking service. We're lucky she's on scene. She's processing footprints."

Relief waved over me. Because of prompt crime-scene management, I told myself. And, yes, because she hadn't been there to romantically mingle.

"She also found this," Sam said.

He held up his phone and a photo that chased away my unseemly relief.

A hammer, hefty, with a flattened head. I pictured Gram's pegboard with its tool outlines. Gram had modeled the board after Julia Child's pot rack. Back in my kitchen, I bet there'd be an outline missing its hammer.

"You keep tools in your storeroom," Sam said.

Meg turned away from the photo. "Gram uses them for book repair. We have some antiques too, like blacksmithing hammers from old relatives."

My family retained a rural frugality. Sure, we kept items that sparked joy, but also anything that might come in useful someday.

Sam slipped the phone back into his pocket. "We'll have to check your tool wall," he said. More gently, he added, "Ellie, you most likely saved his life. A night out and he would have died from exposure."

"That was all Agatha," I said. "She told me to look outside."

"Your cat? I'll put her in for a commendation." His lip quirked but soon firmed back to stony. "Meg, I'll need to ask you about tonight."

Meg took a breath. "I—"

He held up a hand. "I want you to understand your rights first. You don't *have* to talk to me."

I frowned. What was he saying? That Meg *shouldn't* talk to him?

Sam continued. "If you want a lawyer present, that's your right. Both of you."

Both of us?

"We have nothing to hide," I said. "You were there and saw—" I bit my lip. He had been there. I'd talked about booting out Cameron and told him about Meg arguing with her ex. He'd also heard Meg's "Good riddance."

I reached over and squeezed Meg's hand. "We can call Lorna," I said to her. "Marcos will know someone."

"Marcos is an environmental lawyer," Meg said.

True, but Lorna's husband mingled with a lawyerly crowd.

"I have nothing to hide," Meg said stubbornly. "Cameron and I talked about our daughter. I told him to leave. He was disrupting Lorna's mixer. He did. I went up to Ellie's loft to read. That's it."

Sam's face gave nothing away. "Did you hear anyone else go out the back door?"

Meg didn't know. She'd gotten caught up in a book. "There was a lot of noise from the lounge."

"Cameron will clear this up," I said. "He'll know. Meg wouldn't hurt Rosie's father."

Then I thought of something. "Waldon!" I blurted. "He saw Fiona. She was hanging around outside the Chalet before the mixer started." Guilt panged. If Fiona was innocent, I owed her carriage-loads of apology chocolates and sherry.

Meg pinched the bridge of her nose, then addressed the detective. "Cameron didn't tell you what he saw at Joe's?" When Sam shook his head in the negative, Meg shut her eyes and sighed. "That foolish man. Word's gotten around town that he and that telescope saw something. If the killer heard . . ."

Sam rubbed his chin thoughtfully. "We'll talk to Fiona and Waldon. I'll be in touch."

Once again, Meg was the last known person to see a crime victim.

My sister groaned. "I need to call Cam's parents. I hope someone at that resort answers the phone at this hour." Condemned prisoners looked cheerier.

"Want backup?" I asked.

Meg declined. "I need to do this on my own. There is something you could do . . ."

"Anything!"

"Will you call Lorna? She's not going to be happy."

That was an understatement. I feared who she'd blame in the short-term too: the cousin who'd promised not to find a body at her mixer.

✳

CHAPTER 37

Unhappy Visitors

Douglas and Elaina Winfield arrived by private jet the following afternoon. I expected a frigid wind to accompany them. Instead, Arizona warmth swept in.

In the high, dry Rocky Mountain air, sunny and thirty-eight degrees feels like spring. Skiers donned shorts and even bikinis. Diners ate al fresco. I watched over a relaxed bookshop and made sure Meg stayed safely home.

Piper Tuttle showed up near closing. "The Mountains and I are hearing things," she said.

I fancifully pictured Piper communing with the peaks.

She named Mountains of Mystery members and a gossip chain that led to L'Auberge, an exclusive and pricey inn.

"The Winfields have booked two penthouse suites." Piper leaned an elbow on the register counter.

L'Auberge was practically our neighbor. I shot a wary glance toward the door.

"Cameron will be springing himself from the hospital soon," she continued.

I nodded. Meg had texted to let me know.

Piper said, "So one of those suites is his. They say he has a head injury. Needs to be watched over. I'll say! Someone tried to kill him and we all missed it. We should have followed him. I knew it!" She paused for a moment of regret, then said, "Was it *really* your Gram's hammer?"

"Not Gram's." I was splitting hairs. The hammer had been our blacksmithing great-aunt's, as identified by Gram and the outline on Gram's tool wall.

Piper smiled knowingly. "How's your cousin doing?"

For this, I had a prepared line, provided by Lorna. I took a deep breath and let it all out: "Bibliophiles Find Love wishes the victim a speedy recovery but notes he was not a book-matched client nor an approved guest."

Piper flicked her hand. "Lorna should get out of the match-making business while she can."

I studied the woodgrain in the counter, hoping Piper couldn't read my agreement.

"Her husband makes enough," Piper continued. "She wouldn't have to work."

That corrected my treacherous thoughts. Lorna was seeking her work match! I smiled tightly and issued another company line. "Bibliophiles Find Love will be proven to have no association with crimes of law or passion."

"We'll see." Piper went to peruse the Valentine's display.

In between customers, I doom-scrolled news headlines on my phone. Last Word had made the nationals again and the tabloids. *Lothario slain in scenic small town infamous for murder. Little bookshop of mysteries once again center of crime spree.* Did one murder and two assaults constitute a spree? Was Joe Darcy a lothario, a serial seducer? Worse?

"Piper?" I called.

She bounded back. "Yes?"

"Did you find more women who'd dated Joe Darcy?"

She preened, pleased to be asked. "I did! The man got around."

I lowered my voice. "Did anyone mention losing money? Jewelry?"

Piper drummed her fingers on the counter. "Remember the lady from Durango, the second fiancée? I looked up that 'nature resort' where she's hiding out in Costa Rica. It's the kind of place you can get by without a lot of money. She sold a six-bedroom home in Durango's historic district."

I added up this information. Durango was a lovely mountain town by a river. So lovely that, like in Last Word, real estate prices had skyrocketed in recent decades. A house of that size and coveted location might sell for several million. Unless someone messed with her finances . . .

Piper reached over and clasped my hands. Her rings dug into my knuckles. "I hear what you're saying, Ellie. I'll look into it!"

She trotted out, feather scarf fluttering behind her.

Waldon strolled up the aisle, looking extra rumpled. He'd spent the afternoon in what I now thought of as his lair.

"I'll be leaving now," he said. "I have an early class tomorrow."

"Thanks for stopping by," I said, polite, friendly, in no way romantically encouraging.

"How's our suspect Mr. Winfield?" he asked.

"Cameron couldn't have attacked himself," I pointed out.

Waldon tapped his temple. "That's what we said about Fiona and her tumble."

I watched him drive off and realized I hadn't told Sam about Waldon's car. I picked up my phone and tallied problems.

One, I wasn't sure. There could be dozens of electric hatches cruising by crime scenes. Two? Meg, reluctantly, had retained a lawyer, a Stetson-wearing shark by the name of Jay T. Truman. Jay T. had given us "free advice." Shush up. Say nothing to the police unless arrested or subpoenaed.

I was still holding the phone, playing a game of *should I/*

shouldn't I, when it rang. The caller ID made me blink. *Now phones were reading my mind?*

On the other end, Sam Ibarra sounded formal. "Ellie. Ms. Christie. Cameron Winfield wishes to make a statement but requests you and your sister in attendance. Six-thirty tonight at L'Auberge. His parents and lawyers will be there."

"A statement to whom?" I asked. "Us?"

"And us—the police." A pause, then Sam's voice softened. "Ellie, I'm saying this as a friend. I get the impression you might not like what he has to say. Meg should bring that lawyer."

* * *

L'Auberge catered to guests' every need. They offered a spa, hot-spring pool, cocktail bar, library, and a "gathering room" perfect for giving statements to a crowd. Cool blue flames flickered in a gas fireplace. Oil paintings of aspens decorated the walls. A large oval table filled the center.

Meg took a seat. Jay T. Truman and I flanked her. Cameron positioned himself directly opposite Meg, bookended by his parents and a besuited lawyer who, unlike Jay T., had forgone a silver belt buckle, bolo tie, and Stetson. Chief Sunnie and Sam Ibarra claimed the end seats. Like elders at Thanksgiving, with us as the fractious family members.

A staff member provided mineral water flavored with strawberries and mint. I sipped mine and surreptitiously studied the Winfields. Elaina was as I remembered her, as icy and sharp as her platinum bob. Holden was ruddy and chummy. Cameron wore a loose beanie and a sweatshirt advertising an Ivy League college. His skin had the pallor of aspen bark.

"Should you be resting?" I asked him.

Cameron touched his hat, which I guessed was covering stitches.

"We're caring for him," Elaina said. "But yes, let's get this over with. Cameron, tell the officers what you told us."

His head dipped. Silence stretched so long, I worried. But when he raised his chin, he stared at Meg.

I read an emotion rare to Cameron's face. Confusion, mixed with . . . sorrow? Regret?

Alarm prickled up my arms.

He said, "I saw Meg Christie in that house the night of the murder."

I relaxed. "*Everyone* already knows that," I said, ignoring the tut-tuts of Jay T. Truman. Okay, maybe *he* didn't know.

Cameron continued in a dull monotone. "Later, I checked again. The kitchen was dark but someone was there." He looked to the chief. "Something seemed . . . wrong. That's why I hiked over."

"Could you identify the person?" Chief Sunnie asked mildly.

Cameron returned his stare to Meg. "I thought it was *you*, Meg. That's why I didn't say anything. I was trying to help *you*. You wouldn't let me."

"*You thought*," Jay T. repeated. "You did not positively identify my client."

"Because I wasn't there then," Meg said. "I was home. This isn't new information, Cameron." She rose to leave.

"Wait." Elaina Winfield froze the room with a single word.

"Sit," she said.

Meg remained standing, gripping the back of her seat.

"Meg Christie has an additional financial motive to harm my son," Elaina said. "I consider myself responsible for telling her."

"Telling me?" Meg slid back into her chair. "You didn't explain anything."

Elaina issued a frigid sigh. "I *said* we were reconsidering the appropriate beneficiary of the Winfield Family Trust, originally to be distributed to our son when he turned forty."

Not a brain tumor! Forty! Meg and I shared a glance.

"How does that pertain to my client?" Jay T. Truman asked.

Elaina said, "The alternate beneficiary—as I told Meg—would be a *suitable heir*."

"Rosie?" Meg whispered.

Elaina's look suggested we were the ones suffering head injuries. "Obviously. Given the circumstances, we are making no decisions at this time."

Holden thumped Cameron's back. "We're in this together, son."

Cam winced but jutted his chin like a peevish child. "I *tried* to explain, Megs. You wouldn't listen. Then this? You attack me?" He touched his head and raised his voice to drown out Meg's denial. "I heard how you ripped up my shirts after our wedding blew up. You know, I actually felt bad but now I think I saved my life. I don't know you!"

Clearly not. How could he ever think Meg attacked him?

"So," Chief Sunnie said, "to return to that trust. If Cameron had succumbed to his injuries, it would have gone to Rosie Christie?"

Elaina sniffed. "Most likely. With an appropriate trust manager."

"We don't need your money," Meg said. "We're fine."

Jay T. Truman tutted.

I did more than tut. I rose and tugged my sister up with me. "We have nothing more to say."

✳

CHAPTER 38

Second Chances

The following afternoon, the front door to the Chalet inched open with barely a sound. That's what alerted me. The covertness of our guest. I already had a stealthy visitor. Waldon had settled into his nook around noon to "keep a mind out for crime."

I eyed the door suspiciously until I spotted a pink mitten. Rosie slipped in like Nancy Drew. Head ducked into shoulders, finger to her lips urging silence. All she needed was a magnifying glass.

She tiptoed to the register counter. "Mom's not here, right?"

"No. Your mother has a, ah, *thing* with *someone.*" The police had a warrant to search their house. Meg had rushed down earlier. "She said you have after-school work." She'd been relieved that Rosie wouldn't be home to see.

"I do have work," Rosie said. "It's really super important and only you can help, Aunt El. You will, right? Please?"

Who was she asking for assistance? World's Coolest or Most Gullible Aunt? Either way, I was there for her. "What are we doing?"

Rosie broke into a smile. "Planning a date!"

Most Gullible, I realized, too late.

"We're gonna fix up Mom and Dad!"

"Well, ah . . ." I hedged.

"You said you'd help!" She tapped a boot. "It's a good idea!"

Maybe it was. Who was I to say?

"You're in luck," I said. "We have a pro in the house."

Rosie told me her logic on the way to the storeroom.

Marigold sat at the worktable. "Picnics," she said when Rosie and I entered. "Wouldn't that be fun? With books of poetry? We could schedule into the spring or get one of those glass igloos and try it now."

Dear, optimistic Marigold was looking ahead to other seasons and igloo investments. Meanwhile, Lorna was cooking up essential-oil concoctions, a warning sign she might jump the dating ship.

I said, "Rosie and I have a dating challenge."

"Big-time challenge," Rosie amended. "My mom and dad need to talk."

Even Marigold looked worried. "Your parents might not rediscover their love."

"Yeah, yeah, I know," said Rosie. "I need them to see the facts. Mom didn't attack Dad or that other man. Dad's not a Peeping Tom blackmailer, killer, whatever. Stuff like that."

Marigold nodded somberly. "I hear you. They need to clear the air. When do you want this to happen, Rosie?"

"Tonight! The police are searching our house. This is an emergency date!"

"Rosie . . ." I said, preparing to temper her expectations.

Marigold jumped in. "We can do this! Do they like picnics?"

"Their first date was a picnic," I said. Rosie was right. Meg wasn't guilty. Cameron *probably* wasn't either. If they could clear each other, the police could move on to true suspects.

* * *

I hustled the last customers out exactly at closing. Marigold set a table for two. Rosie texted the invitations. I'd suggested wordy explanations. Rosie rolled her eyes and issued orders: *Need U 6:30 B at Chalet.*

"Now I don't reply except in emoji," Rosie said. "Smiley faces. Cats. Hearts. Books . . . If Mom texts you, do *not* respond. You can't be trusted to lie."

"Could I send emojis?" I asked.

Rosie didn't even trust me with those. "There are so many ways to mess up, Aunt El. You have no idea!"

I didn't, but I knew that Meg would sense a plot in the making.

"Good," Rosie said. "That means she'll show. Mom's too curious for her own good."

Indeed, Meg arrived early. "What's going on?"

"Mom!" Rosie hugged her. I issued a don't-blame-me shrug.

Meg focused on Rosie. "Honey. I thought you were working. . . ."

"I am." Rosie tugged her mother to the lounge.

Marigold had arranged armchairs on either side of our largest coffee table—a buffer, made more substantial by a wicker picnic basket, topped with an ornery-faced Agatha. I'd paid a premium for last-minute hamper pickup from a catering shop down the way.

Meg balked in the entry. "What's this?"

Rosie dragged her inside. "You *have* to do this, Mom. You owe me. Kids at school—bullies and mean girls and everyone—they're saying one of my parents is a killer." She led her mom to a seat.

Knocking came from the front.

"That'll be Dad. I'll get it." Rosie ran off through the shop.

"Sorry," I said to Meg. "I didn't have the heart to stop her."

"Cameron does have to see I wouldn't attack him." Meg winced. "The police need to know that too. They took the sweater I wore to the mixer. Something about fiber analysis again."

"You'll be shirtless at this rate," I said, attempting some little-sis dark levity.

Meg forced a smile. "Gram said that too. She says she'll teach me how to knit."

* * *

"It's going super well," Rosie said. "I don't hear any fighting."

I listened. "Nope, no yelling."

Rosie and I had set up camp in the storeroom. Agatha was monitoring the date—or, more likely, the fried chicken in the picnic basket. Marigold had popped out to pick up pizza I'd ordered for us chaperones.

"Last I went by, they were talking about Grandmother and Grandfather Winfield," Rosie said. "That's good."

I agreed. "A shared foe brings people together."

Rosie looked around, as if her paternal grandparents might be hiding behind the coatrack. "Grandmother said they'd pay for me to go to equestrian dressage camp instead of horse camping. She says dressage is more 'ladylike.'"

I raised an eyebrow. "And you said?"

Rosie snorted. "I'm going horse camping! I'll raise the money."

Out front, the cowbells clanged. Marigold arrived with a large cardboard box and the heavenly scent of wood-fired dough.

"Sorry, there was a wait," she said. "I hurried back so it shouldn't be cold."

After we each took a slice, I popped the box in a warm oven. We ate in listening-for-trouble silence.

Rosie was getting up for a second slice when we heard the thump. We all froze.

"What was that?" Rosie said.

Where was that? Somewhere in the shelves? The lounge?

I grabbed the backup bottle of wine I'd bought for the picnic date. "I'll go check." Offering wine was a good excuse to check up on Meg and Cam. Plus, the bottle could serve as a weapon.

"I'm going with you," Marigold said.

"Me too!" Rosie jumped up.

"Nope," I said firmly. "Rosie, you keep watch here."

Rosie rolled her eyes but relented. "Fine. I'll guard the pizza."

When Marigold and I reached the central aisle, we stopped and took stock. Light shone from the lounge. A table lamp illuminated the lobby. In between, the aisles were dark.

"I'll check the aisles," Marigold said.

I offered to go with her.

"You should check on Meg," she said. "I'll be fine. It was probably just Agatha."

"Probably," I said, trying to ignore my panging nerves.

In the lounge, Meg and Cameron still sat with the table between them. The picnic basket was on the floor. Agatha snoozed on top. So much for the blame-the-cat theory.

My sister and her ex looked up, and I saw that they'd been looking at photos on a phone.

"More wine?" I held up the bottle. The picnic basket had come with individual bottles of bubbly, which I now noticed sat unopened on the table.

"Can't," Cameron said. "Head wound."

Meg gave a tight smile. "None for me, thanks, El. We're just looking at photos of Rosie's science fair project."

"Award-winning," Cameron said proudly.

"Okay," I said. "Great. Just checking. Did you hear a noise?"

Cameron looked up so sharply, he reached to steady his head. "What? Wasn't that you?"

I gripped the wine. "No. Marigold's checking the—"

A scream ripped through the bookshop, followed by a sickening *thump*.

Cameron shrank back, holding his head. Meg bolted up and together we ran to the archway. Down the main aisle, a figure— no, two—struggled on the floor. Cowbells clanked and rattled at the front door.

I brandished my wine bottle. Meg surged ahead of me. Marigold Jones groaned and a head rolled into the aisle.

I'd been wrong. Not two people, but Marigold and the bust of Poirot. Meg knelt to help her.

"Mom? Aunt El?" Rosie appeared, wide-eyed. "What happened?"

Marigold groaned and cradled her wrist. "It's okay. I'm okay. Someone pushed by me. I grabbed on to Poirot, but we fell." She struggled upright. "Did you see him?"

"Him?" Cameron stepped up, now that the danger had fled. "A man? You're sure?"

Did he know otherwise?

"I . . . I don't know," Marigold stammered as Meg helped her up. "It was dark. I fell . . ."

Cameron sounded peeved. "*You* were attacked? I thought the killer would come for me again."

Meg and I exchanged a dark look. *Maybe the killer had come for Cameron, but Marigold got in the way.*

✳

CHAPTER 39

Scene of a Crime

"Leave the head where it is," Chief Sunnie instructed.

"Sorry," I mouthed to Poirot. The "real" fictional detective would have been appalled. Such indignity, to be left lying in the aisle with his bad-mustache side facing up.

Sam Ibarra intercepted us. "I'll check the rest of the building, with your permission, Ellie?"

"Please!" I pushed aside concerns about dust bunnies under my bed or kitty fur on my pillow.

Meg and I followed the chief to the lounge. EMTs had arrived at the same time as the police. One was taking Cameron's blood pressure. Another wrapped Marigold's wrist in an elastic bandage. She squeezed her eyes shut and winced. Rosie huddled in a wingback, knees hugged to her chest. Agatha frowned down from a high shelf.

When Cameron and Marigold were deemed fit to talk and the EMTs departed, we each relayed accounts that were basically the same except in interpretation.

"I thought it was Agatha," Marigold said.

"She was with us," Meg said, clearing our bookshop cat. "We thought it was Ellie." She looked to Cam.

He agreed. "We joked about it. Ellie, snooping on us like when we were teenagers."

Rosie had gotten her wish. At least for the moment, her parents were on the same page.

My niece shrugged when it was her turn. "I thought it was just, you know, a noise or whatever."

We'd all heard Marigold's scream and the cowbells clattering.

Marigold flushed. "I'm sorry I wasn't a better witness."

"Oh, come on!" Cameron said. "You had to see *something*."

"Cam," Meg said sharply. "Marigold was injured!"

"Yeah, well, I'm the one in danger here." He rose and declared he was returning to the inn. "They have better security. Rosie? Want to come with me? We can have dinner with your grandparents. Order the tasting menu on their tab?"

Even now, Cam was attempting to buy Rosie's favor.

"I, ah . . ." Rosie stammered as Meg shot daggers at Cameron. So much for parental agreement.

"No worries. We'll ski later," Cam said, covering for his obvious defeat.

"Rosie and I will walk you out," Meg said tightly. The chief accompanied them.

Marigold and I sat in silence until cowbells jangled, signaling Cam's departure and sparking a thought.

"Marigold, was the front door locked when you came back with the pizza?"

She inhaled sharply. "I left it unlocked when I went out. But I'm sure I locked it when I returned. Oh, no! Do you think someone got in when I was getting the pizza?"

I tried to remember. "I only heard cowbells *after* your attack. That means whoever did this was probably already inside." Like in those horror films I was too scared to watch. *The killer calls from inside the house!*

Marigold cradled her injured wrist. "Well . . . whoever

shoved me was strong and . . ." She looked reluctant. "Maybe I felt something? Fabric? Woven fabric?"

"Woven fabric? Like tweed?"

The words came straight from my thoughts but in a male voice. Sam Ibarra stood at the entryway. "Shop is clear," he reported. "Ms. Jones? Marigold? You felt a type of fabric. Was it rough, smooth, crinkly? Any impression would help."

Marigold shook her head.

I stood and gestured for Sam to follow me. We skirted Poirot—now draped with the added indignity of crime-scene tape—and stopped at Fantasy and Flights of Fiction.

The chief joined us.

I gestured down the aisle. "There's a reading nook back there, around the corner. Waldon's been using it. Once or twice, he's stayed after closing. I was rushing tonight, helping Rosie arrange her parents' date. I didn't check the shop thoroughly."

Sam rubbed his chin, considering. "So, he might have stayed late again. And we know he likes to eavesdrop. He overheard Fiona arguing about that ring."

The chief said, "But why shove Ms. Jones tonight? I assume he didn't run off shoving folks the last times you caught him staying late?"

I agreed that he hadn't. "I'm not saying it was him, but if it was, maybe he was embarrassed? He mocks Miss Marple."

Sam sniffed. "Foolish man."

The chief said, "Guess we need to take a gander down Flights of Fantasy. What should we expect?"

I described the best reading nook in the house. "Probably also a stack of Beckett books. Waldon was examining our collection. We let him keep them there." Much to Ms. Ridge's organizational angst.

The officers snapped on gloves and disappeared down the aisle. They were gone so long, I started to imagine them tumbling through a portal.

The chief emerged first, holding a clear bag. "Found this in a book."

I cocked my head to read typed text in large font.

```
Hello, Professor. I saw what you did. I
have proof. Want me to prove it?
I don't ask much. $10,000. For now.
You can't afford to ignore me.
```

I jerked back as if the note might bite. "Blackmail? But who would . . . ?" Too late, I answered my own question. Someone who'd come to town for mysterious financial reasons. A man who'd already been attacked.

"I *saw,*" the chief repeated with emphasis.

A man with a telescope.

But in front of lawyers, the police, and his family, Cameron had accused Meg. My insides froze. Cameron couldn't be that cold, could he? Accuse innocent Meg of murder while blackmailing the real killer? *He couldn't be that foolish!*

Except . . . This was Cameron. Maybe he could be both those things.

The chief used her old standby technique and waited me out in silence.

"But," I said, refuting what we'd both been thinking. "If Cameron were blackmailing Waldon, then Waldon . . ." *Then Waldon was the killer! No, no, no!* The events of last year crashed in. That was it, I decided. I was officially the worst dater.

"Could explain why Dr. O'Grady ran tonight," Sam said mildly. "He came for a second crack at his blackmailer."

I leaned on a shelf for balance.

Sam reached out. "Come sit down, Ellie."

Only Marigold remained in the lounge. Meg, Rosie, and Agatha must have gone to the storeroom. I sank into the nearest seat.

"Waldon told me," I said numbly. "He said he was the killer." And then, cleverly, he'd planted suspicions. Fiona, unstable, unreliable, arguing with Joe, peering in the shop window. Ven, murderously mad at date-deserting Cam. Even Marigold, out to get Waldon himself because of a puppet performance.

Marigold stifled a gasp. "Dr. O'Grady? No! That can't be. . . ."

"Fiona warned me about him," I said. "I didn't listen." I'd been swayed by Waldon's assessment of her. By Lorna's and my own mystery-reader's imagination too.

"You told me," Sam said gently.

Gratitude warmed me, until I realized I'd failed there too. "His car!" I blurted. "I didn't tell you about the car. It's electric, black, tinted windows—like the one that drove by the theater after Fiona was hurt. The rubbernecker, remember?"

The detective's jaw hardened.

The chief had followed us in and been listening quietly. "I'll get someone over to check on Fiona Giddings," she said.

"But why?" Marigold demanded. "Why would Dr. O'Grady hurt anyone?"

Sam rubbed his jaw. He was pondering but he wouldn't speculate.

"Jealousy?" I suggested. "He thought he was in a relationship with Fiona until Joe showed up." I immediately talked myself out of my theory. "But if Waldon knew what Joe was—a conman, a thief—he could have simply told Fiona and been a hero."

Marigold clicked her tongue. "No. No one likes the messenger. My college roommate loved a man like Joe. I told her and she broke off our friendship instead."

I tried to picture Waldon raising a fireplace poker. Or my great-aunt's blacksmithing hammer. During the mixer, Waldon had gone off on long jaunts, supposedly to retrieve snacks. He could have easily slipped into the storeroom, plucked a hammer from the pegboard, and whacked Cameron. Meg had been in the loft. Sam and his undercover colleague, a gaggle of sleuthing mystery readers, and I had all been watching the wrong people in the wrong place.

Sam cleared his throat. "We need more solid facts."

Marigold rose unsteadily. "We'll do better, Ellie. I'll talk to Lorna. We'll improve our dating survey. This won't happen again."

No, it would not! I'd never go on a blind date again.

Marigold left. Sam soon followed, leaving me with the chief and crime-scene techs.

"I'm going down to Ridgecrest," he said, an oblique way of letting me know he was looking for Waldon. "It could be late, but would you like me to come back? I can camp out in your lounge tonight."

Yes! Every bit of me wanted to accept. But I wasn't a blackmailer. I had nothing to fear. I declined with thanks.

Agatha twined between Sam's legs. He smiled and bent to rub her cheeks. "At least you have a vicious guard cat."

When he was gone, I teased Agatha. "You like him, don't you?" I scooped her up. She nuzzled my ear and purred.

"Tell you a secret?" I whispered into her fur. "I like him too." And that was another thing that terrified me.

CHAPTER 40

✳

The Clue in the Books

They say nothing good happens after midnight. For me, that included sleep. I tossed, I turned, I jolted awake to every whisp of a sound. The chalet's old wooden bones groaned as wind wailed through the eaves. Agatha snored in my ear. Then there were my thoughts, banging around like upstairs neighbors with rattles and clogs.

By 5 A.M., I was exhausted but too wired to stay in bed.

"I give up," I announced, much to Agatha's delight.

She bounded downstairs. Early to rise meant more meals. Second breakfast. Brunch. Early-bird lunch, followed by tea-time.

Blearily, I filled Agatha's bowl and my coffee maker and ate half a muffin before realizing it was jalapeno cornbread. Finally, armed with coffee, I tucked my phone in my bathrobe pocket and headed for the lounge, intending to sip and listen to an audiobook. With any luck, I'd make like Gram and fall fast asleep.

On the way, I peeked into the shop. Poirot was back on his pedestal, but caution tape blocked Fantasy and Flights of Fiction. My frayed nerves attempted to laugh it off. *Ha! We'll re-*

name and reshelve. True Crime and Big Deceivers? Cads, Cons, and Blackmailers? Horror.

Soft rustling jarred me from my thoughts. I followed the sound to a row past Poirot and found Agatha in playful attack mode.

"What are you doing, silly girl?" I couldn't help but grin.

Agatha lay on her side, back paws kicking an imaginary ball of string. She flashed wild, delighted eyes and kicked harder.

Wait . . . I frowned down. Agatha wasn't pretending. That was string, a favorite but forbidden toy. Risking my fingers, I grabbed her prey. The clear line caught, not only on Agatha's grasping claws but also on books.

I put my mug on a shelf and knelt to extract it. *The things people left behind!* Most visitors were properly respectful, but I'd found unbelievable items. Half-gnawed apples. Gum! Crumpled napkins, books with sullied pages, and an oboe.

The thread led to a grapefruit-sized clump behind vintage Nancy Drews on the lowest row.

"The case of the invisible thread," I said, attempting to wind the mess into order. My efforts did little to contain the thread, pouncing Agatha, or my questions.

Who brings fishing line to a bookshop? Kids? A messy angler? Why stuff it behind books? A Nancy Drew fan creating a mystery?

Agatha balanced on her back paws and reached. She was undeniably adorable and *almost* irresistible.

"Sorry," I said. "This is for the trash." I stuffed the lump into my pocket, retrieved my mug, and started back for the storeroom. Something about the string made me uneasy, beyond littering and feline safety.

I was about to push through the half-open door when Agatha's ears perked. I stopped. A fresh breeze slipped past, accompanied by the click of a door closing.

Agatha bolted off with a chirpy meow: *Yay, second breakfast!*

A *shhhh* greeted her.

I opened my mouth to issue my own greeting. Or, better, *Do you know what time it is?*

But I knew the time—way too early for visitors. At least, for friends and family.

My fingers twined in the line. My stomach flipped with a sickening thought. I strained to hear over my thudding heart. Soft clinks of kitty kibble in a bowl. An Agatha bribe.

I backed down the aisle. A board creaked, and I winced. As a kid, I used to navigate the aisles blindfolded. I read the spines like braille. I knew each squeak and groan of the floorboards. Holding my breath, I tiptoed in a hopscotch pattern to the center aisle. Once there, I considered. I could sneak down the fantasy aisle and hide, but caution tape wouldn't stop the visitor I feared.

A killer.

I kept going, past Poirot and on to Romance, one row beyond the aisle with Nancy Drew. If I was right, that was the destination of my visitor.

A wingback in plush pink fabric anchored Romance. I crouched behind it, turned my phone to mute, and dialed. A sleep-muffled voice answered.

I whispered, "Don't talk. Listen. Stay on the line."

I didn't dare say more. Footsteps padded down the main aisle and turned into mystery. I heard hardbacks being pulled out. The rasp of covers and soft thuds of books stacked one by one. A sharp inhale, then hardbacks slapping together faster, like the searcher was becoming frantic.

I debated. I could keep hiding, but then I wasn't really hidden unless my unwelcome guest believed an armchair came with six legs, two of them in fuzzy slippers.

"Agatha, did you take it?" a voice whispered.

Blood whooshed through my head. *I know who killed Joe!* No one would believe me, especially not now, with Waldon tied up in a neat bow as top suspect. All I had was thread and a theory, both tangled. I needed proof.

I rose. My knees felt unlocked, like a marionette flailing on strings.

When I rounded the corner, Agatha saw me and mewed.

Marigold Jones gasped.

"Oh, Ellie! You surprised me! I didn't think you'd be awake." Marigold wore a puffer coat in midnight blue. *So dark, it might be mistaken for black and a shadow, shoving Fiona down the theater steps.*

Marigold stuffed something the size and shape of a blackboard eraser into her pocket.

"Couldn't sleep," I said, testing my voice. "What are you doing here, Marigold?"

There, I'd said her name. If Sam was listening in, he'd know. *A lot of good that would do me if I ended up like Joe Darcy!*

Marigold looked like she hadn't slept much either. No makeup. Dark hollows hung under her bloodshot eyes. "I, ah, lost an . . . earring," she said. "Last night, when I fell. I didn't want to bother you."

"So you let yourself in?" I nodded to a keychain dangling from a pink springy band around her wrist. Two keys, a library card, and a ski pass. "You found Rosie's missing keys?"

"Yes, Rosie's," Marigold stammered. "She left them last night. I was going to give them back today. I wanted to tidy up from the picnic date too. It was going so well until Dr. Waldon interrupted. That man! He isn't right for you, Ellie."

True. He wasn't. What wasn't true? Rosie hadn't left her keys last night. She'd lost them days ago.

I drew the tangled line from my pocket. Eyes widened, Agatha's in glee, Marigold's in horror. She took a step back.

"I found this string," I said at a volume that could carry across a theater. "Is it a fishing line? Is that how you made the crash and the cowbells chime?"

"What?" Marigold shook her head. "Ellie, what are you talking about?"

"The cowbells." I stepped closer to her. In a few more steps, the aisle ended in a shelf of classic mysteries. "We all heard the bells last night, after you screamed. You know what I don't remember hearing? The front door slamming shut. What did you do? Rig up the bells when you came back with the pizza?"

"How would I do that?" Marigold reached back and steadied herself on a row of Sherlock Holmes.

I wished the great detective would appear. Sherlock would be confidence itself. I was guessing, teetering on a thin limb. "Puppetry," I said.

"Puppets?" Marigold raised a nervous smile. "Puppets are for joy, for fun . . ."

Creating illusions. I thought of Marigold, stringing up the book-page bunting and teaching kids to tell stories with shadows. Another thought flashed. Marigold hauling in folding chairs, miming a weight lifter strengthened by lugging heavy puppets. Was she strong enough to maneuver the dead weight of Joe Darcy over his balcony? Desperate enough to attack Cameron?

I was afraid so, but I had to keep pressing. Lives were on the line, and mine might be one of them.

"What did you put in your pocket?" I asked. "A tape recorder? Sound effects like Fiona uses at the theater?" Fiona's worked on timers. It would be easy enough, I guessed, except for the extreme risk. After we heard the crash, Marigold had sent me to the lounge, presumably to check on my sister. She'd come back here by herself. All by herself . . .

"Waldon wasn't here last night," I said, upping my volume.

What if Sam thought I was a crank call and hung up?

Help might not be coming. I toned down my accusations. "Marigold, I know you didn't mean to hurt anyone. In fact, you were trying to help, right? You certainly helped Meg last night. She's no longer the prime suspect. We're *so* relieved."

"Oh, me too!" exclaimed Marigold, which admitted nothing.

"Meg would never hurt anyone. She's honest and true. Joseph Harrison Darcy should never have joined Bibliophiles Find Love. If it hadn't been for him, everything would be okay."

I nodded enthusiastically, until a memory froze me. "Harrison," I murmured. "You knew his middle name."

Marigold frowned. "Well, yes. That's his name."

"On our first date in the library," I said. "You introduced him by his full name, but Harrison wasn't on his application. He hardly filled that out."

Marigold fluttered her hands. "A name isn't a secret."

But she knew who he was. I thought of the note, fluttering by his body. *I know who . . .*

"You tried to warn Joe off. I saw your note."

Marigold made a disgusted sound. "He rubbed your nose in that too?"

I blinked. Joe was dead when I saw him again. Had Marigold blocked out the part where she killed him? "Yeah," I said, struggling to keep my voice steady. "He did that to you?"

Marigold clutched at her heart. "He mocked me. And Meg too. He said he already 'had her on the line.'" She nodded to the fishing line in my hand. "I reminded him about his fiancée. The things he said about poor, poor Fiona. Just awful!"

"You tried to warn Fiona too," I said, thinking out loud. "You left notes in her copy of *The Mousetrap*."

Marigold nodded eagerly. "Yes, you do understand! Fiona didn't at first, but she started to see more clearly. I was sorry to hurt her, I was."

Fear must have clawed its way into my features.

"I didn't push her!" Marigold snapped. "She tripped. I was sorry to hurt her heart but it had to be done. He was cheating on her, stealing from her. She wouldn't have believed me if I'd told her. She had to see for herself."

She reached out for me. It was my turn to draw away. As I did, I pushed Agatha back too with the heel of my slipper.

The bookshop queen did not appreciate my shove. Agatha

raised head and tail high and stalked back toward the store-room.

Thank goodness!

"We can keep this quiet, Ellie. No one has to know." Marigold's eyes gleamed. "It's perfect. Waldon—he's not the one for you. He's rude and cruel. He took Fiona's theater. He told their colleagues she was crazy."

"What about Cameron?" I asked. "He saw you that night."

Marigold huffed. "He lied. He couldn't identify anyone, but he wanted to blame Meg. You said so yourself, Ellie—he's out for his own good. Look how he manipulated his own daughter. I only wish . . ."

I drew back. Marigold's wistful smile sent chills gripping my neck. Did she wish she'd finished him off?

"It will all be okay now," she said. "Meg won't be blamed. Cameron has no hold over her. All you have to do is keep quiet, Ellie, and we can move along with Bibliophiles Find Love. Promise me? You will?"

I was a terrible liar. I bobbed my head in what I hoped looked like enthusiastic agreement and inched back until I bumped against cold, hard marble. Poirot. "You will?" Marigold said, coming closer. "Truly?"

I kept nodding. Marigold's eyes narrowed. She closed in until only Poirot separated us.

"Go, Marigold," I said. "Run while you can." If she didn't believe I'd keep quiet, maybe she'd buy that I wanted her to get away. A tiny part of me did. She'd started out with good intentions.

Marigold raised her hands, as if preparing to rip Poirot from my grasp.

"Go . . ." I pleaded and held my breath until I felt dizzy, and Marigold turned and ran.

The cowbells clanged. This time, the door slammed. I scrambled for my phone. "Are you there? Sam, did you hear?"

Nothing. Silence. *He'd hung up!* How would I prove what

she'd done? I had fishing line and a wild story. Then, my phone burst with the sound of a siren that also echoed outside. I ran to the window. Down the lane, a light flashed atop a pickup truck.

I ran outside, heedless of my slippers and frigid air whooshing up my bathrobe. The truck swerved, cutting off a figure running toward the gondola station.

I pressed the phone to my ear and heard Sam, breathing hard. He called Marigold's name. She sobbed, and he said words that brought tears to my eyes for multiple reasons. Sorrow, anger, regret, and most of all relief.

"Marigold Jones, you have the right to remain silent . . ."

✳

CHAPTER 41

Murder Brings People Together

Five days later a small party gathered in the lounge after hours. Sam Ibarra and Chief Sunnie. Glynis, Piper Tuttle, and Ms. Ridge. Meg, Gram, Lorna, Agatha C. Christie, and me. Gram provided cookies. Lorna served up hot buttered rum and spiced cider.

It was Valentine's Day, but none of us wanted to mention it.

"Fiona is going to sell that house," Lorna said. "Ven got the listing, lucky woman. That gorgeous kitchen will overcome the murder problem. Do you think I should get back into real estate?"

"Did you enjoy it?" Gram asked, knitting needles clicking.

Lorna sighed. "It was easier than matchmaking."

"Matchmaking's always going to be tricky," Glynis said. "People put up pretty covers. You don't know what they're hiding inside."

"Love of books was supposed to solve that," Lorna said. "Where'd I go wrong?"

"Going into business with a killer," Glynis said.

"Accused killer," Chief Sunnie said but her heart wasn't in it.

"Admitted killer," Meg said. Agatha snoozed on her lap, always knowing who needed the most comfort.

Meg and I had visited Marigold down at the jail. She'd rationalized her actions, saying how she'd only wanted to help Meg and Fiona and Rosie too.

Lorna huffed. "If Marigold had just *told* me Joe was engaged, I would have kicked him out of our service. Why make things so difficult?"

"Some people enjoy drama," said Piper, who adored every lurid detail and would be reporting back to the Mountains of Mystery book-clubbers.

"But not Marigold," I said. "She was afraid to tell Fiona about her cheating fiancé. She thought Fiona would blame the messenger. That's what happened with Marigold's college roommate."

"Anonymous notes never go well," Gram observed, knitting steadily.

Meg agreed. "Marigold left notes in Fiona's script, along with fingerprints and her handwriting. That's why she needed to steal it back."

I said, "She left Joe a note too. She told him she knew who he was. He rubbed it in her face when she confronted him at his house. He said he was done with Fiona, and Marigold couldn't stop him from seducing Meg. It set her off."

Piper and Glynis harmonized in their murmurs of agreement.

"I saw part of the note by his body." I shivered despite the crackling fire.

Lorna handed me a hot buttered rum, but it was Sam's smile that warmed me. He and the chief had agreed to join us, on the condition that they'd mostly listen. Marigold had spilled confessions to them too, but she still deserved her day in court.

I bolstered myself with spiced rum and said, "I think Marigold considered Fiona a close friend, even though Fiona said they barely knew each other. When Marigold heard about Fiona's fiancé, Joseph Harrison Darcy, she cared enough to look him up. She saw him at the theater too, and recognized him when he signed up for Bibliophiles Find Love. After that first date, she went to Joe's house to confront him. You were there, Meg, so she waited outside."

Meg shuddered, whether thinking of that cold night or the hidden eyes watching her, both Cameron and a soon-to-be killer.

Lorna made a disgusted sound. "A conman! Why did he target my business and Meg?"

"I know why," said Ms. Ridge crisply. "He went after Meg because she's a nice woman with a successful business."

"Just his type," Piper said. "He went for artsy, bookish women who hadn't dated in a while. Trusting types. He swooped in as Prince Charming. Most never reported him because they were too embarrassed. They felt foolish. If they did try to report him, it looked like a bad breakup. Nothing criminal. He was going to try the same with you, Meg. You were his perfect target . . ."

"But, Ven . . ." Meg said. "Why didn't he go after her?" My sister flushed. "Not that I would have wanted Ven to get hurt."

"Too eager?" Piper suggested. "I heard about Ven scoping out Fiona's house. We Mountains of Mystery had her on our suspect list."

Lorna topped off Meg's mug. "I think Ven scared Joe Darcy off. She's too savvy. She wants a partner, yes, but she would have seen through Joe's financial shenanigans in a heartbeat." She sighed wistfully. "She was evaluating that house because she's a born realtor. She has her *thing.*"

Meg frowned. "So you're saying I'm gullible?"

We all heaped praise on Meg's kindness, wisdom, and optimism.

My sister blushed, then rolled her eyes. "I'll say it. I was smitten after one date. He might have succeeded."

"No," I said as supportive little sister. "You'd have caught on."

Maybe . . .

Meg hugged Agatha closer. "Who I feel bad for is Rosie. She was conned too. She thought her father was here for purely sincere reasons. He loves her. I know he does, but he came here to prove himself to his parents and get his hands on that trust."

Cameron and his parents—true to form—had flown out yesterday. He and Rosie would go back to their usual relationship. Big splurgy vacations and holiday gifts.

Meg said, "I think he feels somewhat guilty. I'm going to take advantage of this rare moment and ask him to pay for half of horse camp."

"Ask for all of horse camp, and college too," Lorna said. "Leverage that guilt momentum, Meg."

The chief stretched and said, "I'll admit, I liked your ex for the murderer. Spying. Sneaking through the woods at night. Foolishly withholding information."

Meg shrugged. "In a way, Cam tried to help me. He thought he saw me later that night. He hiked over to help."

"Some help," Sam said. "He's lucky we didn't charge him with obstructing a police investigation."

The chief was more philosophical. "Maybe he helped us too. He scared Marigold off her plan to stage Joe's death as a suicide." She nodded to Piper, who was listening with gleaming eyes. "Here's that exclusive I promised you, Tuttle. She heaved Joe's body over the deck, thinking injuries from the fall would throw us off."

"Cameron has a talent for ruining plans," Meg said.

In her jailhouse confession to Meg and me, Marigold said she'd seen Cameron hiking around the side of the house. He'd even looked inside. She was sure he'd spotted her. She fled, slipping out the front, leaving the door ajar in the hope it might look like a robbery.

Which made me wonder . . . "Did Fiona find her missing ring?" I asked.

"A pawnshop reported it," the chief said. "They're returning it. Her money's still missing, but we're working on that. She'll have to wait in line. Joe Darcy swindled a lot of women."

Lorna huffed. "That's it. No more matchmaking for me. No love potions either. What do you all think about relaxation spritzes?"

We all signed up for those.

Piper's eyes flashed. "Marigold deserves a killer nickname. What shall I call her? The puppet master? The book-clubbers and I were looking everywhere except at her."

"Like in a mystery," said Glynis. "You look right at the culprit but don't notice 'em pulling your strings." She nodded sagely. "Or a real string."

At Piper's urging, I described how Marigold had rigged the cowbells.

"She tied fishing line to the doorbells when she came back from picking up pizza. She set a tape recorder on a timer too, a trick to get us out into the shop to look. When I was out of sight, she tugged hard and yanked the line free. She wadded up the line and hid it behind some books before we got to her. She came back early to retrieve it. She'd found Rosie's keys a while back and held on to them, thinking they might be useful."

"She failed to account for the in-house Christies," Glynis said.

I gave credit where it was due. "Agatha found the string."

"That cat deserves double commendations," the chief said.

"You could make her a deputy," Gram suggested. "Dr. O'Grady should thank Agatha and Ellie too. Maybe he'll send flowers."

"I don't want any more cemetery roses," I said. "But Marigold would have been happy to frame him for the crimes. She said she did that to help Meg."

"My guardian killer," muttered Meg.

"That's a good nickname," Piper said. "But how so?"

Glynis raised her hand like an eager student. "Because Meg

was the obvious suspect. She was there, at the scenes of every crime. She had loads of motives too. Betrayal, getting ditched at the altar, liars, money-grabbers. There's her history of cutting off buttons."

Meg winced. "I'll never outrun those buttons."

"Not when the incident is in print," Piper said.

"Marigold Jones could have confessed," the chief said. "That would have been more helpful for Meg and everyone."

Sam said, "Dr. O'Grady didn't help himself by suggesting he was the killer." He winked at me. "Absurd of him."

That was Waldon.

Meg rubbed Agatha's chin. "Good thing you found that string, Agatha."

Agatha purred.

"And that you showed up," I said to Sam.

He shrugged off my praise. "You had it covered. Although, when you started laying out her crimes, I worried she'd lash out. I've never driven that mountain road so fast."

Meg empathized. "Ellie did that to me too when she fell down the canyon."

"Climbed down," I said with all the dignity I could muster.

Ms. Ridge said, "I still wonder about Dr. O'Grady. Had he seen Joe Darcy before your first dates?"

I shrugged. "I'm not sure, honestly. He said he didn't. I tend to believe him. He's not that interested in other people."

Ms. Ridge patted her immaculate pageboy locks. "Ellie, it's none of my business, but is he right for you? He leaves a mess in that reading nook."

"We decided that without murder, we had nothing in common," I said, unable to stifle a beaming smile.

"Murder brings people together." Sam Ibarra chuckled.

We clinked hot drinks to that. Meg and Gram left first, off to bake a Valentine's cake for Rosie. Glynis left for a date with her bookish love, Lorna headed home to her family, Ms. Ridge to her quiet date with a book, and Piper to a meeting with the book-clubbers for a lurid debriefing.

The chief checked her watch. "I better get going too. I've got a date with a moose."

The family with the game cam had invited her over. The handsome bull moose had been showing up every evening.

"This could be the night," Chief Sunnie said, crossing her fingers. "My first moose . . ."

Sam and I wished her luck. And then it was just him and me and Agatha weaving around his boots. He rubbed her chin before dimpling at me. "Want to get burgers sometime? I know a good place . . ."

A date? He dared ask out Last Word's worst dater? He was brave.

But what about me? Could I take the risk? I'd made vows to stay in, enjoying evenings with myself, Agatha, and my to-be-read tower.

I looked into Sam Ibarra's granite eyes, flecked with warmth, and rationalized. He'd run down a canyon and sped up a mountain to my rescue. Plus, there was so much I wanted to know about the detective. More about his favorite authors, his twenty-pound tabby, and his four-legged running companion.

I grinned and paraphrased Miss Marple. "I'd love to, but let's avoid talk of murder."

That sounded like a better vow, *for now*.

ACKNOWLEDGMENTS

✳

Here's where I find myself at a loss for words because I can't thank everyone enough. My family has always encouraged and supported my desire to make up mysteries. Any writer knows this is a treasure beyond measure. Heartfelt thanks and love to my parents, in-laws, aunts, nieces, and especially my husband. Eric, thank you for our time together and for enduring way too much talk of murder.

Many thanks to my amazing agent, Christina Hogrebe, for believing in my writing and reconnecting me with Jenny Chen, my brilliant editor. Jenny, thank you for your insights and keen edits, which, as always, have strengthened the story and kept the Christie sisters guessing and suspicious at every turn. Thank you, Mae Martinez, for your kind assistance and for keeping me and the many moving parts of making a book on schedule.

I'm honored and humbled to be working with the fabulous team at Bantam Books and Random House and am afraid I might miss acknowledging all who've helped out. If I do, please know you have my gratitude.

Sincere thanks to Kara Cesare, Kim Hovey, Jennifer Hershey,

and Kara Welsh at Bantam editorial. Many thanks to Luke Epplin, production editor; Katie Zilberman, production manager; and Pamela Feinstein, copy editor. Any mistakes remain my own, but your eyes for detail have made the pages sparkle. For getting word of Last Word out to readers, huge thanks to publicist Katie Horn. I've met so many wonderful booksellers, podcasters, and readers thanks to your efforts. To marketers Allison Schuster and Corina Diez, I'm so grateful for all you've done to promote the Christie sisters. Thank you for sharing the book with readers far and wide. All my thanks, too, to designer Ella Laytham and art director Carlos Beltran. I absolutely adore the design and cover, especially those cat-paw hearts and the adorable dead guy! For being Ellie's voice, thank you to talented audiobook narrator Morgan Dalla Betta. Morgan, you'll be narrating this and I don't want to make it awkward, but thanks so much for bringing the characters to life!

Since I began writing mysteries, I've been buoyed by the writers of Sisters in Crime, especially the marvelous Colorado chapter. I'm most grateful for friendships with fellow writers. Laura DiSilverio, thank you for our teas, talks, and inspiration—and for helping me figure out my killer. Cynthia Kuhn, thank you for your friendship, encouragement, and kindest of critiques.

Most of all, thank you to readers, librarians, booksellers, book reviewers, and fellow bibliophiles. Believe me, I know—reading time is precious and my own to-be-read stack grows taller by the hour. I'm humbled and honored that you've chosen to spend time in Last Word.

ANN CLAIRE earned degrees in geography, which took her across the world. Now Claire lives with her geographer husband in Colorado, where the mountains beckon from their kitchen windows. When she's not writing, you can find Claire hiking, gardening, herding housecats, and enjoying a good mystery, especially one by Agatha Christie.

facebook.com/AnnClaireMysteries
Instagram: @annclaireauthor

ABOUT THE TYPE

This book was set in Legacy, a typeface family designed by Ronald Arnholm (b. 1939) and issued in digital form by ITC in 1992. Both its serifed and unserifed versions are based on an original type created by the French punchcutter Nicholas Jenson in the late fifteenth century. While Legacy tends to differ from Jenson's original in its proportions, it maintains much of the latter's characteristic modulations in stroke.